YEARN TO FEAR

Australian Spy Thriller - The Lamarr Series - Book 1

CHAS MURRELL

Chas Murrell

Copyright

Yearn to Fear

Copyright © 2020 by Chas Murrell

For bulk sales, please contact the author via chasmurrell.com.au

First self-published, 2020.

E-book ISBN - 978-0-6450062-1-6

Print ISBN - 978-0-6450062-0-9

Book cover design & Publicist

Gabbi Murrell. Please contact Gabbi via chasmurrell.com.au

Disclaimer

This is a work of **fiction**. Unless otherwise indicated, all the names, characters, businesses, places, events and incidents in this book are either the product of the author's imagination or used in a fictitious manner. Any resemblance to actual persons, living or dead, or actual events is purely coincidental.

Epigraph

THE LONG GAME

If you wait by the river long enough, the bodies of your enemies will float by – Sun Tzu.

YEARN

please enjoy !

Kind regards,

Chas
1/21

Prologue

Leaning forward to push the big red button marked *ALERT*, his six-foot frame confidently squashed the accelerator underfoot. Senior Sergeant Les Coldman sported a reliable and trustworthy face, rugged yet forgettable. With an intellect sharp as a razor and dark wit to match, he was well suited to his law enforcement career, "TAC 4 copies all, responding Code 1," he replied to the dispatcher. Red and blue strobe lights flashed their warnings off the marked police sedan, and everything else they passed. The Ford answered the demand for speed, leaping forward to respond to the urgent call for help. Diverted from interservice training at the gun range, they would now be first response to an armed siege of a man with a shotgun.

Les spoke louder than usual over the yelp of the siren as they transited a red light. "Sorry, I should have asked if you were OK with this first, Henry," he said to his plain-clothed passenger, as a half-statement, half-question.

"I'm all good", said Henry confidently. Following with a less bold tone he added, "Pity back-up is so far away though."

Pleased Henry was taking this in his stride, Les added, "Well, having spent the last couple of days at the range with you, at least I know you can shoot reasonably straight."

Henry smiled as he patted the .25 Walther TPH pistol in his exposed shoulder holster and retorted, "Damn straight, any paper target who crosses my path today won't make it out alive."

Despite Henry looking like an easy fit into the Bondi Beach Surf Club, larrikin sense of humour included, Les had been gratified with the on-range performance of his astute federal colleague. It seemed Henry had lost none of his proficiency from six months ago.

Almost as an afterthought, Les added, "You might be the first Secret Intelligence Service agent ever to shoot anyone, although I doubt you'll do much damage with that peashooter." He beamed with sarcasm. "Best you let me shoot them first!" Les grinned, then became serious, "Standard rules of engagement, Henry, just like we practice."

Their high-speed journey took no time at all, not least because of the way Les drove. Henry braced his feet wide on the floor, keen to keep his body under control. In this moment, he was secretly glad he never skipped "leg day" at the gym. He couldn't help but feel Les was spurring the car on more than necessary just because he could. Clutching the *Jesus Handle* above the passenger door Henry quipped, "Remind me to send Mr Dunlop a Christmas card!"

The patrol car almost slid sideways, under beautiful control, into James Street. Both men observed a small huddle of people around where they thought number 43 would be.

Les said, "I think we've found the welcoming committee." He parked the car near the small group, the two men alighted quickly and finished donning their tactical gear as they walked toward the gathering.

The armed offender's wife, still in her dressing gown and

shaking despite the warm early morning sunshine, confirmed the details from the dispatcher. Her mentally unstable husband had chased her and the children out the back door of number 37, with a loaded shotgun. He'd been off his meds for a week. Her pale complexion exuded shock and yet, considering what her husband had just done, compassion too. She had no idea what he planned to do next.

Les asked a flurry of questions, ending by asking about access into the house. Each question served to etch her distress even deeper across her features. Both men felt enormous admiration for the way she tried, not quite successfully, to hold herself together.

She explained the back door had a security screen, and the front door a typical fly screen. A key hidden under the pot plant beside the rear concrete stairs was for the back door. "Please don't hurt him, he's just sick," were her last imploring words to them.

Les thanked her, affirmed they were there to help, and bid her go inside with the neighbours. Both men started to walk towards the small, single-storey suburban house in question, while Les radioed a sit-rep, from his tactical vest.

Outlining his basic intervention strategy, Les affirmed, "OK, Hens, I'll take the fly screen front door. If I need to enter in a hurry, I'll shoulder it to gain entry. You take the back door, unlock it quiet as you can, and be ready to make entry to support me if things go south. If this guy John is a rabbit shooter like his wife says, he'll be using number 6 shot, that puts the effective range of his shotgun out to thirty-five metres. Shooting us anywhere *inside* that range, I reluctantly point out, is really gonna hurt."

Henry said, "That may be true, but I work for the government, no-one's going to shoot me."

Les could not help pointing out the facts of life to his impromptu partner. "Henry, I work for the government too, been shot at four times."

"Yer, but I'm federal, you're only state." Henry's blue eyes beamed as he cocked his smiling face at Les, who shook his head, not being able to stifle a chuckle. It released a bit of nervous tension for them both.

Approaching the house, Les said, "So, close quarter battle techniques, worst-case scenario double-tap like at the range. Questions?"

"None."

Time to go, thought Les. "Then let's move."

They made their way to their assigned doors, using the available cover that the hedge boundaries provided. They crouched as they walked but with weapons holstered, to seem less threatening if they were seen. They arrived within sight of their respective doors within seconds of each other. Both realised the wife's stress levels were much higher than first thought. The fly screen door was out back, and the security screen out front, the exact opposite of the information given to them. *No plan survives first contact with the enemy - Moltke.*

Les surveyed the front door. Its sturdy aluminium frame with top-of-the-line triple locks was unfortunately familiar. The Tactical Response Group often trained with Crimsafe. The only thing that would break, if he shoulder-charged it, even at full speed, would be his shoulder. He concluded that no key meant no entry, and no entry meant only one option.

Not an overly impressive start, but at least the main wooden front door had been left open so he could see inside. He would negotiate with John from this position of slightly increased safety behind the mesh. Since there were no radio communications between them, he had to hope Henry would stick to the plan - stay put and be ready.

Through the millimetre-thick black stainless mesh, Les observed the agitated figure of a man holding a pump-action shotgun at a near-vertical angle in front of himself. John stood unshaven, of average height but above average weight. He swayed slightly in the middle of the lounge room, barely five metres from where Les stood. Les could not make out whether John's finger was actually inside the trigger guard or not. The gaping barrel of the 12-gauge Winchester Defender was so close to being under John's chin as not to matter. Les spoke to the man for almost fifteen minutes but made little headway. John was forthcoming with nothing other than fervent mumbling, that only added to the tracks of tears already running down his face.

During this time, Les took the scene in, and his tactical brain repeated the actions required to exercise his only option. *Let's hope not*, he thought. His left side angled towards John in a non-threatening stance, while his left hand rested at chest height on the security door to facilitate fast action if required. He relaxed his right arm down his right side, close to his upper-thigh gun holster, which held his Glock 22 securely. The pungent odour of oriental lilies overplanted in the front garden, permeated the air.

MEANWHILE, Henry carefully tilted the orange clay pot plant beside the back-door stairs, revealing the hidden key underneath. He thought no-one needed such a heavy, awkward pot plant to hide a key for such a flimsy door in the first place. It would be notionally quicker and easier to throw the pot plant through the screen, if a little noisy.

After all this trouble, he suddenly realised John's wife had said they all escaped out the back door; did he even need the bloody key? With the level of care it takes to defuse a bomb, Henry carefully pressed the handle for movement and discovered it was indeed, unlocked.

Through the fly screen, Henry could hear Les talking to John, but couldn't see Les because the corner wall forming the lounge room obscured his line of sight. He listened to Les talk for about a quarter of an hour, but never perceived a response from John.

Henry could only view John by standing on the top step at the right side of the entrance. He was roughly six meters away and could see that John faced more towards Les. As the time passed, Henry listened intently to the same mumbles of a broken, troubled man. Henry thought he might be able to move inside and talk to John. *Perhaps face to face assurance will help John see reason.*

Henry always gave himself a slow ten count before doing something potentially dangerous. He did so now, before quietly and slowly rotating the fly screen handle all the way down. With his weapon still in its holster, he stepped softly and cautiously inside.

Taking half a dozen steady steps inside towards John, Henry said the only thing that sprang to mind as John turned towards him, "Good morning, John." Having never faced this scenario before, or even considered it, Henry knew the seriousness of the position he had placed himself in. John had his finger on the trigger. The implications for John if he didn't succeed in talking him out of it were dismal at best. Taking another step forward, Henry could see Les out of the corner of his right eye now.

"John, my name's Henry … I want to help you work through this so you can go back to your family. Your wife and kids love you. They want to come home and be with you, but they can't until you put that gun down." Henry paused, intently searching John's face for any softening reaction.

Henry continued calmly, "You gave them quite a fright, but they still just want to come back home and start today again. Would you like that too?"

John appeared to be struggling to keep his head above water in the tumultuous seas of his storm-ravaged mind. Perhaps he glimpsed some clear sky in what Henry had said, as tears rolled down his cheeks more frequently. Slowly, but steadily, he lowered the Winchester to the floor. The weapon ended up lying on his feet, and John took his hands away. *Maybe today would be a good day after all,* thought Henry.

Call it what you will, from inexperience to bad judgement to bravery, Henry took an overly keen first step towards John to retrieve the weapon. The trouble was, Henry would need five or six more steps before being in a position to assume control of the shotgun. For John, the effect of Henry taking this first step towards him swept the clear sky away, and the gale in his mind raged full force again.

Flashing a look of total betrayal, John snatched the weapon back. Henry, knowing he was too far away to grab the gun, saw the open end of the wide black barrel rising from the floor as John turned towards him. Thinking himself the target now, Henry was forced to reach for his Walther. Henry doubted, at this range, he'd have time to get on target before his own head and ballistic vest filled with hundreds of steel shotgun pellets.

———

LES HAD CHANGED from active participant to bystander when Henry entered the lounge room. Initially Les was far from impressed with this change Henry had forced upon him. Despite that, it seemed Henry's approach was succeeding, John had lowered the weapon to the floor.

Les felt tenuous relief as Henry stepped closer to retrieve the weapon. Within a heartbeat though, this fleeting, hopeful moment was brutally dashed as Les witnessed John snatch the shotgun back.

As if by some atmospheric conspiracy, the sun, bright since they arrived and backlighting the lounge room through the sunroom windows, became obscured by cloud. Because of the black mesh in front of him, Les went from the equivalent visibility of day to night and could only recognise outlines as his eyes struggled to adjust. He made out the Winchester rising fast, with Henry motioning to draw his pistol.

Without any conscious thought whatsoever, Les exercised the only option available to him, and became the efficient and deadly law enforcement machine he was trained to be.

His right hand automatically found the grip of his sidearm. He was as familiar with the feel of this gun in his hand as his tooth-brush, it was just a kilo heavier. Muscle memory allowed his thumb to go through the mechanical motions to release the pistol and allow him full tactile grip as he drew the Glock in the blink of an eye.

Simultaneously, his adrenaline-fueled left hand pushed against the door mesh. Les drove his body down onto his right knee, into the perfect semi-crouching shooting position. Les's left hand met his right as his weapon thrust the short remaining distance to full arm extension. His target, a direct perceived threat to his partner, was already fully acquired. Three bones of his index finger closed on themselves inside the trigger guard.

Instinctive shooting was his forte. He heard no noise. The double buck of his short recoil .40 handgun launched two projec-tiles neatly through the door mesh at over 370 metres per second. As the hollow point projectiles pierced the Crimsafe, they began to expand and distort from their smooth bullet shape. In the instant both bullets took to reach and breach the side of John's head, they had not slowed an iota.

It was quick, decisive, painless, and very, very, messy.

As the familiar smells of gunpowder and burnt gun oil reached his nostrils, the sound of distant sirens reached his ears.

In the end, it didn't matter what the coroner or his colleagues said, Les couldn't ever decide which he hated more, Henry's poor judgement entering the house, or that Henry had forced him to be judge, jury and executioner. From that fatal day onwards though, he never wanted to smell those fucking lilies again.

For Henry's part, by the time the attention of the inquest was over, he'd well and truly had enough of his judgement being questioned. When an apparently cushy undercover job came up at CSIRO not long afterwards, he grabbed it with both hands.

Chapter One

As the only passenger in the car, Madeleine Banner's thoughts were running rampant in her head. *We're not entirely running late, just a little behind schedule. I wish we didn't have to make a stop. Oh crap! Who am I kidding here?*

"We're running late, Marcus," said Madeleine aloud.

"Nonsense, my dear woman, we're just a little behind schedule," teased Marcus.

"Oh my God, I just had that thought! Get out of my head, and don't look around at anything else in there on your way out," she ordered.

Marcus, never one to shy away from banter with Maddy, exclaimed indignantly he couldn't help noticing other specific things inside her head. He added, up until then, he'd always thought she was a good girl.

In the driest of Victorian-era tones she could muster, she scolded him. "How dare you, sir!" Reverting to more contemporary times, she executed a firm backhand to his shoulder. It was an assault of deep affection, not an attempt to inflict bodily harm.

Marcus tried, without success, not to laugh as he protested,

"Hey, don't hit the driver!" But to Marcus, getting a rise out of Maddy high enough for her to slap him was worth three points in the unofficial good-natured game they always played.

Maddy said, "You parked the car before I slapped you, technically, you're not driving anything at the moment ..."

WAITING IN THE CAR PARK, Maddy admired him as he carried the bags of party ice back towards the car from the IGA supermarket. All six foot two of him cut a dashing figure in his best-man suit, and *he's probably got a six-pack too*, she thought. The manscaped black hair and those brown eyes ... There, her musings ended. Suddenly, in typical style, Marcus stopped. He dropped his cargo to help a little old lady lift a heavy bag into the boot of her car. He's a keeper, can't help himself. She contemplated the future ... *one day, Marcus, one day ...*

He finally arrived back at the car and slumped into the driver's seat, managing a *"Now* we're *really* late," before bursting into laughter, which she couldn't resist either.

Maddy said, "You scrub up alright for a nerdy scientist, although it could just be your pink tie."

"Real men, especially non-nerdy scientists," he insisted in his most sincere tone, "do not wear pink! My tie, for your edification, may only be referred to as *man salmon* or *dried shark's blood* in colour. While I freely acknowledge you too scrub up well, I also allow you the courtesy of being able to refer to your own beautiful bridesmaid's dress as pink."

Revisiting her Victorian tone, she said, "You, sir, are a gentleman indeed."

MARCUS TOOK to the lectern and bent the flexible boom micro-phone to suit himself. Tapping the mic to gain everyone's attention, he took a deep breath and proceeded to deliver his speech. "Ladies and gentlemen, distinguished guests," he paused, scanned the room, and smiled. "Oh I'm sorry, after looking around, there do not appear to be any distinguished guests here. My bad!" The guests, seated eight to each round table now social distancing had ended, were nonplussed at that one, so not the best start. It occurred to Marcus that his worst fear of attending his brother's wedding and giving a speech that bombed was well on its way to fruition. Given no-one had laughed at his Google-sourced wedding joke only meant one of two things, so he started the process of elimination. "Can everyone hear me?" Both his distant but helpful cousins seated way down the back, gave him the thumbs up. He knew then his joke was crap. In itself, not a major catastrophe, if he hadn't got every single bloody one of the others from the same website.

He ad-libbed in another direction. "Ladies and gentlemen, it's not that I didn't come prepared to give you an entertaining speech, really I did. I spent hours putting it together. However, it appears the quality of those preparations may be in question. On the spur of the moment, I've realised I can shorten my time standing here, make my speech interactive and prove I really did prepare. If I start a joke you've heard, please clap, and I'll just move on." Surprisingly, most of the crowd seemed OK with this unorthodox suggestion.

"Unaccustomed as I am to public speaking ..." A smatter of clap-ping resulted.

"Moving along, I had thought about making my speech like the groom ... too quick and not very funny." The problem created now was that no-one would clap, unless having heard the line before. Atop that, even if a gag was a good one, his audience wouldn't clap and definitely not for a bad joke either. Unwittingly, he'd dug himself another hole; he should just learn how to drive an exca-vator and be done with it.

"When I wrote this speech, several words came to mind like handsome, debonair, intelligent, clever, even witty. Then I realised it was supposed to be about Bill, not me." At the end of this joke, there was silence. One of his distant and hitherto helpful cousins commented he thought he heard a pin drop. *Not helpful, but got a few laughs.*

Marcus struggled along bravely in this vein for another five minutes, but realised it was futile. He had imagined holding court like a rooster in a hen house, but realised his actual popularity as a comedian was closer to *Jaws* on holiday at a beach resort for slow swimmers.

"Ladies and gentlemen, although my jokes have flopped massively, it may come as a surprise to everyone here that I penned a little poem, which I'd like to read. It's for my wonderful brother, Bill and my equally wonderful new sister in law, Helen.

"Once up a time, two brothers played.
Building sandcastles with hand and spade.
We grew from boys, and now we're men.
Some days I wish, we could return there again.
Bill met Helen, now they are hitched.
Two gorgeous people without a glitch.
I wish you well bro, as you embark down this road.
With your beautiful wife, to lessen your load.
As my final thought, to share tonight.
I love you both, your future's bright."

This time the quiet resulted from people being surprised and delighted Marcus had written a half-decent poem. He'd showed the strength of his character to not give in when faced with adversity, and to fight the good fight for a loved one. It wasn't lost on many people in the room, least of all Bill and Helen, but notably Maddy. Before Marcus could toast his brother, a nice round of applause broke out. Whether they were feeling guilty from their pin comment or in genuine appreciation, his distant cousins clapped harder than anyone.

Marcus held his champagne glass high. "To the bride and groom!" He wet his lips with the last two drops in his flute. All that remained after his sudden cravings for alcohol during his speech.

As the applause subsided, Madeleine sprang to her feet with glass held high, "To the man in the pink tie!" Maddy watched Marcus for a reaction, but the one she got was unexpected. Marcus pretended to take his heart from his chest and offer it to her. The gesture delighted many, but none more than Madeleine. She beamed.

The rest of the night was filled with wine, food and song. By the time the DJ announced the last dance, most of the guests were slurring their speech, but fortunately the bus would arrive soonish to pick them all up. Marcus and Maddy wandered into each other's arms on the dance floor as the last song began. She spoke softly with a hint of a slur, "Hey ... dry ... salmon ... tooth ... man."

"Hey ... wedding ... planner ... girl," he said smiling at her in a make-it-up-as-you-go response.

Any onlooker would think they were a fine looking couple as they swayed to, 'Can't help falling in love.'

Maddy allowed the alcohol and his warm, gentle embrace to let her thoughts roam. She felt safe, protected, and giggly as he stood briefly on her foot. "So much for taking the next step with you, unco pink-tie man."

"It's man salmon," he claimed, with only a little playful enthusiasm, not wanting to play any more tonight. *Next time you can call me whatever you like.* As it happened, she'd also decided that was her last dig at him tonight. Maddy settled back into having her head on his left shoulder which suited him fine, as he inhaled the subtle fragrance of her long, wavy brown hair.

She looked up at him, their faces so close, her soft grey intelligent eyes looking into his, and he wanted to kiss her right then. Did he just imagine her moving a fraction closer, or was it their mutual swaying to the song? The moment passed but a contented smile crept across her beautiful face, as Maddy rested her head on his shoulder again.

For the umpteenth time of late, Marcus found himself in another moment with Maddy. *Oh, the fragrance of that magnificent hair* ... Desperately wanting her, but not able to find the crooning words, the moving or magic words, so she would know, beyond doubt, his incredible attraction to her. He would have to make small talk if he wanted to say anything at all. He was also aware small talk would leave him sounding like an idiot. So, he said nothing and lost yet another of countless opportunities.

Despite their minds and bodies yearning for each other, with neither confident enough to take the initiative, they passed another night as just the best of friends.

Chapter Two

Marcus Hall loved his job as a CSIRO electronics engineer. He worked well with his less qualified and less experienced assistant Henry Henderson, whom he respected nonetheless for his lateral thinking and ability to make things happen on the *Lamarr project*.

The project was named after the new Lamarr chip they were testing. The chip itself, was named in honour of Hedy Lamarr, a stunning Austrian-American inventor/actress/film producer in the 1930s to '50s. Credited today with co-inventing 'frequency hopping" used in Bluetooth and legacy versions of Wi-Fi, sadly she received little kudos then. Given her founding contribution to the science of Wi-Fi, and therefore indirectly, previous CSIRO Wi-Fi research, the chip and the project, were rightly named in her honour.

In the short months both had been working at Lindfield on the embryonic Lamarr Project, neither could understand why Marcus was subordinate to Sarah Pease, the newly appointed project manager. It didn't make sense. She came talented and qualified enough, but Marcus had more runs on the board than she did.

Eventually, they did what most blokes do, for right or wrong, they put it down to the gender equality target and got used to the idea. Although neither man discussed it, nor ever would, they had not missed the fact that Sarah undoubtedly had 'the thing'. 'The thing,' meant she radiated some form of innately pure feminine energy wherever she went, and whatever she was doing.

Besides all that, Sarah had turned out to be a 'good egg.' Sure, she came across as a tad over-ambitious at times, but there was no doubting her personal qualities and, more importantly, her competent project management skills.

Lamarr, the reason all three of them found themselves working together, was a synthetic crystalline material, incorporated into a computer chip of sorts. It was hoped it would demonstrate hitherto unseen properties in the passive reception of broadband frequencies, aligned with new 5G Wi-Fi networks. The government drove this project for reasons dating back to the 1990s. Almost thirty years ago, CSIRO physicists applied complex mathematical calculations such as Fourier algorithms to enable Wi-Fi, as we know it today, to do its thing. That discovery resulted in patents netting the Australian Government half a billion dollars in royalties. The last of those lucrative patents expired in late 2013. The need to reduce post COVID-19 budget deficits meant it was time to lead the field and cash in once again.

So, a quarter of a century later, the writing was on the wall to repeat their earlier success with the development of super-efficient Lamarr chips. When used in Wi-Fi receivers, phones, routers, computers, almost anything internet connectable, anyone would be able to download data much faster than currently possible; all the while achieving this fantastic feat without consuming electrical power.

In a historical context, Lamarr is the modern super-sensitive broadband version, 'mother of all' crystal radio sets common in the 1920s. Back then, crystal radios, also known as crystal sets, allowed their users to listen to a radio broadcast and not need any electrical power. The crystal acted to receive radio station broadcasts, but only at a single fixed frequency. The crystal oscillations caused, were then converted to sound by other basic components. The same theory was now being applied 100 years later.

It was difficult to understate the promise of the Lamarr chip; if they could get it to work.

SARAH TOO HAD a good deal of professional deference for Marcus and Henry, born of their individual technical and organisational skills. As project manager, she was well acquainted with their personnel files. Fortunately, rank has its privileges, and she had no intention of making this a reciprocal arrangement.

How Henry had come to be placed in their small team intrigued her. His pragmatic skills were undoubtedly beneficial, but the fact remained he was not long qualified. It wouldn't serve her purposes to ask around, though, as any inquiry might lead to a review of her own position and how she came to be project manager. She'd paid dearly in more than one way to protect *that* little secret.

She appreciated Marcus was here because he deserved to be, and if truth be told, he should be project manager, not her. Professionally, she considered him a good man and an honest one by all accounts, someone who loved a challenge, loved the science, and was exceptional at his work. Privately, she found it hard to believe these two handsome, affable men remained bachelors.

As the Lamarr project progressed, the tighter they all became, and the more she liked them both. For once in her life, she was working with true professionals. These two men wanted nothing from her and treated her with all due deference. They even surprised her with coffee and the odd almond croissant, bless their cotton socks! The more she liked them both, the more her ongoing deception ate at her soul, which was now all but devoured.

Sarah's mind drifted back months ago to the day she signed her contract with her direct report, General Manager, Peter Esser. She initially classified him solely as a 'PWP,' a Pasty White Person. Unfortunately, she then had to deal with him and came to know him slightly better; but the least she could. Several other classifications were added. These included, but would not subsequently be limited to - being conniving, suffering Napoléon 'short mans' complex, eccentrically smart and ostensibly creepy. Although Sarah didn't know it yet, her second last, yet to be bestowed classification, delivered to his face, would be – *ARSEHOLE!*

They crossed paths when Sarah, desperate for work, had jumped through all the hoops to reach her final interview at CSIRO. Just as naïve as ambitious, she had wanted to get on, resolutely deciding to take whatever offer lay on the table. She, however, was not going to offer to lay on the table for anyone. She would take whatever job was presented, just so long as it did not involve having sex with anyone. That was the *only* deal-breaker. Anything else, she told herself, *live with it.* In this state of determination, Sarah strode with an air of confidence through Peter's doorway, shaking hands before he closed the door, and sitting where he indicated.

"Project Manager?" she tried hard not to sound flabbergasted, but that didn't work out too well.

"Yes, of course," said Peter with a smile, "Why not? Don't you see yourself as management material?"

Sarah had never considered this scenario. Right there dangling on the line and covering the hook, this juicy bait beckoned. Promptly taking the bait, she swallowed the hook, the line, and the bloody bastard's sinker as well. Everything.

Her mind raced to say all the right things and catch up to Peter's proposition. Finally, to her relief, he seemed convinced, except more was to come.

Peter's smile faded to be replaced by a poker face. She would come to know his craggy face well. "Now that my offer is clear, Sarah, I need to discuss the caveats." He proceeded to explain the strict and unethical provisos. Sarah couldn't decide what disturbed her more, what he said, or the casual, confident way he said it.

She kept telling herself the deal-breaker isn't in there ... the deal-breaker isn't in there ...

The contract details were inconceivable. Considering them was unimaginable. To actually agree was ludicrous, but agree she had. All because of a deal done with herself, before a deal done with the devil.

On the dangling carrot side of the ledger, she would always be project manager. The exclusive agreement ran for two years, then reverted to an 'official' contract. If the objectives of the project succeeded within those two years, she would be paid $2M cash while her career leapt forward five to seven years. If the Lamarr project didn't discover anything within two years, Sarah would still be $600K better off, because of the difference over time, between her Project Manager salary and what Marcus was paid. It was a whole Chanel bag of golden carrots!

Given her two year contract as a whole, her feelings of guilt and deception of her colleagues grew. Peter demanded absolute secrecy as a requirement on the project and her 'special' contract. To receive her $2M cash bonus, she must report all progress direct to Peter in person and achieve all key performance indicators in the project aims within two years of signing. He was also solely responsible for the release of any and all information on the project. Sarah would transfer to an account nominated by him 50% of her contract salary for the next two years, or until the project KPI's were met.

She well remembered his parting words. "Sarah, this is purely a financial transaction in which we both benefit regardless of what happens. All you need to do is keep your cool, stick to our agreement, and all will be well. Do you understand?"

"Yes, I understand."

"Are you sure?" said Peter seeking absolute confirmation.

"Yes, I'm sure," she reiterated.

"All is well then. We'll catch up tonight at 7 pm," said Peter.

As also stipulated, she had met him alone at her house that night. Peter orchestrated every detail of this home meeting before they'd left the office. Sarah met him at the front door. He held, of all things, a Peter Alexander carry bag. Sarah wondered, *has he bought me a pair of PJs as a present?* They exchanged greetings, and Peter handed her an unexpected list of instructions. Top of the list was, 'No speaking for the duration of the meeting.' Also included were turning off her Wi-Fi router, and any NFC devices like her phone. He clearly meant business. Last on the list, strange and creepy, was a self-guided tour of the house.

When he'd finished his solitary tour of inspection, Peter handed her a USB, which she copied to her own computer as instructed, printed two copies of the contract and returned the memory stick. They both duly signed the agreement and kept a copy each. It was surreal. She kept waiting for him to take his pants off, demand she strip naked, or say something suggestive at least. She recalled thinking maybe he planned to do something weird, or more bizarre than he was doing already. But apart from what was expected, nothing else, nothing else happened at all. He departed as he had arrived, Peter Alexander bag at his side. Except, as she soon discovered, at some stage during his self-guided tour, Peter had left her bed totally messed up. *What the fuck?*

She recalled recognising she should feel elated, but none of it sat well with her. The randomly messed-up bed, in particular, felt way wrong. The sheets were in the washing machine almost before his car was off her driveway. Sure, she now had a well-paid job and prospects beyond her wildest dreams from a mere twelve hours ago, but it all felt wrong. *Two years,* she had told herself as she reached for a scotch. *Hang in there for two years, and don't fuck this up!*

Back in the real world, several months later, she realised she was going to fuck it up. Despite herself, she intended to tell Peter she wanted out. In the space of a couple of months, deep regret and lower self-worth had replaced ambition. Her growing feelings of betrayal of Henry and Marcus, were no longer able to be ignored.

Chapter Three

Peter Esser's office was a short walk from the lab space; she could see his office entrance through the Perspex of the lab's double doors as she headed there. The end of the day was the best time, not many people about.

Peter sat at his desk and bade her come in, smiling at her. "How can I help you, Sarah? Do you bring news?"

Sarah closed the door behind her and sat in the same chair she did each time she suffered through a fortunately not too often visit. "Not quite. I want to talk about my contract."

"I see, do you want more money?" he pre-empted, in a tone sounding like there was some genuine willingness to negotiate.

Well, she hadn't seen that one coming, but didn't suppose he was really willing to anyway. Not that it mattered. His was an extraordinary knack for keeping her off balance. "I don't want more money," she explained. "I want to be released from our agreement, please." His poker face appeared. Sarah continued, "This is wrong for me, and it's adversely affecting me, so I can't continue with it." He remained silent, so she kept going. "I know you might not be happy with what I'm saying, so I'm more than prepared to

24

give you my word that all progress reports will still come through you." She tried to make herself sound as conciliatory as possible.

Peter's facial expression morphed into one she couldn't decipher. He spoke quietly as he cocked his head towards her. "Thank you for explaining your position, Sarah. I think I understand and appreciate where you're coming from."

She thought he might actually think about it. "I know it's a bit out of the blue so if that suits, can I leave it with you and come back tomorrow?" In truth, she only wanted to leave before her nervous tension gave out, and she projectile vomited all over his desk.

"That won't be necessary," he said with a dismissive wave of his left hand.

She cringed inside, *here comes his answer ...*

Sarah had considered that, with a situation this delicate, Peter might pause and think about his words before speaking. Not so.

"You can't. We've signed a contract and that's that. You can't renege because you're suddenly identifying as an oversensitive Gen Y teenager." He held up two lazy fingers and said, "Two years. We're a couple of months in, you just need to sit tight like I said and go with it." The poker face was back. "Is there anything else? I'm a busy man." Emphasising 'man', while looking down at paperwork on his desk with pretend interest.

Sarah had thought some level of pushback was likely, but surely some possibility existed he would at least reconsider. *Wrong again.* His abruptness, his superiority, the pure dismissive arrogance of this 'man' cut her grass as low as anyone ever had. Attempting to process the psychological brick wall built in front of her, she had unintentionally remained in the chair.

"Are you still here? Go back to work, or have you forgotten the money you're going to make from the opportunity I gifted you?" Not even bothering to look up, his condescension was total.

What a fucking charmer, Sarah thought in anger as she attempted to digest this latest rebuff. *Gifted? Gifted has less than zero to do with his deal. This prick doesn't have a benevolent bone in his entire piece-of-shit body.* Not wanting to admit defeat so quickly, she tried to sound resolute. "I think we should try to reach an agreement. Negotiate."

"Oh, you do, do you?" quipped Peter as his expression morphed again, and he met her gaze this time. His was not a good look. "You didn't want to negotiate when I offered this contract, did you? You wanted a job here. I gave you this one, and you couldn't believe it. You would have done anything at the time, don't you remember? I bet you'd have fucked me if I'd stuck that little gem in the contract as well, wouldn't you have, hmm?"

Sarah was so mad her teeth were grinding, and she cupped her clenched right fist into her left palm to prevent herself from striking out. He wasn't just under her skin, this scumbag had dug way deeper now. Then, right then, Sarah's anger wrestled the reins of self-control from her reason, and she made a mistake of mammoth proportions. "I'll go to the CEO! She'll be more than interested I'm sure. You'll end up in some crappy police cell by nightfall!" She saw him raise his eyebrows, but little else in his expression changed, although his tone turned to one of sarcasm.

"Why would I be in trouble? I'm the victim here, not you."

"You're the fucking what?" she blurted. "How the flying fuck, do you work that out?"

Peter rose and took a casual stroll to a nearby filing cabinet, punching in a combination on the keypad. He turned towards her and mocked her with pious regret. "It's my fault, I should have been stronger." Continuing to pretend rather poorly, he said, "I shouldn't have let you blackmail me like this." He retrieved what she recognised as her original job application and started flicking through the pages.

His ability to throw her off balance had set a new benchmark. Mystified, she barely heard herself say, "What?"

"Oh yes," Peter said. "As I'll tell the detectives," he continued skimming her application, "I should have realised reading her application she would be trouble. Yes, here it is, and I quote, 'I am eager to start and will aggressively pursue any developments which present, as far as possible with all vigour. I will do whatever it takes to achieve every success possible', unquote. And apparently, so you did. This, coupled with me being the unsuspecting victim of a honey trap. Like I said, I should have been stronger." He mocked her unashamedly.

"Honey trap? What fucking honey trap!?!" With zero idea of what he was talking about, and thrown headlong off balance once again, she tried to regain the initiative. She played what she thought was her trump card. "You can say what you like, but you can't lie your way around the contract though, you dumb fucker." She did notice this comment register, and, emboldened. "You gave me a fucking copy with your signature. I'm paying you money every month!! For fuck's sake. You're in it up to your neck!" She spat the words out in disgust and triumph, staring at him. If he were worried in the slightest, he sure as hell didn't show it. It was more like what? It was more like ... supreme confidence. *He's more confident than ever now. How the fuck does that work?*

Peter started again, "Are you telling me after everything you've been told, you still don't get what's gone on here? I thought you'd be smart enough to understand. This isn't a difficult jigsaw. Perhaps I should connect a few more pieces, so you can move on with your life for the next two years, hmm?" She didn't move or say anything. He took that to be a yes. "Tell me, Sarah, where did the unsigned copies of the contract come from?"

Mystified yet again she replied, "You gave me them on a USB."

"Yes, well that may be your memory of it, but it certainly isn't mine, the physical evidence reveals something altogether different. With a little help from some technical associates, the contract file itself shows it was created on *your* computer, and in support of this fact, also printed on *your* printer. I first saw the contract when you forced me to sign it as the jaws of your honey trap sprang shut.

Look at the way the contract's written. Peter doesn't demand Sarah pay up. The legal style reads as if you're the one making the demands, not me. Like I said, I'm the victim." Peter enjoyed her confusion profusely and added almost comically, "You wicked wench."

She felt herself deflating. "But you're extorting *me*, I'm paying *you* extortion money!" It was more a plea than anything. She realised she was done, he would have worked this out as well. As far as legs to stand on went, sitting down would be a necessity for quite some time.

"For god's sake, woman!" he exclaimed in frustration, "your money is paid to me for ongoing services rendered. You're bribing *me. You're* paying me to keep quiet now you have the PM spot. You're paying me to provide you with everything and anything you request. Haven't you noticed how quickly you get what's requisitioned with no questions asked? I'm on your payroll. You're paying me, to remind me who's boss and that you have the power. Need I go on?"

"No ... No need." She resigned herself to abject surrender as her addled mind caught up slowly. "Let me guess, you didn't speak at my house so I couldn't record you. The written instructions provided a guarantee no evidence would exist that might conflict with your version of events."

"Thank heavens. Finally. Correct."

"The bag you brought in had a bug scanner in it. You used it on your house tour to make sure no hidden cameras or recording devices were present."

"Now you're getting it." He paused. "Go on, ask me the one question you couldn't fathom about my visit that night."

He's gloating? Sarah hesitated in total defeat. "I'm not sure I really want to know."

His composure was of the mighty conqueror standing over a vanquished foe.

"I trashed your bed before I made a quiet little video on my phone with the messed-up bed in the background. I spoke so remorsefully. *Oh god, please forgive me for what I allowed her to do to me. I should have been stronger,* blah blah blah. After all, I was being weighed down by guilt instead of basking in the afterglow of our union. Just more proof of how you manipulated me. Would you like a copy of the video for your Facebook page?" he asked as if there were actually somewhere in time and space anywhere in the universe where that question would be funny. "Look, Sarah," he said in a conciliatory tone, as if another person had just stepped into his shoes, "Hang in there, I'll be retired soon. It will all be over before you know it, you'll be 600K richer, if not $2.6M richer if you hit pay dirt. Deals don't get better than this, now focus on the benefits you're getting, NOT THIS SHIT!"

Sarah stood in a semi-zombie-like state and with a single minute disbelieving shake of her head, resigned herself to her fate.

Chapter Four

Sarah wouldn't get another chance if she didn't toe the line. If she persisted in not listening to him, there were other means at his disposal. But for now, Peter would do nothing.

Peter studied her thoughtfully as she left his office. Perhaps he'd told her too much, but he found it irresistible, watching how what he said affected her body language. It was like they were in a boxing match with no referee. Him trading blows with her, but she missing him with those big old haymakers, then receiving his kung fu left/right jabs on the nose every time. Her face couldn't possibly take that much collective punishment, prompting her to throw in the towel and acknowledge his clear superiority in every respect. This fight finished in the first round, and Sarah should never be a contender again.

So, what now? She raised every red flag in his mind. He hadn't trusted her much before, but now that had dropped to zero. Knowledge is power, and he had said more to Sarah than any other person who'd come calling asking the same question. Maintaining his guard would ensure Sarah remained ring-fenced from his other victims. There were fine lines to tread, but having done it for so long, he was sure his plans would hold together. Wouldn't be long until he finished making bank and was ready to cut and run.

His mind returned to Sarah. He'd almost told her he had no intention of spending any of the money she sent him monthly. Tempted as he was to jibe her with that as well, he managed to resist the temptation. Unspent cash in a regular bank would add proof to any investigation he didn't need the money and only acted under duress, afraid of losing his job. In truth, as each of Peter's other two year contracts had come to a successful end, their values had accumulated. Besides, he had a seven-figure sum amassed in a Swiss bank account. This stash of multi-path laundered cash was kindly set up and taken care of by the spymaster. To top it all off, a strong gut feeling told him the Lamarr project would bring home some serious bacon.

Industrial espionage continued being highly profitable for Peter and his sole buyer. Their relationship, built on a need-to-know basis, meant never meeting nor seeking the actual identity of the buyer for his 'products'. There'd never been a problem, when they said they would pay, they paid. His spymaster, Sifu, was master at the city's principal kung fu school. Peter smiled to himself. Over the years, training once a week in this ancient Chinese martial art was the perfect cover for them to meet.

Peter enjoyed the smooth and flowing style that forms kung fu. He grew fond of the paradox that something so gentle and graceful could focus such concentrated energy. Adapting the fighting philosophy of this famous martial art into his own secret work-life, there was only one rule: Win.

Peter was a great believer in, 'if it's meant to be, it will be.' Being a student at the school before he met Sifu was meant to be. He had only joined in the first place after finding a recruiting flyer in his home letterbox. That, along with the other junk mail went in the recycling. It must have been a massive flyer drop though, even the community notice board at the local shop had several. Two incidents happened in the next week which left him feeling threatened and helpless to act. The first, a push and shove match between two drunks in the supermarket carpark, one of them even denting a panel on his car. The second, an aggressive woman having trouble getting into her post-box as he waited to check his. He'd had enough of being helpless when she stood over him and said acidly, "What the fuck are you lookin at ya short arse scaredy cat?!?"

He stopped at the shop on his way home, grabbed some milk he didn't need, and a flyer. Learning martial arts boosted his confidence through the roof, and for the first year, he'd gone three times a week to build his basic skills. Peter never doubted he was destined for great things, kung fu somehow confirmed that.

He had long sensed he was a descendant from some noble family, or ruler. Around 12 months after joining the Kwoon, the training hall, he opened a random Facebook ancestry advertisement offering to find those answers for him. His sense of self was piqued. The $100 fee seemed a little on the stiff side, but he ordered the DNA test kit anyway. Not long after, an honorary name, *Shunyuan*, was bestowed upon him by Sifu.

When the test kit arrived, he took a saliva sample and popped it back in the post. With the day-to-day pressures in his life at the time, he forgot about it. Then, when he received his email results, right then and there, beyond doubt and without question, his true heritage was revealed. The Great Khan, Genghis Khan, was his twenty-second grandfather!

Knowing the Khan's blood coursed in his veins, he found himself obsessing about his heritage. He remembered staring numbly, with rising excitement at the computer screen, when lo and behold, he discovered the meaning of Shunyuan: *Obedient to the Mongol rulers*. Finding his way randomly to the Kwoon to train, thence to his ancient Chinese past, was like finally being summoned home by his ancestors.

Fixated as he was on his heritage, Peter started gathering

records and papers from everywhere and anywhere he perceived might be relevant. His parents, may they rest in peace, had left few documents related to his early childhood. To fill in a gap, he wrote to the hospital where he was born for any records they might be willing to blow the dust off. One of these documents, the delivering surgeon's report, would remain the greatest revelation of his life. During the difficult birth, which his mother survived, unsuspected blood clots were present. The post-operative notes mentioned amongst other trivial activities and medical observations, a clot-like mass found grasped in the baby's right hand upon delivery. Peter was acutely aware Genghis Khan was born with such a mass also grasped in his right fist. This unique and rare occurrence, interpreted throughout history by Sharman and wise men alike, meant only one thing: 'Great Ruler'.

After training at the Kwoon one night some months later, a strange conversation occurred with Sifu. Despite the cryptic and guarded nature of their exchange, Peter understood an offer had been made to him. Life was uplifted suddenly with renewed noble purpose and direction. Both a long-awaited ancestral calling and a parallel, most secretive career, had come to him through a series of complex chance circumstances. Just as the Khan of Khans opened the Silk Road to Europe, he, Shunyuan, would open a new silk road to Australasia.

Chapter Five

Sarah and Marcus were drawn together on first meeting by a mutual attraction, one that neither acknowledged to the other. They stayed strictly professional.

Sarah reminded Marcus of Madeleine in about every way. He tried to forget this thought the second it occurred, but it wouldn't go away. This startling fact presented him with a danger, so he stuck a large mental sticky note on the urgent reminders board in his brain: *never* draw that parallel with either of them! He and Sarah worked in an intense, technical, and absorbing environment and together with Henry, they formed a tight little team in a small but efficient laboratory. He didn't want anything to change that.

LINDFIELD CSIRO IS a sprawling and accomplished research and conference facility in the suburb of the same name. Fridays are the night out to blow off steam for the technicians, scientists, maintenance officers, managers, and admin staff. Sometimes the talented women from the cafeteria turned up too. Tonight's drinkies, as usual, were for no reason other than a pretend Friday night tradition at the Liebig bar.

The Liebig bar had opened not long after the recent expansion at Lindfield and was situated not far from the campus itself. It had striven to become, very successfully, the place where the folk at CSIRO came out to play. The owners cleverly named the bar after a type of condenser used in chemistry. It was a much-appreciated play on words for people of a scientific bent. As the name turned out, it perfectly befitted the unofficial entertainment of progressively taller tall stories. Patron tale-telling was firmly enshrined in the Liebig tradition. Well, what passed for historical practice after only six months of being open. The telling became so popular, a 'Liebig' stage with cordless microphone and stand was installed to accommodate impromptu performances. For those who preferred the words of others to their own, it was also used for karaoke.

For reasons related to blood alcohol concentration, these patrons became known as being from Sisero. CSIRO was way too hard to pronounce after a few drinks. If one did happen to be slurring a word or two, Sisero was about the easiest name to articulate not in the urban dictionary.

Tonight's get together was chugging along as usual, with the nightclub vibe having hips swaying from side to side in time with heads. Incredibly, and perhaps a little sadly, no-one from Sisero would ever find themselves, 'dancing with the stars.'

Marcus, doing the gentlemanly thing, kept an eye on Sarah as she got up from the group's table to head to the ladies. It seemed Sarah was bent on self-destruction for some reason tonight. Unlike himself, drinking hearty amounts of Willie Smiths organic cider, she'd overindulged on her preferred poison, good whisky. Sarah was a little wobbly in her boots, unaware Marcus was flying top cover for her. She chatted with acquaintances as she walked back through the crowd from the restroom. He saw Peter walking in the opposite direction towards her, with his back to him. It didn't take a Rhodes scholar to work out Sarah's disposition towards him. Her face lost that happy-go-lucky look as she and Peter stopped in front of each other. Marcus could see her face, but only Peter's body language from the rear. His arms rose palms up in the universal sign for, 'not my fault, what have I done?' While he couldn't read lips, and most people in Liebig's were in the same boat, he reckoned anyone would have guessed what her words had been.

She'd said, "Please," without a doubt, accompanied by the dip of her head in a pleading manner. What she said next, after a brief pause surprised him. Sarah didn't speak with gusto, apparent anger, or with any gesticulations. It was a simple, "Fuck off."

MARCUS AND SARAH had enjoyed a great social night up to this point. But now, Sarah was not only three parts drunk, she was three parts pissed off as well, and having trouble hiding both. She spied Marcus watching. With her inhibitions at a low ebb from the whisky, her angry encounter with Peter had just unleashed her wild side.

As she walked towards him, the closer she got, the more certain she became. *Oh, how convenient,* she told herself, Marcus is coming to meet me. They met in the bustle of a small gathering. Taking his hand gently in hers, she turned him towards the door, saying, "Why don't we get out of here?" He was easily led. A minute later she found herself standing with him in the warm night air at the not-too-busy taxi rank.

"Got something I want to show you at my place," said Sarah. "We can down a nightcap after that, if you like?"

"Sounds like an idea. Lead the way."

After a short ride to her house, the cabbie departed. Although not a whole lot richer for the experience, the driver appreciated clocking up another Friday night fare, that had not left a six-pack and a pizza on the back seat for him to clean up.

The two walked down the dimly lit driveway, the nearest street-lamp didn't seem to be working properly, casting just enough light to see by. A slight downward angle into the carport took them to a hard-right turn onto the covered veranda. At the other end of the seven-metre extended patio was the front door they walked towards.

Once close to the front door, and noticing the absence of any lighting, Marcus considered suggesting she install a sensor light sometime. At that thought, both his eyes were blinded by the brightest floodlights in the country. "Whoa!" They both shielded their eyes, as Sarah impatiently searched her small Coach clutch bag for her house keys. This led him to the only reasonable conclusion within reach in his state of intoxication, her bag must be an offshoot design of the *TARDIS*.

If I don't find those damn keys pretty soon, she promised herself, *the porch lights will find themselves shattered, and I'll take him on the veranda.* A flirtatious giggle escaped her lips.

That sound was a new one for Marcus. Not knowing it at the time, this evening was about to have a happy ending. All he had to do was say nothing, which, in circumstances of sexual tension like this, came to him naturally.

"Sorry about the lights," she said. "Security, don't you know? Got to keep the riffraff out."

"But I walked straight in," he joked as he found his voice.

"Point made," she played along. "Should get them replaced."

They both giggled a little as they went inside. She clicked some lights on and closed the door behind him.

"What did you want to show me?" Marcus quizzed her.

She looked him straight in the eye. "Me."

Taking his hand gently again, this time not letting go, she led her willing conquest down the hall into her boudoir, neither to emerge until morning.

AS MARCUS SHOWERED, the hot water brought the smell of her alive again. When her scent eventually faded, and with some reluctance, he washed himself clean. He recalled the night of released, pent-up passion, as wild in its ecstasy as previously fantasised ... once or twice. Pausing to think about that, he felt himself stir. Best to pause no longer.

Once dried, he put on last night's clothes instead of the blue bathrobe neatly folded on the vanity, not being quite sure it was for him. Once dressed, he made his way towards the kitchen.

Conversely, Sarah wore nothing more than a short white sheer silk gown, tied loosely at the waist. Her soft, shoulder-length brown hair flowed out over the robe.

She called to him while he padded down the hallway towards her. "Well now, here's an advantage of working together, I know how you like your coffee." She smiled, well pleased with herself. While he'd been showering, she'd been imagining a still wet Marcus in the loose blue bathrobe sauntering seductively out of the bathroom and to her side of the kitchen bench. Scooping her up into his arms, and kissing her lustily like last night. Hmm, hardly surprising the intense spark of deep desire lit her womanhood again.

As though in the kitchen for the first time, the bench took on new meaning. She tried to estimate if the height was suitable for her intended morning delight. By the time she closed the kitchen blinds, she'd noticed how moist and ready for him she was. The delicious preambles of the night before weren't strictly necessary then and wouldn't be required in the kitchen either. After all, they had all day. When her long-lusted-for lover appeared, he was not quite as pictured, and not the way she wanted him to be *this* morning.

"Oh, thank you, you didn't have to do that," said a fully clothed Marcus. He proceeded to plop down atop a bar stool on the opposite side of the kitchen bench to her. He noted she looked delectable as she finished off making a Nespresso in a mug for him. It didn't occur to him to scoop her up in his arms.

"Well, that's the beauty of it," said Sarah, speech awkward and daydream dashed.

Before he realised he had improperly appraised the situation, he proffered in his well-intentioned manner, "Do you think we should open the blinds and let some light in?" Marcus had just jumped into a deep, dark, foreboding mineshaft of his own making. In all reality, saying nothing and just embracing Sarah would have immediately taken this day in a whole new luscious direction. While Sarah had purged her reservations last night, for Marcus, now sober and reflective, they returned entrenched again.

Sarah said nothing as she opened the kitchen blinds. Her inclination for morning penetration on the kitchen bench was lost faster than shoppers barging into Myers for the Boxing Day sale.

Uh-oh, realised Marcus finally, *she wants more than a one-night stand!* As she turned from opening the blinds, her gown splayed, partially revealing her. He glimpsed the erogenous zone he'd delicately massaged the night before, as, writhing on his tongue, she'd tried hopelessly to delay her first release. The thought of her then and the sight of her now stirred his manhood from slumber again. But lust is a cruel master. His testosterone only compounded the unspoken awkwardness filling the room. That all too familiar inner turmoil he shared with Maddy, followed him here. "I'm sorry, have I done something wrong?" he asked.

Sarah took a sip of her coffee, shaking her head in reply, "No, you haven't done anything."

This unintentional double entendre rang true to them both.

Moroseness filled her in stark contrast to the ecstasy they'd shared mere hours before. Marcus felt an ever-increasing claustrophobia he needed to escape from.

"Perhaps I should grab an Uber and go," he offered. "Got an absolute tonne of things to do today," he lied.

"I can't let you go without something to eat." She tried to win him with politeness, but in the months since meeting, she'd become aware of a trait. His subtle fidgeting now, like waiting on a test result print out, meant he'd become impatient, so, not wanting to seem clingy, she acquiesced.

He replaced his coffee mug on the bench, strolling around it to stand in front of her. He held her elbows in his large hands and kissed her lightly on the forehead. He wanted to orchestrate something memorable, something inspiring, but alas, he failed on all counts uttering just two words but with genuine tenderness, "You're beautiful." And with that, she was alone in her kitchen.

———

AS SARAH WASHED the sheets she reflected on the night before. *Did I use him?* she asked herself. Perhaps this distressed damsel had just needed a knight for a night, to feel safe with everything going on. She couldn't decide. But if it were only a one-night stand, so be it, they couldn't possibly come much better than that. Neither, she realised as her mind drifted back to multiple shudders of ecstasy, could she!

———

MARCUS SPENT Saturday at home doing the many things requiring his presence. That wholly consisted of him putting his head on his favourite pillow and sleeping until midday. When he woke late afternoon, he found himself thinking of his rapturous night with

Sarah, but these memories conflicted with thoughts of Maddy. He reminded himself he and Maddy weren't in a relationship. They were just friends. Yes, they got on like a house on fire, but if Maddy wanted more, all she had to do was lead him to a bedroom. He was being unkind he realised, which returned him to square one, internal conflict and confusion.

What he did know for sure was that he didn't want to front up at work on Monday and find an upset or offended Sarah, #awkward. *Perhaps I should call Sarah and invite her to brunch at some swank restaurant tomorrow?* If there was a problem, they'd have a chance to talk about it and clear the air before meeting each other at work. *Bingo.* Grabbing the phone on the bedside table, he called Sarah.

ITALIANO WAS one of the best Italian restaurants in Sydney. It had won several awards over the years for its menu of exquisite dishes. This superb cuisine was served by staff in traditional dress against a backdrop of whole-wall murals and aromas from the kitchen to die for. Everything down to the traditional music piped throughout the seating area by a sophisticated sound system was top shelf. The well-tuned PA produced crisp clear sound in the background that rose above the conversations and general noise, yet was never loud.

Marcus arrived 15 minutes early, so as not to risk Sarah sitting alone in the restaurant and feeling stood up. That would well and truly defeat the purpose of asking her here. He made sure he was already seated at their table, killing some time with a slow drink when she entered. He sat facing the entrance and rose from his chair so she could see him, and as a gentlemanly mark of respect. He gave the maître d' who intercepted Sarah a wave and a smile when the senior waiter looked for confirmation in his direction.

Sarah arrived at the table, and they smiled broadly at each other. "Buongiorno, mademoiselle," he said, trying to inflect a half-decent

Italian accent. The attractive young waitress of classic Italian heritage, who stood at their table pen in hand ready to take Sarah's drink order, looked quizzically at Marcus for an instant before exchanging a look with Sarah. Sarah and the waitress did that thing where you don't want to laugh, so you don't open your mouth, but your stomach still contracts, making a weird sound as you kind of laugh out your nose. With control of herself regained, Sarah spoke to the waitress in the old language, "A glass of Chianti Classico, please. If my friend and I get lost in Italy, he may have to let me do the talking unless we plan on dining in a French restaurant." The waitress nodded at her and did the nose laugh thing again. Both looked at Marcus and smiled the smile of the much amused.

Marcus said to Sarah with a perplexed look, "What? My Italian a bit rusty?"

"Oh no, your Italian's fine. Your French needs some work though."

"My French?" Then the penny dropped, and when she raised her eyebrows at him, they both burst out laughing with such gusto no-one in the restaurant could hear anything else. They were their own sound system, forced to use their napkins to wipe away the tears. At least the ice was broken, he thought, grateful for small mercies.

"Thanks for coming, I thought it might be nice to do lunch and just relax. Clearly, I didn't expect to showcase my superb non-English linguistics so early on today." He stifled another impending round of merriment, as did she. "You seem to speak fluent Italian, where did you learn?"

"My mother was Italian, and like most immigrant families to Australia back in the day, my grandparents only spoke Italian. As I grew up, if I wanted to chat with my Nonna or Nonno, I didn't have much choice but to speak the language."

"Here I thought you studied up for our date," as soon as he said it, he could have bitten his tongue off.

"Oh, this is a date?" she knew he didn't mean to say 'date', but something in her wanted a pound of flesh.

He saw the slight head tilt, the raised eyebrows. He felt like a modern-day fighter pilot in combat, desperately struggling to keep his damaged aircraft aloft over enemy territory. With the missile threat receiver activating again, there were only seconds to live if he didn't punch out. His brain screamed at him, EJECT! EJECT! EJECT!

Sarah observed his discomfort. He was just being well-meaning as usual, but letting him off the hook straightaway did seem like a bit of a shame. "Cards on the table, you know I want this to be a date, right? Don't you want that too?" *Uh-oh*, she didn't mean to say the last part, it just kind of Freudian slipped out. The first bit was bad enough.

"Sarah, I," was the sum total this befuddled Mensa member could manage. His hands unconsciously opened and rolled outwards in the classic gesture of openness.

She watched his almost painful internal struggle. As he took a deep involuntary breath, she lifted her wine glass and sipped. Deflated, to say the least, she interpreted his answer clearly as if tattooed on his brow.

He struggled to communicate again, the first words coming haltingly, "Sarah, I, I'm sorry, I ... asked you here, so we could relax and chat on neutral ground. Clear the air of any awkwardness Saturday morning may have created." Marcus intentionally said Saturday, trying to separate it from the passionate night spent together on Friday.

She surprised herself with her own visceral reaction. His sentence, again as well-meaning as it might have been, nearly finished it for her. "So now we need neutral ground? Are we that complicated already?" She became businesslike. "I'm fond of you Marcus, not much doubt about that now, is there? But if you don't want to explore a relationship, say so. We'll call it one night and move on." Speaking these words, she didn't altogether believe them herself. "Can we try? Do you even want to?"

For Marcus, the jig was up, "I'm not sure we should ... I'm not sure ..."

Sarah paused to gaze at his hangdog face. Having tilted forwards in her chair, she allowed herself to relax back, her hands fell into her lap, stunned. "Wow."

Marcus sounded like a broken record. "I'm so sorry."

She sculled the last of her wine, took the napkin from her lap, slowly, graciously, placing it across the silver knife and fork in front of her. "So be it," she said. Her right hand found the underside of her padded bentwood chair. She moved her seat rearwards with a push from the back of her knees. She stood and, in a voice suddenly devoid of emotion instructed him. "Tomorrow ... don't be late."

Chapter Six

Marcus had become used to the number of security hoops to be jumped through at CSIRO. Their research might radically alter the balance of power in an industry worth a third of Australia's GDP, but it wasn't there yet. A little tense, he got to work early, looking forward to seeing Henry. Despite everything that had transpired over the weekend, he looked forward to seeing Sarah too, and magically redeeming himself in her eyes somehow. He knew the chances of that were pretty slim, less than a nanometre in fact. His face curled up in a frown, *Did I just make a joke? Really? Get your shit together, Marcus, comedy is not your strong point. You need to focus on work.*

Henry arrived a little early too, wandering in as Marcus reviewed the protocols for today's broadband receiver quantitative analysis tests. "Hey, mate," called Henry cheerily to Marcus, "how was your weekend?"

Marcus had his head buried in technical papers trying to distance the weekend. Henry's question, intended as an off the cuff, standard kind of Monday greeting, dragged him back. Marcus berated himself for not having foreseen the question. If he had, he would have prepared a brief generic bloody answer! He had to respond to his friend and sound casual in some sort of short-form. However, he overdid the intended casual short-sounding response with, "Fine." He may have gotten away without being asked an eager follow-up question by pretending his mind was otherwise occupied with work. But, as he had spoken half an octave higher than usual, Henry was at him faster than Phar Lap winning the 1930 Melbourne Cup.

Henry toyed with his friend, "Oh Marcus, take me now, you big stud," he soothed in his best high-pitched wanton voice. "Did you stay for long at the Liebig on 'Fraternising Friday' after I left?" Henry sensed Marcus cringe slightly when he said fraternising. The first rule of scientific research is to check your results against a control. That being the case, Henry said one word, but drew it out so it took three times longer to pronounce than usual, "Frraaatt-teeerrrnnniiisssiiinnnggg."

"I get it, mate!" said Marcus, flushed with mild annoyance and guilt.

Both of them then heard the door open. They turned to see Sarah, looking confident and even more fabulous than usual, Henry decided.

"Morning, gents."

Sarah had purposely gone to the trouble to make herself more attractive than usual today. Some not-so-subtle revenge on her weekend lover turned weekday wussy. She wanted him to want her again, even though it was over."

"Hi, Sarah, how'd your weekend go?" asked Henry out of polite habit. He received the same single word as when he'd asked a few minutes earlier.

"Fine."

Henry knew then he didn't need to finish teasing out the identity of Marcus's weekend fling. His first thought was *oh shit*, his second thought, *I need to be somewhere else for a little while.* Henry had his escape plan up and running in a jiffy.

"Excellent timing, Sarah, I was just heading down to grab everyone's usual," and without waiting for anyone to comment, he slipped, relieved, through the door towards the cafeteria.

Marcus knew they had ten to fifteen minutes before Henry got back and wanted to use the time normalising their professional relationship again. "Sarah, something's been weighing on my mind. What's the go with Peter at Liebigs? Is there anything you need help with?"

Sarah tried to blow him off with a nonchalant, "It's nothing."

Marcus, cognisant of the thin ice he stood on, but knowing this related directly to work, persisted. "OK, but it's not nothing when you tell the GM to fuck off at a social gathering. All I'm trying to say, Sarah, as your colleague and your friend, is if you need help, or you need someone to talk to, I'm here."

Sarah acknowledged his sincerity. "Thanks, I appreciate you saying that, but I'd also appreciate you not saying anything to anyone else. If there is a problem in the future, *I promise*, you and I will discuss it, OK?" She could tell the support he was offering was genuine and decided to respond in kind. No more extra dressing up to try and make him pay. That was over, she needed to focus on more important things.

"Deal. Thank you." That had gone well until he ended with, "Can't say I ever trusted him myself."

This drew Sarah's full attention. *Was Peter putting Marcus through some sort of ringer as well?* "Really? How so?" She tried not to sound overly interested, but her heart started pounding away.

Marcus had shot himself in the foot so often lately, it was surprising he could stand upright, let alone still walk. But it was out there now, and it was too late to dodge away. There was important work to do, and all of this was damn wearing. Marcus confessed,

"Honestly, because he didn't consider me for the project manager's job. There was no process, he gave it straight to you."

Sarah stepped carefully through this minefield. She knew full well the reason.

Marcus took a deep breath and continued, "I mean no disrespect Sarah, but I have wondered about it at times. That question aside, you're more than capable, so perhaps Peter's simply a good judge of character."

Sarah tried to sound confident. "More likely to do with government affirmative action policy, but between you and me, I doubt Peter has any people skills at all."

"More to do with your skillset, if I had to pick," Marcus replied honestly. *Leave sleeping dogs lie*, he thought, but couldn't shake the idea something was up here.

Sarah smiled. "Well, we've got a busy week ahead of us, so we may as well caffeine up, prepare, and launch into it. What do you say?"

"Sounds fair." It certainly did.

When Henry returned, Marcus and Sarah were deep in conversation reviewing the impending test regime. Everything appeared *Ops normal* much to his relief.

Things went smoothly for the next three days until Sarah called in sick with a lurgy on Thursday.

As a leftover from coronavirus, anyone exhibiting flu-like symptoms became an instant pariah, shunned without compunction. The general transmission rates of flu and the common cold were down due to the now ingrained hygiene practices from the 2020 pandemic, but they still appeared wherever people worked in close proximity, eating into everyone's sick bank.

Marcus and Henry remained healthy. In Sarah's absence, they followed the Lamarr test program, maintaining the schedule for most of the following day as well.

Over a Friday afternoon latte in the staff cafeteria, Marcus regaled Henry of his brother's recent wedding. Although relatively new friends, both had taken an instant liking to each other.

Henry was single, and happily so for the moment. Content to focus on work for the time being on the principle that the woman of his dreams would cross his path if he stopped looking. Trying to get something off his chest, he said, "I didn't mean to stir you so badly first thing Monday morning. I didn't realise it was Sarah."

Marcus gazed at him in surprise.

"All good, mate. Just quietly, I wouldn't mention you've put two and two together with her."

"Are you guys an item out of work?" probed Henry.

Nothing like asking what you really want to know, thought Marcus.

"God no, strictly a one-night drunken liaison. The only relationship we have now is professional."

Henry decided to let the subject drop. "Are you both happy with progress on the project?" By the look on his face, Marcus wasn't.

"We're on time with the testing, as you know, and while we're getting inklings, we've not one quantum leap in sight anywhere. The fixed test regime isn't illuminating a path to success. It's a bit frustrating, to be honest."

Henry looked sympathetic. "Well, at least we're only testing the receiving properties. There's no transmitting tests at all. Otherwise, there'd be twice the trouble, don't you think?"

Marcus put his cup down as an epiphany formed. "That may be true, mate." After a brief pause and some profound thought, he added, "That's very lateral of you, Henry. Kind of makes you want to make a basic Lamarr chip free-form wave generator to see if we detect an output signal. Bearing in mind, if it does or doesn't, it isn't going to help the project." Marcus was almost arguing against himself. Having had his interest piqued though, any negativity towards the idea became irrelevant.

Henry couldn't see why not and said so. "Sarah's not here. That leaves you in charge. We may as well enjoy a bit of play this afternoon, might be fun. Let's do it."

Marcus didn't need much encouragement. Quickly, he wrote a list of the integrated circuits, ICs, he needed on a napkin in his best doctor's scrawl. Henry took the list, including other components to sign out from stores. They grabbed their coffees and agreed to meet back at the lab.

Marcus knew what he wanted to do but wasn't convinced his chances of frying a Lamarr chip in the process were low. *How much were these things worth anyway?*

Henry returned to the lab all smiles. He unloaded the box of goodies onto the bench and arranged them all in some kind of order. Meanwhile, Marcus had drawn out a rough circuit diagram to install on a blank 5 x 7 cm PCB. Known as a *printed circuit board*, or, in the trade when blank, a *breadboard*.

This breadboard had eighteen numbered holes vertically, and twenty-six lettered holes horizontally. The 468 equidistant holes were designed to accept the soldering of ICs. The equivalent of a blank canvas for an artist to create magic on, this magic would use small electric currents instead of paint.

Marcus cheerfully soldered a Lamarr chip in centre pride of place on the board. Following his intuitive schematic, he soldered in the remaining components. With Henry's help, they worked apace for nearly six hours until it started to get dark. As the initial excitement receded, both decided to call it quits at seven. However, Marcus changed his mind as their agreed knock-off time approached. He told Henry he might keep going for a bit longer before finishing up, but Henry could get going if he wished.

"Might take you up on that," said Henry. "Besides, you won't believe it, I have someone waiting for me with a drink at Liebigs."

"Didn't know any of the blokes here were so generous," Marcus teased.

"Ha-ha," retorted Henry. "That someone is a woman. I don't

actually know anything about her, it was all a bit impromptu. We just kind of bumped into each other in the cafeteria during the week but were both in a hurry."

"Well, best of luck to ya, buddy," said Marcus, adopting a sincere tone so Henry would know he meant it. Switching back to sarcasm, so Henry would know that too, "You never know, you might spend the whole weekend bumping into each other and not get out of bed at all."

Henry pretended offence. "You are truly disgusting, you know that? Not to mention, you may have just slandered my future wife!" He grinned, then admitted, "She is gorgeous and smart, let's hope so." With the speed and intensity of a man on a mission, he scooped up his car keys and strode briskly out of the lab.

Marcus reflected on his friend. *Henry's a hard worker and a nice guy with a good heart. Any woman would be lucky to have him. Not like me*, he thought, *I can't even enjoy a one-nighter without causing a shit fight thirty minutes after getting out of bed.*

Marcus made a kitchenette coffee, adding a little sugar for an extra hit. Careful not to spill it on the bench, he tested for dry solder joints. Power was ready to be applied after necessities like continuity, resistance, and earth checked out with an auto-range multimeter. Installing a Duracell 9V battery, he flicked the small toggle switch mounted through the casing to the on position. No smoky smell was a good start. He couldn't see the point in affixing the lid. Something was bound to go wrong, then it would just have to come off again.

He earthed himself to the breadboard using the wrist strap, and ensured the oscilloscope was earthed to the test bench. This was necessary to avoid false readings, and not fry any circuits with static electricity that might have accumulated on him. Several measurements were made, but it was evident the Lamarr chip was not broadcasting any signal on a wavelength used in Wi-Fi.

Glad I didn't video my failure, he thought. Drinking the last swig of his cold coffee and about to call it quits for the night, a thought occurred to him. It was born more of desperation not to have a total failure on his hands than any practical reasoning.

Marcus swapped out the usual 25Ghz oscilloscope for the smallest range scope they had, one capable of measuring over a thousand times lower, down to 20Khz. He went through the instrument's set-up procedure and activated his creation one more time. To his utter surprise, he registered activity almost hidden amongst the 'noise' that normally populates the lower portion of the display screen. This indicated the device was transmitting a signal at 20Khz. Marcus was unable to move for an instant such was his shock. While this 20Khz discovery was nothing to a layperson, to him it was a startling discovery of mammoth proportions. He realised straight away that this was within the audible range of human hearing. If he made additions to the printed circuit board, there was a real chance he could hear the amplified signal. Whatever that was ...

Turning the soldering iron on again, he scrounged around for what was needed out of their laboratory stocks. Coming up trumps, he thanked his lucky stars. He soldered in the audio electronics to the breadboard. Once that was done, the 2.5 mm headphone jack was connected through the casing next to the on/off switch. Marcus inserted his faithful Sennheiser IE80 earphones into the headphone jack of his newly created black box, about the size of a six-pack egg carton. Holding his breath, he switched the device back on.

For the first time ever, a human ear detected the naturally soothing, quad pulse tones of Lamarr, oscillating rhythmically with the precision of a quartz watch, at a frequency able to be heard. He had created something. He had discovered something. But there was really no way to be sure what it was. In any event, he felt exalted, holding the device aloft, he exclaimed to the empty lab, "I christen thee the Marc1."

He wanted to call Sarah but talked himself out of it. *It wasn't in the test program. How would she react? She was sick, so he should leave her in peace. Better to spill the beans when she got back, he could manage that with a bit of luck. Who was he kidding, he'd need a lot of luck.*

Worn out from the hours of work leading to his discovery and the associated adrenaline high of the discovery itself, Marcus decided to take his 'Marc1' home. He tidied up without too much fanfare and with a half-hearted attempt at security, locked the circuit diagram inside the lab safe, and headed home.

WHAT A HELL OF A DAY, but an outrageously interesting one, he mused as he lay on the bed. Sleep eluded him. Still on too much of a peak, his usual bedside classical music wasn't doing the trick. Recalling the soothing sounds from the lab earlier today, he rolled out of bed and grabbed the Marc1.

Slumping back into bed and putting in the earphones, he smiled as the new, but strangely familiar sounds filled his mind. After a bit of nesting with the pillows, he fell asleep in minutes, and dreamed.

In his dream, her elegant, slender, naked form stood before him. Her long brown wavy hair flowed across her shapely and smooth face. Her face was hidden but he smelt her soft hair, and knew it was her. Marcus lowered her sculptured body ever so gently to the turned-down antique four-poster bed. They made slow, gentle, and intense love, just as he had always imagined it would be. This was as magnificent a rapture as making love could, or would, ever be.

He woke with a start in the dark early hours. *Damn noisy neighbours always getting home late.* Lying on his back, he saw his aching, raging erection pointed at the roof under his bedsheet. He passed comment quietly as though the neighbours might hear him, "I've been reincarnated as a circus tent." A half-smile and a sip of water saw him pass out again, still wearing the Marc1. The four-poster bed, a face under long brown wavy hair, flowing over beautiful and ready curves, re-appeared. Of course, they were as gentle and he as masterful as ever ...

Marcus awoke in the morning with a smile on his face wide enough to cramp his jaw muscles for a week. He rarely remembered a dream. Only one word completely covered off situations like this: "Fuck," as in *How could I be so lucky?* He eventually ran out of derivations and muttered to himself, "No wonder I've always loved four-poster beds, just like I imagined it ..."

MARCUS DID some of his best thinking in the shower. He enjoyed the soothing, all-over feeling the hot water provided as it ran down his body from the soft flow overhead. *It was just like I imagined it ... like I always imagined it ... exactly like I always wanted it to be with her. Not once. Twice ... FUCK. It can't be coincidence. It has to be the Marc1 doing something dirty to my brain.* These thoughts, together with his fantasy coming into high-definition dream reality, gave him an intense sexual rush. He contemplated what he should do next, including whether to finish his shower. Or not ...

Chapter Seven

Marcus never got used to the sound of the railway boom gates at the end of Bill and Helen's street. He didn't stay overnight often, as he thought the boom warning bell would drive him insane. In truth, it only operated twice during the night, but as with most things he didn't like, Maddy shared his train aversion, although it didn't stop her living there. It was great to be here with her again. Tonight, after dinner and a few drinks, Marcus had his usual spare room.

Marcus felt distant and distracted at the impromptu, 'welcome home after the honeymoon dinner,' for Bill and Helen. Only the four of them attended. The newlyweds were patently smitten. It was easy to imagine them merging into a tidy bundle of pure love whenever they were close to each other, which was always.

Towards the end of the night, Marcus blurted out what he saw as the discovery of a lifetime. Inventing a machine inducing deep sleep in minutes, using earphones and just listening to pulsing rhythmic tones. He didn't reveal everything. Modesty and the likelihood of embarrassment forbade him from mentioning the sexually explicit and self-aggrandising dreams that went with it.

Upon request, a quick trip upstairs produced his overnight bag and the mystery black box. The three showed unashamed interest in seeing what he called the Marc1. They listened in turn to the calming, beautiful crystal-generated melodies. Marcus remarked laughingly how perhaps he'd discovered the ultimate drug-free sleeping pill. Needlessly reminding him he was an audiologist, Bill badgered Marcus into allowing him to sleep with it that night. Marcus resisted at first, but realised it would be an interesting blind experiment, so relented. A late night hadn't been planned, and, as it turned out, that was for the best anyway.

ONCE IN BED, Bill and Helen settled in. Bill inserted an earphone from the Marc1 into each ear. Helen took the cord out of his right ear and placed it into her left, snuggling into him. "I can't let you struggle along with this yourself, husband." Cuddled up, they fell asleep. As they slept, they recalled vividly making love to each other, on the same unforgettable night, atop the sexual pinnacle of their honeymoon.

Waking on the morrow, the Marc1 remained on the bedhead, the earpieces astray in the bed. "Oh my God, I had the most beautiful dream of you and me on our honeymoon!" Looking puzzled and surprised, "Me too, what was yours about?" asked Bill. To their mutual astonishment, they described the very same beautiful and gentle dream, down to the second mutual orgasm.

Silence reigned as they stared blankly at each other, and silence was not a common occurrence with them, not since the day they first met nearly walking into each other as a pair of lift doors opened.

Arriving simultaneously at the same conclusion, they turned, swung their legs out of bed and called in unison, "MARCUS!"

THERE'S something about sipping a latte while the familiar odour of bacon, eggs, and toast wafts tantalisingly in your direction. Bill was a dab hand with a frying pan, and Helen adored those dab hands for other, more personal tasks as well. After last night's mutual dreaming, the smile on her face easily betrayed her thoughts to her husband, and he to her.

Only Maddy held no clue as to what the hell was going on. Why the urgency of dragging her out of bed on a Sunday? Truth be told, she liked seeing Marcus first thing in the morning, lunchtime, dinner time, well, anytime really. She wished Marcus would just drag her straight back to bed for the rest of the day; they could eat later. Maddy chuckled almost silently at the thought, and, without thinking, tugged at her dressing gown in physical attunement to her lusty daydream. Another giggle, a little louder, slipped out.

Helen knew her little sister well. Her thoughts were written all over her smirking face. They smiled at each other knowingly as Helen passed Maddy her favourite mug of Moccona, and whispered the old TV ad punchline in her ear, "For lovers ... of coffee ..."

Maddy whispered in return to Helen, "Lovers have nothing to do with it. As a psychologist *and* my sister, you know getting me out of bed early on a Sunday is dangerous to my mental health without coffee." They giggled and settled in.

With the men of the family settled too, Helen began. "So now we're all here, let me start by saying things took an unusual twist last night after we went to bed."

Maddy, quick-witted and fast in the uptake, couldn't help snickering. "You mean we're having breakfast early because of your discovery it's impossible to hold some pages of the Kama Sutra upside down and not fall off the bed?"

Marcus, tense about what Helen and Bill had to say, was thankful to Maddy for unwittingly providing some light relief.

There was no way of knowing how this conversation would turn out.

"Actually," Helen confided, "Bill and I shared an earphone each as we drifted off last night."

"Oh," said Marcus, trying to sound nonchalant but sounding more like he had a noose tightening around his neck. "How, um, um, did that go for you both?" he stuttered out, hoping not to give away his own intimate experience.

"OH MY GOD!" exclaimed Helen and Bill in unison, "you knew what would happen!"

Marcus tried his best, without success, not to let his mouth lead his foot into the waiting bear trap. "Not quite ..." he began.

"Knew what?" interjected Maddy. "Can you three start from the start please, wherever that is? I have a feeling my coffee mug isn't going to be large enough. By the looks on your faces, maybe we should be having a bubbly brekky instead, if it's that important?" When her half-giggle went unanswered, she repeated. "From the start then please."

Bill and Helen related with a mixture of shyness and excitement for each other, their exact shared dream experience.

"Don't get me wrong, I'm not complaining," finished Helen.

"Ha-ha, me neither!" agreed Bill. "Forgive the details, but for us to dream at the same time of a real past event in such detail, the same precise details for both of us, can't be coincidental. We'd assumed that a memory of our honeymoon was just something to be treasured through the years." Bill was very invested in this unexpected situation and struggled to explain it. "But to also enjoy total recall in the morning ..." He lost the thread of his thought and went to another. "We both experienced the event, while asleep, precisely as it happened. Even down to the instant we knocked Nessie into the spa and flattened the batteries!" The last part about the vibrator was perhaps a little more information than he and Helen had intended to share.

Marcus's and Maddy's amused eyes met. "Um, what's a Nessie and what does it do in a spa?" asked Marcus. Without missing a beat, he followed up with, "Forget I asked."

"Isn't Nessie a monster?" chipped in Maddy.

Not wishing to reveal too much of their intimate marital activities, and aware of Helen's now rouge-coloured cheeks, Bill diverted the conversation. "So, Marcus, I guess we should say thank you for the re-live, but what in creation is in that amazing box you made!?"

If Marcus wanted his leg pried out of that bear trap to avoid further pain, he was going to have to spill the beans on what he'd neglected to tell them the night before. It didn't take long for him to come clean with a summary of what had transpired in the last 24 hours. He quite rightly still left out the bit about contemplating his penis in the shower though. This self-imposed limit as to how clean he was *really* prepared to come, would save a little embarrassment.

While Maddy sat amazed and silent in her pride for Marcus, she could indeed have gone a flute or three of sparkly wine at that point. *This whole conversation would be worth getting up early for a month*, she thought to herself.

"And that, as they say, is all I know," finished Marcus.

"So, you have no idea how this thing works?" asked Helen.

"None," confirmed Marcus.

Looking more puzzled than ever, Marcus asked Bill modestly, "I'm just an engineer, but you're an ear doctor, how can these sounds bring out memories?" Bill confidently assured everyone at the present state of scientific knowledge, they physically couldn't. Not helpful ...

Seizing some sort of initiative to guide the conversation and appear helpful to her secret, but obviously pained beloved, Maddy summarised. "OK, so what do we or don't we know? One, we don't know the mechanism by which it works. Two, it works when you're asleep and generates dreams based on imagination or memory. Three, it picks memories or imagination based on what we most want to be doing. Do we all agree?"

The newlyweds giggled like teenagers. "Yes, I think we can agree on that point without too much trouble."

Maddy powered onward. "Four, Lamarr has something to do with it, and five … is there a five? OK, number five, which brings us back to point one ... I have an evil plan ..."

"Right," said Helen smiling seductively at Bill. "Let's leave the other two with Maddy's evil plan and go invent a naughty daydream of our own on this beautiful Sunday morning."

Bill stood quickly. "Can't argue with logic. We'll do the dishes later." Without further ado, they walked towards their bedroom.

"You two are incorrigible," called Maddy with a smile as they disappeared from earshot. She was over the moon her sister was so happy. Bill and Helen were like two peas in a pod. Maddy turned her beaming face to Marcus, "So, wanna hear my evil plan?"

Chapter Eight

As they arrived at the university grounds, Marcus made a show of wiping his fingers along the spotless dash in front of him and inspecting his fingertips. "You know all this dust is ruining my passenger experience," he taunted her.

Maddy ignored him. No way would she allow a point for that one, but she had an idea for racking up some points of her own.

They drove past the general car park and towards the main entrance where Madeleine lined up her immaculate, modified black G6E Turbo to park in the Chancellor's reserved car park, close to the foyer of the university.

"Of course you are," he murmured loud enough for her to hear, "no lesser level of bad behaviour and disrespect for authority could be expected."

"Oh come on, Marcus, be a trooper," she said. "Look, mate, the Chancellor's away hobnobbing in Canberra for more funding. He's not within 300 k's of here."

"Mate?" said Marcus with a guffaw. "In all the years we've known each other, you've never called me that! But thank you, I'll take that as a colloquial term of endearment. Which brings me to ask, define your intended context of 'mate'? Is it as in *you dumb bastard*, or mateship, or *I'd like to mate with him?*" Knowing that would be a difficult one for her to squirm out of, he laughed again.

Maddy didn't miss a beat. "That last comment does you an injustice, not to mention, but I will mention, you considerably flatter yourself, sir." Switching off her Victorian inflection and exuding mock indignation, she added, "Let's clear up a few things before we alight ... mate."

She looked straight at him, and he looked straight back at her. He could tell the corners of her mouth were curling upward ever so slightly as she struggled to keep from smiling.

'Firstly, any park here, but notably *this* car park, is honoured having a vehicle such as mine parked in it any day of the week. Particularly, instead of that crap red two-seater sports car, cheap Italian Holden Roozamatti thing, or whatever it is the Big Kahuna drives."

"From your description, I take it you're not a fan," he interjected. "And I believe the word your looking for could be, *Maserati*." With his chin almost touching his chest, and eyes towards her, he raised his left hand towards Maddy as if about to take an oath. "No judgement zone."

She pulled up the handbrake. "I'm not finished yet. Please observe proper manners and let a lady continue," she warned. The corners of her mouth began to rise further into a smile against all her best efforts. "I was going to mention, I'm also practically bringing scientific royalty to the campus, and this, therefore, constitutes a twin honour for the area over which we now find ourselves stationary."

"Awesome," he said, clapping at her summary.

"Define awesome," she demanded.

Funnily enough, *he* was on the spot now but didn't mind. "You Madeleine Banner, awesome defines you."

They sat in the car silently as the seconds lingered, both bathing in the rare straight-out sincere compliment he'd afforded her. Both realised with a warm glow what had just happened.

THEY HAD WALKED several metres from the muscle car by the time Maddy operated the key fob to lock the doors with a dull thud. She looked at the car to make sure the indicators flashed twice to show it had locked properly. Apart from anything else, it was one hot looking car, which she had dubbed 'G-Sexy' before even driving it out of the car yard. The leather smell was in the air back then too, kept company by 'Back In Black' loaded into the old-school CD stacker.

Marcus found himself led through a veritable labyrinth of hallways and rabbit warrens. *Holy crap, if a fire breaks out, I'll never find my way out of here in a hurry*, he thought. He closed up a little on Maddy, it was as legitimate an excuse as any.

They eventually entered through a pair of heavily varnished doors and into Madeleine's domain of the Radiological Research Unit. "Are you sure this evil plan of yours is going to work?" he said, seeking some kind of reassurance.

"Well, I am sure because we want to get some answers on a Sunday, and hey, all you need to do is trust me and be a good little guinea pig," Maddy teased him as she turned his way briefly.

He saw her sweet grin again. *Hmm, I missed you*, he thought. "But don't MRI machines use giant magnets? The Marc1 is made of metal. I'll have metal in my ears. Isn't that, like, a bad idea? You see where I'm coming from right? It could be dangerous."

"Jesus, Marcus, did I mention MRI?" she responded in a mock serious tone. "Do you know what YUSSP stands for?"

Marcus thought she *was* serious, "Um no, I'm sorry, is it some kind of protocol or super scanner?"

As the adage goes, sometimes it's best to remain silent and be thought a fool than to speak and remove all doubt.

Maddy laughed. "Not even remotely close, it's how a dyslexic spells pussy." She continued to lose herself in her own humour. "Just man up, everything will be OK, trust me."

They walked through the last nondescript door. The next displayed 'PET scanner' in small blue lettering on the pale white paint. "Behold," cried Maddy, proudly gesticulating at the near new machine before them, emblazoned with 'PET scanner'. "Don't say it," Madeleine warned, pre-empting some joke Marcus was going to drag up about a pet dog. "It stands for Positron Emission Tomography, and doesn't use magnets, so even if that pelvis of yours has a metal hip in it ..." she feigned concern, touching him gently on the arm, "... you don't have a metal hip, do you?"

"Well, not yet at least," he confirmed gyrating for effect. He gazed at the size of the scanner in the room. There was only one other door into the room, about the same size as the door they had come through. It must have been installed in tiny pieces, he thought, a multi-million-dollar mix of Meccano and Lego.

"Then we are G2G," said Maddy.

Although a small thing and of no apparent consequence, he recognised with glee she'd said *we*, not *you*. Marcus smiled, he did so like this girl.

Despite Maddy trying to make the PET bed as comfortable as possible for him to lie on, he believed the university must have bought the cheaper, more uncomfortable model. Even the man of steel would ask for more cushions on this thing. The effect of having almost no clothes on, together with the constant flow of cold air conditioning, made him feel a little vulnerable. Whether the goosebumps were wholly due to chilly air, or the beautiful woman in the room, remained to be seen.

He consoled himself this was the best, and quickest way, to

establish how the Marc1 messed with their minds. The small syringe of radioactive isotopes to be injected before the scan started lay on a stainless-steel tray nearby, and he settled in wearing the Marc1, trying to go to sleep. The soothing tones, in conjunction with the interrupted sleep the previous night, courtesy of New South Wales Rail, allowed him to fall rapidly asleep.

Madeleine, a consummate professional, quickly re-checked everything, knowing she only had twenty minutes from the time she injected the contrast medium to do her work. Knowing also, she shouldn't administer the injection before Marcus started dreaming. She needed the timing to be perfect so the contrast medium would enhance the images the scanner revealed, over the maximum length of time. She hoped it would be long enough to capture whatever brain images were there to be had, and hopefully make sense of them. It seemed fitting the first brain scan of this device in action was being done on a research scanner. It suddenly occurred to her, *how the hell am I going to know when he enters a dream state?*

She waited and pondered. After an anxious eternity of two minutes, she curiously perceived movement. At first, she thought it was the slight breeze from the air-handling system playing on Marcus's gown. Administering the injection through the wrist catheter she had inserted earlier, Maddy returned the syringe to the tray in well-practised movements, then paused.

She stared in open defiance of her self-imposed professional standards to admire the generous partly folded erection, trapped and straining for freedom. *His underpants must be constructed of reinforced carbon steel fibre to withstand that kind of pressure!* Her mirth and desire rose in equal proportion, but she moved to the operation console with experienced efficiency. "Well," she said to the grinning Plexiglas reflection of herself, "he did man up quite nicely, didn't he?"

MARCUS HAD RETURNED in his dream state to the four-poster bed and the naked, gorgeous figure of a woman who lay thereon. Her long curled brown hair no longer covered her face, and Maddy smiled up at him as she shyly but eagerly beckoned him to her.

Chapter Nine

T he four of them sat around the lengthy curved PC screen in the den at Bill and Helens, displaying a series of brain scans from Marcus's examination that morning.

"The resolution is impressive," stated Bill, as he studied the images intently.

"Well, folks, first things first," began Maddy. "Red on the scan images registers the most intense brain activity, while any other colour denote less intense activity." She paused for dramatic effect before adding, "What is holistically shown here is nothing other than love."

"I don't understand," responded Marcus.

"With you there," agreed Bill and Helen in unison.

"OK," said Maddy, "let me explain. The red bloom in the frontal lobe, the tight cluster of red indicating intense activity in the frontal area, is considered to be where our emotions live." She clarified this sentence so as not to be too general. "Not entirely, but close enough for the purposes of today. One favourite student-selected assignment is to show love on a scan. I'm not demeaning your emotions, Marcus, but your findings appear in many assignment results produced over the years." Maddy enlarged another scan.

Marcus shrugged. "OK, that's where my love hides, so ... what's the other long area of bloom in the one on the screen now?"

"That," she replied slowly, less sure of herself now, "is one of two things that hasn't appeared in a love scan result before."

Bill addressed Maddy perplexed, "But they're both blooming at consistent intensities along their entire length?"

"Yes," said Maddy, bewitched by the ultra HD images on the widescreen, "they are."

"Huh?" asked Marcus with a pleading expression.

"Sorry," answered Bill, as if he would explode if he didn't get it all out in five seconds. "Both pathways of your vestibulocochlear nerve all the bilateral way to your primary auditory cortex ..."

Marcus stopped Bill in mid-sentence with a 'please stop' hand gesture, and a more intense look of pleading than before.

"Maddy, can you translate please? Been a long time since I did anatomy and physiology," said Marcus, diverting the conversation away from his brother.

Maddy obliged. "The auditory nerve is showing red from your ears to inside your brain, but it shows a consistent shade on each side of the nerve. The thing is, there are two separate pathways in that nerve. They do different things because they *are* for different things. They always, and I mean *always*, produce two different shades in a scan when the patient hears something.

"I know this because students play different types of music and even audiobooks at varying levels of volume during their prac sessions. You, Marcus, were listening only to the Marc1 through your earphones" Maddy finished the sentence and left it hanging there, expecting some reaction from the others.

All four looked randomly at each other, clearly not all on the same page, perhaps even in different chapters. "I don't suppose you would let me guess what the second thing is you haven't seen before?" Helen asked Maddy.

"Please ... be my guest. I'll give you three guesses."

"There is nothing else," said Helen in triumph. "No other brain activity of significance is indicated."

"Bravo!" exclaimed Madeleine, proud of her sister as always. "Right first time! I take back all those bad things I've ever said about psychologists," she teased as she hugged Helen.

"Don't I get one as well?" inquired Bill.

"No," said Maddy in her cruellest voice, "and you needn't bother asking either," as she looked towards the only other male in the room.

Marcus collected himself after his hug denial. "So ... as I understand it," he said almost painfully, with all the confidence he could muster, which by this juncture didn't amount to much, "you're saying the Marc1 has somehow mysteriously made my brain go into love overdrive and turned everything else off?"

After a bout of deep thought, with head lolling from side to side like a boiled egg on a side plate, Maddy replied, "That about sums it up."

Everyone was lost in their own thoughts at this nascent summary, the power of speech lost to them all. Helen broke the silence and addressed everyone in the room. "I need to ask a question. Please understand, it's purely from a professional point of view, but I think it's important. It may give us another important clue." She delivered this in her clinical psychologist to patient tone, lulling everyone into a false sense of security.

"Let's hear it, it might crack the case," said Marcus, "I'm sure Maddy will be all over it like a rash."

"Shoot," said her sister looking in mock disapproval at her tormentor, "I'm all ears."

Helen smiled her best clinically distant smile at Marcus and asked, "You may well be, but the question is for my brother-in-law not for you, little sis." After the obligatory building-suspension pregnant pause, the question arrived, "Who did you dream about, Marcus?"

The question should not have come like a bolt from the blue, but it did. Given the company in the room, Marcus would have preferred a swift kick to the testicles with an ice skate. His face turned as bright as a male flamingo in mating season.

Never one to miss a chance to add to Marcus's discomfiture, Maddy said, "Yes, Marcus, I must insist you tell us. It could be vital to us cracking the case ..."

Marcus shot her a glance and squirmed in his chair. He told himself, *Generalise enough to keep them all happy.* He noted the total lack of support from Bill, who had that look older brothers get when they have no intention whatsoever of helping their younger brother out of a tight spot. "Just some woman," popped out of his mouth. Marcus detested times like these when his brain was not engaged before his mouth went into gear.

"Just some woman?" repeated Maddy, "Just some woman?" Repeating it a second time failed to cool her sudden rise in passion, and it boiled over.

Marcus felt the backhander from Maddy on his shoulder, which encouraged him to reconsider his position and perhaps supply a few more details. He hoped he could do so while still dodging the question. However, his opinion of himself in this realm as compared to Madeleine was severely misguided. "She had long hair ..."

"Now we're making progress," said Helen as though Marcus was lying on the couch in her professional rooms.

None of the 'steady as she goes' responses satisfied Maddy. "Colour? Curly or straight? How long? Come on ..."

Far from jumping in to help his brother, Bill intentionally

played the complete cad, grinning from ear to ear. "Yes, do go on, Marcus, I support you. This sounds *very* important, please ..." gesturing to Marcus as though inviting him onto a stage as next speaker.

Marcus stared his brother down, "You are ... such a bastard." His next words in an upbeat tone, were in an unsuccessful attempt to divert attention away from the question. "Perhaps now's a good time for a cuppa, there's been a lot to take in."

Madeleine's backhander felt far harsher than even the last one, and probably harder than any other delivered over the years. He suspected she may well have hit him, no point scoring, just actually hit him. It was difficult to miss the warning it implied, if he wanted the torture to stop, he had to cough up the answer. He cringed and confessed, "The same as yours, Maddy, you *could* say ... yours."

Bill squeezed Helen's hand tenderly and broke the silence as he stood, "You're right, Marcus, time for a cuppa. Come, darling, give me a hand with the coffee, will you?" Despite his polite, loving, mildly insistent husband tone, Bill still had to virtually drag Helen out of the room.

When they'd left, the two were alone. Marcus was sure Maddy was livid with him. "I'm sorry, but you made me say it." She landed another but not so hard backhander to his deltoid, this time without saying a word, and he couldn't read the look on her face. "What?" Now desperate and confused, he thought if he said anything else she would just beat him to death with the over-sized stapler on the desk.

"You don't get it, do you?" she said incredulously as her arms snapped out in front of her as if trying to capture a thought for him.

Marcus rose and took a step sideways to be out of range of what he thought was inevitably another hostile inbound. Totally baffled, he grumbled, "Get what, Maddy? I have utterly no idea what you mean." To his surprise, Maddy rose too, her face now a picture of touched contentment, as she stepped with purpose towards him. While caressing his face gently in her hands, for the first time in all these years she kissed him softly on the lips. His arms closed in a loving reflex embrace around her, and they kissed again. Both understood that the torment they had put themselves and each other through, was finally, and thankfully, over.

Chapter Ten

Sitting in the comfort of the lounge room, they spent the rest of the afternoon and into the early evening discussing, theorising, conjecturing, and coming up with one hypothesis after another. It had been a mind-blowing day but at the end of it, they each had a list of action items for investigation the next day.

With the pizza boxes and the empty champagne glasses cleared away, Helen and Bill slipped off to continue their happily never-ending honeymoon.

Madeleine and Marcus found themselves gazing at each other from opposite sides of the coffee table. "So, what were we doing in your dream, exactly?" asked Maddy, one eyebrow raised.

"Nothing." He regretted the single word lie even before he finished pronouncing it.

"Nothing?" she continued to tease, "Strange thing for a naked woman to be doing, is nothing." They both smirked at each other. "Oh, you mean I wore nothing." Their smirks turned to teenage-like giggling. "I want to try it," she said with certainty, "but ... I want to feel safe, will you be there for me?"

"Can't really say no, can I? You were there for me."

"Exactly," she said as she rose and proffered her hand to his. She held his warm hand close to her heart and led Marcus into her room, closing the door and turning on the bedside light.

Marcus felt like a nervous wreck by the time he found himself standing close to Maddy at the side of her bed. What was wrong with him? His mind raced, so many thoughts, nothing made sense, he couldn't speak. If his brain were a computer, it was under a denial-of-service attack. The anticipation of Maddy reduced his IQ to zero, and she knew, and she smiled, and he melted.

With one hand on his chest and her soft grey eyes gazing lovingly into his soul, she whispered, "You didn't bring it, did you?" Smiling back as his right hand squeezed the hand on his chest, he looked at the roof, closed his eyes and opened them as he turned and walked out to retrieve the Marc1. Walking out the door, he thought to himself, *Did I just catch the most playful giggle on the planet then, or was my wishful imagination overacting again?*

Returning with everything in hand, he found Maddy lying back on the pillows having already slipped into something more comfortable, a long white cotton nightshirt sporting a witty phrase.

"My eyes are up here," she said.

"Oh um, I was reading your shirt ... is it true?"

She grinned that seductive grin again. "No, Marcus", she said with feigned indignation, "I do not have more issues than Vogue. Now gimme that headset, and prop yourself up with those other pillows against the bedhead next to me and keep me safe." Accommodating her on all three counts, and, although he didn't know why, he told her, "Always." It just felt right.

HER BREATHING CHANGED PERCEPTIVELY BEFORE LONG, and he assumed she was asleep. He waited to make sure. Not able to believe he was here with her, and conscious of his duty to keep her safe, he began to survey the beauty before him. Never before had he the opportunity to stare at her and take in the soft nuances of her face. As he did so, her brows furrowed slightly, her breathing increased, and her whole body moved slightly on the bed as she released a gasp.

Oh god she's having a nightmare, what have I done?

Marcus, heart pounding, ashamed and tormented at causing such calamity to this gorgeous woman, was reaching for the off switch just as the urgent warning of the railway crossing bells at the end of the street made him jump. The railway crossing had done the rescue work just before he could. She was waking.

"I'm here," he said quietly seeking the confidence he didn't feel. Marcus attempted to keep from his voice, how instantly upset he had become as the cause of her nightmare distress.

Her eyes flicked open to stare at the roof in a temporary, vacant gaze.

"I'm here," he whispered compassionately again, lightly touching her elbow.

Her head tilted in recognition and disbelief as her consciousness swam to the surface. "Still keeping me safe I see," she responded groggily.

"Oh Maddy, you were having a nightmare, it's all my fault, I'm so very sorry," confessed Marcus, as he stroked her locks tenderly.

Maddy smiled broadly and held his gaze, "If that was some kind of nightmare, I hope I get one every night. Now come here and finish what you started in that dream."

Marcus had been wrong, and relief flooded him. His last non-erotic thought that night was maybe he didn't hate that train crossing after all.

HELEN CAME BOUNDING up the steps to Maddy's room, knocking urgently.

"Maddy, Marcus is missing. His car's here, but his bed hasn't been slept in!" She walked straight into the bedroom worriedly, only to spot Maddy lying on the bed, looking like she had been up all night, which of course, she had been. Maddy smirked with a loved-up look Helen had never seen her wear before. Her sister rolled naked out of her dishevelled bed, and slid on her white nightie, which looked like it hadn't been worn all night, which of course, it hadn't.

Marcus stepped suddenly from the ensuite, his body trim and taunt. He often had trouble with towels, particularly in motels, and had wrapped his backside in a somewhat smaller than expected one. It forced him to hold the two top corners together at the front. While this provided more than adequate protection for his rear, it offered none for his frontal protuberance. The too-short white cloth created a distinct inverted V from where Marcus held the top of the towel. Helen did her best to fight Fibonacci's rule of thirds and keep her eyes from being drawn into the middle of this living picture.

"Are you wearing the hand towel?" Once said, Helen couldn't take it back. Once seen, the memory wouldn't go away either. Helen could not contain her laughter, while Maddy's head swivelled at breakneck speed towards this dangling vision.

"Shit, sorry Helen," came as a surprised Marcus, briskly rotated the inadequate garb through 180 degrees around his waist, while turning his body around towards the sanctuary of the bathroom. Either rotating the towel or himself to face the other way would have solved the problem. But doing both, only gave Helen an inverted V towel view of his butt cheeks as well. Hell of a way to start the morning after the night before.

Maddy and Marcus were sure they could still hear Bill and Helen laughing a full five minutes later.

Chapter Eleven

There was no doubt he shouldn't be driving today, so he caught the train.

He spent the short journey distracted with Lamarr, plus silent paroxysms of delight at recalling his night with Maddy. Stepping off the T1 train at Lindfield station, to his utter surprise, he managed to catch the 565 bus. The 565 would drop him off right at the Lindfield Road entrance, a mere nine minutes away. The regular driver was society's classic bus driver, quiet but missing extraordinarily little. He had greeted Marcus, knowing he had caught the bus at odd times before, not to mention noticing his ID lanyard and total immersion in his iPhone. A good-natured prompt from the driver ensured Marcus actually made it to work and didn't take the tourist route looping back to the train station in another half hour or so.

Marcus remained engrossed in his reflections as he checked through the security gate at Lindfield. With his engineer thoughts properly in flow, he realised there must be something else going on with the Lamarr chip. Whatever that turned out to be, he might not be able to measure all the audible freqs with the 20kHz oscilloscope. This scope displayed the lowest frequency range in the lab, but even then was at the top end of the human audible range. It wouldn't be low enough.

He realised dealing with this unknown was exciting, and he felt the thrill keenly. Helen had explained the previous night that brain waves were measured in single Hertz, not billions of Hertz like Wi-Fi signals. His best bet was to beg, steal, or borrow, instruments capable of measuring single-digit frequencies.

It occurred to him with a start that, if the Marc1 could lull you to sleep and facilitate very particular and vivid dreams that you remember, it must be doing something more than being a sleeping pill. He'd discovered from his general, but intense Google searches on the train and bus, that sleeping, dreaming, emotions and hearing, all relate to different parts of the brain. *Have I made a brilliant discovery, or created a monster?* "Perhaps a brilliant discovery of an emotional monster," he uttered under his breath, not being able to decide what he really thought.

His body craved coffee and carbs to drive through the day and find answers to questions the four of them had pondered the night before. He headed straight to the ground-floor cafeteria for a bucket of caffeine and one of their magnificent almond croissants. Two lousy nights' sleep in a row; the second he wouldn't change for the world.

Henry and Marcus spotted each other as soon as Henry came through security, so Marcus doubled his order. Henry too had a penchant for their fare.

"How'd ya end up?" Henry enquired as he caught up with Marcus.

"I could ask you the same question, mate," Marcus said fairly, "but judging by the clown-sized smile on your dial, you ended up fine. Have you even had any sleep?"

"How about we make a deal?" negotiated Henry. "You don't ask me her name, and I won't ask you the name of the woman you slept with last Friday night."

"But you worked out her name the minute she walked in," pointed out Marcus, disputing the fairness of this proposal.

Henry responded playfully, "I know what you're saying but let's not get lost in the detail."

Marcus smiled, "Fair point, and in answer to your original question, we could be on to something. I don't suppose I could stretch our friendship on a Monday and ask a favour?"

Henry laughed. "I'm so glad you're going to ask for whatever it is, coz I forgot my lunch money today. So, you'll have to shout me lunch and today is chicken schnitty day. I hope this is a big favour, so you get your money's worth."

Marcus smiled, outmanoeuvred and defeated again. "An oscilloscope or two ..."

Henry didn't realise Marcus hadn't finished, "But each department already has one ... oh, you need two? We could probably borrow another one for the day ..."

Now was Marcus's turn to interrupt. "No, I don't mean that. We need to be able to measure anything from zero to 20Khz. What I'm trying to detect will be in the ultra to extreme low-frequency bands, which we've not needed to measure up to this point."

"Now I *am* intrigued, and you are *so* springing for lunch," replied Henry. "I don't think I'll be able to find that kind of bandwidth in one device. We might have to buy several to cover that spread of freqs. Could be expensive if stores are short on. But," he smiled cheesily, "as my reputation no doubt precedes me, you are aware of my not inconsiderable sway in said stores, so I'll just march down there and demand everything we need. I rarely need to use the full force of my charms, so I'll be back in a jiffy." Henry was positively bubbling, it must have been some date on Friday night.

Marcus felt his eyes rolling into the back of his head. "You are so not going to be able to get them. Did I mention I need them today?" Henry gave the thumbs up as he continued walking out of earshot.

Sure enough, Henry returned empty-handed in short order. Marcus failed to stifle a smirk, which rapidly got out of control. He continued to tease his friend. "Ah huh, clearly you used, how did you put it? Oh yes, all your considerable charms over the weekend, and left none for today." He clamped his mouth shut to avoid laughing with complete gusto, making his face look like his lips were smothering his teeth.

Henry feigned offence. "My weekend was just that, my amazing weekend ... but I'll make some phone calls and track a few things down." He left the lab ten minutes later with a corporate credit card to go retrieve his booty.

Sometime later, Henry arrived back pushing a trolley of three brand-new oscilloscopes still in their boxes. Marcus looked delighted to see him as he hung up the phone and told Henry, "Sarah won't be in today. Probably make it tomorrow."

As Henry unloaded the trolley onto the bench space, Marcus noticed a six-pack of Wi-Fi location trackers and enquired why Henry had bought them.

Henry, in stern defence of his additional purchases, explained, "What, you think because we work at CSIRO, no-one is going to pinch one of these beauties? I bought the tracker Tiles to put in them, so wherever they end up in the building, we can go grab them back. I'll glue them in later when I get a chance."

Marcus easily saw the sense in that. "Sterling idea, we can deactivate them so they won't interfere with the electronics and no-one will know they're in there." As a joke, he added, "Like those thieving bastards down at Astrophysics. They love getting their filthy mitts on new stuff."

"Damn straight."

Both laughed. They were very fond of the folks down at Astrophysics. And Henry was particularly fond of a new crew member, not that his colleague realised it yet.

They conducted several exhaustive tests in uncharted territory over the following hours, copying a digital recording of all their oscilloscope results to a thumb drive for pondering over later. So engrossed were they in their work, they almost missed lunchtime, and the promised chicken schnitzel in the cafeteria.

Looking somewhat undignified in their pursuit of speed without actually sprinting, both made it to the eatery just in time. More than one person looking on wanted to transfer to the Lamarr Project, because *those guys always seem to have more fun than everyone else.*

Lunch went down an absolute treat. They tried to make sense of their results while devouring some delicious tomato-and-cheese-sauced dead chook. With blood sugar and caffeine levels on the rise, they waddled slowly back to the lab and plonked themselves down on a stool each beside the workbench. They hadn't overeaten, but the walk back helped them feel less bloated anyway.

Marcus felt his mind often seemed to be split in two. Not in a psychopathic way, but in a way that allowed a problem to be mulled over while sleeping or thinking about something else. He knew it was as close to multi-tasking as he would ever get.

"I think, to be fair, we can't know what these results mean," started Marcus.

"With you so far," agreed Henry.

Marcus's brain reactor surged to 110 per cent, fuelled by processed food and absorbed caffeine. This unintended post-lunch surge resulted in him thinking out loud, something he was prone to do when by himself, but not generally with anyone else around. He'd found over the years that verbalising a problem sometimes helped to illuminate the answer. What it did today, however, was share the question on his mind with someone else. "Well, beyond Lamarr producing waves in the single and double-digit hertz range, what other clues might there be about the sleeping or the dreams?"

He stopped abruptly.

A quiet pause arose as Henry continued to digest the overheard thought. He took the diplomatic path and decided to ignore the issue of apparent confidentiality. "Perhaps, I could help more if I fully understood the problem ..." he suggested.

There was no sort of moral or security dilemma for Marcus. He trusted Henry and, in this case, maybe a trouble shared would be a trouble halved. So, over the next hour, he brought Henry up to speed on what had happened, and the capabilities of the Marc1. Henry didn't directly receive the juicy bits, of course, but Marcus knew he had an active imagination, so those bits didn't matter.

"Holy shit," mouthed Henry. "I wasn't expecting to hear that today. I don't know what I *was* expecting to hear today, but that was definitely not it," he rambled.

Marcus continued on now as if Henry had known all along. "You and I are used to dealing with frequencies in the gig or meg ranges, not single-digit freqs. My level of knowledge on longwave freqs isn't beyond the basics. We need to ask someone knowledgeable about extreme-low and ultra-low-frequency transmissions, someone we can bring into our confidence."

"Jezzzuuusss." Henry exhaled as he realised something. Having grabbed Marcus's full attention he continued, "I know someone who will be more than happy to help, keen in fact, and I'm sure we can trust her. I trust her."

With the 'I trust her' ending not lost on him, Marcus asked, "OK, mate, where do we find our expert and when can we chat with her?"

"She's here at Lindfield. I'll give her a call now."

"Sweet," said Marcus cheerily, if a tad surprised.

Henry lifted the receiver on the internal phone attached to the wall. While scrutinising the letters on the number pad, he pressed the numbers, 7384.

Marcus watched and worked out by looking at the keypad which department Henry was ringing. But he couldn't think of a woman who worked there. *All in good time*, he told himself.

The phone answered.

"Hi, it's Henry from the Lamarr Project ... Fine mate you? ... I might have some welcome news for Jane is she around? ... Thank you ... Hi, Jane it's me ... I may have found the source of your anaprop ... Well, it's a bit of a long story, can you pop up to our lab? Marcus is here as well ... oh, you don't have to ... that would be awesome ... Standard brew white and two ... No, we don't need anything else, thank you ... See you in a tick."

Marcus's interpersonal skills with women required considerable improvement, but his observational skills, one of the vital skills in his line of work, needed no such tutelage. "I'm going out on a limb here, Henry. Let me know if I've got any of this wrong. Jane is from SETI, and the same mysterious lady you met in a hurry downstairs, and the same mysterious lady you met at Liebigs and ..."

Henry raised both hands in defeat. "You can stop there. You may consider my connection to Jane well established now. I might as well fill you in on the rest before she gets here. Well, the strictly pertinent information, need to know and all that."

"I entirely understand, mate, and trust me, I do not want to hear any non-pertinent information about, how should I put it, accommodating prowess ... when's the wedding?"

"Ha-ha. Don't forget, this woman's picking us up a latte each on her way here."

"I like her already, Henry, she sounds like a keeper! So, what's the juice?"

Henry and Jane originally planned on keeping their promising relationship quiet for as long as they could. Well, that had worked well! Henry became serious. "Jane is an astrophysicist, and she only recently transferred over to SETI, which is why we'd never seen her before." Henry beamed with more than a little pride in Jane and said, "She's quite a remarkable woman.

At Liebigs, an hour or so after I left here her phone alerted her to a signal SETI had received. It was across the ELF ULF bands. Their computer categorised the signal as weak anaprop, a false return if you will, but because SETI isn't staffed overnight the app notified the scientists. Jane said that on top of her to-do list today was finding the cause of that anaprop."

"Oh crap, I'm with ya now," said Marcus.

"Oh crap indeed," said Henry.

Chapter Twelve

"**H**ere she comes," said Marcus, noticing as Jane strolled towards them, she was a naturally attractive woman. Her blonde hair spilled down to her shoulders. She took long, confident strides like a model at London Fashion Week. In a holder as promised, and balanced superbly, she carried three coffee cups.

Henry had become positively perky and moved forward to open the door for Jane, who smiled more than generously at him as she walked in and handed the coffees to Henry.

"Thank you so much for coming," welcomed Marcus, "I don't believe we've ever had the pleasure of welcoming someone whose job it is to search for extraterrestrial intelligence. You'll probably find no intelligence here at all." He was obviously joking but realised she must have been subjected to that a hundred times since arriving, *#awkward*. Jane was kind enough to smile, although she was already smiling at Henry. She conveniently transferred the last seconds of her smile to Marcus in polite recognition of his well-intentioned, but otherwise mediocre, attempt at humour.

After the obligatory introductions, they all sat down on the white padded vinyl furniture set around a matching coffee table in the corner not far from the door.

"Apparently, I am responsible for your anaprop recording on Friday night," Marcus put forward. He noticed a reaction from Jane, who suddenly did not look happy.

Jane, who had come straight up to the Lab expecting a legitimate explanation, was prepared to pay close attention up to this point. Except now, she was convinced these two were playing a joke, and was now waiting - unimpressed - for the punchline.

Marcus continued quickly, "I inadvertently created a combined extreme-low and ultra-low-frequency generator on Friday night in the lab, and I suspect that caused the false return in your system and the alert on your app."

Jane ignored Marcus and looked angrily at Henry. "Henry, this is bullshit. I thought you were way better than this sort of crap!" She stood abruptly ending their brief meeting, "Enjoy the coffee, boys ..." She saw the look of horror pass between Marcus and Henry. Henry stared at her as though nothing else mattered in his life but her believing him. It gave her just enough reason to pause.

Marcus and Henry started talking at Jane over the top of each other. Their dead-serious flurry of conversation was almost indecipherable. The gist was, they were not joking and begged her to please sit down so they could explain.

She sat down against her better judgement, but more so because of the mutual affection her and Henry developed so quickly over the weekend. She changed to a more understanding tone. "Guys, whatever you think you did, you didn't." With her hands flat on the coffee table, she continued. "I accept you are genuine in your beliefs, but your opinions are mistaken and here's why. No 400-metre tall umbrella antennae has sprung up in here over the weekend. So, unless we've been visited by the very ETs I'm charged with finding, and they dropped off a new bit of kit, or the laws of physics have changed, I'm sorry guys, it wasn't you."

Jane looked to Henry as she prepared to leave. He reached under the coffee table, withdrew the Marc1 from the glass shelf underneath and placed it in front of her. "Not extra-terrestrial, but it is new kit, and I promise you, Jane," as he touched his hand on hers, "it was us. I can prove it, with your help."

Jane, pacified for the moment, played along. "OK, I'm all ears, prove it."

Henry saw Marcus reclining and took this as the signal to continue as the frontman. Henry picked up the Marc1 and, without speaking, simply activated the external toggle switch and turned it on. "Jane, give your office a call, see if the false return is back."

Jane stood and dutifully, if not without substantial doubt, walked to the phone and dialled her office. After a brief conversation, her look changed to one of shocked disbelief. The duty console operator had reported the anaprop signal was back. A weak signal, the operator confirmed, but it had the same profile as the one on Friday night. Henry went to her side and, while she was still on the phone, held up the Marc1 so she could see him toggle the power off. The console operator verified at that instant the false return signal had been lost. Jane thanked her colleague on the phone and hung up. In almost conspiratorial timing, her SETI app alerted her to the test they had just concluded.

Jane followed Henry in deep thought back to the seating area. All she said as she grasped her coffee cup was, "Talk to me."

And talk to her they did. They also reviewed their recorded findings of the oscilloscopes earlier in the morning, with Jane providing insights as they went. *She's one smart cookie*, thought Marcus, *I can see why Henry likes her so much*. After two hours of intense information exchange, Jane asked a couple of interesting questions they had not asked themselves.

"Where did the Lamarr chip come from? Who invented it?"

Marcus didn't know, so Henry replied, "Defence Science and

Technology? Can't think of anyone else who might have. Otherwise it wouldn't be here."

Jane shrugged. "Whose to know what they do at DST, hey? I wish we had some of their budget. As a summary, I'll get the techs to use a bypass filter so all the frequencies we pick up while the Marc1 is operating won't set any alerts off. I'll also amend our Schumann resonance algorithm to the specs you gave me and crunch the numbers. The problem is massively less complicated than the calculations we routinely do, so I'll be able to email them through to you probably early evening. Have I missed anything?"

Henry and Marcus replied almost in unison, "No, that seems about everything."

"OK," said Jane, "I'll head off and leave you two to make more discoveries to stand science on its head for the next century." Everyone smiled, and Jane shook hands with Marcus. "Thank you. Considering I felt like throwing hot coffee in your lap a couple of hours ago, I'm so glad I stayed."

"Well, I can't take the credit for that one. You came highly recommended by my partner in crime here," responded Marcus sincerely.

Jane grasped Henry's hand in a professional handshake, which lasted a fraction of a second longer than a *totally* professional handshake. She looked appreciatively at Henry and said in a matter of fact way, "Henry, no doubt we missed some things this afternoon that we might discuss tonight. What do you think?"

"Absolutely, I can think of a couple of things already," he responded.

"Excellent. Do you remember the address?" she asked.

Henry was almost gushing. "How could I forget? What time suits?"

"Let's call it seven. That way, I'll have time to do the calculations, and you'll have time to brush up," she teased. "Bye."

When Jane walked out, Marcus sat down again and did his own

one-word summary of the knowledge gained that afternoon, "Amazing."

"Isn't she just," agreed Henry.

Marcus thought that one could go through to the keeper. "Well, mate, let's clear the test bench off and hide these new scopes from any prying eyes."

Chapter Thirteen

Marcus pulled up at his brother's house and saw the big black Ford already parked alongside the gutter directly in front. He parked his far less powerful, but equally comfortable, red Honda SUV in behind and walked up the garden path towards the front door. He thought with amusement that if anyone were to presume who owned which car, no-one would guess right!

Madeleine may have coincidentally been passing the front door for the umpteenth time since she arrived there herself, or perhaps she was more loitering with intent to embrace. Whatever the truth of the matter, Marcus didn't get a chance to push the doorbell before the door magically sprang open and he became blissfully beset by the full-length, hard-pressing warm body of his enthusiastic lover, who felt at that moment that her world was complete.

Marcus was taller than Maddy but standing inside the door frame made her marginally higher such that their height difference became minimal. They wrapped their arms around each other without a word and kissed passionately as if it was something to be savoured, as indeed it was.

"I missed you ... Can't believe we've been apart less than a day," he whispered as he smooched her again.

"Me too," she whispered back in total contentment. "It seems so long." As she said that, she pressed even harder against him. As though in response to some sudden primeval urge, she tilted her pelvis towards his. His growing hardness massaged into the crutch of her jeans. The accompanying rush of sexual tension was almost excruciating in its pleasure. "Mmm, so long ..."

Helen poked her head around the corner from the hallway and saw the 'collision' at the front door. "For God's sake, Maddy, at least let the poor man into the house before you have your wicked way with him!" Helen's teasing tone belied her joy these two had finally kick-started, or rather slap-started, a relationship.

Reluctantly, and not without another quick peck, they parted, and Marcus followed Maddy inside to the lounge room.

All four sat around the dinner table. The discussion commenced on their success in answering the questions on their respective lists, developed from their conversations the previous evening. The goal had been, if they could get answers to these questions, they might reach some conclusions tonight as to how the Marc1 worked. Maddy's particular list though, as everyone present understood, was more about looking to the future than the present.

Helen started the ball rolling. "Who wants to start?" When no-one offered immediately to kick off the proceedings she continued, "Well, I can. Mine is probably a little time-sensitive anyway ... So, I spoke surreptitiously to Frank, a colleague neurologist, in his rooms today. He was at our wedding."

Bill interrupted cheekily, "Did he speak *frankly*, as usual, darling?"

Helen turned her head patiently towards her husband, closing her eyes as she inhaled and opening them again as she exhaled. She did think it vaguely amusing, and unfortunately for the rest of her life and the thousands of as yet untold dad jokes, he knew it. Helen continued, "Not long after I started talking, he was looking at me like a patient, and about to write a clinical diagnosis of 'she's lost her marbles' on my case notes.

I realised early on in our conversation that I would need to show him the PET scan results, so we loaded them up on his laptop. I don't know if gobsmacked is quite the right word for his reaction, but it has to be close. He asked me a series of questions but said my answers didn't make any sense against a backdrop of a normal functioning human brain. That was because areas of the brain essentially have their functionality dialled down to practically zero. The phrase he used to explain what happens was ..." She flipped open a Spirax notepad and read, "... *Polymorphic artefact waves appear to be cancelling out other organic waves and turning parts of the brain off by default, at the same time over-stimulating the frontal lobe*. He may have been sceptical at the start, but I got the idea he wouldn't be thinking about much else for the rest of the day. He is well and truly invested in getting to the bottom of all this. Frank suggested, no, wrong word there, *insisted*, I give Marcus two EEGs tonight and email him through the results. That will allow him to piece some things together. He'll give us a call tonight after he's finished his hospital rounds. I did bring the machine home, so shall we do that now?"

"Guinea pig two days in a row," said Maddy with a smile as Marcus rose from the table. She and Marcus had been furtively playing footsie with each other under the table as Helen talked, trying not to make eye contact with each other. Now she snuck the opportunity to run the top of her right foot up the inside of his left calf, a sort of, 'until later' kind of footsie goodbye.

A MODERN EEG machine is quite small compared to its relatives of old. In the digital world, the resultant file of a brain's natural electrical activity, its neural oscillations, can additionally be sent to a smartphone or any other blue-tooth device for reading, or merely forwarded on by email. The file can be read by any device with the right app, as well as printed out conventionally.

Marcus put the headpiece on, paradoxically simple overall but complicated in its construction. It resembled a World War One fighter pilot's helmet, but inside the headpiece, spaced one centimetre apart at their closest points, were dozens of sensor pads. Each pad had a wire connected into a multi-cord lead, itself braided into a trio of quick connectors at the rear of the diagnostic headdress. It made him want to shout, "Tally-ho, chaps!"

Helen set the digital frequency settings of the non-invasive electroencephalogram at their widest. A range of .1Hz to 70Hz. She explained the significance of the two tests and how they would proceed. She told them an EEG is used to help diagnose conditions like sleeping disorders and other neurological conditions. Importantly, they're also used to gauge the depth of anaesthesia of a patient and will provide a perfect supplement of highly accurate information to complement the PET scan. So, from these points of view, it was critical data they were about to gather.

Because they were looking for something particular in known ranges, the typical test time for the first test would be cut to ten minutes. The first test was a control to establish the expected level of activity in Marcus's brain. The data would then be used for comparison to the second test, which would take twenty minutes with Marcus wearing the Marc1. During the second test, she would disable the differential amplifier function, usually a vital EEG function, for the initial ten minutes, then turn it back on.

Using a layperson's metaphor, this was like turning off and on the noise-cancelling functionality of a pair of headphones. With the noise-cancelling off, you hear everything that is going on. With the noise-cancelling on, you only hear the range of signals you are trying to listen to. Both recordings would be critical for Dr Frank to understand what was going on.

The tests themselves involved Marcus lying on the couch in cliché psychiatric-patient fashion. The first test was easy. In the second, he was asleep in minutes, and Helen woke him twenty minutes later.

Marcus missed all the action between the sisters. Helen, not so graciously declined Maddy's lascivious offer to wake him herself, by slapping Maddy's hand away as it approached his inner thigh. Maddy glared at Helen silently as though they were children again and her older sister was denying her use of her favourite toy. "Incorrigible," was all Helen said, in a fun-loving repeat of the word Maddy had used to describe her with Bill on Sunday morning.

Helen blue-toothed the three files to her phone and emailed them to Dr Frank.

"I'm about done until Frank calls," she said. "What did you find out, Marcus?"

Marcus rolled upright on the couch and said, "Frank sounds like a bit of a bonus. I hope he can fill some gaps in. From my perspective, Henry thinks Lamarr originated at the DST - Defence Science and Technology - but he's not sure when. As far as I know, it's only been at CSIRO for a few months before our project started. Probably reasonable to assume Lamarr's been around about two years, eighteen months minimum, because of how long it generally takes to get funding and a research program up and running."

Marcus continued, "Background-wise, CSIRO supposes Lamarr has unique properties which they hope will form a new generation of 5G Wi-Fi receivers. Near Field Communications - NFC - is the field. Dollar-wise, the rewards for better products in this field when CSIRO succeeded last time in 1997 were staggering: half a billion dollars. That's over $870M in today's dollars. Our project has been focusing on the receiver side, because logically it would be easier to discover a new receiver and, if it couldn't receive, there was no point in seeing if it could transmit. So, no work has been done on the transmitter side because that doesn't form part of the project test regime. But a unique, ultra-low-frequency transmitter is what the Marc1 really is. No-one foresaw the possibility because, to be truthful, I think no-one spent any time thinking about the transmitting side of things.

"What Henry helped me discover by accident, and the last thing I was looking for, or expecting to find, was a love-dream device, or a make-you-fall-asleep machine. Or even the ability to see someone incredible that had been in front of you for years." He glanced at Maddy, who looked like she would explode with happiness as well.

"I'm assuming you're allowed to tell us all this?" asked Bill. "So, this is solely to develop another type of Wi-Fi transmitter/receiver and make the government some more money?"

"Well, yes and no," said Marcus looking over everyone's heads into space for the train of thought he was seeking. "Lithium-ion batteries are near the end of their developmental life." The silence in the room encouraged him to go on, and he looked straight at his brother. "The advantage of Lamarr is that, as a crystal, it is exactly like the old crystal radios you saw me build as a teenager. It can receive radio signals but doesn't need power to do that. The offshoot of this is higher graphics resolutions for new smartphones."

"I'm sorry ... I ... don't see the connection," said Bill ponderously.

Marcus tried to explain, "Digital displays are made up of pixels. The more pixels per given area, the higher the resolution, but, the more power you need to make each pixel work. Your average consumer doesn't realise battery life and higher screen resolution are inextricably linked together."

"Still don't see," said Bill. It seemed he was not the only one in the room either.

Marcus continued unperturbed, "If we can get Lamarr to work by receiving broadband signals from a commercial 5G network or private 5G Wi-Fi network, and that function requires no power ..." he paused to let them digest this first link, "then the power that would otherwise be used to receive those signals, as in a present-day phone, could be diverted and used for higher-screen resolutions instead. In new smartphone designs, battery life and screen resolution are two of the most contested elements in a mobile phone. Again, the rewards to the market leader are in the billions."

"I'm assuming given what the Marc1 does now," said Bill, "and whatever it could do in the future, would be worth billions as well?"

"You could pretty much pluck any figure in the tens of billions and you'd be fairly safe." Bill gave a low whistle, "Should we like, be having more security or something if the stakes are so bloody high? How far would unscrupulous people go to get their hands on new tech that will make them or some corporation that kind of money?"

His question hung in the air as they all considered the ramifications. No-one spoke for what seemed like ten minutes but was probably only thirty seconds. It was a prophetic question.

Chapter Fourteen

During the serious thoughts regarding their safety, Jane rang Marcus's phone.

"Hello, Jane, thank you so much for all your trouble today and calling me tonight."

"No problem at all, Marcus, always a pleasure," which, considering Henry was at her place, was likely pretty close to the truth.

Marcus could tell he was on speakerphone. "Hi, Henry!" he said in a voice like he were playing hide-and-seek and had discovered who he was looking for.

There was a brief clearing of a throat in the background before the reply croaked out, "Hi, mate."

"Jane, you're on speakerphone and in the room is Maddy, who's a radiographer and my girlfriend ..."

OMG, thought Madeleine, *he called me his girlfriend!*

"Bill, my brother, an audiologist. Helen, my sister-in-law, a psychologist and the brains in their relationship." Bill smiled at the jibe. Everyone said their hellos as Marcus did his audio tour for Jane's benefit. "As you good people here know, Henry is my esteemed colleague, and Jane, if memory serves me correctly, is an astrophysicist ..."

"Got me in one," interjected Jane.

"... and esteemed *new* colleague," added Marcus, "who works on the SETI project."

Jane rarely appreciated flattery, but she did appreciate she was amongst friends. "I do have a theory, but I'm not sure how much use it will be to you," she said, not wanting them to get too excited. "I did reprogram and run the Schumann resonance algorithm as I said I would, but, as suspected, it was inconclusive for the reasons we've previously discussed.

The expected result from Schumann was that with the milliwatt output of the earphones at that distance to the eardrum, some waves would transmit straight through the eardrum in their pure waveform, but some waves would not. That, of course, considers the low amplitude of the multi-frequencies emitted into the eardrum cavity. The waves that pass straight through will be heard as audible sounds as they are up around 20 Hertz.

The longer waves that did not initially pass through would necessarily bounce off the surface of the eardrum and return towards the transmitting earphone. That process repeats such that the energy within the ear cavity rises as these return signals corrupt themselves and others. According to the algorithm, the physical point of maximum energy build-up turns out mathematically to be the centre of the eardrum. Hardly surprising when you think about it because the earphone is pointed right at it."

Bill interrupted with an idea, "Jane, it's Bill. That being the case, do you think the eardrum could be acting like a satellite dish and focusing the corrupted energy through the eardrum into the inner ear?"

Jane couldn't say so either way. "Difficult to say, that's outside my area of expertise, Bill. I can only offer you up information where I can apply known calculus to the problem, and I don't know how to progress beyond what I've said here." Jane thought for a moment. "I'm sorry, folks, perhaps my explanation has made this sound more complicated than it needs to be. If I can use the analogy of a microwave oven, it might make more sense. A microwave oven is a box with six sides. One of those sides you can always see through, which is the door. The door has metal mesh under the glass specifically designed so the microwaves cannot physically pass through the mesh at the frequency the microwave oven is designed to operate on. Are you all good so far?"

They all made affirming noises.

"OK, if you made the microwave oven operate on a different frequency or frequencies, the door mesh would allow energy to pass through it. I believe this is what the eardrum may be doing. Beyond the eardrum, though, we should defer to Bill. That's about all I have for you, I'm afraid."

"Thank you so much, Jane, for another piece to the puzzle," said Marcus. "We can't tell you how much we appreciate your help."

"Hey, Marcus," said Henry, "do you mind if we start at ten in the morning? How about we meet in the cafeteria?"

"Not at all, mate, I like the way you think. Let's lead with a latte!" replied Marcus and smiled at Maddy, who did not make her displeasure known. That being because she had none.

Goodbyes passed between them, and the phone call ended.

Bill took up the thread. "I think I can take Jane's information and put that together with the physiology of the inner ear. I postulate that the inner side of the eardrum is focusing energy getting through the outer eardrum onto what is called the round window." Bill continued in response to the blank looks directed at him.

"Because the frequencies are wave energy, they are not converted into sound in the earphones themselves like normal. If I stick with my satellite dish theory on the back of what Jane said, the earphones form an antenna, which radiates a mix of energy focused on to the middle of the outer surface of the eardrum. The drum then acts like a flat double-sided satellite dish, concentrating signals on the outer side, and then those signals are pushed through to the inner side due to the energy build up. To give you an idea of size, the eardrum is twenty times larger than the oval window in the inner ear at the cochlea, which significantly is where the auditory nerves start.

So, if this is acting as I think, from there the signal is still not sound and travels along the auditory nerve straight into the brain. Both the auditory nerve pathways carry the signal in equal proportion as if made to. But they are not made to and never function this way. That, again, is something new and unique." Bill finished off. "I'm sorry if this doesn't make sense. I'm still trying to get a handle on it myself, but all I'm trying to say is what Jane has said is making more sense the longer I think about it. I believe my basic theory of how the signals get through into the aural nerve holds true."

The three nodding heads were what he needed to see. That meant, if they didn't follow the detail, they at least understood the summary.

"My turn?" asked Maddy, and again three heads nodded.

"In the research field, as you never know what line of research might be of assistance to another, the university never discards or deletes information. That includes all student research and assignments. I checked for any results of students having done PET scans trying to capture emotions other than love. I couldn't for the life of me remember a student ever doing a research assignment on an emotion other than love. Appreciating I'm only one of four radiographers there, I thought there was a reasonable chance it had been done, I just had to find it."

Maddy continued, "I didn't just want to straight out ask the other three technicians, despite us all being friends, because that would have led to awkward questions that I didn't want to answer. To be honest, I couldn't find anything on the PET and was feeling quite deflated, like I'd let you all down. Then I realised, while focusing on the PET scanner results, the obvious had escaped me, and I finally caught on to the fMRI scanner. Similar to the PET, the fMRI was the second scanner in the department after the MRI and has been there for years. The *f* stands for *functional*. It shows which parts of the brain are experiencing greater neural activity as they consume more oxygen from the blood.

"To cut a long story short, I found part of what we're looking for," she said pleased with herself. She held up a white USB. "On here, are the fMRI scans of two different people. One brain experiencing Fear, the other, Hate."

"Incredible," said Helen, "but how do you know they're valid?"

"Ah, that's a question I asked myself too. So, I dug out the papers that went with the scans, and I don't doubt they're valid and represent the emotions they say they do. I reached the same conclusions as the assessors did. The Fear scan was from the brain of the second-year student who prepared the paper. He always knew he had a predisposition towards claustrophobia but managed to face his fear, so to speak, even to the point where he would ride in a small elevator for short distances on purpose, to de-sensitise himself. The trouble was, he got trapped in a small shopping centre car park elevator for nearly forty-five minutes instead of his planned twenty-second ride. It tipped his phobia well and truly over the edge."

Maddy continued with evident empathy, not lost on an admiring Marcus. "The scan was done three months after the car park elevator incident, as the poor young man tried without success to wrestle himself back to normality. In the end, the phobia became so bad he couldn't lean forward into the fMRI when standing alongside a patient waiting to go into the machine. Just doing that gave himself symptoms of heart palpitations, hyperventilation and nausea. For the Fear scan, he foolhardily, or bravely depending on your perspective, stuck through the scan in apparent severe distress. He was shaking like a leaf when he finally got off the machine's slide bed. According to the notes, he took a strong antiemetic beforehand. That was his last day in training as a radiographer, but he went on to complete a degree with distinctions in aquaculture, in the wide-open spaces of the sea, I guess."

"I'm surprised it got past the ethics committee, that being the case," thought Bill aloud.

Maddy replied, "Well, interesting you say that, neither the Fear nor Hate scans came before the ethics committee. They wouldn't have got approval, given the personal suffering involved, even though in both studies the suffering was to the student who was seeking the results."

A phone rang again, this time Helen's. She answered without using speaker.

"Hi, Frank ... Fine ... Oh. OK ... Yes, me too. I'm glad you concur ... Sure, we're all still here, you're most welcome to, of course, that would definitely be easier ... No, not a thing, thank you, we're all good." Helen gave Frank the address and hung up. "Frank will be here in ten or fifteen minutes. He said it was way too much information to try to discuss over the phone."

Helen frowned not sure whether she wanted to ask her next question, but her curiosity got the better of her, "And the other student, what was their background?"

Maddy took a deep breath. "That one, like the last one, took great courage as well. A female student hated her father with a vengeance for his, shall we say, mistreatment of herself, her sister and her mother, over many years. She and her sister blamed the father for the untimely death of their mother. The student prepared by meditating in the fMRI room and then being put into the machine. An audio file that her similarly abused sister had prepared, and which she had not heard before, played during the scan. Pictures of her father were stuck on the inside of the scanner, providing both visual and aural cues. According to the notes, by the time the results were in, she was mentally exhausted, her hands were pale from being clenched, and she was sweating profusely. Her sister, now a nurse, was present for moral support, and also upset herself, administered 10 mg of diazepam and took her home ..."

Everyone in the room was in genuine awe at what both students had put themselves through. "There's no doubt these two case studies are legit," summated Maddy.

The doorbell rang. Marcus leaned forward to stand and said, "Best I get that, in case Maddy thinks it might be me. Helen knows what happened last time." The slap landed swiftly and surely on his shoulder. *Man, that woman is quick*, thought Marcus, as he blew his assailant a kiss.

"Why, what happened last time?" asked Bill.

"Nothing you need to worry your handsome head about, husband," replied Helen closing the subject. "I'll tell you later, maybe."

Bill headed into the kitchen for more wine and another wine glass.

Chapter Fifteen

Frank entered the room and, although they hadn't all got the chance to meet at the wedding, a good feeling of familiarity was felt by all. With the formal introductions of this fifty-something-year-old, grey-haired, distinguished-looking gent completed, Frank sat, and they got down to business.

"I have to say," he said with great passion, "this is the most fascinating thing I have ever read about, heard about, or seen in my career. I am so glad to be part of this infinitely fascinating discussion."

Bill chipped in good-naturedly, "Are you charging by the hour, mate? I'm not sure we can afford you."

Frank raised his glass in Bill's direction and shot back, "We both work in the public system. If you can afford this bottle of Pinot Grigio, you can afford me for the night!" There were smiles all round.

"Here," offered Marcus as he passed the Marc1 over the table for Frank to hold and gaze upon. Saying nothing, Frank held the device with such reverence as though he were a knight of old concluding a lifelong quest to find the Holy Grail. He placed it carefully on the table before him without saying a word, as he was, literally, speechless.

After taking a breath of air and another swig of his white wine, he rallied his considerable mental troops and began. "OK, here we go. Let's start with the easiest explanation first, actually, the only easy explanation in all of this. The normal sleep process starts with a neurotransmitter, a chemical not an electrical connection, blocking histamine from attaching to H1 receptors in the brain. This causes drowsiness, like you experience using the Marc1, or by taking a common first-generation antihistamine drug such as Phenergan. The longer the Marc1 stays on you, or, the more drug you take, the deeper you sleep, up to a point." He raised an index finger in emphasis.

"Just to be clearer, I don't believe the Marc1 acts like a relaxant such as diazepam. Diazepam discourages neurons from firing in the first place. The end effect of sleep is the same, but we can see neurons firing on the EEG. So, my money is on the Phenergan-type antihistamine effect. After reviewing and considering everything you've supplied me with, I've reached a conclusion. As an overarching comment, and this will come as no surprise to any of you, the Marc1 is stimulating psychological and physiological responses from the brain, using what could best be described as artificial brain waves. I don't know how else to put it."

He went on, "The brain is like your heart, run by a superbly interactive and timed electrical and chemical system. For instance, most people are familiar with defibrillation these days. In a nutshell, that works by passing an electrical charge of extremely precise energy at extremely precise intervals, across the heart. This energy is designed to stop the heart momentarily, thereby giving the normal electro/chemical processes within the heart, the opportunity to restart in their normal sinus rhythm."

With no-one looking like they were about to ask a question, another sip of his wine brought more information. "This is similar in principle, although different in practice, to what the Marc1 is doing. The Marc1 is passing electrical energy into the brain, and that's doing three things. Number one, as you now know, it is blocking histamine from attaching to H1 receptors, causing drowsiness and deep sleep. Number two, it is successfully targeting and hyper-stimulating the part of the brain related to love. The yearning for a person, and the specific over-stimulated part of the brain, makes the temporary neural connections to allow memory, or daydreams, to be experienced as a vivid dream with total recall. Number three, and this is where the defibrillator analogy comes into play, it turns off some higher-function activity in the brain, and this last feature is why we see what we see on the PET scanner results. When the Marc1 itself is turned off, all electrical activity in the brain resumes its normal function."

What Frank said was engrossing the four others in the room, so he moved on. "The equivalent to a defibrillator in a brain is ECT or electroconvulsive therapy. Most people know of this in a bad way. ECT shocks the brain where it causes a seizure, which is intended to allow the electrochemical activity in the brain to reset, thereby treating things like severe depression. Whether ECT even does that is up for debate. The Marc1, on the other hand, is infinitely more subtle by comparison, turning specific activities off. When the Marc1 itself is turned off, normal brain activity recommences with no neurological deficit or perceptible side effects. This is astonishing and unprecedented." Frank couldn't get the smile off his face.

Maddy was the first to say anything. "Frank, do you think at some time in the distant future we would be able to tune the Marc1 to be able to hyper-stimulate another emotion instead of love?"

Frank gave a small chuckle, which Maddy took as a sign that a straight-out 'no' was on its way.

Bill chimed in, "Interesting question, Maddy."

Against Maddy's expectation, Frank now answered with an

emphatic, "Yes, I do. Helen, your sister is obviously as talented as you." He became visibly thoughtful, then clarified his answer. "It would seem reasonable to think if you can target one emotion, you can target another in the same way. But, although my initial reaction is yes, it would depend on whether it is technically feasible, and I have no idea on that side. What do you say, Marcus?"

"To be honest, Frank, I've given that zero thought. In the last few days, my mind's been taken up with how it works, not what else it could do. You're right, though. She is talented. We'll put our heads together later on and see what we can come up with," mused Marcus.

As there were no other questions, and he had a busy day tomorrow, Frank gulped the rest of his wine and stood up. They all shook hands and bid him goodnight. As he walked across the front lawn, he turned slightly to Marcus, who stood on the landing, "The big Ford suits you, Marcus."

"Oh it's um ... a great car, thanks," replied Marcus, not knowing what else to say.

Marcus returned to the lounge room, where the others had obviously been continuing their discussion.

Bill was recalling the question Maddy had asked of Frank. "Hey, Maddy, you asked Frank a question about other emotions. Why did you do that?"

Maddy assumed they'd all noticed that, and she was glad no-one had said anything at the time. "I couldn't stop thinking about your security comment earlier and whether this thing should be kept undercover. We should be trying to limit who knows what the Marc1 can do, so as few people as possible realise what it could become."

"As Frank told Maddy, you're as talented as your beautiful big sister." Bill added in 'beautiful' on purpose, and Helen's batting eyelids told him she'd heard.

Still looking at Helen, Bill continued, "I know you have a bit more information to top the night off, honey. Shall we do that and call it quits for the night?"

"Sure," replied Helen. "It's the last thing on my list for tonight."

Marcus and Maddy snuggled into each other on the couch, indicating they were ready.

"OK, there are eight primary emotions. We are all born into the world with these eight emotions hard-wired into our brain. That wiring, in conjunction with cerebral chemical processes, causes our bodies to react in certain ways and even to react physically when relevant emotions arise. Since I am speaking totally professionally, I can give a quick example ... Maddy."

A look of horror crossed Maddy's face. "Why bring me into this?"

"Come on, little sis, this is pure medical professional-patient confidentiality stuff."

Maddy wasn't convinced. "Hmm, OK then."

"So," continued Helen, "when Marcus had his PET scan ..." Maddy's alert level upgraded to Defcon1. "Did he get an erection while he was asleep and you were taking his results?"

"You bitch!" cried Madeleine with a laugh, following up with, "That is so not fair." Maddy avoided looking at Marcus next to her. Bill started to shake with unsuppressed laughter.

Marcus gazed at her innocently before asking, "Yes, Maddy, did I?"

As Maddy's face grew to a shade that would embarrass a beetroot, Helen voiced her triumph, "I'll take that as a yes." To avoid anyone getting a word in edgeways, she carried on, "Right here are two examples of a physical reaction to an emotional situation, one from Marcus and the other from the beetroot here.

Of the eight primary emotions hardwired into our brains, Love is sourced within one of these primary emotions called 'Interest'. Love itself is not a primary emotion. That seems counter-intuitive I know, because you'd think love would overarch, but it doesn't.

Interest includes others like devotion, affection, kindness, trust, acceptance and friendliness."

"While we're on the subject, what are the other seven then?" Bill asked.

"Why, thank you for your question," Helen responded in mock seriousness to her husband. "It's been a while since uni, but I believe them to be, Joy, Anger, Disgust, Sadness, Fear, Surprise, and last, but not least, Shame.

"How impressive is that? How impressive are you?" said Bill giving her a peck on the cheek.

"Oh, get a room, you two," Maddy groaned.

"'JADS FISS' was the acronym we all used to remember the list of emotions at uni," Helen continued. "We rote-learned it for the exams and it seems to have stuck in there." She smiled, pleased her husband was delighted with her. "That brings me to the last question on my list, why is the Marc1 hyper-stimulating love? Initially, I conjectured the reason was that love is amongst the greatest emotions, with the strongest neural pathways and the most potent reflexes across the brain. But, after putting everything together tonight, it would seem the love aspect must be totally random. It also appears, and as we've touched on tonight, that if the same mechanism of operation can be adjusted for other emotions, there is a good chance it would work for them as well.

If you were to sit down and do a mind map of the possibilities, the implications in any and all directions would simply be mind-blowing. I don't want to shock you all, but I agree with Bill. Seriously, we should keep this under wraps for our own safety and anyone else who knows."

Everyone took this further warning to heart, and she could tell by the look on their faces that they'd all got the message.

Maddy sought clarification from Helen, "While we're on the negative side of things, where does hate sit in all this?"

Helen replied thoughtfully, "We aren't born with hate. Sadly, it's something we learn because something has happened, or tragically, even criminally, are indoctrinated with. Hate is a composite of emotions like rage, disgust, resentment and our old friend, fear."

"Gotcha," said Maddy.

Bill suggested, "Maybe until after this all settles down, we should all stay here together, you know, congregate in the safety of numbers and all that." As Maddy and Marcus looked thoughtfully at each other, he added, "I'll add some extra security in, to help keep us safe. I'm sure nothing will happen, but we'll take some extra precautions anyway."

"Sounds like a good idea," agreed Marcus, and with Madeleine also nodding her head in accord, the deal was sealed.

"I don't know about you guys, but it's been a long day, and I'm ready to hit the sack," said Helen with a genuine yawn.

No-one was going to argue. The kitchen could wait for the morning this time.

Chapter Sixteen

As the door shut quietly to Maddy's room, Marcus put the Marc1 in the middle of the bedhead. They began undressing on opposite sides of the bed. Maddy looked down at her shirt to undo her buttons more quickly. Every now and then she glanced warmly at Marcus as he raced through his clothes removal. The anticipation developing between them was unmistakable, and given their state of increasing undress, what Maddy said next caught him a little by surprise.

Maddy stopped unbuttoning, briefly closed her eyes, trying to reset the persistent, non-sexual-related thoughts invading her mind. She soon found her words, "Please bear with me for a minute, I can't turn my brain off!"

Marcus, unaware of the torment she was experiencing replied half seductively with a huge grin, "Oh, I'm almost *bare* with you now."

Madeleine raised an eyebrow, and didn't miss a beat, "I can't stop thinking about what Helen said regarding the potential of the Marc1. It is *staggering* and *mind-blowing*, and those words are major understatements." Maddy was assembling an idea. "We know from the fMRI scans I found in the archives where Fear and Hate are focused in the brain. Using the information from them and the Love PET scan with tonight's EEGs as a baseline, do you think you could work out how to hyper-stimulate other emotions instead of Love?"

Listening to her talk about his project with such passion was endearing. He paused to look at her appreciatively and said sincerely. "I can only try. I've had a couple of ideas about how to modify it, and I'll give those a shot in the lab tomorrow … after 10 am." He beamed and she grinned in return.

As the last remnant of clothing slid down his legs to his ankles, Maddy lost herself in the distraction of his body as she ticked off a mental checklist. *Fit and muscular, but not a gym junkie, smooth skin, everything in proportion and as it turns out, a perfect fit.*

In an attempt to regain her attention, and mimicking her dig at him the previous evening, he said, "My eyes are up here, darling."

Marcus had never called her darling before either …

They slipped towards one another, between the soft flowing, dove-coloured bamboo sheets, their gazes not parting, even momentarily …

… "OH MY GOD," whispered Maddy breathlessly, her face inches above his as she lay astride him. Her breathing finally calming down, "I may never walk again," she quipped.

They smiled and kissed tenderly again. "Me neither," agreed a similarly recovering Marcus.

He cupped her face in his hands and kissed her as she slid off him to snuggle her head on his shoulder.

As he lay on his back, Maddy sensed a change in his demeanour and looked up at him, "Now it looks like you have something on *your* mind?"

Marcus, currently doubted his own ability to add up two single digits, did his best to answer as he squeezed her lightly. "It might be a little late now, but I had a thought earlier on tonight and wondered if you would be up for a quick experiment involving no clothes?"

"As long as it doesn't involve me trying to walk in the next half hour my love, I'm in!" she flirted, but realised she had accidentally said the 'L' word. Not in the way she genuinely wanted to say it, but said it, nonetheless. She need not have worried, as the man next to her heard every word and had no intention of going anywhere. He tried vainly to look down at her to provide reassurance, so kissed her on the top of her head to provide the same message instead.

"My idea, and I have no clue whether it will work or not, is we share the Marc1, like Bill and Helen did, but turn the volume down to zero so it doesn't make us fall asleep. The idea is to see if the love emotion is enhanced while we're still awake."

"The things I do ..." sighed Maddy, as she sat up and rearranged her flowing hair with an intricate and perplexing flourish of move-ments, with all the practised skill of a magician's sleight of hand. The resultant transformation from a beauty queen's flowing curls to a business-like 'bun' on the back of her head made her locks infinitely more manageable and exposed the pale softness of her long neck.

Marcus watched, altogether impressed as she accomplished this remarkable feat of instant hair rearrangement. He found his thoughts considerably distracted by her actions and believed himself unable to add one and one together for the second time in five minutes. He struggled to continue with his original train of thought and get it straight in his head. "It kind of makes sense if we turn it right down, so if we can't hear the audible part that makes us sleep, we should stay awake."

"Sounds fair so far." Maddy appreciated that this was important and followed along closely.

Marcus tried to remain logical. "Since the signals we can't hear shouldn't be affected by the volume setting, they should still get through and be effective, as long as we don't mute it, because muting will break the circuit."

"I understand what you're saying, strangely enough. You know you don't need a ploy to keep me from getting out of this bed, right? Besides ... this is *my* room!" She sealed the plan with an enthusiastic, "Come on big boy, let's do this thing."

Marcus paused. "Oh, one more factor, if it works at all, it will take a few minutes to affect us like it does when we're asleep."

"Ok, I'm ready" was all she said.

Marcus turned on the Marc1 and she placed an earplug in her right ear, and he in his left. They lay facing each other, eyes wide with excitement as they waited for any effect that might happen. As the minute's past between them, at the outset, there was no discernible jump in emotion.

SPEAKING SOFTLY, Marcus said, "I can't tell you how many times I imagined this moment." His eyes fixated on Maddy's, "I thought we would only ever be friends, and now this machine has somehow ..." She raised a finger and gently placed it on his lips, motioning him to stop talking. In that instant, his words strengthened their new relationship, and she smiled.

Holding her hand, he lightly kissed her fingertips and curled her fingers over his. He inhaled against her skin.

"I wanted this to be real too," she whispered, "imagine if you'd never discovered what you did, we would still be having awkward moments that went nowhere."

His mouth left her fingers, and he moved his hand down her arm to her waist. As his hand settled into the small of her back, he firmly pulled her forward toward him. Her heart was beating so hard, she thought he could hear it. She wrapped her leg over the top of his hips, feeling the radiated heat between them.

What they initally felt, could be likened to walking outside in the sunshine after the rain, everything so clear and vibrant. As they lay, with their bodies clamped around each other, the building of breathless urgency consumed them. Then they felt *it*, the uplifting, fulfilling, *surges of pure unadulterated LOVE.*

Engulfed in the moment, he rolled her onto her back in one graceful, powerful movement. He looked down upon her in wonderment, drawing his hand gently down her forehead, fingers twisted the hairs around her ears. He pulled her closer to him, she tilted her head back, enticing him further. He could feel the heavy rise and fall of her chest as he savoured her. His dark eyes were aglow as he tenderly kissed and teased her lips apart.

With his hips cradled between her legs, he gathered her up in the strength of his arms into a sitting position. His large warm hands firmly around her rib cage, he lifted her. Then slowly, with powerful restraint, he guided her down. She gasped a short breath, as his pressed into her, resisting her efforts to have him thrust. Her hair came loose from the bun and tumbled down around her shoulders, their eyes staying locked upon each other.

As the overwhelming emotions swept over them, they both, inexplicably, burst out laughing, neither knowing why. The intensity between them was such there was no holding back a mutual, sudden, but brief flood of tears either.

Earphones no longer attached; it didn't matter. They were finally both equally enmeshed in each other, and ... in their *Love.*

Chapter Seventeen

I t being Henry's turn to shout caffeine and calories, Marcus arrived at the cafeteria and seated himself at a table to await him.

They shook hands in greeting, which was pretty much a first. Neither would have said the other offered his hand first, but it seemed natural to signify their friendship and trust.

It was such a great way to ease back into work, and 10 am at that! The Marc1 had brought the two of them rapidly closer in their friendship. With this growing camaraderie, so too had other feelings for their respective partners grown. Today was a new day. For the first time, they openly discussed the women in their lives and how happy and lucky they felt. Marcus also brought Henry up to speed entirely with the current state of play. The 'committee of inquiry,' as Marcus had randomly and affectionately dubbed it, collectively understood how the Marc1 operated.

Both men agreed the committee would comprise *only* those who were briefed on everything, or those they could trust, or had no choice to trust. To maximise safety, the committee would be kept to an absolute minimum. On the list at present were seven people: Frank; Marcus and Maddy; Henry and Jane; Bill and Helen.

THEY WERE SOMEWHAT surprised to see Sarah strolling past the canteen half an hour after they arrived. "I thought she was away today," said Henry matter-of-factly.

"Me too," replied Marcus, "but since she's arrived, and we're technically not there yet either, best we get the boss a latte with a pastry and high tail it to the lab, my friend!"

Both men chatted intently as they walked. "The more people we tell until we confirm what the potential and dangers of this thing are, the more people *you and I* put at risk. I propose, for the time being, we protect Sarah and don't tell her everything just yet, agreed?"

Henry readily concurred. "Agreed, not to mention Sarah being here today will also put the stops on us building the module we planned. That is, unless you can come up with a bold and cunning plan, Baldric."

They arrived at the lab to find Sarah seated on one of the chairs around the coffee table, reviewing the test program on her laptop.

"Beware of colleagues bearing gifts, but we hope you're feeling better," opened Marcus at the same time Henry placed their purchases before her.

"So, this is how you keep yourselves entertained while the cat's away, hey? Spending your days in the cafeteria," she answered light-heartedly scanning them both. "You certainly know the way to a woman's heart you two, and I'll take it. So, what's been going on in my absence?"

Marcus and Henry stared involuntarily at each other, and since Marcus was the senior, he was the one to deliver the update.

"Would you like to start at the mundane and build up to the exhilarating, or the other way around?" he asked Sarah.

"Let's go mundane and build up from there. I'm intrigued as to just how exhilarating this could get though!"

Marcus explained how they'd followed the testing program on Sarah's first sick day and up until lunchtime on Friday, providing a rudimentary summary of the results.

Sarah knew something was coming. "So, I guess the mundane finishes at lunchtime on Friday?"

Henry spoke up and directed his question, delivered in a please-excuse-us way, to Sarah, "Have you ever heard of the saying, *sometimes it's better to ask forgiveness than permission?*"

"Oh, it's *that* exciting?" came the sarcasm, with a hint of humour. "What exactly did you two get up to? Smash our budget for the month on coffee and chicken schnitty?"

After taking a deep breath, Marcus said flatly "Apart from the chicken schnitty ... no."

Something in the way Marcus's voice inflected let Sarah know the casual repartee was over, and the unburdening of consciences was about to begin.

Not knowing how this would go, Marcus became more upright in his chair and used a formal tone. "I had an idea over lunch on Friday about running a Lamarr *transmission* test, and I decided, off my own bat, to depart from the planned program to carry out that test."

"We," added Henry, "we decided," in an unnecessary demonstration of solidarity, but one that Marcus appreciated, nonetheless.

"Come on, guys," placated Sarah, "this isn't like you've carried out some kind of coup d'état, it's only one transmission test! It's all good so far, and I'm keen to know what you've found out."

Marcus retrieved the Marc1 from his backpack and placed it on the table in front of Sarah. "This is what we found out."

"You built a little black box, installed with what? And what does it do?" she asked, intrigued.

"How about if I blurt it all out and then you ask questions later. Is that OK?" queried Marcus. Sarah shrugged, then nodded assent.

Marcus went on to explain, in summary form, and without any gratuitous sexual references, what the Marc1, as he had unofficially christened it, actually did. He said nothing of how they thought it worked, or its future potential. Henry chimed in at odd intervals but, as per their conversation walking to the lab, steered clear of these two issues as well. Anyone would think the briefing was thorough and that both men were reading the same script. While both were definitely doing that, there was a purposeful lack of thoroughness. However, from Sarah's point of view, you can't know what you don't know. What the two men told her was enough to make her extremely excited indeed!

Sarah's thoughts sprang to her contract with Peter. *This may well be my ticket to release my bonds to the devil.* "I'm speechless, other than to say, well fucking done you two! Now give me a big hug!"

Sarah stepped forward to hug Henry, then Marcus, with a strength and sincerity that surprised them both. For all intents and purposes, she came across as well pleased with what they had done, providing substantial relief to the nervous men standing before her.

They sat again, and Sarah continued to speak. They could tell she was trying to contain her delight and not become too excited. "OK, to confirm I've got this straight in my head. You two have invented a little black box with earphones that will send the listener to sleep in a few minutes?" She let the question hang.

"Yep," said Marcus as Henry nodded.

"OK, while you're asleep, you dream vividly of someone you yearn for or love, and you can remember the dream in detail, like it really happened, when you wake up?" This question received the same response as the last. Sarah stared at the Marc1 on the table and picked it up with all the care customarily attributed to a Ming dynasty vase. She heard her dumbstruck self say softly, "Fuck ... me," and *knew* she had just uttered the words of her deliverance from tyranny.

The co-conspirators sat patiently in silence while Sarah further contemplated the Marc1 in her hands.

"So, tell me what you *do* know about how this thing works?" asked Sarah.

Marcus was very aware she framed the question to persist in an area of inquiry he had already covered. Similarly, he thought, *I will have to persevere in my broad response to parry her thrust.* He spoke politely and with candour, "Like I said, Sarah, beyond thinking sound waves are being generated into the brain, I can't tell you anything else." His gut told him this wouldn't be the end of it. He had to come up with a distraction for her if he wanted to get away with this vagueness for a day at least. "Henry and I were discussing expanding the Marc1 with a diagnostic module while we were in the canteen this morning. Hopefully, this should speed up our quest for answers."

Not what they'd agreed upon, thought Henry, as he nodded in affirmation. *I wonder where this is going?*

Marcus had her attention. "The idea is we install variable low and high pass filters to help us isolate signals and find out what's going on." He tried to sound conversational. "We add in some menu controllers and other stuff to make the whole thing self-contained. This will save us loads of diagnostic time in the long run."

"Sounds fair," agreed Sarah, all smiles.

Before she could continue thinking, Marcus tactfully tempted her. "I have a schematic in the safe. I just need to add a couple of extra circuits to it, and you can build your own starting now. We have all the bits needed for a duplicate, and it would be better to have two working prototypes. What do you think?"

"What a terrific idea! Thank you, I'm *so* grateful to you guys."

Sarah smiled warmly and could hardly contain her jubilation as she headed to the lab safe to retrieve the schematic for Marcus to amend and to start her own construction.

Henry looked at Marcus knowingly. In one stroke, Marcus had not only secured Sarah's blessing for how they planned to adapt the Marc1, but they could now do it right in front of her! Besides, he suspected Sarah would be so engrossed in her build she would likely not pay too much attention to theirs. Genius!

Henry bet Marcus was relieved they had stashed their new oscilloscopes away. If they had still been on the test bench, their little deception could have faltered big time.

THE DAY PASSED with Marcus working intently on the diagnostic module, and Sarah excitedly on the Sara1, as she now liked to call it. Henry moved backwards and forwards between them, able assistant to them both.

Around mid-afternoon the Sara1 was complete. Marcus loaned Sarah his earphones to confirm audio was being produced. After a quick tidy up, she intended to pop into the music store on the way home, as the same Sennheiser earphones had to be considered part of the original specifications. With the Sara1 in hand, she sincerely thanked the other two once more for such an uplifting day, and told them she was heading home to give it a shot. After all she couldn't really go to sleep at work now, could she?

They bid her a good night and good luck with it. Having failed to explicitly mention how vivid and lurid her dreams might be, they expected she could only be pleasantly surprised at worst.

With Sarah distracted earlier on, Marcus had carried out minimal modifications to the Marc1, and create an externally attachable module for it, held in place by an over-centre latch system. He didn't want to modify the internals of the Marc1 any more than he absolutely had to, in case it caused a fault he would need to trace. As a hundred per cent working prototype, it was best to leave it that way. When attached to the new module it doubled the size of his invention. The module would support different tests, but the Marc1 itself could now remain unchanged, thus providing a constant baseline. To add the module, all he had to do was latch and attach. Latch the modules together, attach the multi-pin connector, and the coupled device was off and running.

On the security side of things, it was more secure to experiment with advanced features using a modular system. If their Project was compromised, or they were directed to hand the Marc1 over, they would only have to produce the Marc1, not the test module. That was because no-one outside the Project team, apart from the committee, knew the module even existed. Using this approach to Marc1 advanced capabilities research, they could keep as much of it secret for as long as possible, from as many people as possible. Primarily, that would also keep the 'committee' as safe as could be.

The module they created contained a concoction of features all there for an express purpose. The three main items powered by extra batteries were controlled by a separate on/off toggle switch just like the Marc1. When connected, both switches had to be on, or nothing would work. There were a digital multichannel controller, a modified Butterworth frequency filter, and a single 3.5-inch 20-watt subwoofer cone. Rough calculations determined a speaker of this size would produce about 2000 times the power output of a pair of earphones. As with all earphone equipped devices, when the earphones are connected, the speaker doesn't operate. There was no point in spending any time on more precise calculations because it would either work or it wouldn't. The issue was if it did work, and assuming no attenuation, what range would it work at? Their ballpark figure indicated about three metres.

With the installations completed, they attached the module to the Marc1. Both agreed, to save confusion when in this configuration, it should be referred to as the Marc2. When not attached the module would be called the Marc2 module. Thus, the Marc2 *and* the Marc2 module had the same birthday. After a series of connectivity and functional tests, they declared it ready for service.

The idea for an experiment arose during the previous evening, so before they left the lab for the night, they quickly set it up. Marcus simply wanted to establish if it were possible to use Bluetooth earphones instead of wired ones. Neither man was sure, because Bluetooth operates on a frequency billions of times higher than the Marc1 transmitted. Both men rather knew this difference would somehow interfere with the Lamarr chip during transmission, and nothing would be heard through the earphones. As it turned out, their collective educated guess was correct, but neither was pleased to be so.

Marcus turned to his friend and colleague. "Not meaning to impose anything on you, but since you and Jane are on the committee, would you like to take the Marc1 home tonight, to, um, increase your practical exposure to the device?"

Henry smirked. "Well, I never thought to ask ..."

Marcus retorted, "Oh, you so did too! Liar, liar, pants on fire!" They both laughed at the aptness of this children's taunt from the 1920s, the very decade crystal radios had become popular.

With Marcus grabbing the Marc2 module to show 'the committee," he was ready to say his goodbyes for the day. Henry, taking the Marc1, closed up the lab and they walked away together. "I guess we should be here at eight tomorrow," said Henry, "since the boss is back, I'll be interested in hearing what she has to say about the Sara1."

"I'll be interested in what you have to say as well, mate," Marcus teased him. "See you tomorrow."

Chapter Eighteen

Marcus and Henry had been in the lab since 8 am sharp. Henry returned the Marc1 and locked it in the lab safe. Marcus was expecting Sarah would arrive at any time as well, but that never eventuated. At 8.30 am, Marcus sent her a welfare check SMS to make sure she was OK. There was a short delay in her response, but then she texted she would be in the office about 11. She had some things to sort out and some calls to make before she came in. Also mentioned in the text was a meeting with Peter she has shortly after she arrives. Both realised they only had two and a half hours of programming time with the Marc2 before Sarah arrived, and they were not going to waste them.

"OK, Henry, crunch time," said Marcus. "We need to make a decision and then get on with it. There are pros and cons for both. We could do this scientifically, or ..." He produced a dodecagonal object from his right trouser pocket and held it up in front of him. It was the third-largest coin in Australian circulation, the fifty-cent piece. "Heads for Fear, tails for Hate." Marcus tossed the cupronickel coin, sending it spinning vertically into the air, until gravity returned it to him. He caught it in the palm of his right hand. With one blurry movement, he turned his right hand onto the top of his left, while leaving his right hand in place so the coin couldn't be seen, until Henry made his choice.

"Heads," called Henry ...

"Tails it is," responded Marcus. "Looks like we try to program Hate."

"You know, now we've finally made a decision, I'd rather do Fear. There's enough hate in the world, let's not try and make more. What are the chances of us reneging on the toss and being badass rebels and going with Fear instead?" asked Henry.

"Pretty good, I'd say. Helen mentioned Fear is one of the eight emotions we're born with, but Hate isn't, it's learned or taught. Maybe there's something in that, who knows?" said Marcus. "Badasses we are." He paused before continuing, "Henry, without any, you know, personal details, can you tell me if the Marc1 worked as you understood it should have? You know I'm trying my best not to grin here right?" said Marcus grinning uncontrollably. "Purely professional interest only, to see if it has the same effect on everyone who tries it."

Henry found his colleague's grin infectious. "Well, suffice to say it worked as advertised, my friend." He then looked thoughtful and continued, "One thing, though, do you think using it could be accelerating people's genuine feelings of attraction faster than normal? I ask because my feelings for Jane are pretty intense and not like anything I've felt before, and over how long? Not even a fortnight. Jane has said pretty much the same thing to me, and is talking about commitment, which I'm fine with. I want that too. She says she's been bitten before and all she needs to go further now is absolute honesty. How's that for not including personal details?"

"Well, right back at ya, mate, I know what you mean. Maddy and I are in the same boat. Regardless of any effect it might be having on any of us, I have to say, I've never been so utterly happy to be with someone ever ... Bloody hell, Henry, we've taken thirty seconds to go from badasses to falling in love in two weeks!"

The two friends exchanged grins of happiness for themselves, for each other, and for their precious partners.

―――――――

AS HENRY surreptitiously locked the lab door, Marcus logged into his secure emails to access the collective information the committee had amassed in less than a week. The actual process they had to go through to find what they needed was a bit of a mashup. Effectively, the fMRI scans and EEGs would provide baseline information and, together with a little calculation and some pertinent research, they would find the appropriate settings for the Butterworth filter.

Their Butterworth frequency filter would block unwanted frequencies above and below the required frequency range. Once the theoretical Fear frequency for input into the filter was established and set, there only remained the practical setting up. After reviewing the data according to all their parameters, they came up with the 'frightening' figure of 4Hz. This would cause the audible frequency range to be filtered out by default. Theoretically, Fear could then be set with the push of a button on the digital controller, but would it work in practice?

Once they accomplished that, and they would be pushing to get it done before Sarah arrived, they would be in a position to carry out a trial run. If it worked as well as 'Love' worked, they pitied the poor bastard volunteering to be the test subject. It seemed somewhat ironic the test subject would have to be rather brave in the first place.

More speed and less haste ensued.

As they were about to congratulate themselves on having completed their ground-breaking tasks before Sarah arrived, Sarah arrived. She paused at the door while Marcus moved to unlock it and let her in while Henry checked there was no 'incriminating' evidence laying around.

Marcus became aware of something unusual about her body language. It was like she was tense or stressed, but also excited, and all thrown into a melting pot. Being a realist, he didn't trust himself making those kinds of certain judgements but knew something was up somewhere. She seemed nervous and agitated. "Good morning," he said, trying to sound upbeat.

She looked Marcus directly in the eyes. "My God, Marcus, this creation of yours is something utterly amazing, I had an incredible experience ... thank you."

"Oh, I'm glad Sarah. I hope it wasn't too torrid." Marcus was joking about sex dreams, assuming that's what Sarah was talking about. But the look of bewilderment on her face said she didn't get what the hell he was talking about. Realising, he digressed quickly, "It's important we gather as much information as we can, will you sit down with us and share what you're comfortable with?" Now Marcus was the one bewildered. *Does it do more than love or lust? What the hell did it do?*

The three of them sat around their well-used coffee table in the corner. Henry had overheard the initial conversation when Sarah had arrived and was keen to know as well. Both Henry and Marcus felt something left field was coming, they just didn't know what.

"Well," said Sarah looking at her suddenly bashful audience, "I'm guessing you two have had at least one experience with the Marc1. By the way you're both looking at the floor right now, I'd also guess it wasn't what mine was. But, I'll share mine, then you can share yours, deal?"

Sarah, who had lots on her mind today, noticed Marcus's eyes widen slightly and Henry look even more intensely at the floor. Both men felt they had no choice but to agree, and did so.

Once Sarah began, both listeners knew this was intensely

personal for her. "I dreamt of my parents," she said sombrely. They both died of *that* fucking virus. I'm an only child, we were so close. I wasn't even able to see them … I never got a chance to say goodbye …" Sarah trailed off and looked off somewhere in the distance, then said flatly, "Until last night."

"Jezzzuuusss," exclaimed Henry, "That was not on my list of possibilities, but I'm thinking now we're just scratching the surface here. Are you OK with what happened?"

"Strangely enough, it might even have given me some sort of closure, I wouldn't have missed it for the world, again, to both of you, thank you so much. At least something good has come of all this crap," she added as a softly spoken edgy afterthought, more to herself than the other two. "But tell me what happened to you, tell me about yours."

Marcus started off with an explanation, having his professional, dispassionate hat pulled down tight on his head. "I'm not putting your question off in any way, but I think I need to put some context into what our answers will be, already knowing what Henry's experience was. Before what you just said, our understanding of the types of events the machine facilitates had a fairly narrow focus, in that it caused you to dream of someone you love, or yearn for. Having established that with you now, I can tell you both Henry and my experiences have all been of a sexual nature."

Sarah raised a single eyebrow, Henry lowered both.

Marcus continued, "It would seem now, and steering away from considerations of stereotypical male behaviour, that what defines love or yearning is way wider than Henry and my personal experiences led us to believe. You've revealed something new and astounding, Sarah."

"Well said," added Henry.

All three sat in deep thought trying to assimilate the new pieces of the puzzle they had just fitted into the picture.

Sarah stood, and to the concern of the others, had clearly

changed demeanour. She was clearly agitated now. "Right, more of this later I dare say, but for now I'm going to see Peter and tell him about the Sara1. I need your blind trust on something, can I count on you both?"

"Yes," came one reply. "Of course," the other.

"I'm not going to tell Peter the Marc1 exists as well. For the moment, all I will be telling him is the Sara1 is a machine that makes you sleep by mechanisms unknown. I'm specifically not going to mention my parents, your experiences, or that these added experiences even exist. Are you both good with that on trust, and nothing of any of that goes outside this room?"

Both men verbalised their agreement and added in words of unconditional support.

Marcus said, "There is something else you should know since we are all in this together now. The Marc1 may well be useful as an anti-depressant and morning sickness treatment as well. The same neural pathways doctors target PTSD and these other conditions with drugs are evidently used by the Marc1 as well. If the device could be developed as a treatment, the worldwide market is over a trillion dollars. That's US dollars!"

It occurred to him that saying it was a time machine would have elicited the same bland reaction from her. Her mind was clearly on the impending meeting with Peter.

Sarah nodded, "OK, that's a big number. We probably need to keep that quiet as well for the time being. I trust Peter as far as I can kick him, for reasons I can't disclose right now. Speaking of the devil, I'd better get to that meeting." She was about to leave.

"Sure, no problem, Sarah." Without thinking, Marcus moved a little closer and took her by the elbow. He intentionally spoke loud enough so Henry could hear. "I can tell something is wrong. Let one or both of us come with you to see him. Whatever this is, nothing says you have to go it alone."

"Thank you, but I'll be OK," Sarah smiled briefly at Marcus, and

Henry. Her two colleagues were genuinely there for her. She could use another hug right then from either, preferably both of them. Sarah maintained her resolve not to dissolve and turned away, walking briskly towards Peter's office. The men remained riveted to the spot as they watched her walk away, both thinking the same thing. *What the fuck is the problem with Peter, or what is Peters problem with Sarah?*

Henry broke their deliberations, "I feel like this is about as calm as it's going to get before the storm."

"You got that right mate, somethings brewing and it's not good."

SARAH WALKED towards Peter's office. She'd rung ahead to make sure he was there. Not for Peter's convenience, only so she didn't stress up to now if that shithead happened not to be at work. She was suffering massive internal conflict involving her potential release to freedom or continued overthrow, producing distressing levels of anxiety and almost incapacitating stress if she dwelled on it. At least her parents and the lab visit had taken her mind off it for a short time.

Arriving at his door, he beckoned her to have a seat, but did not look up from what he was doing, a tactic he used regularly, designed to intimidate. Having a seat in Peter's office held all the attraction of sitting in an electric chair, a thought that led her to the next one. Although she didn't think Peter would be physically violent towards her, something inside her would need more convincing.

Peter pretended to be in a good mood when eventually he turned his attention to her. "Hello, Sarah, what news from the lab?"

Sarah didn't bother with pleasantries. There was too much bile rising in her throat for that. She proceeded with her preconceived plan. "We've developed a cure for insomnia," and she leaned forward to place the Sara1 on Peter's table. According to her plan, no earphones were attached. Thus, he would not be aware it required a headset, nor be tempted to try it out.

Peter seemed unimpressed. "Why am I only hearing about this now? When did this happen?"

As usual, she was instantly thrown off balance. None of the countless scenarios she'd run in her head included either of these questions. Accordingly, she had no answers ready. It meant she would need to resort to a concept she wanted to avoid as far as possible: the truth. "A bit less than a week," she replied.

"A bit less than a week?" Peter repeated her statement as a question, letting it hang in the air like a bad smell. "Well, I suppose that's kind of interesting in a way. Give me some more details."

Sarah responded in an intentionally broad manner but was like a child trying to play chess with a Grand Master. "It puts a person to sleep in five minutes or so. Not unconscious, just a deep sleep they can be routinely woken from. It's way too early to know how it physically works." She gazed at him knowing as she said so, it would not be enough. *Offer up what Marcus just told me? Shit, I only asked them to keep it quiet five minutes ago, can't I do anything right by those two? Desperate times demand desperate measures ...*

"There are several other potential benefits," she added. "Sleep and depression drug treatments target the same area of the brain, as do morning sickness and PTSD. With development time and investment, the keys to our discovery will likely unlock a new range of drugless treatments as well."

"That all sounds very promising," praised Peter mockingly as he slid the Sara1 back towards her, "but that's not why you're here, is it?" His gaze was as cold as the inside of a mortuary fridge.

Sarah found her reality confronting, *it's not gonna happen.* Unintentionally, she discovered her more resolute, perhaps more foolish self, trying to extract some concession before she left. "Insomnia and depression are two of the biggest mental health problems in the world, a cure for either is worth hundreds of billions. Can't you see that? You should be prepared to consider my contract well and truly fulfilled based on an effective treatment or cure for either condition, surely."

"Oh, I should, should I? My dear Sarah, it appears you do not appreciate your untenable position. Apart from this not being a negotiation, I pointed out the last time you sat there that your contract refers to developments concerning 5G. The only connection I can see between 5G, sleep and depression, is that you'll probably contract depression yourself if you can't make a breakthrough!"

She should have taken the hint, but her anger rose in direct proportion to the unwise use of her power of speech. "You have to be fucking kidding me! Small in stature, small in mind!" Calculated to wound, she threw the 'Napoléon complex' insult at him, and for the first time ever, she hit a nerve, an old, but still very raw nerve.

His anger started ballooning. Peters initial response came as cold as his stare. "You come in here and presume to tell me what I should do? You waltz in here, bold as brass, with a little contraption making spurious claims and spruiking grand theories, which by your own admission, require even more investment. We are here for a return on investment, not to find sideshows to throw money at! To top it all off, these discoveries were made while you were on sick leave!"

Peter suddenly wound up, face flushed and rapid fired his speech at her. She felt his balloon was about to burst. "This is nothing to do with 5G, the very reason I gave you the PM's job, and I can only assume you were home in bed when the discovery was made! You want to pass this off as the kind of success you entered into your contract for, so I pay you out and release you? I think not, I know not, I will not. Mutton dressed up as lamb, nothing more. Put it in the safe before you go home." Then, as if Mr Hyde was suddenly gone and Dr Jekyll had returned, excused her with, "Good chat, we're done."

She stared back, <u>almost</u> blankly at him. But almost blankly still shows *some* emotion. He could tell she had something she could say but wouldn't reveal. The only real weapon she could wield against him now or ever, was knowledge he did not have. She wanted to say something to wound him again, one-up him, threaten him, or all three. He realised he had not misjudged her but underestimated her reaction to being told no. *The bitch is holding out!*

"You're holding out, what are you not telling me?" pursued Mr Hyde as he materialised again without warning. "You are making a grave mistake if you leave here and don't tell me. Actions speak louder than words, and I will not ask you again, *I will act instead!*"

Sarah rose. "You know what? I've had enough of your shit. You'll find the rest out soon enough. I've made an appointment to see the CEO tomorrow, I'll take what's coming to me and you can take your medicine too. *YOU LITTLE ARSEHOLE!*" She walked angrily but determined from his office.

At least one of them was sure she wouldn't be back.

Sarah couldn't escape thinking. *Was I just having a conversation with two people in there? That 'man,' is seriously fucking demented!*

ONLY HENRY WAS WAITING, and visibly worried, when Sarah returned. She was the antithesis of the cat on a hot tin roof she had been before leaving for Peter's office.

She entered the lab and placed the Sara1 on the workbench.

"Excuse me the bathroom's calling, be right back," she whirled around for the door again and was soon out of sight.

Henry moved to the workbench, Philips screwdriver in hand. Not wanting to look a gift horse in the mouth, he removed the top cover of the Sara1. Retrieving the already activated tracking Tile from his left trouser pocket, together with a small tube of quick-set super glue gel, he set to work. With the Tile held in his left hand, he coated half of one side with the gel and slid it under the printed circuit board where it couldn't be seen. He used his handkerchief to wipe away the excess gel forming a slide mark where he first placed the Tile and slid it undercover. In quick order he re-secured the lid and removed any evidence of his actions from the workbench.

He retrieved his smartphone from his right pocket, walking to the coffee table area and sat down. With no time to lose, he checked the tracking map. Signal was confirmed. Tracking validity assured, he de-activated the Tile and closed the app, just as Marcus returned from the canteen with Devonshire tea for three.

"We've never had jam and scones here before, so hopefully doing something left field like this might help to distract her, and she'll feel a bit better about whatever it is. Is she back yet?"

"Yep, gone to the ladies," said Henry.

Sarah walked in, still looking worse for wear, but in better condition than before she left for the loo, thought Henry. She sat down and looked at the afternoon tea with surprised appreciation, but still without saying much. There seemed no intention to give them a debriefing on what had happened, so they would have to ask. As Marcus did the honours with the scones, Henry took up the mantle of friendly neighbourhood inquisitor.

"What happened with Peter?" asked Henry.

Sarah inhaled deeply and began to reach for a teacup. Suddenly she changed her mind and stood. "You know what, I'm just going to get out of here for the rest of the day and see you both tomorrow. Thank you for what you guys do, for being the best colleagues I could ask for, and let me go so far as to say good friends as well." And with that, she scooped up the Sara1 into her work bag and was gone out the door.

They watched her go. Henry fumed, "I said to myself before she left for Peter's office, and now I'll say it to you, what the fuck is it with Peter? He has some kind of negative effect and maybe even a stranglehold over her somehow. There must be a bloody good reason she detests him. If what she said to us was true before she went to his office, we're withholding what you would think is pretty standard information from our boss. Even if he is a complete slippery little bastard, none of it adds up."

"I'll give her a couple of hours," said Marcus, "and then I'll go around and pay her a visit, kind of the least I can do. I wish she would let me help her with whatever is going on. We're stronger if we all stick together, but she doesn't want to for some reason I can't fathom. No doubt Peter has something to do with it … somehow or rather."

Since the tea for three was now tea for two, Henry was able to convince Marcus he needed some cheering up himself. Consequently, they enjoyed a somewhat serious afternoon tête-à-tête as they savoured the lemonade scones with jam and cream, washed down by Yorkshire dark tea. After faffing around a little longer, the Marc2 was secured in the lab safe and Marcus told Henry he was heading to Sarah's house for a welfare check after making a few stops and maybe picking up a good bottle of scotch, in case she was in the mood to chat.

Chapter Nineteen

I t was no facade Peter had presented to Sarah before she left his office. She had well and truly pissed him off by holding back information and planning to meet the CEO tomorrow. If she thought it was possible to insult and treat him with contempt and avoid his total control, she had 'another thing' coming. That 'another thing,' would come to her today.

On the other side of the coin, he was close to his 'retirement.' He found himself excited, despite the steep peaks and troughs of his negative emotions, at the prospect of making some unexpected bank with the mental health treatments. It wasn't the money, he had plenty of that now, it was the *win*. He had no doubts an expanded Lamarr project would be successful, if not straight away, then after some development. The quality and inventiveness of their people made CSIRO great. Despite his tirade to Sarah, investing in the research was a given. While most scientists here may well be gullible to his ways, and able to be manipulated by his unsurpassed skill, they were all brilliant beyond doubt and compare.

HE WOULD NOT USUALLY CALL Sifu as he was able to legitimately see him once a week on training nights, but her withholding information and meeting the CEO tomorrow made things different. He wasn't sure what form that meeting would take. Peter had enough, more than enough counters and deceptions in place to stop the CEO taking immediate action. But it would, more than likely, lead to closer scrutiny and greater oversight. Either may well represent a significant threat to him and his client. This could not be ignored. His own independent plans under such circumstances, required immediate action. The situation was to be restored ASAP to his full control again.

Peter was a rampant contingency planner. In Sarah's case, all he had to do was pick the relevant plan off the shelf and execute it. Probably her along with it. He already permanently rented a "safe house," which he had used for a variety of purposes including the springing of honey traps.

Over the years he was not aware of any interest by the AIC, Australian Intelligence Community, in the foreign organisation of which he was part, and did not want to start now. The AIC was small, but technology heavy. The quality of its people was very high, and they used two other vital virtues: patience and stealth. They also played the long game well, how well, was yet to be seen.

Peter focused on the plan for his next victory. *I, Shunyuan, will be victorious; I, Shunyuan, will always WIN!*

Sun Tzu – *Mystify, mislead, and surprise the enemy.*

HAVING smartphone research in Near Field Communications under his auspices brought him easy access to new smartphones and SIM cards. This was important, but not as important as both items being untraceable.

Any member of the public wishing to buy a new phone or SIM card has to supply various forms of identification. The individual telephone and SIM serial numbers are recorded and attached to that individual. Thus, these devices could be tracked and traced very quickly if the authorities were inclined to do so. Not so for Peter. In his position, he had a stash of hard-to-trace throwaways kindly supplied by the federal government.

However, Peter had survived and prospered in his field of industrial espionage for years by acting only with purpose and building multiple layers of security on any electronic platform. Telco's were one thing, but it was vital, he stayed under the radar of the Australian Signals Directorate. The ASD motto, "Reveal their secrets, protect your own," was ominous, yet inspired him to greater efforts.

To make any electronic interception one step harder, he got his phones from Sifu, who supplied him with brand new iPhone or Android phones direct from their factories in China. Sifu explained it was a simple process. A factory quality assurance inspector would fail several phones in between the product being completely manufactured and their Telco/Trace Identification Numbers being attached electronically. These phones were as clean as a whistle. The same applied to SIM cards, but Peter rarely used these unless part of a deception plan, as Wi-Fi was infinitely more secure. But, there were times in the espionage business when it served your purpose to be found.

Peter presented his right thumb into the scanner port on the bio-metric lock of his office wall safe. He retrieved a brand-new smartphone in a click seal bag. Peter knew the process he was about to use offered the best guarantee against location tracking. He powered the Samsung up and skipped the 'Insert SIM Card' prompt. After selecting aeroplane mode, he connected to the cafeteria Wi-Fi and opened 'Elsewhere'. Smirking piously, he entered into 'Elsewhere' his current location as 25 Rue des Saints-Peres, Paris. He'd always wanted to go there.

For anyone attempting to track his GPS data legally, or illegally, he would appear to be staying right there at the Hotel Da Vinci, apparently relaxing in the beautiful surroundings of the luxurious top-floor spa, inspired by the tranquil colours of the Mona Lisa. He created a text message, which said simply, 'Test'. This seemingly innocuous message was prearranged and would cause the recipient to take immediate action. It conveyed the urgent message the integrity of Peter's activities was being put to the 'Test'.

Using inspiration from the easy way to remember the SETI internal phone number, he could readily recall the sequence he now touched into the keypad. He typed in the first four digits of his regular work number, followed by the corresponding digits for the word 'Master'. He pressed send and saw the notification, 'delivered'. To complete his security precautions, he turned the phone off, and wiped its surfaces using alcohol lens cleaners to remove fingerprints and ruin any attempt at DNA sampling.

He returned it to the click seal bag, then placed it in another, thicker opaque plastic bag. Peter positioned the phone across a three-inch-long piece of inch-diameter dowel, then stood on either end of the mobile until he heard it break. He rechecked the contents of the bag to ensure the phone was destroyed, and then sealed the bag. He would dump it randomly in one of the many council roadside bins on his way home.

If anyone in the intelligence community tried to track the source of his single word text, it would be 'almost impossible'. Trying to locate where the mobile text recipient was geographically located would be even more 'almost impossible', whatever that level was. Peter knew his SMS was sent to the *M* mobile phone with its software permanently arranged similarly to the phone he had just destroyed. The *M* phone was located in Melbourne 800 kilometres south-west. It was ingeniously operating hidden in the roof of an unknowing domestic household that had insulation installed under the federal government's Home Insulation Scheme.

It had been a simple matter for an installer on their payroll, to tap into a power cable in the roof and use a small trickle charger to keep the battery topped up. The old couple living there even gave the install crew the Wi-Fi password during the two installation days, so the 'lovely young men' didn't have to use their prepaid data, very considerate indeed, and it meant no SIM required. The *pièce de résistance* though, wasn't the *M* phone GPS falsely reporting it was in Brisbane 1800 km to the NNE.

It was that *M* call-forwarded to roof phone, *P*, in Perth, twice as far away to the West. *P*, also falsely reported it was physically in Brisbane, 4000 km ENE of where it really was. With all this subterfuge, the *P* phone was in fact, forwarding the message to the intended recipient a mere forty-minute drive from where Peter had initially sent the text. Peter finished his mental side-track and wished anyone trying to track and trace the text to enjoy their wild goose chase. It was an outrageous high for Peter's ego every time he used this system.

As the second part of this elaborate, but remarkably effective counter-surveillance process continued, Peter removed an iPad from a locked drawer in his desk. He turned it on and confirmed *ExpressVPN* booted during start-up. With this active, Peter knew his IP address was hidden, and any data between his iPad and any router being used was encrypted and could not be intercepted. He was anonymous. His work router of choice was the CSIRO cafeteria. He recalled the day long ago, when he worked his magic there, and silently thanked the operators of the cafeteria for letting him use their system, even though they didn't have a clue he did.

Most people are ignorant to the ways of the internet, and it remains an enigma to the cafeteria staff. He started by sitting in a quiet corner of the cafeteria with his iPad and an orange juice. He typed in 10.1.1.1 into the iPad browser. Pressing the enter key led him to the admin area of the cafeteria router, where a password prompt appeared. He guessed correctly they wouldn't have changed the default password from their internet service provider when they originally installed it, so typed in 'admin' and pressed the enter key again. Bingo, he now had administration rights. He uploaded ExpressVPN, then rebooted it to complete the installation process.

When Peter saw the staff notice the internet was down, because the EFTPOS machine wouldn't work, he casually walked over and offered to help. All he needed, he said, was the network key and to be shown the router. He said he would work his magic and have it up and running in a jiffy. Of course, Peter didn't have to do a thing, except wait a couple of minutes while it finished rebooting. They thanked him kindly, and he left the canteen with a giant complimentary glazed jam doughnut, their network key and by virtue of his covert talents, two additional layers of security when communicating with the Spymaster.

Returning himself to the present, he looked at the desktop of the iPad. He used his right index finger to tap the icon buried deep in a multi-level hidden folder entitled 'car sales'. This opened a free chatroom portal. He scanned for a visitor logged on in the last five minutes, with the name of a luxury brand of car. He spotted 'Bentley'. A quick message was appropriately responded to, and they transferred to a private chat room. They continued their discussion away from prying eyes in a format again virtually impossible for the authorities to monitor in real time. If they were scrutinised, it would mean a traitor in their midst.

Peter aka *Audi*: *Car playing up badly. Needs fixing today. Diagnostics one hour?*

Bentley aka Sifu: *OK. Black and Red*

Audi: *Recommend replacing. Done?*

Bentley: *Done*

They both exited from their seemingly innocent conversation, but innocence had little to do with their business. Peter started the countdown timer on his phone, as did Bentley, or as he was otherwise known; Sifu. They synchronised their timers, from the exit time displayed when they both left the virtual chat room.

He knew he would meet Sifu tonight after training at the Kwoon, but now saved the information he urgently needed to pass to Sifu on a triple-encrypted and double password-protected thumb drive. It included information on the Sara1 and that Sarah herself was withholding unknown information, that the information needed revealing, and she needed to forget about meeting the CEO tomorrow. He impressed she was a direct threat to them both and the client and everything they had built. If she wasn't co-operative, she needed to be, "replaced tonight." Peter added in her address from her personnel file and removed the USB. He left the office and walked to his car.

Peter had been a good student of various spymasters. He had not only learned the lessons they gave him well but had also taken them to new heights using his own particular skills.

His white Holden Commodore was not the latest, greatest, or even top of the range, but it served its purpose exceptionally well. What it was, was one of the most common, and that meant 'forgettable' cars on Australian roads. He was not in the business where he wanted to be remembered or noticed. When he'd bought it, it was *almost* perfect for his needs, and after having made substantial modifications to it, it *was* perfect for his needs.

His car was a mobile electronic surveillance and counter-surveillance masterpiece. In the boot, he had added a single 3000-Watt inverter. It ran off two 170 Amp Hour Gel batteries, to supply household quality power to the array of devices that he had, not without a twinge of pride, fitted himself. There was more than enough 240-volt power available in the back of the car to boil two kitchen jugs. In fact, to test the surge capacity of the system initially, that was precisely what he did. Peter had also uprated the alternator for faster battery charging and installed start protection for the engine, in case the system drained the voltage too low over an extended time.

He unlocked his car remotely and sat in the driver's seat but did not as yet do up his seat belt. His practised hand reached under the dash and located the red switch guard covering the spring-loaded toggle. These guards are typically fitted in aircraft cockpits to protect an essential function from accidentally being activated, and to easily confirm by sight, or in this case by feel, that the function was off. With the switch guard closed, the function had to be off, because the guard physically moved the toggle to the off position when the guard closed.

Peter flipped the switch guard up with his thumb and then pushed the silver toggle switch up. This quick and positive manoeuvre operated the master power switch for all the 'non-optional extras' secreted in the rear of his vehicle. There was an ever so slight sound of fan noise from the boot, easily disguised by starting the motor. He started the two litre V6 engine, spinning up the input shaft to the 9-speed automatic transmission. Compulsively, he took a second to check his CF-98 PLA 9 mm pistol was holstered under his seat before releasing the hand brake. This pistol was rugged, functional and manufactured, as was his other far more exotic and deadly weapon, by the People Liberation Army of China.

He drove from the work car park and turned left onto Bradfield road for a kilometre and a half, then left again onto Lane Cove Depot road. Shortly afterwards, he entered the long straight stretch bordered by nothing but forest. While he listened for any radio traffic on the frequencies he was scanning, he gazed intermittently in his rear-view mirror for other vehicles. He kept his maximum speed to 50 kilometres per hour, despite the speed limit being nearly twice that.

His high-tech radio scanners would not only to pick up voices, but also 'burst transmissions'. Although these types of law enforcement or intelligence service transmissions were not decipherable, their mere presence meant the enemy was in his area. That was not a good sign by any means.

By the time he reached the 'T' intersection with Max Allen drive, he had seen no-one and heard no-one. He turned left again and headed towards the nearby shopping centre, a mere ten minutes away. After parking, he pretended to be reading something on his smartphone until fifty-nine minutes after he terminated the chatroom call. He alighted. Five seconds exactly after the dual electronic sounds of his car locking sounded, he heard a car door slam. *Courier here. Coast clear.*

Peter walked to the central parking meter machine ostensibly to obtain a parking ticket, while the six hidden cameras fitted to his car did their 360-degree work.

As he approached to get a ticket, he spied a short but stocky man wearing a black baseball cap and a red shirt. Peter had not expected the man in the red shirt and black hat to be Sifu, nor was it. Peter stood in front of the parking machine and inserted a $1 gold coin into the slot, then feigned that something was wrong, cancelling his transaction by pressing the coin return button. The legal tender jangled its way from where it was held inside the validator mechanism, all the way to the coin return slot. Peter retrieved his dollar coin from the return, simultaneously placing the USB in the slot. He walked away, making a gesture the machine was broken, to the next person in line. The male in the red shirt, now standing directly behind him, went through a similar process as had Peter. At the end of his process, the man retrieved the waiting USB from the return slot.

FOR SOME REASON THOUGH, the machine declined twice to refund his money. He felt robbed and toyed with the idea of taking his revenge later with a little plastic explosive. *Fucking parking machines!*

Chapter Twenty

H enry was packing up the remains of the near demolished Devonshire tea when his mobile rang. The caller was using Crypto-Cone, which meant only one thing, it was his principal employer. He went through the necessary process to access the app and connect with the caller.

This call would not be secure, but neither would give anything away.

Henry answered, "Call you back within five."

"Within five," was the only reply as the VoIP call terminated.

Henry had recalled his instructor's training on secure comms before answering the call. She wisely counselled, "There's not much point in having an end-to-end encrypted mobile call to the ZRTP encryption protocol standard if you're somewhere that's not secure. Having a target, or device potentially able to listen in on a single-sided conversation is NOT acceptable, people, EVER! Move to somewhere secure. The DST has gone to a lot of trouble to develop Crypto-Cone and not even they can listen in, so let's not make it easy for the bad guys."

As Henry walked out of the building, he realised why this

particular lesson stuck in his mind. It was because of the new arse the instructor had torn him for suggesting DST named it after the cone of silence on the old TV series, Get Smart. Despite the bollocking, Henry maintained he was right, then <u>and</u> now.

Once outside in a secluded spot, he opened the app again. He just looked like some guy trying to have a conversation away from his colleagues, which was in effect true, it was only that this discussion was about national security, not a domestic difficulty with a new flame, or an old one.

Henry returned the call, and both parties went through the secure connection procedure.

The original ASIS caller said without preamble, "7,0,4,8."

Henry knew if his screen showed the same number, their call was secure from man-in-the-middle attacks where their conversation could be overheard by a third party. Sure enough, 7048 displayed, so he touched the 'secure' icon. When the caller on the other end next actioned their icon, both knew they could speak freely without fear of electronic interception.

The directives passed to Henry were as a result of intel he'd provided to ASIS in the last few days. Despite this, it took him by surprise, took him aback, and took him back into the building at a brisk 'man on a mission' walking pace to lockout the safe and grab his car keys. Amongst other tasks, in his brief, he was to urgently locate, retrieve and secure in the lab safe, the Sara1 and the Marc2, with all documents. He was to use the override code to secure the safe from access by anyone else. He knew the Marc2 and the circuit diagrams were already in there, half his problem was solved already. The Sara1 was with Sarah, hopefully she was at home by now. His mission clock was ticking ...

He continued walking with purpose to the car park and used the keyless entry to unlock his new Mazda CX-5. Opening the driver's door of his *Titanium Flash* ride, he sat in the driver's seat, closing the door. He leaned over, reaching under the front passenger seat to a small squat black box bolted to the chassis. Locating the mechanical keypad lock by feel, he pushed in the four-number access code that protected his 'business partner'.

The lid fell open towards the floor, and he withdrew his trusty Walther TPH from the metal gun bunker. His pistol was always stored ready for action, held secure in its Cloak Mod holster. With a quick lift of his shirt and a push of the holster downwards over his belt on his left side, his physical switch from lab technician to armed intelligence service agent was as complete as his mental transition.

Henry too had learnt his lessons well. A right-handed agent caught in the driver's seat of a car could cross draw their weapon with great stealth, unlike the blatant posture required to draw a sidearm from their right-hand side while seated.

He activated the Tile Tracking App, and re-armed the Sara1 Tile to make sure he was travelling to the correct location, oblivious to the sequence of lethal events he had just instigated.

As he looked up from confirming it was Sarah's address, he saw Jane walking towards him. At this distance, he could just make out her mile wide smile directed right at him. He smiled back, that part at least wasn't hard. *Wow, she's gorgeous.* The problem was, he had to drive right past her as he made his way from the car park, *so how can I not stop?* It was all the harder as the two of them had become almost joined at the hips. He would just have to make it bloody quick and explain later.

He pressed the button on the door armrest, automatically winding the driver's window all the way down. As he stopped beside her, Jane didn't say a thing as she leaned half her svelte body into the open window and put her hands on his shoulders and kissed him gently. He responded by hugging her as affectionately as being seated in the car allowed. At the moment their lips parted, Jane let her right hand run down the left side of his body, more in an act of intimacy than anything else.

They both realised at the same time what happened next. Jane put her hand on his Walther. She guessed it was a firearm based on the shape of the handle and it felt like it was in a holster.

She straightened abruptly, but remained beside the door, "Henry, you're scaring me, why are you wearing a gun in the car park?" Her question seemed absurd to herself, *why the fuck is he wearing a gun anywhere?*

Henry went straight into damage control. This was unexpected, to say the least, for him as well. "Don't worry, Jane. I work for the government."

"Honey," said Jane trying to remain calm. "I work for them too, same division and in the same complex you do, but they didn't give me a gun!!!"

He had imagined in a hundred different ways how he would tell Jane he was a spy, the car park at work never being one of them. All he knew was, he had his orders to expedite his mission. "Jane, I work for the good guys, you have to believe me. I have to go do something *right now*, and I'm on the clock."

Jane could be no-nonsense when the occasion moved her, and now, she was very moved. "You'll have to do better than that if you ever want to see me again, total honesty, remember?"

An ultimatum was the last thing Henry needed or expected right now, but he knew, being the strong woman she was, she would not have said it if she didn't mean it. "I'm an undercover agent with the Australian Secret Intelligence Service."

"No, you're not," she said incredulous, "you're a lab technician ..." Jane could not have been more astonished if she'd just discovered the unified field theory merging general relativity and electromagnetism.

"Well ... yes ... that too, sweetheart, but I'm foremost an agent. You can't tell anyone just yet, do you understand? No-one. Because, strictly speaking, I shouldn't have told you already, but I don't want to risk living without you either. I'm so sorry I have to go, trust me,

I'll call you later tonight, I promise." His eyebrows rose silently pleading for her trust.

Jane swore uncharacteristically for the second time in a minute, only this time out loud. "Henry Henderson, if you're not fucking careful today and every other day," as she leaned in the window to kiss him firmly, "I'll be so angry, I'll kill you myself." She accepted he had to go in a hurry, so took a step back from the car to allow him to depart on whatever his urgent mission was.

Henry the larrikin surfaced. "Honey, hold that thought, the make-up sex will be amazing!" Before she could reply, Henry had planted his foot on the accelerator and was gone.

FEAR

Chapter Twenty-One

Sarah turned left and drove off the street into her driveway. The white picket fence bordering the front of her property had thick brush running along the house side of its length, roughly bordering the lawn. White gravel comprised the first fifteen metres and most of her unusually long, slightly downslope cement driveway. The gravel made its usual loud announcement as her car drove slowly over it, then along the remaining length straight into the attached open concrete carport, at the left of the house.

She alighted, work bag in hand, walking back towards the front door of the modest rented weatherboard home. An extended, unfenced, wooden deck formed the front veranda along most the length of the ground-floor dwelling. About a dozen steps found her at the front door, having walked past the generous living room windows overlooking the veranda.

She behaved autonomously in mental neutral. Her learned behaviours, conditioned responses, and muscle memory allowed her to stroll into the lounge room with the thought she couldn't recall driving home. *Wasn't there some social rule about not driving angry?* She'd flaunted that well and truly today. *How the hell did I make it home in one piece? Whatever. Need Alcohol.*

Standing in the kitchen, adjacent to the back door, she held her first glass of superbly chilled Pepik Tasmanian Cuvee. Inside the champagne flute, bubbles lost their quest to remain attached, and rose upwards in a procession of alluring effervescence. Watching the bubbles was a welcome mindless distraction from her shitful day, week, longer? What she didn't need was accidentally knocking the bottle hard off the bench into the sink and chipping the top. She couldn't see any chips in the sink, so it must have gone into the bottle. She'd be mad to drink any more out of it! *Typical me, so close to something I really want, but at the last minute, for whatever reason, I can't have it. Might have to drink the emergency cheap scotch. Fuck My Life ...*

Sarah didn't hear a thing before the doorbell rang. She might have been home twenty minutes or so, she couldn't be sure. Sarah took a gulp of the sparkly before opening the unlocked solid wooden door. Hardly an ideal habit to forget to lock her front door, but she sensed no threat, why would she? The metal security door between her and the person ringing the doorbell was locked. *It was locked, right?*

A jolt of unease coursed through her as she opened the door and was confronted by a tall, muscular and athletic male she didn't recognise. Of Middle Eastern descent wearing jogging gear, he stood directly in front of her, less than an arm's length away, and sweating lightly. There was no water bottle to be seen. His hair was unkempt, and a thin faded facial scar ran across his left cheek. The security screen was fully open and folded out of the doorway against the front wall of the house. As Sarah tried to read his face, she noticed something was dangling in his left hand, but didn't want to take her eyes off him and glance down to see what it was.

"Are you Sarah Douglas?" he said.

Oh fuck, he knows my name! Peter said I'd get what's coming to me!

Realising the surprise, even alarm he was causing, the visitor tried allaying her fears by speaking quickly, "Hi, I'm Mo from number 14, the postie must be going blind, this is marked for number 74. He held up an international postal satchel.

"Yes, that's me." *Thank fuck for that,* she thought, and put her non-glass hand out to receive the parcel as the stranger smiled and handed it to her. She smiled warmly in return, thanked him for going to the trouble of delivering it, and stepped back as he shut the security screen. Closing the wooden inner door, she practically trotted to the kitchen to grab some scissors, finishing off her Pepik on the way. She told herself she was cleansing her pallet, but knew she was going to have a little bender at home.

She also knew what was in the satchel, a selection of fine drams offered up by a company called Master of Malt. The whisky came from some of Scotland's most legendary whisky distilleries, now closed. Rare samples indeed, as reflected by the price tag for these twenty-five to thirty-seven-year-old masterly matured beauties. Alcohol is never the solution to any problem, short or long term, but today it sure was going to make the latter part of her day a damn sight more enjoyable than the rest of it! The forthcoming single malt enjoyment, added to the relaxation of her dark mood, giving her another idea.

Fortunately, as angry, frustrated and uncertain of her future as she was, she had prepared for this delivery weeks ago. The whisky had travelled halfway around the world, only to be snavelled by Australian Customs at the border, awaiting her paperwork to pay GST on the import. Delay one. Delay two, obviously thanks to the local postie, who was unfortunate enough in his line of work to suffer from macular degeneration, or maybe he just misread the address?

There are broadly two types of whisky drinkers, the haves and the have-nots. Sarah was a have-not. She did NOT have Coca-Cola with her whisky. Such heathens should be banished to Laos, and only allowed to drink the famous Laotian national rice whisky with their caramel soft drink mixer. Any true artisan would not so sully, or completely ruin, any damn fine authentic vintage scotch. These were best delicately consumed with celebrated pomp and ceremony by learned connoisseurs such as herself. She was keen to take the edge off, although the quick glass of Pepik had likely already seen to that. Sarah found herself unable to completely shrug off the state she'd arrived home in, even with the delivery of her precious drams.

Sarah commanded herself to *calm down, level out, try to relax and just enjoy this.* Placing the parcel gently on the kitchen bench, she worked the scissors and released the trapped Scottish air within the satchel to mix with that of her native New South Wales. She withdrew the armoured cardboard container, which held the five aged samples. The pantry provided a packet of plain, but most importantly, unsalted, Saltine crackers, and a pack of ground coffee beans. She concentrated on her usual preparations for cleansing her nose and pallet. Folding back the thin metal tabs holding the furled coffee packet tight, she unrolled it before taking a deep inhalation of the aroma. Opening one of the two sealed packs within the Saltine box, she devoured one of the biscuits with the appreciation that, *now I'm ready.*

Next, Sarah placed two of her beloved Rauk Heavy Tumblers on the bench. These unique gold-standard whisky glasses were born of machine-pressed molten crystal and thought to be named after a derivation of an old Scots word. She individually placed a handful of ice cubes into one. Not being a person for delayed gratification, she slowly and with pronounced veneration for the craftsman who created both tumbler and whisky, liberated the dram over the ice. Her nose was soon upon the glass, inhaling the vapours now released half a world away from their place of rest these last three score and seven years. Her intricate, and therefore *Peter* distracting experience continued. The precious amber liquid, its flavour enhanced by a small amount of melted distilled water from the ice, wet her waiting mouth. She sipped, savoured, and sipped again ...

After repeating the entire ritual with her second Rauk and rapturously sampling her next dram, she sauntered around the house. She found it freed her mind to focus on the identification of the most subtle flavours within her soul-warming drink. That achieved, she decided to try and reconnect with her parents again for some salient advice on her internal conflict and her Peter issues. Ironically, the source of most good *and* bad things in her present life, Sarah collected her creation from her work bag and placed it on the daylight lit bedside table. Replacing the thin daytime ineffective curtains in her bedroom, which didn't quite fit either, had been on her list for a while, but she closed them now as best she could. That done, she continued around the house in no particular direction, trying to think of what questions she would ask if she could see them just one more time. With the last sip tasted from her ornamental tumbler, she gazed inside at the extruded chevrons radiating from the centre, willing them to refill with whisky, but alas, they did not. With a shrug of resignation, she returned to the bedroom and lay back on the bed. The mix of wine and whisky was doing its work. She slid the earphones into her ears, not even taking off her shoes let alone any clothing, because today, she *couldn't* be bothered.

Chapter Twenty-Two

As she fell asleep, and despite her intentions, her mind replayed a recent tv episode she watched at home, where she imagined herself as the leading lady to her favourite Witcher. Perhaps she had overused the rewind function on the remote, but that part had stuck in her mind for days. It was this erotic dream that came to her in her slumber, not her parents. The Witcher captivated her, massaging the arches of her feet, which, as soothing as that was, only made her body tingle further up. He lightly kissed her toes and gently, tenderly, moved his way around the inside of her ankles. He massaged her skin ever upwards with his lips, his soft hands trailing slightly behind, stroking the goose-bumps towards the ache and longing Sarah yearned him to reach. His weight shifted on the edge of the bed; the patient bastard teasing her deliciously.

His mouth was now directly and firmly on hers, *but how did he get there?* He pressed harder. *Too hard!* Her brain grasped a real-world threshold had been crossed. She was not dreaming of the pressure on her face! The neurons in her Medulla Oblongata could fire off orders for adrenaline to flood her body 200 times a second.

As her conscious awoke from its deep slumber, these neurons fired at primal top speed. Barely awake in that instant, epinephrine-triggered glucose, fuelled her fight or flight reflex. It also dilated her pupils to full size, forcing her eyes to allow in the maximum amount of light possible.

As her overly sensitive eyes sprang open, the late afternoon light through the curtains half-blinded her, forcing her to squint to make out the brute with one knee on the bed edge, and a hand jammed down hard over her mouth. A second, unshaven intruder stood by the bed, holding the index finger of one hand vertically in front of his lips to signal her to be quiet, and indicating with his other hand not to struggle.

She willed herself to calm down, but the pounding of her pulse in her ears and throat was taking no notice as yet. Relaxing herself was confounded by the forced nose breathing, at the same time her sympathetic nervous system surged the rate and rise of her breaths. The jolt of the attack, plus the alcohol, required her to ferociously resist the impending barrage of puke welling inside her.

It took time, but with superhuman resolve, she calmed herself, and nodded to the man indicating for her to be silent, that she would be. With her house set well back from the road, she held little chance of anyone hearing her scream for help anyway. Entirely at their mercy, she wanted, she needed, to get off the bed, a place she thought herself totally vulnerable.

At last her mouth was uncovered and she was allowed to sit on the bedside. Her direct oppressor produced a gag from his pocket. Having seen enough movies to know what it was, and not forgetting she had less than no choice, she acquiesced as he applied it. The man who had signalled her to be quiet handed some silver cloth Gaffa tape to his accomplice, who taped her hands behind her. The older man stood her up, and they walked to the living room. To her monumental relief, whether she survived the night or not, at least she wouldn't be violated in her own bed. If there was any comfort to be had, however cold, that was it.

The man in apparent charge looked to be in his late forties. Probably handsome in his earlier years, solidly built with short black hair. He stood about six feet tall and his eyes were bloodshot. One, perhaps both, of her assailants had body odour. The younger, a Eurasian in his early 20s, thinner and shorter, with some sort of radical haircut, quick-stepped behind them down the hallway. The older man took a kitchen table chair and dragged it along the timber floor as though it were too heavy for him to lift. He continued to drag it over the dense pile carpet, leaving it upright in the centre of the living room. Sarah guessed what was in the Jerry can beside the front door, which only added to her compounding fear. She also identified a tin of Zippo lighter fluid and two long-necked barbecue lighters and a set of keys on the kitchen table.

She could see the younger man looked somewhat worse for wear with two front upper teeth completely missing.

"Tape," the older man ordered. The other headed to her bedroom to retrieve the rest of the roll.

"Hurry the fuck up, dipstick, or you'll lose your other front teeth as well." The older assailant conveyed the impression to Sarah he would indeed do that if given the slightest cause. Sarah was sat on the chair, her arms behind her over the chair back in a stress position.

The junior party checked that the knot in her mouth was not in too deeply, just enough to stop her screaming if she thought to. He tested the gag was secure behind the nape of her neck. That he made sure she was breathing as comfortably as possible was not done out of compassion; he simply didn't want to suffocate her before they had what they'd come for. As he taped her legs to the front of the chair, he knew full well his senior would punish him without mercy for any kind of avoidable mistake.

Sarah wrestled with her thoughts. *Who are these guys and what do they want with me? It's not the obvious or I wouldn't be out here!* It dawned on her that she might get out of this alive if she played her cards right.

It was no consolation, but at least she was starting to think more clearly now, as she watched the taller of the two home invaders.

The tall man with the black hair stood at full height in front of her. He spoke with a sharp tone, indicating beyond any doubt that he was used to being obeyed without question. "Let's get this straight ... *Sarah*, I don't give a flying fuck about you, and I don't care who you are, or what you've done. If you don't answer any question I ask, with the truth, the whole truth and nothing but the fucking truth ..." He paused as he withdrew a small gun from his back pocket with his right hand and pressed the end of the barrel down on top of her left knee, hard enough to dent the flesh.

Sarah knew nothing of guns, but like most people recognised bullets. She was transfixed by what was a snub-nose .38 revolver. He pulled back the hammer of the weapon with his thumb.

There was an audible click, as the projectiles rotated anti-clock-wise in the cylinder, and she felt a rush of horror seeing the trigger move rearward. She was sure she'd never walk on her left leg again. Her eyes widened but nothing happened. She realised this scumbag was mentally torturing her. The tactic was highly effective. He most certainly did not seem to give a shit about whether she walked with a limp for the rest of her days, or passed from this life to the next. "Ready to talk now?"

"Is this how you did the insurgents, Shane?" interrupted the young man, with all the eagerness of a new world of discovery before him.

The resultant glare from Shane silenced him with an intensity to melt glass.

As much as she wanted to tell him anything he wanted to know, it was hard enough breathing through her nose, let alone talking with a gag in her mouth. She furiously tried to make coherent noises and nod her head to signify compliance. Her situation was hopeless; he would do what he wanted to do, when he wanted, and how.

"So now that it seems we understand each other, lady, we're gonna take the gag off. You should know if you scream, there will be no ifs or buts, the gag will go back on, I will shoot you in both knees and leave you here while we burn your house down around you." He leaned closer to her, and she smelt his stale breath as he exhaled, which without doubt, was his intention. From what he said and how he established control, this certainly was not his first time.

Shane, the man in charge, nodded to his accomplice, who lowered the gag to rest on Sarah's shoulders.

"There's some mistake ..." spluttered Sarah between gasping breaths.

Shane cut her off with nothing more than a casual lift of his right index finger. "Tell me about the little black box you were listening to in the bedroom. Don't leave anything out if you want to be able to walk."

Sarah felt no temptation to hold back. She quickly explained as best she could about the Sara1 prototype. It was basically a dreaming machine, putting you to sleep in a couple of minutes, and allowing you to have vivid dreams of someone you yearn for, or love. Twenty minutes of hard questioning ensued, but apart from mentioning Lamarr, which meant nothing to her captors, she had no idea how it actually worked. Just that it did.

When you're already telling the truth, but aren't being believed, it's life-threatening if your interrogators are both armed with revolvers, but neither with a conscience. Peter had warned in the USB files not to trust her, so Shane was initially not inclined to believe her. However, Sarah was right about Shane; he had done this type of thing before and was not without savvy when it came to his savage vocation of choice.

"So, you're trying to tell me this black box, makes the love part of your brain take over in a vivid dream after it makes you fall deeply asleep? When you wake up, you can remember everything fully?" clarified Shane in stilted phrases, while gathering his thoughts.

"Yes," she replied.

He believed Sarah to be telling the truth as far as she knew. They'd gotten everything possible to get out of her, plus, they had the working prototype to report back with.

"And love is it? Just that, nothing else?"

Sarah squirmed uncomfortably in the chair, wanting to play for time, with as close to the truth as possible. She didn't know how much time she had left, so kept talking. "Well, I guess it includes things like people you respect, people you know deep down you can trust with your life. People you miss so very much that you feel at times you don't want to go on without them. Those you'll never see again because maybe they've passed away before their time, or some other reason or another. Love means different things to different people for different reasons. But you can do that within this machine, and quite a few people have already."

She looked at Shane, trying not to look too hard, but she didn't have to, he hung on every word. Something she said, or was saying, resonated deep within his psyche to another person who was not the thug in her lounge room.

"Including you, right?" asked Shane looking for exact confirmation.

"Including me," she continued. "Apart from actually assembling it, I'm the head of the project, so for all these reasons, I know it works. Probably for the same reasons whoever sent you realises that as well." Talking about the Sara1 this way to a man who might murder her yet made her realise the potential and infinite value of this machine. *Jesus Christ*, she thought, *unless whoever sent these guys needs me for something, I'm toast.*

Shane turned to his young accomplice and ordered, "Go recheck our escape route."

The young man knew better than to ask questions, so walked casually out the back door as if without a care in the world and closed it gently behind him.

Oh fuck, thought Sarah, *this can't be good.*

"The next questions are private between you and me. If you have a death wish, just breath a word of our conversation to anyone else and I'll find you, understood?"

"Understood," said Sarah, but too afraid to ask if that meant he wouldn't kill her tonight.

"If I had a person in my past, that I, um ..." he trailed off.

Sarah broke the pause, unsure where her compassion for this evil but perhaps troubled man came from. *Probably some fucked up mini Stockholm syndrome.* "It means different things to different people," she reiterated, appreciating the need to be bloody careful here. "I truly believe this machine can connect you to one or more of those people in a dream it induces. Like it does for me. I was doing that when you woke me up." If he asked for any more details, she was prepared to lie through her teeth, because there was no way he would get those specifics!

The back door opened, and the young man strolled back in. "No problems," he reported.

Shane held the Sara1 in his hands while instructing his subordinate, "I'm going to test what she's told us. Let me sleep for ten minutes and no more. Wake me up then, understood?" His eyes bored into the younger man, and his right index finger waved at him like a magic wand to complete a warlock's spell.

"Understood," nodded his underling.

Shane lay down on the long couch in the living room with the earphones in. He was asleep in under five minutes. It might otherwise have been hard to assume when he'd nodded off, but the decibel level of his snoring left little doubt.

If she'd thought about it, like really thought about it, she would not have done what she did next. Halfway through the designated snore time, Sarah decided to test the frozen waters between her captors, whispering, "Does he always treat you like shit? He doesn't seem to trust you at all."

He looked at her, then at the ground in front of him and exhaled in apparent shame.

She decided to keep walking further out onto the frozen lake where the ice was even thinner than what she already stood on. "How long do you think you'll last with him? He's a psycho, you're not, I can tell. You're just caught up with the wrong people." Getting no response, she continued to press her luck. "Let me go, and we can both escape quietly while he's asleep. He won't wake up for hours with the device on. You saw how deeply asleep I was. We'll be long gone and safe by then. I'll speak up for you, tell the police what a decent young man you are and that you saved me. This is your chance for freedom. Come on, what do you say?"

Ambling towards Sarah, he stood directly in front of her, not staring ... glaring at her. She knew she had gone too far and fallen through the ice into the icy waters below. *Why couldn't I have kept my fucking mouth shut?* She grasped her misjudgement of him, having mistakenly seen shame because that's what she needed to see to have any hope herself. Contempt, though, was what she'd truly seen. Not for the cruel brute in command, but for her, the woman tied up directly in front of him.

In a slow-motion move similar to what his sleeping boss had performed earlier, he reached behind him and a gun just like the one brandished by Shane, came into sight. She looked into his eyes to see nothing, no emotion, no humanity, nothing. Continuing the re-enactment of earlier, he pushed the end of the snub-nose barrel into the top of her left knee. Sarah closed her eyes and started to tremble at the thought of the impending agony about to befall her. The cocking of the hammer sounded familiar as she felt the gun press even harder into her leg. Sarah waited for the inevitable suffering to begin. The only sound was that other bastard snoring.

Opening her eyes at her tormentor, he was smiling a toothless grin, silently, wickedly, cruelly. In wretched defeat and expectation, she followed his eyes down to the gun still jammed down mercilessly on her leg. She witnessed his finger enter the trigger guard and close the distance slowly to the trigger as if he was relishing the moment. She knew this time she would never walk properly again, if she survived at all, and resigned herself to the fact, closing her eyes once more. He pulled the trigger the remainder of the way back. The hammer released as it sprang forward from its cocked, ready to shoot position and struck metal ...

Time almost stood still. She had read stories of soldiers being shot in battle and experiencing no pain, as she felt no pain now. A full three seconds passed before she contemplated opening her eyes to behold her smashed and ruined joint. What she saw shocked her. His gun remained in position, but her leg remained miraculously whole. *What the fuck?* Sarah suddenly realised she had heard the click, not recognising then what it was, or what it meant. It wasn't luck or anything else that had saved her. *There's no fucking bullets in his gun!*

"Like ya said, he don't trust me at all. He certainly don't trust me enough to keep me hardware loaded all the time ... yet." He touched his left back pocket, "So I keep them in here. Now shut da fuck up, or I'll gag ya again, whether he's asleep or not ... Actually, I have a better idea ..."

Chapter Twenty-Three

Dusk had passed by the time Marcus arrived at Sarah's place.

There wasn't much traffic around; she lived in a pretty quiet street. He parked out on the roadway as he knew from his Uber pick-up that awkward Saturday morning that the white gravel made a mountain of noise when driven on. Not knowing whether she would be awake or asleep, he didn't want to be unduly noisy. He decided to leave the expensive bottle of Glenfiddich *Winter Storm* he'd bought for her on the back seat of the car for now.

As he approached the end of the driveway it was darker than he remembered. It caused him to look at the closest overhead street-light and note the bulb was now fully blown. *Thanks for nothing, City Council!*

As expected, there was no porch light, and he was still well out of the short range of the front-door sensor lights.

Marcus walked down her dark driveway with the contrasting white gravel helping him to see the way. Grabbing the phone from his pocket, he decided not to use its torch as his eyes were adjusting well enough. Another car pulled up quite abruptly but quietly in the street somewhere near where he was parked. Their headlights remained on. As he walked in front of the first living room window, Marcus thought he heard snoring, but saw movement in the living room through a small gap in the curtains. Something didn't feel quite right, and his heartbeat quickened.

He paused at the curtain gap and peeked in. If Sarah was there, he would knock on the door; if not, he'd head off. Incomprehensibly, he spotted Sarah bound to a chair in the middle of the living room with someone holding a gun up in front of her. She looked utterly terrified, trembling perceptibly from where he stood. Marcus was rocked, and his immediate ingrained reaction was to dial triple zero.

He didn't consider when he rotated his phone up to use it that the backlight would illuminate his face in the curtain gap. In the instant it took for him to realise his mistake it was too late; he'd been seen. Sarah screamed, "RUN, MARCUS, RUN!" He recoiled mentally, as disbelief initially brought inaction. But then, turned and ran for all he was worth directly up the driveway entrance towards his car.

MEANWHILE, inside the house, Shane sprang awake, but as is typical after waking from the Sara1, he awoke more slowly than usual. Still half-asleep and on autopilot, he shouted at his young partner, "Go bring that fucker back here!" It was just as well Shane yelled when he did, her young torturer had his gun raised and was about to pistol-whip Sarah.

The younger man obeyed instantly and moved the short distance to the front door, but Marcus had a head start by the time he'd opened both doors and made egress. The thug's hand fumbled to retrieve a couple of bullets from his left back pocket. As he made chase, the passive infra-red sensor, which controlled the two 150-Watt floodlights attached to it, detected him. Taking their cue, the sensors activated both halogen lanterns. One of the outdoor bulbs pointed roughly parallel to the front veranda and the other towards the start of the driveway.

The young criminal, hell-bent on misdemeanour, ran up the driveway, superbly backlit and highly visible, as cold white floodlights turned night into artificial day. His wild scream at Marcus of, "COME BACK HERE OR I'LL PUT A FUCKIN BULLET IN YA!" was heard by his intended victim, and one other ...

MARCUS SPRINTED up the driveway and nearly slipped over disastrously as he turned sharp left, covering the distance to his car in what could only have been a personal best time. Even before he reached the roadway, he was *pat running* trying to find which pocket he'd left his bloody keys in. He only had a few more car lengths to where his Honda was parked parallel to the gutter. As more luck than good management would have it, his car was pointing in the right direction for a fast getaway. At last, he found the solid lump of his keys in his right leg pocket and ripped open the Velcro pocket flap, only to find his keys stuck fast on a tangle of threads in the bottom of his pocket! He cursed, this wasn't the first time!

Surprising himself, he did the next best thing and fumbled by feel for the unlock button. With hopeful relief, he heard the door lock mechanisms shunt as the indicators blinked twice, while the interior and park lights came on. Because of the lack of nearby street lighting and the dark driveway, the bright flashing amber lights and park lights of his car acted like lighthouse beacons. His night vision was severely degraded.

Several steps from his driver's door, a car door slammed somewhere close by up ahead. While Marcus heard feet getting rapidly louder on the gravel driveway, he realised he was being converged on from both directions. Knowing he wouldn't make the driver's door handle in time, let alone the seat to be able to drive away before catching a bullet, Marcus strained to see ahead at what he instinctively saw as his nearest threat. At this close distance, his glare-affected eyes struggled to discern any details of the human form rushing towards him. He knew he was a goner when that person stopped suddenly. He made out the double-handed grip on *another fucking gun* pointed directly at him, already raised to the shooter's line of sight.

It's all over, he thought, as his beloved and beautiful Madeleine flashed before his eyes. In the microsecond the bullet left the gun barrel in a short blast of flame, with his world slowing from ultra-slow motion to frozen, he saw Henry's face, arms outstretched, pistol clasped in both hands, shooting him. Killing him. He accepted his fate with resignation and waited for the homicidal slug to strike him down.

Chapter Twenty-Four

Marcus was struck then by an acute, debilitating episode of a complex neuro-physiological reaction, afflicting even the bravest of men. When he was spotted at the window, he already had adrenaline in his system from the growing unease he'd felt that something wasn't right. This was followed by a full adrenaline rush peaking his heart rate, redirecting blood flow towards his muscles. The airways of his lungs relaxed to open themselves fully and provide every muscle with more precious oxygen. In turn, this made his breathing rate faster but shallow. After his record-breaking sprint from house to car, he gasped for air in rapid shallow breaths. His body was trying to re-boost its depleted oxygen levels, under the additional pressure and stress of trying to help Sarah.

With his body already in this heightened but mostly spent physiological state, Marcus was confronted with the added profound revelation that his friend Henry, was also his killer. With imminent death at his door, his tenth cranial nerve, the Vagus nerve, mediated his reality by a vasovagal episode.

Neurogenic effects counteracted the adrenaline, as vasodilation made him suddenly lightheaded. Marcus felt no warning his blood pressure had plummeted; his limbs just started to shake, and he found himself unable to stand. He abruptly collapsed to his hands and knees, and retched with such gusto, not a skerrick of the Devonshire tea he'd shared with his assassin remained within him.

HENRY HEARD WHAT MARCUS HAD, but saw what Marcus could not; the criminal's gun pointing towards Marcus's back.

THE YOUNG THUG to his utter dread, saw Henry running towards the driveway entrance, holding a firearm about to become fully stabilised in a double handed grip. Whoever this might be, had just stopped abruptly and was a split second away from shooting him. The young offender reversed direction as fast as he could, to sprint back to Shane and the comparative safety of the house.

Henry's single shot rang out just as the reprobate turned and lost his footing on the gravel, ironically on the slide just created by Marcus fleeing. The young man fell violently to his right knee but lost little momentum recovering.

It was an incredible piece of luck depending on your point of view. Henry's single .25 calibre bullet slammed into the top of the slipping young man's left shoulder instead of centre mass, Henry's actual aim point. The bullet entered the AC joint, wreaking considerable destruction on bone, tissue, and ligaments in the fraction of a second as it passed through. The gunshot wound would ensure he could not use that shoulder anytime soon, certainly not without the further insult of a surgeon's knife.

The offender scuttled back towards the house with no perceptible pause in pace, a gut-wrenching shriek of pain adding self-motivation to his footsteps enroute directly to the front door.

THERE HAD BEEN no time for a second shot. Henry continued to cover the driveway opening using the rear driver's quarter panel of Marcus's Honda for protection. He continued to shield Marcus, still puking for all he was worth on all fours directly behind him, fortunately, he was puking the other way.

His friend was his priority for the moment, so he didn't pursue the villain back down the driveway. Henry's actions were guided by two principles. *A bird in the hand is worth two in the bush,* and *don't kill one to save one.* He recognised with the floodlights on, the driveway entrance stood as nothing more than a killing zone to funnel or lure an enemy into. Henry gave himself a ten count and time to appraise his tactical situation. "Marcus, it's Henry. Are you hurt, are you hit?" demanded Henry urgently but calmly.

The abdominal muscle spasms powering Marcus's intragastric events were relentlessly trying to expel his empty stomach lining. He managed to shake his head and gasp haltingly, "No... Not hurt ... Sarah ... Sarah ... Help Sarah," was all he could muster as his small reserve of physical and mental energy spent itself. Exhausted again, Marcus trembled as he collapsed low against the Honda.

Henry swapped his Walther into his left hand. Although he knew he couldn't hit a barn door at two paces shooting left-handed, he had no reason to suspect anyone else in the espionage world knew that. Taking out his mobile, he opened the Crypto-Cone homepage, unguarded a red button and tapped it. Taken to a second page, he tapped a sizeable red icon marked EMER, and the symbol started pulsing.

Henry had never anticipated using the recently upgraded emergency function. The powers that be had gone to great lengths to make it entirely understood that anyone who activated this feature had better be in deep shit, because if they weren't, they bloody well would be. He knew with the EMER icon pulsing, urgent pre-recorded assistance from the Police Service was being mobilised and his service identifier added to the end of the message to help police identify him on site.

On the lower half of the same screen, two more coloured icons marked *Amb* and *Fire* shared the space. Pressing Amb, he made sure it too was pulsing before sliding his phone back into his trouser pocket. The whole process to get the cavalry mounting up and on their way, took a bare ten seconds, infinitely faster than making a triple 0 call.

Henry felt reassured again with his ability to protect himself and Marcus, as he swapped his handgun back into his dominant hand. With the front yard floodlights still operating, a scan of the limited area he could see, identified no immediate threats. But then came the sound of a single, maybe muffled, gunshot. Hunkering down closer to the vehicle, he couldn't tell if they were being shot at, or a weapon had been discharged close by for some other reason. He discarded the former rationale because, if someone was shooting at him, and they hadn't even managed to hit the car, they were about as dangerous as he was shooting left-handed.

Next to draw attention, were two loud and distinct, cringe-worthy sounds of glass panes being smashed in succession. Henry continued listening intently and scanning around them when he heard what he thought to be two people running. Judging by the Doppler shift, they were running away. The deep and very loud WUMP of an accelerant igniting in a confined space drowned out any other noises.

No-one could avoid the noxious smell of thick black smoke, as the structure fire propagated rapidly. Henry used his app to swiftly summons the last of the three emergency services.

He glanced at Marcus, not sure now how well he was coping,

considering what he had just been through. Satisfied no clear and present danger existed, and with no thoughts of another ten count on his mind, it was now or never. Henry stood and pushed forward in tactical stance, gun held in a classic double pistol grip in front and, in this case, two grades below horizontal.

One grade was standard for searching in threat environments, so he wouldn't risk obstructing his vision if a target presented itself. The additional grade was because any potential target would be downhill and, again, he did not want to risk some mortal peril being obstructed by the very gun he would unhesitatingly shoot that threat with.

Whether the front-yard floodlights were on or off at that moment became immaterial. The amount of light from the tongues of ferocious flames already darting ten metres skywards into the night sky through the smashed front veranda window was startling. More than sufficient light was present to see clearly. Atypical thick black smoke billowed through the opening, as the diesel accelerant, ignited by the lighter fluid, the original cause of this instant conflagration, was consumed.

The breaking of the large viewing windows, one at the front of the house, the other at the rear, facilitated cross ventilation of the fire. Rather than be starved of oxygen as it would have been had the windows not been smashed, the arsonist's touch had ensured this structure would not be saved. Even if the Fire Service response time was four minutes, not the actual fourteen it would take them from the nearest suburban station, this building would not remain standing.

Henry made his way as close as possible to the already fully involved house, where the radiant heat was scorching and oppressive. No-one could conceivably be alive in there.

Feeling like his clothes, but definitely his hair would catch fire, he retreated reluctantly up the driveway. He holstered his weapon as he saw Marcus stumbling down the driveway towards him, dishevelled, distraught, and damn near demented.

Marcus yelled ever more desperately for Sarah, becoming increasingly manic as he totally disregarded Henry's presence, even with arms outstretched, blocking his intended path to the engulfed house. Tears tracked down his cheeks, although he wasn't sobbing. He looked from side to side around Henry at the front of the blazing inferno that minutes earlier had been Sarah's home. Marcus continued to scream out her name.

Henry said everything he could think of to break through the sensory overload and disbelief Marcus was struggling with. Henry needed two things, his friend *compos mentis and some quick answers.* Hoping he would forgive him, Henry took half a step back and slapped Marcus hard across the face. He may have slightly over-done it. Marcus wasn't steady on his feet *before* he struck him and was less so now. Henry stepped forward quickly for support and to keep him upright. But, he had at least stopped yelling. Considering the rising welt on Marcus's left cheek, it was lucky Henry managed to snap his friend out of his mania, and not snap his neck instead.

But Henry was in work mode and couldn't afford to dwell on it. Using a formal voice of authority Marcus would not attribute to who stood before him, and right up in his face, demanded, "Where did you last see Sarah? What happened here?"

MARCUS'S tortured mind began to rouse, and his eyes, having been swept savagely to the right with the rest of his head, stopped sweeping the burning building. "I don't understand what's happened," he said. Marcus was not only looking at Henry now, Henry felt he could see him and comprehend more of what he saw.

"Jesus, Henry, where the fuck's Sarah? I spotted her through a gap in the curtains, strapped to a chair in the living room, some bloke holding a gun like he was about to backhand her across the face with it. There was another one asleep on the couch, snoring his head off, I think. I didn't see any others. She had a gag around her neck, but it wasn't over her mouth. She saw me and yelled to warn me." His next words flowed, but came loaded full of realisation and pain, as Marcus tenuously clung to the present. "Sarah sacrificed herself for me, Henry. She saved me, and now she's gone. This has to be about us, or work. We failed to protect her, shield her. Why the fuck did they kill her? Why not me or you? Why have you got a gun?!? None of this makes any fucking sense! … none!"

"I'm sorry, Marcus. It was all happening after I got here. We weren't to know," apologised Henry again, placing a comforting hand on his colleagues' shoulder. It initially occurred to Henry, if he could have saved the time in the carpark with Jane, things may have been different. He rationalised the same could be said for the red lights and the road repair truck he was caught behind on the way here. For these valid reasons, he dismissed any potential guilt out of hand. If Jane made the same connection, he would make her understand that too.

The blaze continued devouring Sarah's home. Even her car in the carport burned at an ever accelerating pace. It was a paradox the flames were unaware of. The faster the fire engulfed and destroyed the building, the larger the inferno would become, and the quicker its mindless determination would lead to its own fuel-starved demise.

APPROACHING sirens from several directions were nearly drowned out by the noise of the fire, until those responders had almost arrived. First on scene was a highway patrol vehicle diverted from a routine patrol of the nearby motorway; the closest unit when the call came over. They received information from dispatch that federal agent *5335* was on scene requiring urgent assistance, and an all-services response had been required.

While responding urgently to the scene, they received an update from the ever-calm dispatcher. "Multiple triple 0 calls, shots fired, house well on fire at location with single person reported, TRG BearCat responding, approach with caution, no further information at this time." As the Patrolmen travelled in the direction of whatever the hell was happening, the dark thermal column of smoke was silhouetted by the glow of the surrounding suburban streetlights.

The two male police officers therefore had a broad overview, but not a lot of detail as to the exact nature of the incident they had been called to. *Ops normal.* They were cautionary but, it would be fair to say, ready to react professionally without fear or favour, to any eventuality presenting itself.

The officers quickly parked their high visibility Chrysler SRT8 across the street from the driveway and alighted. The big red trucks were not far behind, and they knew from experience the Fire Service would want the driveway to run hoses and equipment to the dwelling. They had already spotted the two men standing beside the driveway leading to the house fire, apparently waiting to speak with them. Both walked briskly towards the two, who did the same, and they met on the roadway.

HENRY IDENTIFIED himself as per interservice protocol.

"I'm Federal Agent Henderson service number 5335. This is my colleague Marcus Hall from CSIRO." Henry stepped subtly more forward than Marcus, maintaining his urgent but calm persona. Henry displayed another trait Marcus had not seen in him before, *Command Presence*, and he held the attention of the police officers. "I believe this is the result of a planned home invasion by at least two men who escaped out the backdoor immediately after they set the house on fire. We believe Sarah Douglas, a CSIRO manager in her 30s who lives here, is still inside. She was last seen forcibly strapped to a kitchen chair in the living room by a male holding a gun about to pistol whip her." Henry pointed at the front of the house. "That's the room at the front between the carport and the front door. I believe I hit one of the armed offenders in the shoulder near the driveway entrance, just as the bastard was about to shoot Marcus here in the back with a small revolver."

With that, Henry walked back to the top of the driveway where, with the light of the fire raging far into the night sky, he could easily see several drops of blood on the white gravel. At the top of the driveway, he saw a bloody splatter mark, which any forensic examiner would determine came from a bullet shot from the direction Henry had approached from.

One of the constables stepped away a few metres, turning his head towards the microphone slung over the left shoulder of his Hi-Vis armoured vest. He was difficult to make out over the sounds of the intense fire, no doubt as the officer intended. Marcus identified intermittent words and phrases like, "Federal agent ... home invasion ... trapped inside ... driveway ... be on lookout for ... rear entrance."

"When you say hit one, you mean shot one?" asked the other highway patrolman.

"Yes, I shot him with my service pistol ..." Henry patted his left hip to indicate under his shirt, "... secure in holster here, safety on, one up the spout, 4 in the mag."

"And what about you, sir? You've obviously been assaulted. Are you armed as well?" asked the patrolman to Marcus, who stared back at him with quizzical revulsion.

"No. No, I'm a colleague of Sarah's from CSIRO." Saying her name again made him grasp for self-control, which he was most relieved to hold uncertainly again. "I don't know anything about guns, or being assaulted," he added distantly with a touch of his sensitive cheek, and an unappreciative sideways glance at Henry. Marcus felt his overloaded emotions vacillating between sheer gratitude and outright anger.

Henry knew the next question would be coming because it was standard law enforcement practice. Typically, at any scene like this, the only people police can easily authenticate are other emergency service workers, partly because they're familiar faces in their area. Everyone else, until proven otherwise, may not be who they claim to be. The deadly threat others are out there searching for might well be standing right in front of them.

The officer, finishing his radio call, remained vigilante towards both men at a short distance and oblique angle. For Henry or Marcus to rotate towards him quickly as a threat would be difficult. Both men were unknown quantities to the police, so by remaining apart this officer effectively, if casually to a layperson, covered his partner. Henry recognised their practised professionalism and appreciated that run-of-the-mill cops covered their bases like they should, without a word passing between them.

"As you're no doubt aware, I have to take your firearm into my possession, Agent Henderson. Carefully and slowly, I reiterate carefully and slowly, place your firearm on the ground in front of you, keeping it at all times within the confines of the holster. Do NOT attempt to withdraw the weapon from its holster for any reason, we will perceive that as a direct threat and may use lethal force against you. Do you understand me?" spoke the officer in a severe, forthright manner. Both officers had their gun hands empty and ready near their quick draw weapons.

Henry observed the officer standing just away from them now had a pad of traffic infringement notices in his non-gun hand. These guys weren't threatening but weren't playing around either. It was by the book. He knew if he attempted to draw his Walther, the ticket book would be thrown at him as a distraction and four bullets would arrive in his centre mass before the ticket book even reached him. To Henry it was procedure, to Marcus, it was intimidating.

"I understand." Henry did as bid and stepped back three paces pre-empting the officer's next requirement. Because handing over a weapon to police was practised on his regular firearms training days, he also knew he and Marcus were about to get body searched. The nearest officer to him retrieved the Walther.

Another two police vehicles screeched to a halt in quick succession and disgorged another four officers onto the scene. A third response vehicle arrived hot on their heels, this one, no standard police car. The truck-sized, dull black and brutish-looking armoured response unit was known as a BearCat. This ballistic colossus belonged exclusively to the Tactical Response Group. To Henry's great relief, his inter-service firearms instructor, who trained him every six months or so, stepped from the vehicle and walked briskly towards them.

SENIOR SERGEANT ROSS 'ROSCO' RADCLIFFE may have just turned fifty, but there were very few in 'the Force' outside his specialist team capable of keeping up with him on a morning beach run. His 194 cm frame, slightly taller than Henry, filled out his tactical apparel nicely with his long legs. His rugged, some would say handsome face had seen more than most. Like most coppers, Rosco maintained a good sense of humour, if not a little dark at times. Tonight, however, he presented as short, sharp, in charge and all business.

He recognised Henry as he walked over to him in between tactical scans of the area. Everyone else wearing a police uniform, in blue with a cap, or black with a ballistic helmet, were fanning out into the neighbours' yards to form a perimeter. "Hi, guys,"

Rosco addressed the highway patrolmen first, "I'm Senior Sergeant Radcliffe, and once I get a sit-rep off you two, I'll assume Incident Control. Wanna give me a quick handover?" In no way a request, it was merely the standard way of dispensing with unnecessary niceties to get on with the business at hand.

The handover was quick and thorough. Finally, Rosco turned to Henry and extended his hand; they shook briefly and firmly. "Hi, Hens, I'm guessing since you're here we need to talk in private. We can do that in the BearCat in a minute."

Before they moved, Rosco had two other things to clear up. To the officer holding Henry's confiscated gun, he said, "On my authority as IC you can return this firearm. He is a federal agent known to me, and by the sounds of things, it could have been a damn sight worse if he'd been unarmed tonight. Make sure you write some detailed notes in your notebooks before the shift's out, OK? Oh, and gents, thank you, job well done."

Both officers nodded, and Henry gratefully reacquainted himself with his pistol. As pleased as he was to have his Walther returned to him, he also knew it remained cocked and ready to shoot. He would have to clear his weapon when he got the first opportunity.

Roscoe turned to Marcus, who, by any stretch of the imagination was a mere bystander these past few minutes. Marcus tried to wrap his head around what had happened, and *how the fuck am I suddenly in the middle of guns, arson, and death?!?*

Henry spoke up, "This is Marcus, he's with me." With an almost comical darting index finger bouncing back and forth between them, Henry introduced them. "Marcus, Roscoe. Roscoe, Marcus." Roscoe and Henry saw Marcus's eyes following Henry's pointing fingertip, his head hardly moving, it didn't look natural.

Roscoe offered his hand to shake and Marcus accepted with a little delay. Mild shock Rosco decided. "It is nice to meet you Marcus, my condolences. I have to ask if you'll come down to the station a bit later. To be honest, I don't think you should drive after what you've been through, I'll find a driver for you, is that OK?"

"Sure," replied Marcus flatly.

Following a conversation regarding his Honda still parked outside the burning house, they headed across the road to the Bear-Cat. Their timing coincided with the first Fire and Rescue appliance responding into the street, powered by 320 thoroughbred racehorses.

Chapter Twenty-Five

The Scania heavy pumper arrived at the driveway head amid the warning of its blinding strobes and Techtronic siren. Similar sirens could be heard not far away. Station Officer Russell, in full turnout gear with red helmet, and thermal imaging camera, took the three steps to the ground and began talking on his tunic-mounted radio. His head was a swivel as he sized up the task before them.

Rescue was his priority. He had already directed his team to aggressively knock down the fire through the smashed living-room window. The aim was to survey the living-room floor area for a victim, without making entry to the building proper, all the while being wary of the collapse zone. The fire, having fully penetrated the roof space, was venting flames above the height of nearby power poles. The lack of structural integrity of the building was beyond doubt. Making entry was not an option. Alas, no special skills were required to know anyone still in that house would only be coming out in a body bag. Given the extreme heat over time, probably a small one at that. As SO. Russell and his crew continued intervening, another two heavy pumpers and an aerial appliance arrived and deployed.

MARCUS WAS ASKED out of the BearCat by ambulance officers to be checked over. While he protested he was fine, it was never a discussion he had a hope of winning. He did, however, successfully decline the invitation to go to hospital, because he knew his only chance to find out what the fuck was going on, remained with Henry. The ambos did give him two much appreciated going away presents. Some green minty liquid to finally rinse the taste out of his mouth, and an assurance the red mark on his face would be faded tomorrow.

As Marcus re-entered the rear of the armoured vehicle, Henry and Rosco were wrapping up their conversation. Marcus, fine just a moment ago, now struggled to maintain control of his emotions and be polite. It had suddenly gotten the better of him. He blurted out questions as his voice cracked. "Who do you really work for? What did you have to do with Sarah's murder? Are we really friends?" Helplessness descended upon him, he needed some real answers and soon, or he would definitely lose his shit. That would be neither courteous nor dignified.

Despite the things he had seen and done over the years to keep the peace, not to mention the professional thickness of his hide, Rosco had not lost his human perception or empathy. He knew when people needed some space. "I'll step outside for a minute." He gave Marcus a compassionate smile, and a friendly gesture to take a seat on his way out.

Henry looked sympathetically at his friend and colleague, "Marcus, I'm sorry, I couldn't tell you I'm a federal agent. I was undercover until this afternoon."

Marcus sounded exasperated, "If I hear federal agent one more time, I'll break someone's nose! Federal agent means nothing to me! Who the fuck for?"

Henry saw the unmistakable need to pass on clear information quickly, to prevent the mental health of his friend, snapping. Significant beans had to be spilled in Henry's next breath. "OK, mate, I work for the Australian Secret Intelligence Service." Some tenseness flowed from Marcus, his face less pained, so Henry continued to answer the questions Marcus had already asked tonight, thinking that would assuage him most. "I came here tonight because the service ordered me to. It was pure coincidence I turned up when I did. We are good friends, that's entirely genuine, believe me, and I hope we always stay good friends. I've never *ever* lied to you, but I have been forced not to tell you everything. Prime example; I'm a spy placed in the Lamarr program. I'm sorry you have to hear that under these circumstances."

As Marcus soaked up these truths, the door opened again, and a young, slim, raven-haired policewoman stood there.

"I'm here to take you to the police station now if it's convenient, Mr Hall. If you give me your car keys, we'll get it dropped back to Lindfield after SOCO have finished and leave the keys with gate security." She spoke in the polite, understated manner police exude at times like this.

Marcus felt reassured by the answers, look Henry cast him, and by the way she spoke.

"I'll be about five minutes behind you," said Henry. "Got some things to tie up with Rosco and I'll meet you there, I promise. We can continue our conversation there, no more secrets."

"No more secrets," responded Marcus, "but one more question before I go. Is your real name Henry?" He looked directly at his friend, who could see in his eyes he desperately wanted it to be true. For *something* to be real, but this in particular, if it meant he could hold on to Henry, he could share his burden.

"Yes, mate, my real name is Henry. But in the trade, they call me 'Hens.'"

"That will do for now ... Henry ... thank you," acknowledged Marcus with several nods. He'd barely gotten these last few words out before he started to choke on them, but the sudden feeling passed, succeeded by a stronger urge to maintain self-control. He continued adapting to his roller coaster of emotions and had enough answers for now at least.

Marcus departed with the young policewoman, appreciative of her kind and understanding face. She wasn't apprised of all the facts and who fitted into what in tonight's melee, so couldn't decide whether to make small talk or not. In the end, she decided not to, and given her passengers history with small talk, that was probably a good thing. He sat in silence in a kind of half-stunned thinking state, but thinking nonetheless and lining up some ducks in his head.

Chapter Twenty-Six

M arcus was shown to an interview room and given a pot of percolated coffee. Appreciating the thought, he knew there was no way he could stomach it right now though. He sat in solitary contemplation for a few minutes, then, faithful to his word, Henry joined him.

As Henry walked past to take the chair next to him, he put a hand briefly on Marcus's shoulder in commiseration again. Henry said, "I'm sorry we lost Sarah. I had no idea what was going on at her place until I saw you running, then heard and saw the guy with the gun lining you up."

Marcus was listening intently as Henry continued. "Because of the brilliant discoveries you've made in the last week, the project was re-classified *top secret* due to the national security implications. I was tasked to Sarah's to retrieve the Sara1. I knew you would be there because you said you would be. I intended levelling with you both, which I thought would work out well ..." With a wave of his hands he said, "Then, all this shit hit the fan."

A brief knock at the door preceded Inspector Les Coldman. Les kept himself in good nick and still wore the dark uniform of the

TRG. Given the nature of the evening's events, it wasn't the time for a reunion, even if this meeting brought back happy memories, which it didn't. To this day, Les still couldn't abide the smell of those fucking lilies.

He carried an A4 manilla binder marked, 'ASIS Ops'.

"Hens, they told me it was you." They shook hands firmly. "I've been given a precis already," said the TRG head.

"Les. Congratulations on the promotion," said Henry with sincerity.

Marcus looked backwards and forwards like watching a tennis match in slow motion as the ball went from one side of the court to the other. It reminded him of his introduction to Rosco, but something was different he thought. *Their tones were familiar, respectful even, but perhaps a little wary?* Marcus was introduced and they got underway.

"Before we start the debrief, Les, if you don't mind, I need to explain and confirm some things to Marcus. I owe him that much, given everything that's gone on. Some of it will be good background info to start with too; some of it you will already know."

"Sure, Hens, you talk. I'll pour myself a coffee. Anyone?" Both shook their heads.

"Marcus, Henry Henderson *is* my real name, I *am* a real lab technician, but my main job is with ASIS, as you now know. Since this isn't over, I have received approval such that you are both cleared to listen to everything I am about to tell you. You must realise, though, this information is classified top secret and cannot be divulged outside this room. Would you both please sign the relevant indemnity form Les brought in?"

"I've done mine already," said Les with mounting curiosity, fishing out Marcus's form from the manilla binder and sliding it over with a government-issued black BIC pen. Marcus didn't go beyond reading 'Top Secret - Crimes Act 1914 Part VII' at the top of the page, before signing blindly and sliding it back towards Les.

Henry intercepted the paper, appended his signature as witness, pushed the page back to Les, who replaced it in the binder.

"The Lamarr chip was invented by DST - Defence Science and Technology - several years ago. As it was suspected that Lamarr had the potential to revolutionise both 5G and 5G Wi-Fi technology, it was classified as sensitive." Henry continued, "Apparently, the AIC, the Australian Intelligence Community, became aware of foreign government interest in the potential of our Lamarr research even before we got started, so we're talking pretty early on. As a result, by the time funding for the research project proper was established, I'd been given training as a lab technician and placed as the third member of Sarah's team, to act as lab tech and also as a covert security investment.

"The government never imagined you would develop what you have. The initial, and stilted thinking, just hoped the project would find a better way to build on Australia's old cutting-edge Wi-Fi profile. It was never, ever, suspected that anyone would be in physical danger doing Wi-Fi research. The problem is just that, though, now it's become something other than Wi-Fi research, something wildly unprecedented.

"Given my prior reporting to ASIS, I was informed by my superiors this afternoon, of the re-classification of the project to top secret. I was directed to secure all data and prototypes at Lindfield, ASAP. My existing tenure at CSIRO was also to cease. Given the prior foreign interest in Lamarr, and knowing now what at least some of its capabilities are and potential might be, I was to carry my sidearm at all times. I was told being armed was precautionary as the security situation was not clear. Tonight, I think it's fair to say the security situation is abundantly clear. Someone wants our project and will kill to get it."

"Tonight, I went to Sarah's house to get the Sara1. I knew it was there because I'd activated a tracking Tile that I'd glued under the PCB earlier."

Marcus raised an eyebrow. "Really? So, you've been tracking me too? The whole being able to track the scopes in the building was bullshit?"

"No, not at all," denied Henry. "I put it in there on a hunch, it was all I had at the time. Come on Marcus, they're probably the least efficient outdoor tracker we could think of. You know now I have access to a lot better tech than that."

With everything that had happened tonight, Marcus looked Henry steadily in the eye and tilted his head slightly, repeating the question with body language as surely as if he'd asked it aloud.

"I can prove I've never tracked you, Marcus," said Henry. "We both know that if Bluetooth were activated near the PCB, it would interfere with the Lamarr chip, right? Has the Marc1 ever malfunctioned or seemed faulty?"

"No," acceded Marcus.

"I've only used the tracking Tile on the Sara1 once, and that was this afternoon to make sure it was at Sarah's because I had to retrieve it," insisted Henry. "You and I have been honest and open with each other about the research, Marcus. If I needed to know where you were, I'd have just asked. Nowhere near the same with Sarah. She didn't share complete information and trust with us and we reciprocated. She didn't know where we were with the research until today. We'd been trying to protect her. The main point here is, there is at least one other person in the mix we don't know about."

Henry talked for another twenty minutes and answered a multitude of questions from both men. All three seemed to arrive at the same conclusion. Anyone who knew the details of the real research needed protection.

Henry said, "If Sarah had talked to the fullest extent of everything she knew, and there was no reason to suppose she did otherwise, who could she have intimated had knowledge of the Sara1, or the Marc1? The only people Sarah knew was aware of either machine, was me, you, and Peter Esser. The service is in the process of contacting and looking into Peter again as we speak, so we don't have to worry about him. In keeping with 'no more secrets' Marcus, they're also doing more background checks on Sarah."

The coffee pot on the interview room table had run out, just as their questions had for the time being.

HENRY SPOKE on his phone to a very relieved Jane. She'd been watching the evening news, it didn't take much imagination to put Henry in the middle of the headline story of shots fired at a fatal house fire. She was shocked when he said it was Sarah and couldn't be angry with him anymore. After all, he'd lost a friend. Jane had never met Sarah, knowing her by reputation only. Sarah had been a decent person, her co-workers had liked and appreciated her.

MARCUS, on the other hand, found himself in a completely unhappy place. Neither Maddy, Bill or Helen were answering their mobiles - alarm bells rang their warning in his head! A black hole was forming in his abdomen, devouring him from the inside.

Henry was still talking to Jane when he caught the look on Marcus's face and knew whatever he was about to tell him was going to be bad. "What's up, mate?" queried Hens.

"No-one is answering at Bill and Helen's, Maddy included." Marcus was most definitely having the worst day of his life. His look to Henry said one word and one word only: *Help!*

The inspector already looked serious listening to the exchange.

Henry shot Les an apprehensive look. "Oh fuck, are we playing catch-up here?"

Les quickly got the address, and the two nearest uniform patrol cars were dispatched Code 1 to Bill and Helen's house. Even as the three of them jogged from the interview room to the police car park, they each harboured their own separate but similar fears. Had tonight already reached its destructive potential, or not?

Marcus went with Les, and Henry drove his own car, providing Jane with instructions as he drove. She was to make sure her house was locked up tight and wait for the Police to arrive. She was NOT to open the door to anyone, no matter who they were, or who they said they were. She must ONLY open the door to two police in uniform arriving in a marked patrol car, AFTER they quoted 5335. Anyone else who arrived she was to pretend she wasn't home and call him first, then 000. "Oh, and by the way honey, pack a bag for a few nights away ..."

Chapter Twenty-Seven

Sifu had been unusually hard on the sweaty physiques before him tonight. He habitually espoused some wisdom after each night's training, and tonight was about the nature of training. "Training should not only stretch and exercise the body, but broaden and sharpen the mind, to free the harmonious spirit on its journey to achieve kung fu."

With those final, meaningful words spoken and humble bow taken, the class ended. The physical relief for some students was definitely more pronounced than others, and many deep breaths were still being inhaled as gym bags were quickly retrieved, and the Kwoon emptied.

On this occasion, as on random others, Peter remained alone in the hall to speak with Sifu in his office.

"Shunyuan," Sifu began, using Peter's honorary Chinese name. "Whatever you have planned must surely be in difficulty. A woman is dead, and a house burnt to the ground, these things are most regrettable. My masters had already decreed this mission would be your last in this country, so in this, you are perhaps most fortunate.

They have also ruled you have two days to salvage a rich success. As a consequence of your, shall we say, impending triumph, the masters honour your long-standing loyalty, with appreciation and reward. You are permitted to travel and remain in the land of your forefathers for as long as you wish. Under heaven, our masters request you continue to serve them as a consultant, to share your wisdom with others who will carry forward your great work. You will hold the title of Sifu yourself."

Sifu's use of his honorary name, had great significance to him, as it had been given him before he knew of his connection to the great Genghis Khan. "Sifu, I-I am humbled," stuttered Peter, trying hard not to blush at such honour and privilege bestowed upon him.

"Shunyuan, tonight we go to the consulate to collect the items you requested to complete your plan and prepare your travel. Are you ready?"

"Of course, Sifu." Peter suggested they take his car, knowing it was more secure.

"Then we will leave now." He was not a man prone to wasting time on unnecessary chatter.

Shunyuan drove in silence towards Camperdown and the waiting Chinese Consulate. He drove down the one-way street and approached the fortified entrance to the primary vehicle and pedestrian access into the Dunblane Street legation. A shadowy figure stood with hands crossed over his stomach near the glass walk-in entrance doors.

Sifu instructed, "This is our man. Stop on the road beside him. Remain in the car. Our man will walk to your window and hand you a large envelope and take your photo for security purposes. It will be digitally compared to your staff photo before he allows us to leave."

Shunyuan did as instructed, stopping on the roadside with the driver's window down. The Chinese man, resplendent in a spotless grey suit with white coiled earpiece, walked around the rear of the car and stooped at the driver's window to confirm who the driver and passenger were. The man took one flashless photo using a ruggedised tablet.

"Greetings, Sifu, I was told you would be coming." Both men offered a nod to each other. The suited man pressed his earpiece tighter to his ear. "Welcome Shunyuan, here are your items ... Thank you, you may leave now." He nodded again to Sifu, who returned the gesture.

Sifu said nothing more than, "Drive."

Peter drove off, feeling nothing short of elation. Everything Sifu had promised him was in the envelope, of that he had no doubt. The security official even knew his name! Sifu was understandably held in some veneration at the consulate. Peter was mere days from the land of his ancestors, with few deeds left to be done. Those actions remaining were planned for success in a way that would have made Sun Tzu proud.

They returned uneventfully to the Kwoon and Sifu accessed his office. Both sat down, one either side of his desk. Shunyuan held the silk diplomatic pouch reverently. The ceremonial diplomatic wax seal of the People's Republic of China, stamped upon it.

"Allow me," said Sifu as he proffered his hand, and the pouch was handed to him. He broke the seal. In one smooth motion, he emptied the small bag, moving it left to right across the desk in front of him. Of note were two identical A4-sized official proclamation posters, a red PRC diplomatic passport and two diplomatic vehicle plates.

Sifu stood and offered his hand in felicitation. "Congratulations Shunyuan, by virtue of this passport, which I now present you, you are a member of the technical staff of the People's Republic of China diplomatic mission to Australia."

Peter stood and accepted Sifu's hand with a glowing smile.

"Thank you, Sifu." As if to solidify trust in himself and vindicate these great gifts, he followed with, "The final phase of my plan is being implemented as we speak, and I *will* be successful."

Sifu smiled as he nodded and replied, "Of that, I have no doubt, because I trust this plan is as good as your previous ones."

Chapter Twenty-Eight

C harcoaled human remains were discovered in the lounge room where the initial intervention of the Fire Service had focused.

It had taken several hours for the Fire Service to complete *Overhaul*, the search for hidden fire and hotspots. Thermal imaging cameras were used to detect and manage hotspots to be dampened down. Although the smell of the burnt-out house hung in the air seemingly everywhere, even far down the street and upwind as well, no more steam rose from the ruins. At this point in the incident, fire and crime scene investigations formally commenced.

Witnesses heard breaking glass and saw clouds of thick jet-black smoke that followed a very deep and loud wump. Investigators knew this could only be the unique sound of an uncontained fuel-air vapour explosion, causing the fire to spread rapidly throughout the structure. Uncontained hydrocarbons like petrol and diesel, even LPG, burn with thick jet-black smoke. House fires, unless started that way, do not.

A kitchen chair lay in the front and back yards, with accompanying smashed windowpane glass, being carefully photographed by

Scenes of Crime. These chairs had ostensibly been thrown through each window from the inside out, allowing air to cross ventilate the fire. An empty Jerry can lay open and brown inside the back door, its paint completely burnt off, and testing positive for a hydrocarbon, probably diesel. Another, much smaller hand-sized tin also tested positive for hydrocarbon, undoubtedly butane.

Liquid butane, such as Zippo lighter fluid, is extremely volatile and easily lit. Spilt diesel, in itself, is notoriously difficult to ignite with a naked flame, so another accelerant such as liquid butane is best used to ignite the diesel rapidly.

The sheer weight of physical evidence surviving the ensuing inferno culminated in the easily reached conclusion: Arson.

The fire investigator, satisfied beyond doubt as to cause and effect, started packing up his gear, leaving the police forensic people to finish doing their thing. He'd been unable to locate the small metal box mentioned in his brief but was told not to include it, one way or another, in his report. Both his and the police report would be submitted in evidence at the coronial inquest. Unusually, the Government Medical Officer, who sometimes doubled as the Medical Examiner, had shown up. *Interesting,* thought the fire investigator, *there's more to this than meets the eye.*

The GMO donned her PPC and met one of the forensic team in the front yard. After a brief discussion, they moved inside to the living room, where the corpse lay cordoned off and undisturbed. The in situ medical examination of the body commenced. There was much quiet discussion with nodding and shaking of heads as the pair examined the grisly find before them. After ten minutes and much prodding and poking, the GMO finished up. Exiting the house, she went through the prescribed safe process of removing her personal protective clothing, and sealing it in a yellow biohazard bag for incineration tomorrow.

Chapter Twenty-Nine

I
t's a common night-time occurrence in any community when two police cars pull up in quick succession with lights flashing, that neighbours take a sudden interest in what's gone on. It's a reactive, not proactive, neighbourhood watch of sorts, occurring the wrong way around, after the event, not before.

Helen and Bill's street was no exception. You would think the noise produced by smashing in a partly open wooden door held by a security chain with enough force to splinter generous pieces of wood into the hallway would have attracted the neighbours' attention. Apparently not. However, that was what the first responding police found upon arrival.

After passing a sit-rep over one of their portable radios, both crews drew their weapons, identified themselves and made tactical entry, pushing their way down the hall. The urgent call for an ambulance came soon after.

The dwelling was deemed clear of everyone, except the unconscious male lying half prone on the lounge-room floor. A blunt trauma wound and laceration afflicted his forehead. Given the presence of a collapsed coffee table beside the victim, it was a reasonable assumption the mechanism of injury was compounded by a fall onto the table, then the floor. Head wounds tend to bleed profusely, but these guys had seen worse. There was no spectacular amount of blood, *but he will have a hell of a headache when he wakes up*, one officer thought. The officer carried out a primary survey of the patient, quickly noting he was breathing adequately, as indicated by rise and fall of his chest. With the assistance of the other three officers, he carefully placed the patient into the HAINES recovery position to protect his airway and manage his cervical spine. HAINES is the acronym for High Arm In Endangered Spine, a modified Australian version of the standard recovery position, named after it's developer.

Bill received the best care available until the Intensive Care Paramedic Unit arrived. The police officer tending him had been, by chance, an Emergency Medical Technician Instructor before joining the Force. Like many applicants for the emergency services, he hadn't been particularly fussed which service he got into. As it happened, the police were his second choice, not that he told the selection panel that.

But now, another member of the public was receiving the benefits of his prior experience. A head injury is deemed to be a cervical spine injury until proven otherwise, and the position Bill lay in now was the best way to achieve 'C' spine support in the circumstances. With him rolled onto his side and his head on his left arm for support, a secondary survey was completed. Fortunately, nothing remarkable was found. The officer stayed kneeling on the floor monitoring his patient until his relief arrived. Two cheerful folks carrying soft packs and wearing dark blue uniforms with, 'Intensive Care Paramedic' on their epaulettes, strode confidently in.

The patient was administered oxygen at 15 l/min through a high concentration mask, and a cervical collar was fitted. As an assortment of other equipment gathered around him, it gradually seemed the oxygen was having a positive effect. Bill slowly opened his eyes.

BILL'S VISION WAS BLURRY, and his world was now a world of acute hurt. If he hadn't thought of Helen and Maddy right then, he would have chosen, without reservation, to fall right back into his previous pain-free realm of unconsciousness.

Marcus and Les arrived into this hive of faultless pre-hospital care, Henry not far behind. While Les sorted things with the on-scene police, Marcus came forward.

As Bill's eyes focused more, he thought he could make out his brother watching over him. "Marcus?" he said meekly. Relief washed across Marcus's face.

"I'm here, Bill," said Marcus, equally quietly, trying to stay out of the way. "You're in great hands," he added, trying to put a positive spin on a situation no-one understood. "What the hell happened?"

Bill, excessively groggy, but with grim determination, forced some words from his lips, "I ... I ...tried ... to protect them ... get my phone ... kitchen ..."

Marcus had no idea where this was going. Bill agonised, trying to focus and pass on something. Marcus went to the kitchen and found his brother's phone on the charger and retrieved it.

"Here," said Marcus holding the mobile where he thought Bill could see it, being careful not to drop it on his brother's already injured head.

"5 ... 6 ... 7 ... 8," Bill said forcing the numbers out. Marcus assumed he must mean the code to unlock the mobile, so he entered the numbers into the keypad and, as Bill intended, he had access.

"Arlo App," came the next instruction. Bill swallowed hard, like there had been a lump in his throat he had to overcome first before he could swallow past it.

With no prize for second, the penny dropped for Marcus. It seemed weeks ago but only two days since Bill had said he would upgrade security in the house. Now Marcus thought about it, the door chain smashed tonight never used to be there.

Marcus looked at the agony on his sibling's face and said simply, "I understand now, mate. Thank you. Rest now. We will find them."

That was as much time as Bill had. He was laid on the stretcher, with an accompanying whimper of breakthrough pain.

Bill needed to rest now, closing his eyes, having done what he could to identify their attackers. As he was wheeled to the ambulance, he tried to focus on his Helen, his beautiful wife, the love of his life. *Please be alright, please be alright.*

He was taken to hospital for a plethora of tests and hopefully a speedy recovery, despite the hospital food.

Marcus was doing something approaching multi-tasking as he watched the stretcher being loaded into the ambulance. Arlo is one of the most popular home-security camera systems in the world. Bill had probably bought a pack of them at Bunnings hardware when he purchased the security chain. He silently thanked his brother for his diligence and his strength.

Selecting 'library' on the bottom menu of the app, there before him was the HD security footage from the front door as the two crims approached. Other footage showed the hall as they broke the door in, and the living room as they knocked Bill out and gagged both girls before marching them out. Each piece of footage had been automatically stored in the cloud when recorded, so all Marcus had to do was save the video files to Bill's phone. In the age of high-resolution digital freedom, he emailed copies to himself, Henry and Les.

IT WAS FAST APPROACHING MIDNIGHT. This whole long day seemed surreal, but it was, real. Despite suffering physical and nervous exhaustion, all they could think of was their intense need to find the girls. Tomorrow was undoubtedly going to be a long and arduous day too. Les asked Henry in exasperation if he recalled the last time they'd worked together, when they had perhaps both displayed poor judgement. The surest path to doing that again was to not have enough rest. Marcus did not know what Les meant, but he saw Henry's resolve finally break. The considerable federal and state resources now pouring into this investigation would carry on without them for the rest of the night. Les managed, only at length, to convince Henry and Marcus the best thing they could do for the ladies, was to get some sleep.

The issue now was, where to sleep and be safe? The project manager of this top-secret research project had been murdered and her prototype stolen. The partner of the senior researcher had been abducted, together with his sister-in-law, his brother seriously assaulted and now under armed protection in hospital. The only remaining people with direct knowledge connected with the project and who had not been kidnapped or assailed were Marcus, Henry, Jane, Peter and Dr Frank. Dr Frank, woken at midnight, had said there was not a snowflake's chance in hell he wasn't going to work tomorrow. Henry made a phone call, and an ASIS purchase order was provided for two hotel suites. Two large interconnected rooms would be protected by rotating shifts of seemingly innocuous plain-clothed people in the hall outside. There was, however, some serious weaponry under their jackets.

Jane would be transported by the patrol car, and they would meet there safe and sound. They should all try and have some 24-hour room service to keep their strength up for what was possibly to come. Whether Marcus could actually eat anything, or hold it down, or eventually get some sleep, was another matter.

Chapter Thirty

Shane and passenger arrived at Peter's rented safe house, after escaping near capture at the hands of the authorities. Fortunately, Shane had brought the diesel jerry can as a bluff, to make Sarah *think* he was going to torch her house. Thus, his emergency exit strategy was simply his bluff executed for real. There hadn't been a lot to say as Shane hastily initiated the fire-bombing from the back door. In the distraction, he had managed to make good their escape.

Despite the close call, there were three bonuses in all this. He wouldn't have to put up with that young psycho anymore because he lay crispy on the living-room floor with a .38 slug through the forehead. Secondly, he had the Sara1 with him, and although it had failed to work completely for him, the third bonus would take care of that. Sarah, alive and well; would fix it for him!

Sarah found the events shocking and nearly overwhelming as she sat still in the escape car. Given what she'd just been through, it seemed ridiculous Shane insist she wear a seat belt.

She wasn't bound or gagged. Shane thought she probably should be but acquiesced to the kinder side of his inner self, which, coincidentally, he hadn't seen in years. He would have to bind her soon enough, and Sarah gave no indication she would try to escape.

Sarah was surprised how quickly Shane had killed to protect her. She would keep her word and get the Sara1 working properly. She didn't plan on trying to escape. After all, he had just saved her life, she doubted he'd done that just to take it later.

After they made their way inside the house, Sarah sat on one of the rustic bentwood chairs surrounding the oversized wooden dining-room table. As she did so, she placed the three remaining drams of whisky onto the table in front of her. She had reflexively scooped them up off the kitchen bench into her pocket as she fled the murder scene, or what was nearly the scene of her own murder.

She knew it required no excuse, and tonight of all nights there was no time like the present. Forgoing her almost ecclesiastical practice of preparing to savour good whisky, and without a second thought, Sarah twisted the top off one. She recalled her mother's voice as a little girl encouraging her to take her medicine. *Down the hatch.* So, down it went in one gulp. It burned all the way down. She hoped when the taste and burning of the whisky faded, memories of tonight would fade with it.

She realised Shane had been watching her in dull curiosity. He stepped to the opposite side of the table, placing the Sara1 and a small tool wrap in front of her. In a pure reflex action at him putting something down in front of her, she retaliated in a fashion, and placed one of the remaining drams in front of him. She picked up the Sara1 to examine it. He picked up the nip of whisky and examined it briefly before it went down his 'hatch.'

Sarah unscrewed the lid of the little black box and exposed the circuitry. No discolouration on top of the printed circuit board or any of its components indicated anything had failed. She unscrewed and removed five of the six small Philips-head screws holding the mainboard to the shell of the box. As she began to remove the last screw in a corner, the board pivoted slightly around the screw. She stopped. *Something's underneath the board. What the hell's that? Epoxy? It wasn't there when I assembled it, so someone's done something since I built it!*

Rotating the box allowed the less than optimal overhead fluorescent lights to fill the dark void under the circuit board. There, glued to the inside of the Sara1 under the board was a thin, white, square-shaped object. Sarah knew exactly what it was. 'Tile' stamped on its flat face was superfluous. She knew what a tracking Tile looked like, and given her expertise, knew now why the Sara1 wasn't fully functional all of a sudden. Because this little bugger was creating interference. However, the sensational upside to this, if Sarah kept the Tile with her, was her location could be tracked, assuming one of the good guys put it there. A burst of hope surged through her to be dashed as she looked around and could not see a Wi-Fi router anywhere. If the house had no Wi-Fi installed, the tracking Tile couldn't broadcast its position and whoever put it there could not find her.

Shane hovered a few steps from the table, ready to swoop in and take what he was waiting for. It would not be good for Sarah if he discovered there was a tracker in the black box on the kitchen table. Equally, it could be as bad for her continued health if she just told him. She struggled to think of some way of diverting his attention but needn't have worried. Shane had been waiting for the whisky, the best he could remember having, to evaporate from his lungs. He started paying particular attention to the empty whisky dram in his hand. Then, he walked away towards the kitchen, not out of direct eyesight if he chose to look, but far enough away for her to do what she needed to do.

Sarah seized the opportunity and a short, wide flat screwdriver to lever up the Tile sufficiently for her to remove it. In the absence of anywhere else to put it, she slid it into her pocket just as she heard the sound of Shane's little Scottish glass thudding into the bottom of the kitchen tidy, she was surprised it didn't break.

"That was a bloody nice drop, if I can say thank you," said Shane, almost asking permission.

"In reality, I'm the one who should be thanking you. You saved my life, so ... thank you," said Sarah in all sincerity. "I thought he was going to shoot me in the head."

"Oh, he was," replied Shane matter-of-factly, as if giving some rudimentary answer. "That wannabe was skitz, I'd already told him never to load his gun. He was fixated on you when he ran back into the room wounded. Guess he loaded it outside before he got shot. He intended to pop you off plain as day, and you were going to be his first. He'd been itching to kill someone, it was only a matter of time before he found an excuse."

A subdued Sarah asked, "Why didn't you let him?"

"Pick a reason. He'd been seen by the coppers and was wounded. He would need medical attention, which made him a liability connectable to me. I wasn't willing to go down for that twisted little fucker. Anyway, we weren't supposed to kill you, just get the information you were holding back and ensure your silence. You don't do that sort of thing when the boss tells you not too. I want you to fix the box so it works, and ... I believed what you said. There's a couple of other reasons, but those will do." He paused, as he noticed two things. His long gone self had mysteriously re-appeared again and with a brief spark of caring.

She had stopped working. "Have you fixed it? That didn't take very long ..."

"Yes, I think so. Only have to put it back together, and I'll do that now," said Sarah.

"Whose Marcus and why does he carry a gun?" asked Shane.

"Marcus is my 2IC, a scientist, I don't think he knows one end of a gun from the other, any more than I do."

Shane persisted, "Who do you know carries a gun then?"

Sarah answered honestly again, "No-one, absolutely no-one."

As he thought about it more while rubbing his unshaven chin,

Shane believed she was being truthful. *It would have been around about the time the coppers would have casually turned up if a neighbour had seen us in Sarah's yard and called them. Maybe just bad timing ...*

Shane got his thoughts back on what needed to happen. "Best you're done before the others arrive, and they won't be long. I'll be tying you up again before then, you understand?"

"Gotta do, what ya gotta do. Ahead of that, is there anything else electronic needs fixing? How good's the Wi-Fi here? Do you get a decent download speed?"

"I don't know why the hell you're interested in a Wi-Fi we don't have," Shane replied.

Sarah went for deflection and narrowly succeeded. "Whose arriving? What others?"

"Best you don't ask, the less you know, the better." Shane's tenor put an end to any further questions. Before she was due to be tied up again, Sarah pretended to need a drink of water from the kitchen to get close enough to the flip-top bin to drop the Tile in. Getting caught with that in her pocket would definitely not be good for her well being!

Sarah was bound firmly by her feet, but not too tightly, on the queen-sized bed in a closed bedroom. The sheets were clean, that was something at least.

It didn't really matter her bonds weren't tight, she still wouldn't be able to run anywhere. Hobbling was about as fast as she could go, and she didn't think she could hobble much further than the toilet. But she was thankful, and even a little surprised Shane had not tied her as tight as he might. She kept *those* thoughts to herself. He had tied her wrists in front of her, palms together, and left her ungagged, for now anyway. The stipulation was, if she so much as whimpered, she would live to regret it. Somehow, he had made living seem like a worse proposition than dying, and she was reminded of precisely the type of man he was, one to whom brutality and violence came easily. He could have said she wouldn't live to regret it, but either way, there'd be no whimpering.

Ungagged as she was, Sarah knew there was some chance of getting a little sleep, although she didn't like the thought of sleeping at all in this house.

The front screen door sounded like it slammed several times and she could hear muffled voices. The voices got closer, she could tell it was two women who sounded submissive. *Were they gagged?* There were two male voices, obviously captors, but she didn't recognise their voices either.

Who the hell could these two possibly be? There are no other women associated with the Lamarr Project, so why would female prisoners be here?

The males were busy talking together, although she couldn't make out anything said. She could recognise Shane's voice out of the mix though. Without a doubt, he was calling the shots. Sarah got the impression he was laying down the law to the other two men in his foreboding, 'You'll live to regret it,' tone.

SHANE ENTERED HER ROOM, turned on a night light in one of the power points and flicked off the main light. He slumped on the bed beside her, as much of a respectable distance from her as the queen bed permitted. She wished he'd had a shower to get rid of his man smells, she'd already moved as close to the edge as she could. At least they remained fully dressed.

"You don't have anything to worry about from me. None of you have anything to worry about from us as long as you shut up and do as you're told. The men know if they get friendly in the slightest, they will have me to worry about, apart from what the boss will do for disobeying him."

"Who are they, Shane? Why are they here?" She hadn't used his name before and decided if she survived the next thirty seconds, she wouldn't make that mistake again.

He rolled towards her, raised his left index finger in front of her face and with the look and the fiery voice of Satan himself, conjured a single word, "Don't!"

Sarah wasn't sure whether that was don't call me Shane, don't ask questions, or don't pretend we're friends. She decided a blanket 'don't' to be the safest and most prudent message to draw from the man beside her.

He used the TV remote by the bed to channel surf, but despite trying several shows for a few minutes each, nothing seemed to take his fancy, so he settled into Channel 24, the ABC news. He appeared to watch aimlessly until the headlines came around, and Sarah saw her house burning down on national television.

'Police say they received a call of two men behaving suspiciously at the location. When they arrived, officers found a man being threatened with a handgun in the driveway. Police shot the armed offender who retreated to the house before it spontaneously burst into flames. A body was later discovered in the burnt-out rubble. The Coroner and the Police Professional Standards Unit are investigating ...'

At this, Shane switched the TV off, and replaced the remote on the bedside table. *So, it was the coppers.*

SHANE ROLLED to his side of the bed and opened the drawer of his bedside table. From it he withdrew the Sara1. Shane knew this was a bloody dangerous game. He had told Peter the Sara1 had been destroyed in the fire, and his own strictly sanitised version of how and why Sarah was now advantageously their hostage. Dismissing these thoughts, and without further ado or sound, he put in the earphones, switched it on, rolled on his back, and promptly closed his eyes.

"I might take a pillow and sleep on the floor, if that's OK?" asked Sarah with some trepidation.

"Suit yourself, you know the rules," came the to-the-point reply.

Sarah moved off the bed and into the confines between the bed and the wall. It felt strangely safer there, even though it offered the same protection as the bed, which totalled absolutely none at all. The rest of the house had already fallen silent, so she surmised the other men would also be trying to get some sleep. She doubted the other two hostages would get much, if any, sleep tonight.

Five or six minutes passed when she realised Shane was talking in his sleep. She was astounded to notice such gentleness and tenderness in his voice as he dreamt. She felt like a spy inside him. An intruder privy to the deepest secrets of his self. Witness to a love revealed and laid bare. Shane could be further tormented, or mercifully healed by this encounter, she knew not which. As she listened, she was certain this was not a sexual experience of any kind. She recognised the pain, the hurt, the regret, and the yearning to re-connect with the woman, his only love, whose life had been prematurely and unwillingly torn from his.

Regardless of how brief the respite from his earthly torment might be, he connected with her in his vivid dream, he held her, and told her everything he felt remained unsaid these many years. He spoke of regrets and failure. He spoke of them as he had always wished to, but never could have hoped, or dared to, until tonight. As she faded from his embrace, lured away from him yet again by another heavenly summons, his parting words came wrenched and ragged through his tears of reconciliation, "I understand Sarah ... Yes my darling ... I love you too ..."

As the real-world Sarah lay bound and uncomfortable on the thin carpet of the bedroom floor, she remained a participant under duress.

Without choice, she had listened to a one-sided conversation of deep love and longing that had concluded with the most profound of heartfelt farewells. Despite what this horrible man had done and continued to do, she could not help but be moved by his tidal waves of emotion, which swept her humanity along with them. She struggled to control her tears and wished her namesake eternal peace. Marvelling in the machine that had made this all possible and wondering, strangely, if she reminded him more of her than just by name.

His sobbing subsided, and when he spoke, she almost jumped with the unexpected sound of him speaking.

"Are you awake?" Shane asked quietly, but loud enough.

What could she do? She could hardly pretend to be asleep, could she? "Yes," came out from her dry larynx as if she were half choked.

"Thank you." It sounded like as much as he could struggle to say and still maintain any semblance of self-control. But the utter gratitude in his voice was unmistakable.

Sarah realised Shane had no idea she had heard his side of the conversation as he spoke in his sleep. She planned to keep it that way.

Shane left the bedroom, and in the space of a few minutes, water was flowing through the pipes in the house, and she guessed the shower was on. Sometime later, a clean, freshly shaven and deodorised Shane lay back on the bed, just before the pleasant smell of mint toothpaste reached her. Sarah knew his yearning experience had taken him back to a much happier time and place. Perhaps being reminded of that, was going to make him change his life style, so he could more easily hold those thoughts. *Perhaps.* For the second time that night, Shane started snoring his head off. *Some things never change ...*

Given the noise, her mind wasn't exactly about to slip off to sleep easily, so she got to thinking instead. Who could Shane have been talking about when he mentioned getting the information from her she was holding back? She was only holding back Lamarr results from one person. *Could this all be Peters doing? There had to be another explanation surely ...*

With her hands tied in front, she managed to retrieve the last dram from a pocket, and it became her deluxe 'down the hatch,' nightcap.

As her cramping muscles became painful being squeezed between the wall and the bed, and wiggling to grab her whisky, she decided she might as well sleep on the mattress. His snoring didn't miss a beat as she climbed back on the bed laying restlessly near the edge again, determined to sleep with one eye open.

Chapter Thirty-One

Room service arrived at 7 am. Marcus had already been up for an hour, long enough to shower, compose himself and shave. Although the left side of his face felt like it burnt a little with the shaving crème, no red mark remained. But it did remind him why it was tender. It wasn't so much his body clock as his brain not wanting to sleep. It had been a restless night; he always had trouble getting a decent night's sleep in a strange bed. Compounded by the painful thoughts of the last 24 hours, slumber mostly evaded him.

Breakfast was a bit of an Aussie staple, good ole bacon and eggs. While he didn't feel like eating, he knew he should, so pretty much forced it all down. Not to be ungrateful, but he couldn't abide the *bitter beyond belief* room coffee. He was surprised when his experiment to stand a teaspoon vertically in the horrid mixture failed. Even if it were drinkable, he couldn't fit a finger through the handle of the tiny white hotel cups. Salvation lay close at hand though. Inside the small kitchen cupboard waited a coffee pod machine and several mugs.

He tried not to worry excessively about Maddy and Helen. But clearly, the more he tried not to worry, the more worried he became. So, he may as well stop trying not to worry, *because that makes complete sense, doesn't it?*

There was a knock on the room door that connected his room with Henry's. Walking over, he opened it to find Henry and Jane, similarly showered, dressed and ready to face the day. Struggling to smile and put a positive face on things, they took a seat on the settee, and Marcus sat on one of the plush grey velvet lounge chairs.

Marcus forgot to start with 'good morning,' plunging straight in with one of the thoughts that plagued him all night. "Do you realise I thought *you* were shooting *me?*"

Jane didn't flinch, she evidently knew the situation.

"Sorry about that, mate, I really am," apologised Henry. "I hoped, maybe you hadn't seen it that way, but thought you might have. I am sorry."

"Seeing Sarah like that, then you like that, I've never felt so utterly stunned and betrayed, and now, she's gone ... and I feel guilty for failing her and doubting you ... This is all so fucked up, huh?" confessed Marcus.

Henry agreed, just as downhearted, "Everything, is fucked up."

"Speak for yourself, honey," said Jane lightly.

Both men seemed distracted and taken aback by her surprise input. They looked at her, then back to each other. They smiled. She had judged her words and delivery to perfection.

Jane had purposefully joked to keep the boys from wallowing. She knew from previous research 'brick walls', a touch of humour can break the 'wallow cycle,' and allow clear thinking to resume or 'kick along.'

Henry followed on from Jane taking her prior subtle hint to heart, "Rosco is going to stay as our liaison. He'll call me this morning before nine, so we should all hang here for the time being. Keep your phone on the table and charged up, mate. If someone tries to contact you about the girls, we don't want to miss the call."

"Done and done, mate. Done ... and ... done," reiterated Marcus. "By the way, I understand why you hit me in the driveway, but please Henry, if I ever get like that again, can you not do it so fucking hard next time?"

Chapter Thirty-Two

Peter loved elaborate deception and misdirection plans to achieve his ends. This last plan, however, of all those he'd ever put in place, toyed with law enforcement, so extra care was required. The law was the worthiest of opponents, but in some respects, also the most predictable.

There was little doubt in his pious mind, he played the long game extraordinary well. The deciding factor in originally picking the rental house where his three kidnap victims were held, had nothing to do with home comforts, and everything to do with bearing and distance. He knew when he signed the lease, he could use these two factors in a deception plan if need be, and now he would. The bearing and distance that interested Peter arose from a mobile phone communications tower. The bearing from the tower to the rental house was 242 degrees true, at 6.5 kilometres.

This was integral to his current plan, as he intended to use one of his modified phones to call Marcus. Sometime after that, he would get what he wanted and leave the country, and a trail of victims behind. This phone had several unique features to negate anyone's ability to track it rapidly, or even slowly for that matter.

By rapid, he knew under normal circumstances it took less than five seconds to pinpoint a mobile's location. Triangulation was the most common, but not the most accurate method of location tracking. This phone was a D phone - D for deception, what this plan called for. The D mobile had innovative software for use explicitly in the rental house where the hostages were held.

In everyday normal operations, a mobile phone 'pings' every nearby telephone tower, then selects and uses the tower radiating the strongest signal to make and receive calls, download data etc. The phone continually updates the strength of the other nearby towers, so when the phone moves, it's ready to jump on to the next tower with the strongest signal. It repeats this process continuously. Weaker strength towers can still be used simultaneously for location tracking.

Peter's unique software forced the D phone to only utilise the tower with the weakest signal strength and exclude all others. The upshot being, no triangulation of the exact position Peter was physically calling from would be possible. A far less accurate than usual location picture was all the authorities would get. The authorities would only glean a rough bearing and distance from the single tower the D phone communicated with. A far less accurate than usual location picture. The greater the range, the less accurate this picture became. The tower, according to his plan, was at maximum range.

Knowing the specialists behind signal tracking used rigid methodology, he could reliably predict them to behave in certain ways. Accordingly, when Peter called Marcus, Telstra would instantly commence position fixing. For some reason unbeknown to them, the D phone would only be reporting to a single, distant tower, bearing about 240 degrees and around 6.2 to 6.5 kilometres away. The D phone might literally be in any one of a hundred houses or anywhere within that area. So, the Telco would move to the next option. GPS location tracking.

Sun Tzu - Do not repeat the tactics which have gained you one victory.

Peter had installed a different GPS location-changing app on the *D* phone.

He had no intention of developing a modus operandi as predictable as his foe. This would show the location of his phone at 242 degrees true from the tower at 7.4 kilometres.

This information, from the authorities' tracking perspective, would show *precisely* where the phone was located. In truth, it would show precisely where Peter *wanted* the *D* mobile to be located. Cross-checking of the location fix by Telstra, would reveal 242 degrees was within tolerance. The distance of 7.4 kilometres was perhaps slightly further away than first thought, but not overly so. Once the address was identified, a Police raiding team would be dispatched to the location indicated by the GPS.

PETER COULD NEVER LOVE another human being, all that passed for love inside him was reserved for himself. He had nothing to give, nor wish to give it, to anyone else.

Peter also loved to rub his superiority in, to him, being anything else was simply incomprehensible. The meeting in his office where Sarah had tried to squirm out of her contract was case in point. He'd piled it on thick, hitting his usual benchmark and utterly loving himself by the end. So, he would do the same this time, only on a grander scale. If his demand for no police turned out to be ignored, they would raid the wrong house. A hidden mini surveillance camera was mounted on a streetlight facing the decoy residence. The camera was hooked into an insecure Wi-Fi provided conveniently by the neighbours, or perhaps ironically by the decoy house itself, it didn't matter. No-one would ever notice it there.

An elderly couple in their late retirement years lived in the decoy house. If they were raided by the TRG, it wouldn't take long for the TRG to appreciate they'd been had. Badly. Worst-case scenario for them, outsmarted with no idea who had fooled them, or how to proceed from there. Hoping for a spontaneous heart attack into the mix from the stress of the raid on the old folks, would rub salt even deeper into the wound. He smiled at his guile and cunning.

Peter considered the icing on the *D* phone cake, the voice-changer software. He did like, actually no, he adored the idea of talking to someone whom he knew personally, making demands and being in control when they were clueless as to who was really speaking to them.

Although quite partial in some childish way to the Dalek voice, he considered it unsuited. As a direct modulation of his voice, it therefore would only take one step to reveal his real voice. Apart from that issue, no-one would take a Dalek voice seriously. Daleks will be forced to grapple with this issue if they ever decide on an extermination time hop to earth.

The voice he chose to sound like possessed the best of both worlds and a bonus … sovereign misdirection. Not easily undisguised, it struck sufficient terror into any recipient: Russian. The bonus would result in official inquiries and focus away from China, his generous beneficiary.

Shane made sure 'the presents' had all been put away before Peters arrival. Peter parked his car opposite the safe house, activating all the sensors before alighting.

Lao Tzu: There is no greater danger than underestimating your enemy.

A neat, clean, and clear-eyed Shane met Peter at the front door, the change was not lost on Peter. There was even tea waiting on the kitchen table. Most civilised, but surprising. They exchanged the required information, without general chit chat. Peter retrieved the

D phone hidden in a compartment near the lounge-room TV and activated it. He checked everything was *on* that needed to be, and *off* that needed to be.

He dialled Marcus's number.

MARCUS MUST HAVE BEEN a little more tense with anticipation than he thought. Hearing his phone vibrate on the table just before it rang made him almost jump out of his seat as though a small electrical shock had been delivered. The display read, 'No Caller ID'.

Chances were, it was just another pesky cold call. Maybe the bank, or someone else who considered themselves so important they were above such etiquette. They had discussed what to do for each call received, in case one was the kidnappers. The call was to be put on loudspeaker and recorded onto Henry's mobile, or vice versa if the kidnappers called Henry. An open writing pad with two pens lay on the settee coffee table, just in case. Only the person called was to talk, anyone else in the room must be completely still and silent.

Announcing himself, Marcus never expected a Russian gangster to reply! Plainly, neither did Henry as he listened to the accent on the speaker.

"Dobroye utro. Good morning, Marcus Hall," said Peter in his processed voice. He tried to exaggerate his pronunciation and style infusing classic Russian structure. He had even gone to the trouble of learning several Russian words as another layer of authenticity.

He didn't wait for a response, it wasn't a social call after all. "I have two ladies with me. Both miss you very much and want to go home. You can do that for them. They are unharmed ... for now. Do you understand me so far, Marcus Hall?"

"Yes, I understand you. Just tell me what I need to do please so they can come home." Marcus spoke slightly slower than usual in case the Russian had trouble understanding him.

"Do as I say, and you will prove to be as wise as you are inventive. On the other hand, if you do not do what I say, you will have to, how do you say in Australia? Dah, pay the piper."

"I understand," said Marcus reiterating, "I will do whatever you want to get them back safely."

This was going as well as could be expected, Marcus got a thumbs-up from Henry.

"First, Marcus Hall, do not involve the police. This part is essential. You must understand this. Second, you will build another Sara1, I want a working prototype. Third, you provide me with the circuit diagram to produce more, and all your research data. You will bring all this to the location I will send you. Should the police come here to this place, Madeleine and Helen will not be coming home. Do you understand this? Do you agree this?"

The Russian hadn't said their names up until this point. Hearing them spoken like that urged Marcus to be braver for them. Whether out of sheer anguish or misplaced hope at the prospect of a reunion, he replied, "I will do as you ask, but please, please, let me speak to them. I ask nothing else only that ... please."

Peter knew he was on a winner, "But of course!" He said as if he was now Marcus's new best friend. *Precisely as intended.* "One moment," said Peter, who had of course expected this eventuality. He muted the microphone, disabled the voice changer, and handed the phone to Shane.

Shane walked briskly to the bedroom where Maddy and Helen were seated on the end of a single bed. He nodded to the guard who took the gags off them both. Shane unmuted the microphone, and Marcus heard a click on his end.

"Maddy, Helen, can you hear me? Are you OK?"

Shane nodded his head to the girls to indicate they were permitted to reply.

Both answered simultaneously, if a little awkwardly due to the gag just being released, "We're OK."

"Bill's in hospital he's OK too." Marcus rattled the sentence off quickly in anticipation of getting cut off, just as Shane muted the call again and left the room.

Shane handed the phone back to Peter. With the voice changer activated and mute off, he resumed, with any pretence of friendship gone. "Marcus Hall, I will contact you tonight between five and seven. Be ready." Three rapid beeps sounded as the call disconnected.

Chapter Thirty-Three

arcus stared at his mobile on the table in front of him. Henry went through the agreed procedure, texting the audio file through to ASIS, Les and Rosco. They all realised a trace had started on Marcus's phone the second he answered the call. Telstra were prepared and already knew the mobile tower Marcus's number was connected to. The monitoring computer waited for his number to pop up as receiving a call, record which number dialled him, and where the caller was located.

Henry mentioned with attempted levity that he was ASIS and not police, so he should be OK to know considering the Russian's no police requirement ... *Fail*. Marcus's face of thunder looked back at him. Jane gave him a 'Jesus, Henry' glare which nicely topped off the whole experience for him. *I tried.*

Henry regrouped and went for the staid professional approach. "Rosco will call us back in five minutes or so with the tracking info and any updates. We assumed he had the Sara1, was it destroyed in the fire then?"

"Regardless," said Marcus, "the Russian can have the Marc1, and in twelve hours the girls will be home."

Marcus caught the briefest of glances between Henry and Jane.

"No, no, no," said Marcus in rapid succession, "what does that look mean?" A response from either was not quick enough coming. "What? Tell me!" added sharp encouragement.

Henry sat awkwardly, "We're with you, a hundred per cent."

"Okaaayyy. Where's the problem then?" queried Marcus.

"The problem mate, is that we three don't make the decisions about any of this. The state and federal governments do. The police will only want to raid the address when they find out the location, rescue the girls and catch the crooks. They won't negotiate."

Marcus sat in stunned silence, searching for comprehension. Henry's phone rang; it was Rosco. An intense conversation followed for several minutes. Jane and Marcus watched Henry's facial expression change a dozen times during the call. After hanging up, he said flatly, "Rosco's on his way over, be here in ten. Some weird shit is going on here. I'll fill you both in. I think the situation might benefit from both your analytical minds."

Henry went on to explain the details and discrepancies so far. He included the exhaustive search of Sarah's burnt-out house not finding the Sara1, nor any parts attributable to it. Why would the Russian go to this trouble to demand another Sara1 if he already had the original? There was a lack of triangulation to locate the Russian's mobile. Only a rough bearing and distance from a single tower was available. Another thing not right was the GPS position set against the bearing and distance. One point of reference was off. The bearing was within tolerance. But the range was too far away, and what did that mean?

"The question stumping me most, and the answer which might lead us somewhere, is where the hell is the Sara1?" Henry posed the question deep in thought, but thinking out loud.

"Why not track it again with the Tile?" said Marcus as if it was an original idea.

"I've tried, believe me," said Henry. "I've got the Tile set to report as soon as it comes near a Wi-Fi, if that ever happens. But nothing overnight."

Jane chipped into the conversation, "Where *exactly* did the tracker last report?"

Both men looked at her quizzically.

"Oh, come on, guys, I'm a space and time girl, all about the detail. The smallest detail can throw a result off by light-years. In this case, maybe not that much, but enough to matter," said Jane. Marcus had already recognised her as a quiet but exceptional thinker. She didn't always speak up, but when she did it was well worth listening to.

The boys still weren't getting it. She drew a breath and spoke to Henry, "You tracked the Tile to Sarah's place. If the Tile left Sarah's before her Wi-Fi melted, does it show itself moving in the app history? If it did move, which way and how far?"

The logic was almost embarrassing. Henry opened the history section of the Tile app and grinned, gazing lovingly at Jane. "How can one beautiful astrophysicist have so much talent?"

"Why thank you, honey," acknowledged Jane and pecked Henry on the cheek.

Marcus looked on, and Henry felt those eyes keenly. "It shows the last reported position as having moved briefly into the middle of the backyard."

Jane, being Jane, stayed another three steps ahead. One thing her job instilled in people, was the ability for completely open and clear thinking. She wouldn't usually announce a leapfrog answer amongst her peers, she would let them work through an issue and arrive at the conclusion she had already reached herself. However, this was different, time was of the essence. "May I continue?" requested Jane modestly.

Two heads nodded affirmation.

Jane stood and strode the room slowly. Walking sometimes helped her think more clearly of specific details along the path to a conclusion already reached. "Let's make some assumptions and see where they lead us." Two heads nodded again. "Let's assume the Sara1 is intact and trackable, but in the hands of bad guys somewhere. The only possible location we have for it after Sarah's house is the poor quality directional data from the Telstra tower to the Russian's phone. Such being the case, we need a mobile Wi-Fi on a trailer, like companies install at outdoor events. We could start towing the trailer just beyond the limit of phone reception range from the tower, and drive towards it on the back bearing, until if, and when, we detect the Sara1.

If we are looking solely at locating the Sara1 and the girls by proxy, this would be my Plan A." Thoughts complete, she sat down next to Henry again.

MARCUS LIT UP. "Jane, we have a mobile Wi-Fi! It's the centrepiece of our remote area test program. Better still, it was designed from the get-go with twice normal Wi-Fi range." Marcus caught himself speaking as to solve a scientific question and as if life had a hope of returning to normal. He had ever so briefly forgotten his deep fear, it would not. "It's perfect for Plan A!"

FOUR KNOCKS on the door heralded the entrance of a plain-clothed Rosco, while an ASIS operative closed the door behind him.

"Hi, folks,' he greeted everyone in the room. "You must be Jane. I'm very pleased to meet you." Pleasantries exchanged, Rosco sat in the spare lounge chair. He handed Henry a click-seal bag containing a small brass object. "I brought you a present, figured you'd still be one down."

Henry accepted the .25 semi-jacketed bullet gratefully. Not surprised at Rosco's thoughtfulness, he may well have been a little touched, except for the deadly nature of the consideration. "Thanks, mate, appreciate it."

Rosco didn't miss a beat. "I spoke to the Telstra Signal Tech after I spoke to you; smart guy, sounded like an eccentric signals encyclopedia. He said we're being hoodwinked, and someone is manipulating the tower signal data, or the GPS data, or both."

"Is he sure?" asked Henry.

"Strangely enough, Hens, I asked him the same question. His reply was, and I quote, 'There's fuckery afoot and no doubt about it,' unquote. Please excuse the French, Jane. Unless something comes up in the meantime, there is no option but to wait until the Russki gives us an address for the exchange."

"Rosco," asked Henry tentatively, asking in a way that leveraged their personal friendship, not their professional one. "Is there any appetite to simply concede to the Russian's demands? Just do a clean swap to get the girls back, without anyone getting hurt, or worse."

"They won't do it that way," said Rosco. "No offence intended, but should we perhaps take this discussion into the other room, Henry?"

"Rosco ... mate, if the elephant in the room called Les needs to be talked about, we can talk about him right here. We're all security-cleared, all invested in this one way or another, and Marcus has more to lose than any of us. We could do this without anyone getting hurt, or worse. I understand Les may not trust my judgement as much as he might otherwise, but what happened, happened years ago. This is an entirely different kettle of fish, and I've recommended on my side of things we do a clean exchange."

"OK, Henry, looks like we're calling a spade a spade, cards on the table then. Les has also made a recommendation, that being, once we receive a location from the Russki tonight, a tactical team will hit the address ASAP. The plan is to rescue the hostages and cork the bad guys. Les's plan has been accepted by the powers that be and will be implemented tonight."

"Cork?" asked Marcus automatically. Not familiar with the term, his brain preferring to deal with that, than the prospect of Maddy and Helen being close to the use of deadly force.

"Capture or kill," replied Rosco in a quieter tone. "I'm sorry on every level I used that word. I do apologise. It's … just the business I'm in."

"Don't worry, mate, I'm sorry on every level I asked," said Marcus.

Henry looked briefly and silently at Jane, then Marcus. "Plan A?"

"Plan A? Do I want to know?" asked Rosco.

"Probably not, but you probably should," replied Henry, who went on to explain their Tile-tracking plan.

Rosco was surprised, intrigued, and supportive of the plan. But. The but came in the form of them being under protective custody. "Les is responsible overall for your close protection. He would need a pretty solid case put to him as to why a relaxation of your security should be made. Despite the protective agents being federal, it's the state's call."

There was a relatively brief but ardent discussion, on how best to present 'Plan A' to Les. In the end, for several reasons, they decided Jane would stay put in the hotel, guarded as now. The three men would carry out Plan A under prescribed security conditions to be explained to Les. Henry tossed in an afterthought that he already had approval for the plan from the service.

Rosco looked at Henry, "Fair dinkum?"

"Do you *really* want to know?" asked Henry.

Rosco smiled back in answer. "I love working with you service guys. You could never get away with this sort of shit in the coppers."

Rosco excused himself and went into the next room via the adjoining doorways. He came back barely two minutes later to see Henry and Marcus standing by the exit door, ready to go. "Bugger me, approval received."

Chapter Thirty-Four

The three men arrived at the CSIRO carpool in rather good time considering the traffic.

Marcus checked out the 5G trailer. When he switched the battery pack on, the portable transmitter showed only a quarter charge from sitting in the yard. That wasn't concerning, as once the trailer's twelve-pin plug was connected to the car, charging would be automatic. The dull green canvas tarpaulin was faded after it's time out in the elements. Marcus re-arranged the tarp to cover almost the whole trailer to hide the transmitter better and get road-ready.

As his friend checked out the trailer, Henry booked out the oldest vehicle in the carpool with a trailer plug.

Jane called Henry on cue. "Hi, handsome, would you like the long or short story of how I worked the number out without a calculator, or only the number?" asked Jane cheekily.

"Just the number please, amazing woman. Oh, maybe the long version later ..." he teased back.

With the affection out of their respective systems for the next ten seconds maximum, Jane said simply, "Thirty-seven."

They quickly drove the soon-to-be-retired, slightly beaten-up, but unmarked, grey Mitsubishi Triton to the trailer, connected it, and headed out the security gate. Marcus drove the utility, leaving both armed deputies to ride shotgun. They managed to scrounge three baseball caps which they wore backwards and three dark pairs of sunglasses to complete a basic disguise.

"What did the walking computer say?" asked Marcus, intending a compliment.

Henry appreciated the gesture, despite the circumstances they were in and advised, "Thirty-seven k's max while trawling."

"OK, I'll bite, what does that mean?" asked Rosco uncomfortable at continually playing mental catch-up with these three.

"Well, as we've got nothing better to do for half an hour or so, I'll give you the long story," quipped Henry.

"Sweet," said Rosco, hoping he could follow along with whatever explanation was about to be served up for him to digest.

Henry commenced, "Well, if we drove past the tracking Tile at sixty clicks, by the time the app registered, we would have long since gone past. That being the case, we'd need to turn around to re-acquire the tracker and allow the app and Tile the time required to improve position accuracy. This is best done if we're stopped, assuming it's not moving either. Turning around could be difficult depending on where we are, or look suspicious too."

"OK, with you so far," confirmed Rosco.

Henry continued, "Cool. So we need to consider the range threshold of our Wi-Fi, taking into account suburban attenuation, and any shielding of the Tile signal itself. We then calculate in the time delay of the Tile to respond to the Wi-Fi, and comms time of the app. All these active criteria give us a maximum speed of advance down the bearing line to the tower. Staying below that speed, we will detect the tracker, and have time to stop and obtain the best position fix possible."

Rosco interjected, "And we know now, thanks to Jane, our maximum speed of advance must not exceed thirty-seven k's!"

"Give that man a prize," said Marcus, releasing nervous energy in mock jubilation, and trying to distract his deepening mood of apprehension from what tonight might bring.

There was a collective realisation that precise and effective trawling was vital to improve the chances of the only outcome they wanted, the girls coming home safely. It sobered them.

They commenced trawling with their mobile Wi-Fi at the pre-agreed position of 242 degrees from the tower at the rounded-up distance of ten kilometres, just beyond maximum mobile phone range. Because of the traditional square layout of the suburb, it was necessary to go off track and come back on again at the same waypoint to provide continuous coverage down the planned bearing line. Akin to a modified creeping line ahead search. The maximum speed of thirty-seven kilometres per hour was problematical, being below the forty kilometres per hour limit for the cruise control to engage.

They innovated. With Henry seated in the front passenger's seat, Rosco could look over Marcus's left shoulder from the rear bench seat and see the Triton's speedo. On the occasions Marcus reached thirty-five kilometres per hour, Rosco would call, "Speed," prompting Marcus to slow down slightly. Marcus felt the additional anguish by finding himself torn between trawling as quickly as possible, yet not too fast and being inefficient, or, at worst, ineffective.

Depending on how their progress went, they expected to cover the entire bearing line in an hour or so.

Marcus slowed the car to a crawl before he negotiated a cul-de-sac "U' turn. Barely twenty minutes into their high-tech search, they struck the gold they were so meticulously mining for. Realisation and adrenaline were upon them all. They stared at the tracking app as though the combined intensity of their eyes would force the software to do its work more vigorously. The Tile jumped position twice, and finally settled, not moving again from a house on the far side of the dead-end road. The exact address was easily deduced, and the deception revealed. A bearing of 242 degrees at 6.1 kilometres from the Telstra tower. The trio had succeeded, they were elated, and they were also tempted ...

Rosco said what they were all thinking, "Kind of makes you want to go look, huh?"

A "yes" and a "hmmm" rose from the front seat. Rosco reconsidered and said firmly, "Best we leave here, right now, in case we're pinged, or our valour gets the better part of our discretion." It could not have been interpreted as a topic for discussion, the others knew it was an order.

Marcus put the vehicle into gear, released his foot off the brake, and completed the turn back towards Lindfield. He stared irrationally in the rear-vision mirror for a glimpse of Maddy or Helen. So engrossed was he with the slowly shrinking rear-view, Marcus didn't notice a parked car dead ahead until a precautionary, "Mate!" erupted from Henry beside him.

Henry's timely warning preserved the sale value of their Triton, by narrowly avoiding the unoccupied car parked on the side of the road. Not the best look at any time, let alone under these circumstances, but at least they missed.

With Marcus mentally back at the wheel again, the three successful gold diggers decided what they should report, how they should make their report and what outcome they sought. All of them knew their finding confirmed the opinion of the Signal Tech, 'Fuckery, was afoot.' They similarly believed as much which only added to their already firm convictions to play along with the Russian, and just give him whatever he wanted for the safe return of the women.

Rosco had managed one win with Les today and was urged to try for two. The call connected. He made their pitch, only to be instructed to finish up and head back to the hotel. Those on higher pay grades would consider whether the already chosen course of action would require amendment or review. That decision would then be passed down. It wasn't your classic all-beer-and-skittles type call by any stretch of the imagination. There would be no second win for Rosco today.

By contrast, Henry's jubilant phone chat with Jane went rather better, even to the extent of resulting in sumptuous room service arriving minutes after they did. Their stomachs were in turmoil at the decisions being taken. Decisions that were never going to be left in their hands. The only thing their hands could productively do for them now remained to eat something. They might need all their energy in case of a long, but hopefully successful, night ahead.

ROSCO STAYED WITH THEM, having proved himself a good stick and fitting in comfortably in his liaison role with the trio. Rosco felt he was in it with them. However, as one of the few senior sergeants in the TRG, he knew he might well be leading men into danger that night.

Rosco found himself enmeshed in the personal struggles and aspirations of the three victims of circumstance he just shared a meal with. Not relishing the outcome at all, given the mire so far, he had counselled his superior passionately. He'd warned of the risk versus high probability the hierarchy's plans would turn into a giant cluster fuck vs a clean trade. He wasn't sure he'd been heard, and he wasn't sure the current Henry/Les lack of mutual trust situation was helping.

Rosco's phone rang, it was Les. Rosco excused himself and went next door as was his usual practice when talking to his boss. The call wasn't a long one.

He returned to the trio and flopped back into a lounge chair. "The powers that be still plan to hit the address the Russian will provide later tonight. If that's different from the house we located the Tile at, they'll hit both addresses at the same time. Sorry, I pushed as hard as I could," he told them with an air of despair.

He wasn't expecting the sheer depth of gratitude backing the thank-yous directed to him from everyone.

"Two more things," said Rosco, "and I'm glad you're all sitting down. I'll tell you in specific order, for reasons that will become apparent. I've been ordered to lead the second raid, if required. I'll leave for home shortly, grab a power nap and get my head in the right place."

"You can sleep in the room next door, if you like. We won't disturb you, and it'll save you travel time," offered Jane.

"Thank you, but I'll head home. I might be able to catch Anne before she starts the late shift."

"Geez," responded Marcus, "must be hard both of you working the same job."

"Oh, she's not in my job; she spends her life patching people up, not locking them up," said Rosco. "Anyway, sorry to take us off track. The last thing is a bit of a mixed bag, and I genuinely have no easy way of telling you." He held their attention but didn't want it in the first place. Not to mention, *why couldn't someone else tell them this?*

"The GMO has determined that the only body found after the fire in Sarah's house was not Sarah." His audience sat, open-mouthed, and stunned. He continued quickly because he knew what would be coming. "The body was a male, missing two front teeth and, here's the rub, he had two bullet wounds probably of different calibres. One to his forehead and one to his left shoulder."

Even Jane joined in on the emotional chorus of, "What the

fuck?" As with any news difficult to fathom, and this news being no exception, indecent surprise rapidly gave way to obscene disbelief. "Are you fucking sure?"

"They're sure, meaning Sarah may still be alive," said Rosco hopefully.

"I don't give a shit about someone else putting a bullet in that guy's head, but I do care Sarah is alive. But where the hell is she? Has the Russian got her too?" asked Henry.

Rosco shrugged his shoulders. "They have no idea. But it stands to reason he does."

"So, we possibly have a third hostage in the mix, we're blind to everything, we don't know if the location of the Sara1 ties into the hostages, and yet they still won't think about a clean exchange?" asked Marcus incredulously to Rosco.

"Correct, and to be honest, it wouldn't matter if it were a dozen hostages, they won't negotiate, end of story," replied Rosco. "I'm sorry, I do need to go." Jane rose and unexpectedly hugged him. Marcus and Henry rose similarly, shaking hands firmly. They wished him luck for tonight.

THE NEWS that Rosco imparted only served to reinforce to Marcus this was way out of anyone's hands to fix. This was spiralling further beyond reach or understanding the longer it went on. All because he'd discovered the Marc1. He felt the almost overwhelming frustration of his impotent position start to boil into anger. The Russian was patently way ahead of everyone in the game, and he sincerely doubted the current path of action would see anyone currently in peril, released alive by the end of it. Marcus had been grieving the loss of his friend and colleague, even blaming himself for that, only to find out she may have survived. Now it seemed they might really lose her as well, because the government was too damn stubborn to simply do a clean swap!

He sat down on the lounge chair again, where his anger boiled over. He slammed both fists down hard on the armrests, three times in unison, once for each word of his rage. "FOR! FUCK'S! SAKE!"

Chapter Thirty-Five

In anticipation of 5pm, Henry and Jane were already on the settee, waiting for the Russian to contact Marcus, so the information could be forwarded as stipulated, direct to Les.

Marcus received the text message from 'No Caller ID' at 4.50 pm. Apparently, this bastard couldn't tell the time, or his watch ran ten minutes fast. He texted like he spoke. The message started with, 'Marcus Hall'. Marcus was very relieved he didn't have to go through the stress of talking to him again.

The SMS provided the address of the house per the GPS data gleaned from the Russian's initial phone intercept. He wanted Marcus there alone in one hour with a new Sara1, the circuit diagram, and the research. Warning again: no police.

Marcus had the mother of all stomach cramps as he agonised whether to go there by himself after collecting the Marc1, so he could rescue them himself. However, it re-dawned on him there was an armed guard at each door who wouldn't be disposed to letting him go unless he received permission first. The two men standing strong outside their rooms were as much jailers as protectors, and the three of them as much prisoners as protected.

Marcus forwarded the text direct to Les. An acknowledgement came twenty seconds later. All they could do now was wait.

They knew as soon as they were in place and coordinated, the two separate TRG teams would raid both houses.

They feared for Rosco now as well.

Chapter Thirty-Six

Peter calculated it at three to one against Marcus delivering a replacement Sara1 to the house. He had not liked those odds and was worldly enough not to accept them. Not to say he wasn't disappointed in Marcus; he had given his word, albeit to a Russian kidnapper, but he had given his word. Tonight's exchange could, and should, have been simple and straightforward.

Peter's best-case scenario would have been to see Marcus arrive alone via the surveillance camera outside the decoy house. The Russian would have called Marcus on his mobile and redirected him to the house where Helen was held only a few kilometres away for the real exchange. If that went smoothly, he would hand over the other two. The job would already be done, and all this would be over.

But no, they wanted to do it the hard way; *so be it.*

The resolution of the HD camera on the pole outside the decoy house was surprisingly good, Peter noted. He could see very clearly the TRG approaching the house in tactical formation.

Peter had orchestrated events purposefully. Considering the

time it would take the police to deploy from the time he messaged Marcus, he calculated the assault on the decoy house should it occur, would be just before sundown. Hence his early text at 4.50pm. This meant the assault team needed to decide whether to equip with clear or yellow lens eye protection or even wear night-vision equipment. The sun would be low on the horizon, causing by default, intensely bright glare. This could, in turn, lead to operational difficulties, as searching eyes were forced to rapidly adjust from glaringly bright light in an area facing westerly, to comparative darkness elsewhere in the house. *Perhaps small considerations foisted upon my adversaries. Perhaps not.*

However he looked at it though, his master plan was coming together nicely.

Peter guessed the ageing wife in the decoy house would be in the sunbathed kitchen on the westerly side at the time the raid took place. Couples this age, tended to eat early, go to bed early, and get up early, it was the natural elderly way of things.

He didn't give a rat's arse about the unsuspecting old couple in the house; it wasn't his fault anyway. Peter had been fully prepared to walk away peacefully, but the government wanted armed confrontation. The old couple's major life event, or perhaps, end-of-life event, was about to take place.

Sun Tzu - Victory may be produced out of the enemy's own tactics.

'TAIL-END CHARLIE' of the six-man police tactical assault team Bravo, was on the third operational assault of his TRG career. He waited half crouched outside the kitchen and adjusted his chosen protective eyewear for this operation; yellow lens glasses. The smell of a roast cooking somewhere nearby had already done its work on his gastric juices. He couldn't tell if it was from the target house or not, but could see one of the sliding windows half-open. *Maybe the smell's coming from there?* He knew they would make entry via the backdoor at the same time Alpha entered another home a few kilometres away.

He saw the lead assaulter hand signal rearwards, to be ready to make their time-sensitive, explosive breach entry.

The sun, brilliant on the horizon, reflected off the tinted kitchen windows. Tail-end Charlie could only partially see into the kitchen, but the dazzling glare made it almost painful to look that way. His yellow glasses were designed to make distinguishing a target against its background more pronounced in near dark conditions, like those <u>after</u> sunset. However, the insidious glare of the sun, still setting, was exactly the opposite circumstance. Multiple glare afterimages now dominated parts of his eyesight. Bravo leader had already signalled entry was imminent. Charlie grabbed the tinted glasses, half throwing them softly on the ground towards the kitchen wall, and promptly lowered the clear protective goggles from his helmet. *Fucking glare!*

PALE AND STRICKEN WITH REMORSE, Charlie reported to his team leader for a hot debrief. He explained his pre-entry vision issue and how he had sought to remedy it, by removing his glasses and lowering his goggles. It was then he intermittently saw the head and shoulders of a person inside the house through the now somewhat less dazzling window reflections and the remaining afterimages plaguing his eyesight. Charlie maintained his composure with difficulty. "This unknown person, whom I regretfully now know to be the wife, but had not known was there previously, appeared suddenly, and seemed to be walking quietly away from the nearby back door, which had our explosive charges rigged to it.

This person then ducked down out of sight as if trying to hide, and I heard mechanical-type sounds. Suspecting we had been compromised, and this person may have been retrieving a weapon, I detached a Flashbang from my vest. I removed both pins and tossed it inside the building through the partially open window. I threw it deliberately in the direction of this person whom I judged an imminent threat to our team. A second or so after my flashbang exploded, the breach charges detonated on the rear door and Bravo made entry ..."

MINI SURVEILLANCE CAMERAS were hidden in and around the safe house soon after the lease was signed. Peter was always sure if any police action were taken against this house, the raiding party would choose to stage and deploy in the view protected cul-de-sac at the rear. Accordingly, two hidden cameras had long covered this eventuality.

PETER HAD KEPT an eye on the cameras all day through smartphone alerts in case he discovered a clue the police had found the safe house. The only thing of note all day had been three fools towing a trailer who had nearly run into a parked car! These were the same cameras through which Peter first saw the black SUVs with the dark tinted windows, pull into the dead-end street behind the hostage house.

This was NOT part of his master plan, but was part of his contingency. What interested him more was HOW they knew it was there, because they should not have known. This counted as the second time in two days there had been a significant issue, although Sifu remained pleased Sarah was alive. At the heart of it though, he didn't like surprises, regardless of how far ahead of the other players he kept. *Why don't those damn fools guarding Helen answer their phones??*

Chapter Thirty-Seven

Uniform police had thrown up a secure cordon around the safe house. The house was effectively ringed so the public were safe, and no-one could escape. This done, the TRG could go about their work within the *hot zone*. The yard of a wooden dwelling formed a passage to the rear of the target safe house from the dead-end road behind it. Six black-clad body-armoured assaulters of Alpha team, moved in tactical formation through the yard, close to the side of the weatherboard house.

As the six pushed silently forward, a grossly indignant voice hissed from ahead. "I know you're there, out of my yard you cheeky little bastards!" Alpha were suddenly confronted by a giant, over-weight behemoth, who confidently leapt out from behind the corner of the house ahead, wearing nothing but a blue singlet and matching Bonds undies. He came armed with both fists clenched at the ready. His feet were afforded all the protection a pair of double pluggers could offer.

The behemoth, now startled, was staring down the lead barrel of a black submachine gun, with another five carried close behind. "Strewth!" he exclaimed, as he moved to return inside. These domestic warriors were obviously not there to pinch the succulent carrots from his back garden as some of the local kids often did. Both fists unclenched with that insight, and that he hadn't even brought pants to a gunfight. His continued retreat was discernible by the rhythmic flip-flop of his thongs. Rosco's late afternoon facial stubble pinched painfully on the chin strap of his ballistic helmet as he grinned briefly and tried to unsee this most Australian of apparitions. This encounter just had to go in the TRG war stories diary.

Alpha moved on again and found themselves crouched, mutually protective, at the back door of the safe house. Having finished placing their explosive breach charges on the door, Rosco paused for comms with Bravo team, deployed at the other address given by the Russian. He overheard Bravo breach early. *Somethings gone wrong; they were supposed to wait! Shit, do they know we're coming?* Rosco quickly changed back to Alpha teams tacnet to expedite their own entry. To his initial shock right then, he saw the superbly camouflaged lens of the micro surveillance camera under the nearby windowsill.

Without hesitation, he spoke into Alpha's encrypted, frequency-agile tactical network, (tacnet), "Compromise, Compromise, Go, Go, Go." Immediately, the back door explosively lost its' hinges, and Alpha rushed through the empty door jamb, aggressively lobbing flashbangs to commence their rapid primary search.

The Flashbang, aka M84 stun grenade, aka Thunderflash, produces an explosion of sound at around 180 decibels two metres away. Up to twelve times louder than a clap of thunder or a jet engine screaming at take-off, it is dramatically above the level at which sound is painful. The accompanying blinding magnesium flash is a million-candela strong. In any confined space, a person on the receiving end, whether unlucky or deserving, is left momentarily stunned and blinded.

The progressive and rapid updates of "Kitchen clear ... Hall clear

..." were broken by, "Police! Put down your weapons! Put down your fucking weapons!" There was no mistaking the command, or the lethal threat. But the two gunmen, not gifted with high IQs in the first place, had emptied a bottle of good *Stolichnaya* vodka before the police arrived. Now, inebriated, and temporarily deaf and blind from the Thunderflash exploding at their feet, they chose poorly. Having recovered enough to react using their woefully inadequate, but still lethal revolvers, both should have called it quits. Instead of surrendering and eating prison food at her Majesty's pleasure, their final act was one in a long line of bad choices, brutality, and violence.

Both officers in the room judged correctly their rules of engagement were met. The only option to prevent themselves or their colleagues being targeted was to use lethal force. In the black humour of the TRG, each offender received two warning shots through the forehead. Both armed captors died by the sword they lived and threatened society with. Society, would rightly not mourn them.

In the remainder of the safe house, Rosco's team rapidly progressed their primary search of the premises. Rosco could hear their repeated shouts of "Clear! Clear! Clear!" He had not heard the explicit shouts indicating this operation had achieved its primary objective. He grew apprehensive. To his immense relief, the keyword came twice in rapid succession. "Hostage! Hostage!" Helen had been found, bound, and gagged, with no apparent injuries. She lay on her side, fully clothed, on the only single bed in the last room searched.

With the house cleared of threats, Rosco gently guided a mentally frayed, edgy Helen towards the care of two waiting IC paramedics. She wept as she looked for any familiar face but could find none. She desperately needed a hug and someone to hold her hand for a while. The much younger medic was a bright-eyed woman with blonde hair, not dissimilar to Helen's own, not looking old enough to be out of high school. Despite her youth, this talented pro exactly deciphered Helen's most pressing need solely by looking at her. Without a word and with much tender care, she embraced Helen. One woman comforting another, holding hands all the way to the hospital. They didn't let go until Helen was reunited with her beloved, sore and sorely missed, husband.

———

BACK AT THE scene of Helen's captors' demise, Les was not a very happy man. *Where the fuck is Madeleine? She must have been here; she was with Helen when the Russian called. No sign of Sarah either.* Their intel was at an end, and that wasn't good, no fucking good at all!

Les listened on tacnet as confirmation came that the secondary search was complete. The house was clear … Tempting as it might be to order Rosco to do another secondary, he knew his teams were thorough. Ordering another search in a home such as this would only serve to flag a lack of confidence. No, he wouldn't do that because he had supreme confidence in them. Anyway, Les, as senior officer on-site, was bound to do a walkthrough himself, since lethal force had featured. When he came to the room with the two dead offenders, he pulled his phone from his pocket and found the camera footage from Bill and Helen's house. The two bodies laying on the floor were the two that had kidnapped Helen and Maddy. The black humour surfaced again, *Won't do that again in a hurry will ya? TRG two, grubs nil.*

———

THE SCENES OF CRIME OFFICERS, SOCOs, wanted to start work on site. They assured Les if the tracking Tile were in the house, they would find it in five minutes flat. It was, and they did, using a simple search technique. Henry had set the Tile to ring continuously when in range of a Wi-Fi.

The SOCOs set a smartphone to hotspot, which acted as a weak Wi-Fi, and simply walked around the house, listening. The ringing Tile revealed itself in the kitchen bin, alas no Sara1 was anywhere to be found, but they did note the kidnapper's expensive taste in whisky. One mystery solved, another revealed.

―――――

LES DROVE to the decoy house to receive an after-action report in person. Already unhappy, he listened to the precis by the assault leader, and what had transpired before the flashbang flew through the kitchen window. Tail-End Charlie wasn't taking it well.

The most significant points were damning. They'd assaulted two perfectly innocent aged pensioners in their own home. This resulted in the wife sustaining large second and some third-degree burns and incapacitating shock. The husband had suffered stress-induced severe chest pain, of cardiac origin. It seems, the wife had been sitting at the kitchen table unseen by the attack team. She had only moved to the stove to turn the roast. This accounted for the movement prior to entry, and the mechanical sounds that led to the M84 being lobbed through the window. Both had been admitted to hospital in an unstable condition, she to the burns unit, he the cardiac unit.

Les felt sick to the stomach for the old couple. They were suffering because this was the cluster fuck Rosco had warned him of. To top Les's night off, as he left, a veritable parade of media vehicles began arriving. He expected some less-than-flattering airtime for the TRG, and a call from the Commissioner, but wasn't sure which he would have the pleasure of listening to first.

Chapter Thirty-Eight

About 7 pm, Marcus watched Henry finish up his discussion with Les on his phone. He could tell from Henry's body language that things had not turned out as planned, or even as hoped for. Marcus understood from listening to one side of the exchange that Helen at least had been rescued. She was OK, and on her way to the hospital to be with Bill. Both would remain under police protection. Henry thanked Les for the call and hung up.

Marcus and Jane waited patiently for Henry to get his thoughts together and tell them what had transpired with the two raids. Apart from the great relief of Helen's rescue and the finding of the Tile, the only other news was grim indeed. Everything they had done appeared to have been anticipated. It did seem the Russian had been genuine in his desire for a clean exchange but also hedged his bets using two locations. The surprise appearance of the TRG had released Helen but had now perhaps condemned Maddy and possibly Sarah to an early grave! Marcus was over this continuous emotional roller coaster!

"For fuck's sake, why couldn't we have just done a swap?" cried an exasperated Marcus. "Now it's too late, too fucking LATE!" His voice cracked noticeably in despair. He stood and walked to the bathroom to wash his face with cold water. Why he wasn't sure, it just seemed a necessary thing to do to recover something of himself. Which 'something' he didn't know either.

In the last couple of days, he'd become aware there seemed a lot he didn't know. If he had the time over, he wouldn't let the powers that be play politics with the lives of those dear to him. He stared at himself in the mirror until he'd convinced himself he could hold it together.

He returned to his lounge chair, with his hair still slightly wet but feeling somewhat more composed. "What the hell is the next step in this cluster fuck?" he asked.

Henry was taking a breath to respond when, as if by design, the mobile on the coffee table rang into life. 'No Caller ID' displayed on the screen. Marcus's heart accelerated like a Formula One race car.

Jane spoke straightaway before Marcus's hand had reached the mobile. Her words articulated what they all were thinking, "Say what you have to, do what you have to, but get them back. Forget everything else."

Chapter Thirty-Nine

Peter considered how much planning had already gone into this next phone call. It started when he was first interviewing for the Lamarr project. As is the custom in his adopted homeland of China, he always played the long game and it continued to serve him well. Sarah had been judged correctly. She would achieve for him only the minimum to free herself. This had been borne out. She was easily coerced initially with the promise of money and position. But had become troublesome to control, even for a man of his skill. Marcus, on the other hand, confirmed himself as deeply moral. He'd accepted he didn't get the project manager's job, put it behind him, and went forward with all his usual fervour.

This application to duty was the long game litmus test for Marcus. Peter knew these two personalities would turn out to be the way of things and knew he could easily manipulate his morality. All Peter had to do was prey upon those Marcus cared for.

Sun Tzu - Begin by seizing something your opponent holds dear, then, he will be amenable to your will.

HENRY NODDED READY, and Marcus swiped his finger across the screen to answer and tapped the speaker icon. "Marcus Hall," he said.

"Marcus Hall," came the Russian accent sternly, "you are not a man of your word. I said no police and who arrives? I said come alone, and now two of my men will return to the Rodina in caskets ..."

Marcus tried to apologise in rapid-fire succession. Gone was his concern that the Russian wouldn't understand him if he spoke too quickly. "They wouldn't let me! I beg you! Give me another chance! I can give you everything, so much more than you even know exists, please ..."

Peter had planned the conversation, and now seemed as good a time as any to up the ante. The sternness in the Russian's voice rose to complete the suppression. "Shut the fuck up, do you hear me? Can you at least do that? Do not speak again until I command you to speak! I told you not to fuck with me, now you must pay. It could have been so easy. But do not worry, I will tell this Madeleine, your precious Sara1 is worth more to you than she ever was."

Having dealt with a lifetime's worth of anguish and anger in the last two days, Marcus could no longer contain his rage at this Russian. Two words burst from within him in a duo of pure contempt and loathing, "You cunt!"

Peter couldn't altogether blame him for saying that, it was the outburst he had goaded him towards. *Perfect*, thought Peter, *he is amenable to my will.* If a mastermind was directing his own out-of-control life these past days, he'd probably say the same himself. Best to let him sweat on the insult. Nothing like a good, long, pregnant pause to raise the anxiety level. Peter would wait. *He who talks first, loses.*

The other two faces in the room had gone white with shock at Marcus's uncharacteristic expletive.

There was still silence on the other end of the call. All three stared at the screen; they could see it was still connected, just silent. Marcus buried his distraught face in his hands. He'd blown it the first time by not speaking up; now that he had spoken up, he'd blown it again. The Russian was still there, obstinately not saying anything.

"I'm sorry," said Marcus, "this is too much for me, I just want it to be over ... please."

Peter smiled to himself, *that was quite the heartfelt apology.* Marcus wanted his life of plain sailing back again. *Now to reel this fish in.*

Far from being angry when he finally spoke, the Russian was surprisingly subdued. "Marcus Hall ... Mushka ... it is a great shame, is it not, that this intense emotion within you did not surface earlier? Your government values a little black box you invented more than these two fine ladies. They are to blame, not me, do you not see this now, Mushka?"

Something profound shifted inside Marcus. He might not see Maddy again in this life and perhaps not Sarah either. He had wanted to do an exchange to save them but now it was too late, and he blamed himself. He feared both would be lost, more than he was afraid of anything in the world. "Yes. Oh, I see that, I see that all too clearly now." If Henry and Jane had not been in the room, he would have said the same thing and needed no pretence of sincerity.

"As you say in this country, better late than never, Mushka."

Did the Russian just leave an opening then? Henry and Jane again motioned silent encouragement to keep talking. They knew if the conversation could be kept alive, Maddy and Sarah might be too.

Marcus rallied desperately. "I can give you the advanced capability prototype. We can still do the exchange tonight ..."

The Russian interrupted his pleading. "Ah, little fly, you think me a fool? You seek to trade something that does not exist. <u>Be careful</u> with your friends' lives. Such a pity, perhaps there will be no exchange after all."

"I can prove it because I built it. It's called the Marc2. It cures insomnia and will probably do the same for depression and morning sickness. It gives powerful, believable, vivid dreams of those you love or yearn for, with total recall afterwards. With more research, and using it in various ways, the Marc2 could be a revolutionary advancement, used to strengthen or poison someone's mind. Its value will be measured in *trillions* of dollars. I will gladly give it to you freely tonight in exchange for them both back. Unharmed," he added tentatively.

Jane had been scribbling furiously but quietly on the writing pad that had been ready on the table all day. She rotated it and pushed the deftly written note calmly towards Marcus. *Ask Russian to confirm with Sarah/Maddy as proof. Get personal messages from both to confirm they're alive.*

"Mushka, as I have said do as I say and you will prove to be as wise as you are inventive. But just because you say you built it does not prove it exists, perhaps you are being unwise again now?"

"You can ask Sarah and Madeleine, they will both confirm it exists ... I beg you ... when you do that, would you please ask them both for a personal message, so I know they're still alive." Marcus tried to speak with a neutral emotional bias to engender only curiosity, nothing adversarial, in the Russian.

There was a hiatus until the Russian commanded, "Wait," and another silence followed.

Shane stood near Peter, this conversation was awkward for him to listen to. Any slip of the tongue, and he might be pushing up daisies before the hostages. "Go ask them," Peter instructed.

Sarah and Maddy were the ones doing it tough in bondage and had well and truly had enough. They just wanted to go home, wherever home was from there. Faced with the knowledge their captors already knew, both girls freely admitted the truth. Shane memorised two personal messages for relay back. The information was relayed to Peter, who smiled that smug, superior grin Shane so detested. Due to all the unnecessary shit he was embroiled in at the moment, Shane would have much appreciated if Peter would just fuck off now and not come back!

"It would seem you speak the truth, Mushka. I will contact you very soon. By the way, your French sucks, and your tie was pink." The Russian's absence was marked by the usual three beeps.

Peter knew all along that with this conversation, his Russian alter ego would get precisely what he wanted. He just hadn't anticipated it would be so easy. Not to mention extorting infinitely more than he thought possible. Marcus had run true to form. His moral code dictated handing over anything and everything in his possession, if he thought it would protect those precious to him.

Peter's next call to Sifu would also be an uplifting one. Not only would he be able to inform him that the plan was back on track, but that it had been redeemed far beyond anyone's expectations.

A WAVE of cathartic relief washed over Marcus. He looked at Jane. "Thank you, Jane, thank you so much. Henry, don't ever let this incredible woman get away."

Determined to do whatever it took this time, Marcus would hand over the Marc2 and get his beloved and Sarah back. "We need to find a way to escape out of here and make the exchange," he said.

Chapter Forty

Henry wasn't expecting the service to call him, but it couldn't be anyone else on Crypto-Cone. If he'd been using a standard phone, Henry would have put it on the table on speaker so everyone could listen. Crypto-Cone, however, disabled the speaker so no conversation would ever be overhead that way. It also reminded him by default, what was said was for him only. He scooped up the notepad from the table and answered the call. He pointed to the room next door as he headed there for privacy, but not before Marcus and Jane caught a puzzled look on his face.

Several minutes later, Henry returned. "You won't believe this," he said.

"I'd believe aliens are real after this week," said Marcus mindlessly. His face screwed up as he realised what he'd said. He opened his mouth again to apologise to Jane, but her raised hand and friendly smile told him none was necessary.

Henry was excited, as he read from the pad. "Hear the main points out until I finish. The service supports our exchange plan in principle. No police will intervene this time. Marcus should go by himself to make the actual exchange. The service will deny any involvement. We can leave now for Lindfield, the guys outside already know we can go. Some background info ... Oh, and so you know without having to ask, yes ASIS listened in on the call."

Marcus was at the point where he really *could* believe in little green men. All he could utter was, "Well I'll be, that's a first!" He looked at Henry, who raised an eyebrow. "Maybe not then," added Marcus.

Jane stood first, "Well, no time like the present. Questions and discussions can be had in the car." As they walked from the hotel room, their armed protectors turned their backs as they moved past, resuming their positions once they had egressed.

Enroute to Lindfield, Henry did his best to get away with the line 'Some background info'. He could probably have fended Marcus off on this relatively short trip, but Jane, not a snowflake's chance in hell. She was as tenacious as two like magnets determined to repel each other. It was as though she was an immutable law of nature unto herself. Henry appreciated that genuine modesty forbade Jane from seeing herself that way, but that didn't help his predicament!

Henry even tried quoting The Crimes Act. He told her it promised an all-expenses-paid, site-specific holiday with room service, if he revealed such things. When Jane said seriously that she would come and visit him in prison, or perhaps not see him at all after tonight, he knew he had to cough up.

Henry said ASIS had received shared intelligence from 'Five Eyes.' He didn't know what, but as a result, the service now supported doing the swap. That was all they said and all he knew. Marcus and Jane couldn't appreciate the big deal about 'Five Eyes'. What, if anything, did that have to do with handing over the Marc2? Neither had even heard of it. Henry explained it involved an alliance of Australia, New Zealand, the USA, Canada and the UK to share intelligence. In the end though, with neither of them ever having been exposed to the Australian or International Intelligence Community before, Henry's honest explanation, which he had been so reluctant to share, was useless. Well, that one was anyway ...

"And," pushed Jane.

"Jesus, Jane, I've known you all of five minutes and you're reading me like a bloody book already!" protested Henry mildly, then exhaled. "Sarah is to be considered hostile. Les's decision."

"WHAT?" exclaimed Marcus. "I saw her tied up! We know her! No way. No fucking way!"

"With you, but I understand how he came to that conclusion, even though I don't believe it either," agreed Henry.

"And how does that work?" asked Marcus.

"I can't remember it all, but along the lines of, she's alive, one crim's dead, her house burnt down with no evidence of anything left. Her partial print was lifted off a dram in the rubbish bin at the house Helen was found at. So was the print of a Special Operations Command Lieutenant invalided out when he went off the rails after he tragically lost his wife and unborn child. The Sara1 is missing, the tracking Tile has been removed, and the Russian doesn't have it. The assessment was the Lt and her were celebrating something with a toast, blah blah blah. I don't believe it, but you get the idea. There's no way she could be a threat to us ..."

Chapter Forty-One

Mid-evening had come around by the time the three arrived in the lab and Henry used his admin code to retrieve the Marc2 from the safe. They sat around the coffee table with the twin black box in the middle, waiting for the Russian to call.

Henry spoke up, "I think we need to do a test to confirm the Fear we programmed really works."

"Why?" asked Marcus forthrightly. "We're not going to use it tonight, just hand it over. Whether it works or not, whoever has it will find out sooner or later. All we need to know at the moment is where to offload it and get the girls back."

Henry looked slightly guilty at eliciting that response from his friend, both Jane and Marcus picked up on it.

"Why do you think that, Honey?" said Jane levelly, "and when we get a chance, I may have some useful thoughts on this whole thing as well."

"Look, I'm just being open," said Henry, "and I think it's prudent to know if it works in case we need a diversion or something to work with. Like an insurance policy for contingencies, or in the event we're forced into a demonstration, or whatever." Henry found himself a little frustrated by what seemed to him like constant second-guessing from ASIS and Les. It was an all too familiar feeling he hadn't expected from these two.

Exhaustion and stress were sneaking up on them all. Jane saw his point and agreed it would be better to know whether it worked or not too. Marcus followed suit. "OK, mate, let's do it. Got any thoughts on how we should run it?"

Henry detailed his thoughts. "We know it should take around six minutes to have an effect if we're within three metres. I suppose the easiest way is if we stay sitting right here where we are, set a timer and turn it on. Jane will stay 10 metres away for 30 seconds and then come and sit back with us and monitor us both, we keep an eye on Jane too. We should all take our pulses right at the start. If our pulses quicken around the five-minute mark, we'll know there may be more to come and can try to be ready for it. But if anyone starts to freak out, Jane is our control and turns it straight off. Agreed?"

"Yes, but I think my heart rate's elevated just thinking about it," noted Jane holding two fingers on her radial pulse as she walked away.

Marcus concurred. The trepidation of this unknown was enough to unnerve anybody. He flicked the toggle switch to the on position. The Marc2 was silent, it had no moving parts.

"So, while we're waiting, what thoughts did you have, Jane?" inquired Henry.

"Oh yes, it seems with all the anticipation of what's to come, I'd forgotten. Correct me if I'm wrong, but the Russian thinks the Marc2 only works when you're asleep. He must also think it only operates with earphones, because only you and Marcus know of the speaker mod, right?"

Two heads nodded in agreement.

"Similarly, he will have no idea you installed fear. If I recall properly, you said something like, 'using it in different ways, it could be a revolutionary advancement.'"

Two heads nodded again.

Jane concluded her thought process. "Well, if this little experiment we're about to conduct proves successful and we all survive, all that, may be important. Not to mention your revolutionary advancement will have become a revolutionary weapon."

That thought chilled them all.

AT THE FOUR-MINUTE MARK, no-one felt any different, and their initial heart rate increases had subsided back down to an average seventy-five beats per minute. Four minutes and fifteen seconds came and went, as did four minutes thirty and forty-five. Still no change.

As the digital timer passed six minutes, Marcus felt unsettled, it was just there, no build-up, no nothing, just there. He looked at his colleagues. Henry looked a bit that way too, Jane less so, or at worst not as comfortable and relaxed as she had been. For Marcus, only the briefest of seconds existed between consciously feeling unsettled, and the hyper-aroused sledgehammer of the fight, flight or freeze response. For the second time in two days, a massive sympathetic nervous system hit of adrenaline, made his entire body reel. Was it possible to be more terrified now than at Sarah's? This time though, he knew the fear and panic was all in his mind, nothing would hurt him here, but that didn't seem to matter at all.

He was petrified of nothing, yet everything. Nothing in the lab evoked rational fear, but the irrational and absolute panic he felt was horrifyingly real, yet fake. The wide-eyed look on Henry's pale, sweaty face irrationally horrified him further. He became paralysed with fear, unable to save himself from any threat, real or imagined, had there been one. His now chilled body might not have been able to move, but his bowels prepared to. He was literally about to shit his pants.

Neither men spotted Jane turn the machine off. Marcus was focused on his reducing ability to keep his sphincter clamped shut, amongst the avalanche of pure dread afflicting him. He was beside himself even as the physiological responses triggered by the Marc2 gradually released their grip on his body. He could feel himself not calming down, but instead being less afraid, less panicked, two manifestly different things. Thank goodness there were no real threats in the lab. Who knows how much worse and out of control that would have made things?

Jane moved to Henry embracing and comforting him. It took a minute for all three painful hearts to stop beating out of their chests. The men waited to arrive at the point where their mouths retained enough moisture to contemplate speech and for the post-adrenaline trembling to subside. Jane was grateful for the delayed start, but even so, the trio had been to hell and back in their heads, but they had made it back, physically unscathed at least. Time would tell of anything else that lasted. Henry was so very glad he'd used Jane as a control and not made her suffer needlessly to the full extent he and Marcus had.

This was one experiment they all swore never, ever, to repeat. Anyone who suggested mind over matter did not exist, was welcome to try the Marc2.

As if they hadn't done enough to deserve a month away on a tropical beach somewhere, Marcus received the address from the Russian in a text message. It was in Lindfield of all suburbs. Instructions were stipulated too. *Come alone. Bring the Marc2. Bring the circuit diagrams and research. 11 pm sharp.*

Someone at ASIS supposedly still kept tabs on Marcus's phone, as Henry received a Crypto-Cone call. It stipulated the Russian was *not* be followed after the exchange. Henry was shocked. He made the point they had just tested *fear* in the Marc2 and had suffered the most severe panic attacks imaginable. Was the service sure they would allow it to just disappear? As per usual with any unexpected question posed, Henry didn't get an answer, only a reiteration of what was required. Do *NOT* follow the Russian after the exchange.

Marcus subsequently departed on his life-or-death mission, while Henry and Jane remained at the lab biting their fingernails. Fortunately, the kitchenette was stocked with a decent stash of tea and coffee, even cream biscuits. Henry had the agency arrange an ambulance to stage there with them, in case anyone needed medical assistance when Marcus returned with the hostages.

IT WAS the most straightforward job the two highly qualified female ambos could remember. It was also probably the most cloak-and-dagger assignment they'd ever encountered. They considered themselves a little over-qualified for playing nursemaid. But, taking the good with the bad, all they knew was two women might be arriving soon for a check over, and it was open slather tea, coffee and bickies.

Chapter Forty-Two

P eter had two things to prepare before receiving his 'guest'. Should the police turn up, the signs he posted would delay them long enough for him to slip away. No-one would dare stop him once they knew who he was. International law would protect him.

In the under-house garage, he retrieved a Philips screwdriver and in barely ten minutes had ticked one job off his list. He checked that the weapon under his driver's seat was loaded, and as it should be.

The other task was to activate the counter-surveillance scanners in his car. If he got so much as a whiff of police this time, his two hostages would pay the price for this repeated treachery. *Well,* he thought, *there's nothing to stop me making them pay for their earlier duplicity. I might just kill them all anyway ... I'll decide later.*

Chapter Forty-Three

Marcus pulled up his Honda SUV in front of the address the Russian had provided. It was a charming double-storey house surrounded by a business-like black metal panel fence at eye height. The neat garden was well maintained, with an old gum tree, nearly a metre wide at its base, up the driveway end of the block. The garage was integrated under the house on the left end, and the front door was smack bang in the middle. It looked like an expensive property in a nice neighbourhood.

It popped into his head that this house would be ideal as a TV series backdrop starring some wholesome family. He walked through the open pedestrian gate and closed it behind him. He berated himself for even thinking that while life and death hung in the balance beyond the front door, half a dozen steps away. The mental distraction has also caused him to close the gate behind him - *how was that a good idea?* He held the Marc2 tightly, it was the last thing he wanted to drop. He pressed the doorbell with great trepidation.

Something finally registered with him. The A4 poster affixed to the front door looked the same as the poster on the front gate. *Probably important*, Marcus thought. He'd had tunnel vision with stress and gazing at the house, and hadn't read the first one, so thought he'd best read this one. The porch light made it easy.

Very official looking. 'Diplomatic Notice: UN Vienna Convention on Diplomatic Relations 1961.' Directly underneath read, 'Diplomatic Immunity, Articles 29 and 30.' The subheading preceded some paragraphs of long-winded text. Essentially, this is the private residence of a diplomatic agent to Australia ... blah blah blah. It's afforded the same protections as an embassy or consulate of the country whose seal and flag appears below. Unauthorised access by any person or government agent is prohibited under international law ... blah blah blah.

Oh fuck, thought Marcus. *This Russian shithead is protected by the UN. No wonder he's so fucking brazen. The police can't touch him, even if they do manage to catch him. He'd only get sent home with a smack on the wrist. For fuck's sake!*

His eyes continued to the bottom of the poster, and he shook his head in disbelief. He didn't know any official seals apart from the one plastered behind the US President at every media event. But he did recognise a couple of flags and knew Russia's was a tricolour. That wasn't what he saw. What he *was* looking at made no sense whatsoever. The bright red flag had five stars in the top left-hand corner. This country had nearly one-fifth of the world's population. The flag of the People's Republic of China. *What? The Chinese and the Russians are working together? I guess they're both communists ...*

The front door opened. The stereotypical Chinese man he'd imagined was not who received him, nor was his language as expected.

Shane stood in the doorway, neat, clear-eyed and clean-shaven. "You must be Marcus, and that must be the Marc2." The tall, solidly built Aussie seemed surprised at the size of the Marc2. "The boss is upstairs." Shane stood close enough to make anyone feel their personal space was being invaded. He used a low, dangerous tone. "Listen to me very carefully, Marcus, just do the exchange and go. Don't fuck the boss off and you'll probably walk out of here alive with the other two. I'm warning you, savvy?"

"Got it," said Marcus quietly. *Probably?* Before Shane moved away, Marcus asked, "Are the girls here? Are they OK?"

Shane gave his one-word habitual response when asked a question he had no intention of answering. He held his index finger vertically in the limited space between their respective noses and said, "Don't."

Marcus figured if he did nothing and said even less to this man, he'd be safely compliant. Shane frisked him, found nothing, and bade him go up the stairs to the upper level in front of him. He strained his ears to hear any sign of Maddy or Sarah but heard nothing. They stepped from the staircase and walked left around the end of a dividing wall, towards what he guessed was the lounge room. Marcus thought if they'd turned right, they would have gone to the bedrooms.

A plush-looking armchair with a man seated facing him was revealed as Marcus rounded the dividing wall. A glass-topped coffee table was positioned in front of the armchair. *Holy shit, they've got Peter too!* Peter Esser was such a surreal and unexpected sight, his mind paid no attention to the fact that he was not bound or restrained in any way. He appeared to be sitting comfortably, as though casually waiting for someone to arrive.

"You too?" exclaimed Marcus more as a statement than a question. "Don't worry, I'll try to get you out too when we leave."

Peter smiled in his faux style as he was apt to do when about to be a condescending prick, "Au contraire, Mushka."

Marcus had recently been reminded his French was terrible, but he knew what *au contraire* meant. *Why did Peter use that Russian's word? He wasn't Russian, was he?* Marcus became befuddled. When he spoke next, he only wanted one thing. "I don't understand what the hell is going on here, and I don't want to know. Here is the Marc2 and everything else the Russian demanded. Can I just take the girls and go now please?"

Marcus amused Peter. With the truth confronting him, he still had no idea about anything. Even with the lighthouse of reality shining blindingly out before him, Marcus was still all at sea. Peter believed his deception plan had been remarkable and knew now that it was complete. Who could argue with that? *Well, no need to make life easier for him, surely?*

"The Russian asked me to do the swap for him," said Peter trying to sound helpful, but just intent on torturing this man's mind. That at least seemed to make sense to his visitor.

Marcus placed the Marc2 on the dark wood of the polished mahogany dining-room table nearby. It had a zip-locked bag containing a USB and a set of earphones Gaffa taped to the top. Feeling like he needed to state his affairs to get that part over with, grab the girls and leave, he pressed on. "All the documents, including the circuit diagram, are on the USB as required."

Peter nodded at Shane, who returned in the direction they had come, but walked past the stairs into one of the upstairs bedrooms. Shane returned with Maddy hobbling along in rope shackles, hands bound in front of her, gagged. Marcus instinctively moved towards her, but the big Australian guard stepped forward, holding up an index finger in warning to approach no closer. He met Maddy's terrified eyes, for now, that would have to be enough. Shane pushed her into a kitchen chair. *Could it be true? Could they get through this in one piece and be whole together again?* It tortured him. All he wanted was the girls returned.

Shane returned from whence he came again, and Marcus saw Sarah. He had grieved her loss, and here she appeared before him, clearly a prisoner, Les had judged her wrongly. He did nothing to agitate Shane this time. Her eyes met his as they had with Maddy. A message of silent mutual relief that they were close to freedom passed between them. With Shane's help, Sarah's backside found a kitchen chair beside Maddy. Sarah had hoped Shane might become a turncoat and an ally, since he had voluntarily turned over a new leaf after using the Sara1. However, it was apparent to her now by the way he handled Maddy and her, that was a bridge too far.

"May we go now, please?" asked Marcus, suspecting already that the answer wouldn't be the one he wanted to hear. There was something about Peter. *Why is he acting so piously?*

Peter's faux smile faded in again. "I thought you'd have questions?"

Marcus had learned at least some things over these horrible days. "No, no questions, I just want to leave ... please. I've delivered everything, you have more now than the Russian ever expected. Peter, I've kept my word, why won't you let us go?"

Peter was well aware of his major and vicious character flaw, his tendency to seek gratification for himself every chance he got. It was not just the perverted kick he got from the subjugation of others. Their *total* subjugation was the goal. He would sink his boot in hard, and as often as possible, when his victim was already flying the white flag trying to walk away. If he hadn't had enough fun with them when they wanted out, he found a way to stretch out their pain, maximising his pleasure. As with Sarah and others before her, he disliked people leaving before they knew just how very superior he truly was.

"Not quite yet, Marcus," Peter said, asserting his authority, "Sit."

Shane turned to procure another kitchen chair. Marcus noticed for the first time the gun handle sticking out of Shane's back pocket. Shane set the kitchen chair down near him, and the would-be rescuer sat down. Marcus followed a series of instructions before realising, or perhaps before he could admit it to himself, where it was all heading. Shane handcuffed him behind his back, and ankle bracelets followed. The keys to both, Shane threw onto the kitchen table. He was in no position to argue, now fully at the Russian's mercy. *Maybe the Russian would make an appearance now?*

SHANE MEANDERED his way casually back past Sarah and Maddy. At a point near the kitchen, he stood behind everyone but with a clear view of all three captives. The dividing wall from the stairs to the lounge room meant he was just out of Peter's line of sight. He made sure he couldn't see Peter in any of the window reflections. If he couldn't see Peter, then the reverse would be true. Shane promptly and quietly withdrew his silenced mobile phone from his front pocket. Keeping it at arm's length for maximum discretion, he opened the green message app with only thumb movements, careful not to drop the phone. As soon as the ready to send, but empty message had been sent, he slid the mobile back into his pocket. For now, he would just have to play it cool, and hope help arrived in time.

"SO, Marcus, ask me a question. I can clear anything up for you and make life that much easier to understand. You look like you're wandering helplessly in the woods at the moment."

Understandably, Marcus did not want to play. "Look, I've done what I promised. The girls are here. Why not let us just walk away now?"

Peter would never allow his fun to be taken away so quickly. "Mushka, that's not how the game works. Ask me a question and make it a good one, or someone might accidentally get hurt." Peter thought ahead to his glorious days teaching young Chinese to master the art of industrial espionage and what a lesson for them tonight's victory would be. He would be venerated.

What the fuck, thought Marcus, *is this the Peter, Sarah dealt with? No wonder she was messed up from the strain.* Marcus didn't like it one bit. *For fuck's sake, it's a no winner, damned if I do, damned if I don't.* Looking around him for inspiration, his eyes caught Maddy's moistened, dread-filled eyes. He saw the almost imperceptible nod for him to go ahead and ask a question. She was scared, petrified, the same as him. But she would be strong if he could be, and the sum of their parts would be stronger still.

Maddy, with an amazingly simple yet personal gesture, had gifted her resolve to throw the dice and play this sociopath's warped game. If he lost, they lost together.

"Who is the Russian?" he asked, his voice ringing out as confidently as if he held all the cards.

Chapter Forty-Four

Henry's blood ran cold as he read in surprise the urgent text on Crypto-Cone. "Oh shit," he said out aloud. Jane got the meaning, but it merely served to confuse the paramedics. They didn't know what was going on in the first place. Henry informed the ambos they needed to relocate urgently about ten minutes away. The likelihood of there being injuries had risen now, and they needed to be as close as possible.

The well-seasoned ambo in her early forties replied firmly but with all due deference. "It doesn't work that way, you can't just relocate and stage us around the countryside." The portable radio handsets over both the paramedics' shoulders crackled to life with their call sign, and a brief message was passed. "Or evidently you can," contradicted the much younger of the two medics. "You CSIRO types seem to have a lot of pull. How is that?"

Henry shrugged and left the question hanging. "We all work for the government, don't we?"

Henry thanked Jane for agreeing in advance to stay put in case this eventuality came to pass. They kissed each other goodbye with trepidation. Jane remained, as the others walked promptly out the lab door heading towards the ambulance. Henry was privately glad Jane didn't have her car here. He suspected this wonderful woman of his had a bit of a stubborn streak and might be tempted to follow him. He immediately felt ashamed of himself for this lack of trust.

Jane made a show of sitting back down around the coffee table and waving them all off. With them out of sight, she stood and walked to the internal phone on the wall, the same one she'd used on her first visit to the lab. She flipped out the directory and found the number she wanted. "Hi, guys, it's Jane from SETI. I'm having problems with my vehicle. Can you sign me out a pool car please? … Ten minutes? … Awesome, thanks!"

Chapter Forty-Five

Peter was only half impressed. "Good delivery for a poor question. I don't know how many hints I have to give you, so I'll make myself plain. I used a voice changer to make me sound Russian. It was ME you called a cunt."

Peter is the Russian? Oh, fuck, FUCK! His intellect screamed at itself for another, less provocative question to quickly move ahead. But, if he didn't know what the answer was going to be, how the fuck was he supposed to know what would be less provocative? He recalled being warned as he arrived not to tread in this territory. Marcus pressed on with this game of double or nothing, or, considering Sarah now, triple or nothing. Marcus stared at the floor as if it would help him. "How long have you worked for the Chinese?"

"Boring," responded Peter. "That isn't even worthy of an answer." Peter took a turn by default, "What does the Marc2 do that's so different from the Sara1?" Peter added, "Shane, while he's answering, put the Marc2 on Mr Marcus here, I want to see what happens."

Marcus answered in more detail than he was quickly able to supply the Russian on the phone. Nevertheless, deciding not to mention the *Fear* programming, the delay, being awake, the speaker, the effective radius, or two 'on' switches for that matter. Peter was clearly showing his intent not to do the exchange, and for all Marcus knew they'd all end up dead before midnight anyway, which wasn't far away. As far as Marcus was concerned now, this twisted *ARSEHOLE* could well and truly get fucked!

Shane dragged a side table over to Marcus and placed the Marc2 on it. He had never seen the double-decker Marc2 before tonight but noticed, though, that the lower half looked identical to the Sara1, and *that* he was familiar with! Retrieving the headset taped to the machine, Shane inserted them into the headphone output but only turned the Marc1 on. He threw the click-seal bag holding the USB into the backpack and placed an earphone into each ear of his handcuffed male hostage.

As designer, Marcus knew he wouldn't be affected by Fear unless the Marc2, including the module, is switched on. He also knew he wouldn't be affected by Love as the earphones were disabled when the Marc2 was connected. But it did give him an idea for later.

Maddy had seen the Marc2 module only once, knew what it was designed for, but assumed it could only still be set for *Love*. She wasn't apprehensive for Marcus though, as the last time they used the Marc1, they were awake, and it had been pure intimate magic for them both. At least he'd be thinking of her, and she knew it wouldn't hurt him, after all, an aching penis didn't genuinely count as an injury. Thinking of their playful banter, she half *wanted to slap* her knight for *taking so long to rescue her*. But, in their current predicament, an aching penis would have to do.

"What makes you think you can get away with this?" asked Marcus, scratching for a question, and making a point of subtly looking at the lounge-room wall clock occasionally, like there is some time pressure to worry about.

"Marcus, you're going to have to do better than that. Is it not plain to you I've gotten away with it already? You're here with the Marc2, and I'm in total control. As you would have guessed, I like being in control, there's something ... invigorating about it."

There might be something invigorating about being in control for Peter, but his answer gave Marcus the creeps. He felt like he had glanced inside a mind with something very wrong with it, very wrong indeed.

There was one question Marcus wouldn't mind being answered, "You're the bloody GM, why didn't you just take it all and leave us alone?"

"See, Marcus," said Peter, "now that's a better effort. I do believe you're getting the hang of this now. The answer is relatively straightforward. Sarah *should* have told me everything she knew. Indeed, we have a contract whereby she got the project manager's job without having to apply for it, and she agreed then to tell me everything, always. Today, she would have met the CEO and tried to ruin everything I've built. Years of work. All of this, Marcus, is because that bitch lied to us all. It's because *that bitch* tried to double-cross us all. It's because THAT GREEDY BITCH wants everything for herself! All this, everything that's happened, how you came to be here, all of it, is her fault. It's all down to her!"

Marcus didn't take his eyes off the megalomaniac and in doing so didn't see the truth and pain etched on Sarah's silent face. He hadn't looked at Sarah's face on purpose, and felt for once in his life at least, he'd judged an emotional situation correctly. To look at Sarah would have indicated to her some belief in the outburst. But more importantly, indicated to Peter that he believed him, and he wouldn't give that prick the satisfaction while demeaning someone he called a friend. The outburst, Marcus realised, was probably all true, and it certainly answered many other questions, but no-one was responsible for this fucked-up mess but Peter. Peter's snide attempt at divide and conquer, while disassociating himself from all responsibility, had failed.

Maddy and Sarah continued sitting in their chairs gagged and doing nothing, wishing whatever Peter was playing at would end. Sarah knew the Project Manager cat was finally out of the bag but had decided well before this moment that so be it, she couldn't give a fuck about that secret anymore. Maddy had not known Peter previously, but knew now, just as Sarah did, all his loose screws were rattling around in his head tonight. That knowledge was not promising.

"My turn," announced Peter as if it was his go for some party game, which it was in his mind at least. "How did the Police find the address where Helen was being held?"

Marcus couldn't see why he shouldn't just tell the truth. After all, he had been warned when he arrived not to fuck the boss off, and Peter was without doubt the boss, as unstable as he was. "There was a tracking Tile in the Sara1."

Shane nearly had a stroke at that one! If he'd been a God-fearing man, he would have felt considerable fear of meeting his maker at the pearly gates in the not too distant future.

Shane remained where he was, out of sight of Peter. He didn't want to give away any body language to Peter, the astute bastard.

Peter was very much not aware of the tracking device. Judging by the way he went from the 'smug in control of everything type bastard' to 'let me connect some dots, not so confident as I just was, type of bastard'.

The minutes ticked by in the background. Peter was already expecting Marcus to have fallen asleep. Peter had no idea, nor would he ever accept, that if he hadn't been such a draconian mongrel with Sarah, maybe she would have told him everything when he had the opportunity to know.

"Where is the Sara1 now?" Peter blurted out in his eagerness to know, with a slight hint of paranoia escaping, together with a suggestion of loss of self-control.

"I've no idea, we thought you had it, until the Russian, well, until you, asked for it," replied Marcus.

"Well ... well ... well ... Are you still there, Shane?" inquired Peter.

"Sure," responded Shane in as even a manner as possible, moving several steps forward so Peter could see him.

Shane had not heard any indication that Peter had produced a Type 64 suppressed SMG, but he certainly saw it pointed at him when he came into view. It's surprising what comes back to you at different times, and now was no exception. He knew from his military days the Type 64 was close enough to be the silenced Chinese version of the AK47.

His five-shot revolver, still in his back pocket, was no challenge. Even if it was, it might as well have been on the moon for all the use it was going to be. He only hoped if Peter shot him, it was on semi-auto; if not, at that thing's rate of fire, there'd be thirty rounds in him before he could say, 'Don't shoot.'

"Perhaps, I should ask you, Shane? Since you were the only person who could have taken it from Sarah's house, maybe you're a spy in our midst? But, first things first, turn around and lift that toy out of your back pocket with thumb and forefinger."

Shane complied while his back was to Peter. "You've got it all wrong, boss; it was Sifu. It's here in the house. I can go grab it for you now if you like ..." He tried to sound as convincing as possible.

In some way, the three hostages were glad the heat was off them for a short while at least. They were all sure Peter was playing one of his fucked-up games and didn't intend to shoot Shane, any more than Shane would return the favour.

"Why the fuck is it here, and I don't know about it?" demanded Peter, sounding like maybe he would put half a mag into Shane after all. That hint of paranoia was back and more pronounced.

Shane knew he had to be careful, he'd prepared a cover story. "It's like I said, it was Sifu's idea. On his instructions, I briefed him about what happened at Sarah's house straight afterwards. I told him the Sara1 didn't work, but I had Sarah so she could probably fix it. I was to say to you it burnt in the fire.

You weren't supposed to know. He wanted to give it to you as a gift for your achievements. To take with you wherever it is you're planning on going. I'm sorry, boss, I was between a rock and a hard place. I work for Sifu, and you hire me like others do. But, I'm no fucking spy, he doesn't have me spy on you, or anyone else. It's easy enough to verify with him." Shane held his hands out from his body, signifying he had nothing to hide. He hoped Peter would accept his explanation.

The closer this mission came to its end, the less anyone could be sure what the hell Peter's response would be to anything. It was like he was trying to go out with a bang, but the harder he pushed, the less that seemed likely, and the more it screwed up Peter's head.

As if by coincidence, but it was most definitely not, the phone lying face up on the coffee table in front of Peter started to ring. In the grand scheme of things, he wouldn't answer a call from anyone at a time like this, but he could see this caller was the only exception to the rule: Sifu. Peter knew he had five rings before it went to message bank. Realising he wouldn't be able to hold the heavy weapon steady with one hand, he unfolded the gunstock. The stock made pointing the 4½ kg SMG at Shane far more stable with one hand, as Peter answered the call on speaker. He resumed his two-handed aim at Shane, who was still facing away from him, holding his pistol with thumb and forefinger. Peter would keep him facing that way, just in case.

Peter greeted Sifu, "Sifu, you are on speaker, and everyone here can hear you. How may I assist you?" It was intended as a pertinent warning to be careful what was said, and not to undermine the image that Peter was in control.

Sifu's tone was surprising. It was severe, without greeting, and embarrassingly berating. "Shunyuan, what Shane told you is correct about the Sara1. However, you are not acting as I directed.

Your games are to cease, the final success of your plan has already been achieved. Now, you <u>must</u> prepare to depart. What you have to deliver is too important. I will be there myself in minutes. But, in the meantime, <u>stop playing your games!</u>"

A more balanced man, or a less unbalanced one, would have taken Sifu's words, reflected, swallowed their pride, and moved on. Peter had been demeaned, insulted, offended, and humiliated in front of people he did not consider worthy of his respect, and who were far below his station. To be so stained by Sifu in this way was not only inexcusable, it would be punishable when the time was right and the odds favourable. Peter promised himself, this transgression would not remain unanswered.

Chapter Forty-Six

Sifu drove towards Peter's home at a speed he would lose his license, car and liberty for. He knew Peter would grasp his home security system was compromised. Sifu had watched Peter's increasingly paranoid behaviour lead him to sweep his house for bugs every day. Sifu recalled having concerns with Peter's conduct erring on the delusional side about four months ago. He decided on a hunch to hack into Peter's home system to keep an eye on him and allay his personal fears that his minion was losing the plot.

Far from allaying his fears, Peter merely confirmed his suspicions, and the depths to which Peter's troubled mind was plunging. It wasn't hard to get a psychiatrist to review the footage and observe the trappings of dissociative identity disorder, paranoia, megalomania, and narcissism. A second, independent opinion also saw obvious symptoms pointing towards these conditions. The puppet masters decided then that it was time for him to 'retire' before he created some situation Sifu would have a hard time sorting out, make go away, or both. Tonight, was such a situation.

Sifu knew Peter would never consider a security system he had set up himself could fall victim to hacking. Peter saw himself as the wolf and everyone else as the lamb. Sifu had been warned after the clandestine psychiatric reviews that if Peter started seeing himself as a lamb, he would likely suffer a severe episode of cognitive dissonance. If that happened, he could turn on anyone, everyone, or even himself, but there was no way of telling how he would react if his beliefs suddenly and severely mismatched his perception of reality.

It had, in every way, been quicker and simpler for Sifu to access Peter's home network than try to install bugging devices and hidden cameras. Peter had thoughtfully password-protected his internet router with a twelve-digit alphanumeric code including both capital and lower-case letters. The possible combinations of his passcode were 19x10 to the power of 21. Although an enormous number, it was only twelve and a half times the potential combinations of a WW2 German Enigma cipher machine. A reasonable home computer is 8000 times faster than the world's first computer the Allies used to crack the Enigma codes. Considering the supercomputers Sifu had access to, it was distressingly easy. It reminded Sifu of putting his photos in for development before digital cameras. You dropped off your film one day and picked up the results the next.

Everyone who was listening in the room, Shane included, was relieved Sifu was coming and had instructed them to proceed with the exchange. What they were not relieved about was how Peter was reacting to his perceived public humiliation, and control being wrenched from his iron grasp.

Paranoia or no, Peter had realised the only explanation in which Sifu could have overheard or watched what was going on, was that Sifu had penetrated his home security system, which wasn't even on at the moment! Peter held all the cards and was home sitting in the loungeroom holding a submachine gun. Shane was armed as well. Sifu must have hacked his system, he would have detected any stand-alone bugs during his daily scans. He felt vindicated for what others might call, 'over-caution.'

It's dangerous for someone who leans towards or has full-blown paranoia to have proof handed to them on a platter that their paranoia is justified. The next step in that delusional mind is *any* such feelings are vindicated by association with the original proof, thus causing the condition to deepen, perhaps acutely so.

Peter lowered his weapon with no hint of an apology. "Would you be so kind as to get the Sara1 for me, Shane?"

"Sure," came the response, and Shane disappeared down the hall to retrieve it. Returning, he placed it in front of Peter, who no longer threatened him. It was as if that whole episode at gunpoint had never happened. Shane had seen this Jekyll and Hyde aspect of Peter more often in recent months and, although he would only admit it to himself, it scared him a little.

Peter directed his next question to Sarah. "So, did you fix it?"

As Sarah was still gagged, she just nodded.

"And the last big Sara1 question, Marcus, is who exactly put the tracker in there?"

Marcus had no doubt a wrong answer would not go well for him or the girls, but he also remembered from somewhere the best lie is close to the truth.

"Henry," he said.

Marcus caught the briefest flash of mortal concern pass across Peter's face; he did NOT like that answer. Marcus added earnestly, "We bought quite a few things that day, mainly oscilloscopes, and we put trackers in everything. It was just local routine; they weren't GPS trackers, just Wi-Fi Tiles for inside our building. You know how different departments like to borrow other areas' assets and accidentally not return them? You must get complaints about that sort of shit all the time."

Marcus could tell this explanation was far more palatable than the last, but Peter's poker face was on.

"I'm not stupid," said Peter vehemently. "There was no Wi-Fi in the building Helen was taken to. You couldn't have tracked her there. You're lying, and that's the last one you'll ever tell me."

Marcus tried desperately to explain. The trouble was there was way too much information in his brain trying to get out at the same time. He needed to clear his head. He took a deep breath as Peter's eyes drilled into him from his lounge seat. Plainly, being hand-cuffed and shackled to a chair wasn't an excellent indication that the wish for peace and goodwill to all mankind filled the room. *This game won't last much longer.*

Breath taken, thoughts collected, Marcus proceeded to explain how they had towed the 5G trailer down the bearing line from the tower and found the house. Marcus thought it would add some authenticity to his explanation if he included almost hitting a parked car while he was negotiating the cul-de-sac.

"MOTHER...FUCKER!!!" screamed Peter loudly and angrily, mostly at Marcus but a little at himself, as he recalled seeing the incident on the two hidden cameras.

Not a person in the room had ever seen Peter display such a lack of self-control. Peter was losing not only control of this situation in his mind, but in actuality. A sane man would have returned to the path less travelled and walked briskly away before any further surprises came his way.

Peter's recall of the incident also included there being three people in the car towing the trailer. Perhaps he was onto something that would put his stamp of control back on the discussion. "Marcus, think very carefully how you answer these next questions. Who was in the car with you?"

That's a loaded question if ever I've heard one. "Henry and a bloke called Rosco were also in the car." Marcus thought he would go with *the best lie is close to the truth* maxim again. "Rosco was our police chaperone, there in case someone tried to kidnap either of us as well."

"Yes, I can understand that ... Who else does Henry work for?"

Marcus felt the walls closing in, if he lied, they'd all be dead. "Some ... federal agency," he stammered out, trying to sound unsure.

Peter had only been fishing but felt a good bite. Although he could not see their whole faces, this was fresh news to the ladies, but not so Marcus.

Peter proceeded, "Let me be more specific then. Which federal agency does Henry *spy* for? Don't play games with me, Marcus. Henry is everywhere in all this, don't think I haven't noticed. I was directed to give Henry the lab tech job. He was barely qualified, there's three parts of nothing on his personnel file, no actual job application, no résumé, no references."

Peter didn't have a lot of time on his hands before Sifu arrived. "Shane, please point your weapon at one of our lady guests. If this obstinate prick doesn't give me a decent answer, pull the trigger without further recourse to myself."

Shane retrieved his revolver from his rear pocket again and pointed it at Maddy's centre of mass.

"Now ... do I have to ask again?" Peter coerced Marcus.

Marcus couldn't give Peter the acronym quick enough, but had to make it sound like he wasn't holding out, "ASIS, I, I, think ... "

This time Peter caught himself as, "Motherfucker!" sprang forth again.

Shane looked surprised, and considering the answer took it as *stand down.* Shane returned the Smith and Wesson to its pride of place in his back pocket.

Chapter Forty-Seven

Henry arrived a couple of streets away in the ambulance. During the trip from Lindfield, he sat in the rear behind the driver, on the seat paramedics use to treat stretcher patients. From there, he could speak clearly to the older of the two medics, seated in the front passenger seat.

Henry had put the mobile number assigned to this ambulance into his phone. That way he could call them direct if he needed them in a hurry. He made sure they understood that, if they heard gunshots, or reports of shots or violence over the radio, they were to stay put until he called them. It would not be safe to come closer, and he asked them to park a couple of blocks further away after he got out.

As they were nearing his drop-off point, Henry waited until his new medical friend wasn't watching and drew his sidearm. It was better to load a bullet into the chamber by cocking the action in the ambulance than walk down the street at midnight and, with his luck, having some insomniac see him.

The trouble was, when he slid back the action of his pistol, it made several distinct mechanical sounds. While it was nowhere as loud as doing the same thing to a pump-action shotgun, the sound was pretty much the same. When he'd finished re-holstering his weapon, he looked up, and she was looking right at him.

"We may all work for the government, but no-one's given me a gun yet," she deadpanned. "Which department did you say you work for?"

This whole conversation reminded him of the one he had with Jane in the car park. He had to come up with a better explanation, so he thought he'd try a different tack. "Law enforcement."

The paramedic smiled at that. "Not that you need to know, but I'm on my second marriage, both to coppers. Appreciating I should have learned my lesson the first time, you don't operate like any copper I've ever seen. You see where I'm coming from here?"

"It's like you said," replied Henry with his sweetest smile. "It's a need to know kind of thing. I'm sorry."

The ambulance driver picked a spot and was getting ready to pull off the road into the kerb and park. "I think this is as good a spot as any, Anne. I'll call it in as our new location."

Henry's brain felt like it had been zapped with a cow prodder. He tossed up the pros and cons of whether to ask the question.

"Anne, do you know a bloke called Rosco?" Henry tried to sound conversational but failed miserably.

"Holy crap, I've just realised too ..." responded Anne, as the facts dawned on her almost simultaneously. "You both have a lot in common, and he speaks very highly of you. Why don't we all got together when this one's over?"

"As long as I don't need more than three battlefield dressings tonight, it's a date!" accepted Henry as he slipped out the van via the rear door.

THE AMBOS WATCHED Henry move commandolike in the direction of the address he had given them. The driver remarked, "Don't worry, I won't ask, I'm pretty sure I don't want to know at the moment. I'd rather watch it on the news."

"If this seriously goes to shit," said Anne gravely, "we're gonna be first on scene at a bloody mess, and I don't mean that figuratively."

Anne now totally understood their predicament and was determined to provide the best clinical care response possible. Their standard kit would need some additions to help deal with this potential multi-casualty response.

"We need to prep for up to four gunshot victims. We won't have time to come back to the ambulance for any supplies, so here's a bit of a list to start with. Let's stuff our spare battlefield dressings into our trauma packs. If the O2 cylinders are not on full, change them out now. Pre-connect the multi-heads with high-flow masks. Pack the spare bags of plasma expanders in the O2 soft packs. That'll do for starters. Let's jump in the back and hop to it."

Both practitioners knew that gunshot victims require 10 times more blood units, and were 14 times more likely to die, than a person seriously injured in a car accident or stabbing.

The driver took it all in her stride as she was trained and dispositioned to. "Do you want me to park further away, like Henry asked?"

"Not on your nelly. Henry's lucky we can't park any closer." Anne mused, "I just hope we're parked close enough for his sake, or I might have to ask you over for dinner instead."

As they worked quickly and efficiently, Anne's younger partner made good use of her multi-tasking skills. She thought they'd forgotten something. "So ... are we rating him on the COMA scale, or what?"

Anne pretended offence. "You can't do that to my future dinner guest! That's only for patients!"

"Well, he did ride in the back, let's not split hairs."

"Good point, go on then," encouraged Anne, who wanted to know what she thought.

"Straight eights," came the assessment.

"What? My, my, my, I do believe thirty-two is an equal best from you," commented Anne, who then said nothing.

"Come on, you know the rules … give," was the demand for Anne's score.

Anne thought for a moment. "Cute: seven; Orthopaedic: six, he's a little muscley for me; Manliness: nine, he's got that together; and arse: without doubt you'd have to go an eight, wouldn't you?"

They both chuckled while they continued preparing as if *their* lives depended on it.

"Hey, Anne, what does CSIRO stand for anyway?"

Chapter Forty-Eight

The surveillance package in Peter's vehicle had been busy doing what it was designed for, scanning for nearby electronic signals. The app Peter was using to monitor the results made a unique warning sound, and when he heard it, he retrieved his phone from the table. It showed an emergency service vehicle, an ambulance, had transmitted nearby. It had been a day and night of surprises, and only his planning had kept him at least one step ahead. Peter stared hard at Marcus for an instant, then realised no ambulance would pre-position before the police if there was an intention to storm his house. It was probably on a routine call.

No matter, they can park as close as they like, but they won't be able to save this lot when he's finished with them. Still, once is happenstance, twice is coincidence and three times is enemy action. He was well over three unexpected turn-ups for the books today.

Peter directed Shane to remove the Marc2 from Marcus and place it in the backpack on the table in front of his chair, he would need it soon enough.

Peter decided to go downstairs to the garage and, as much as it pained him, he would open the garage door to make it look to Sifu like he was still obedient and preparing to leave. Once down the stairs, he made sure the interior light was off in the car, the keys were in the ignition ready for departure, and there were no lights on in the garage.

He refolded the stock of his Type 64 before he opened the roller door. It would be much harder for anyone to recognise the silhouette of a gun if it wasn't in the classic gun shape. You never know when anyone could be walking or driving past.

HENRY WASN'T DOING EITHER. He was busy standing behind the big gum tree in the front yard near the driveway, and too close for comfort to the garage. *But it is as it is,* Henry thought to himself while cursing his foolhardiness for being exposed this way. He checked as efficiently as he could that he wasn't casting a shadow anywhere on the ground, and that he was safe for the moment. He'd just have to wait until whoever had come downstairs had the good grace to bloody well go back up!

He thought he heard a door close in the garage, and perhaps someone going upstairs, but it was difficult from his position to tell exactly what direction the noise had come from. He waited and took the precaution he did in situations like this: he gave himself a ten count.

He was only at seven when he heard the car approaching and slowing down. *Uh-oh,* if he went back towards the road, he was exposed without question. How blatant that exposure would be depended on a variety of things. It was a forward or backwards Catch-22, and he chose forwards. The open garage door offered the only other cover, and he walked towards it. He was trying to be so quiet, it felt like walking on tiptoes, like a child trying to sneak up on someone. This time, however, it was a little more serious and a lot more dangerous. The closed door to the stairs linking internally with the house came vaguely into view, and he realised, with not a small amount of relief, that his desperate move forward had paid off.

There were two minor drawbacks in being forced to take cover in the garage, well three now the car he'd heard had just pulled up out front. If someone turned the light on, decided to move the vehicle, or saw him walk in there as they drove up and asked him what the fuck he was doing. He drew his trusty Walther, magazine fully loaded again, *thank you, Rosco.* He felt safer, but it made it infinitely more likely he would shoot someone.

He could see where the car out front had stopped. The driver was out straight away and made a beeline to the electronic gate. He used a key fob for entry, a far more elegant way to get into the yard than Henry had used. The visitor walked to the front door and was let in without delay, more sounds of shoes on steps. Henry decided to have a cautious look around in the garage.

Time spent on reconnaissance is seldom wasted - The Duke of Wellington

WHILE PETER WAS DOWNSTAIRS, Shane had duly removed the earphones from Marcus, unplugged them from the earphone jack, and tossed them into the backpack. Marcus could see Shane preparing to turn the device off and whispered to him intently, "You warned me when I first got here, let me return the favour. Do *not* turn it off, it has thermostat timer protection, so it heats up and cools down evenly. To start the protection timer, just turn the other switch on and leave it go, otherwise you'll fry both mainboards, and you might as well throw it all in the bin."

After that shit with the submachine gun Peter had put him

through, and being a return favour under these circumstances, it made sense to Shane. He nodded and made sure both switches were on. No-one could tell it was on or off anyway, it made no noise, so what did it matter? Shane slipped the now *fearsome* Marc2 into Peter's grey backpack.

Chapter Forty-Nine

Time *1202:00am*

As Peter arrives back upstairs and resumes his chair, Marcus takes note of the precise time on the lounge-room clock, but for very good reason this time.

Peter places the Type 64 once more across his lap. The back-pack containing his diplomatic passport and the Marc2 are on the glass-topped coffee table directly in front of him and within easy reach. The three-step, anti-theft zipper-latching system is engaged, so the Marc2 and his passport cannot quickly or easily be removed. All is as it should be.

"Peter," says Marcus, keeping his voice neutral, "I hope this whole thing will be over for all of us soon, and we can go our separate ways peacefully. I ask you in good faith to please, please, allow the gags to be removed from Maddy and Sarah and let their arms free. If they make a sound or try anything, you can punish me, since I'm the one that asked."

The idea of someone paying for another's misdeed, and the pressure that places on all parties, amuses Peter. "Shane, you can release their hands. Gags stay in."

"Thank you, Peter," acknowledges Marcus.

Before Shane has time to do anything, though, he hears a sound and says, "I think Sifu is here. I'll go let him in."

Peter speaks while staring at his backpack. "Tell me this, Marcus, why didn't it work on you?"

Marcus, anticipating that question, has prepared a plausible answer. "It's probably the earphones again. We've had the same problem before. It's not the quality of the phones, they're good quality. It's just the machine seems to do something to them after they've been used a couple of times and we have to replace them."

Time 1203:10 am

Shane greets Sifu at the door. They leave the front door unlocked in case they need to make a quick exit. Sifu comes straight to the lounge room. "Greetings, everyone, I apologise for the delay. You will be out of here very soon."

He has come unarmed. It is best that way on several levels. Unarmed, he can probably talk or fight his way out of a confrontation with Peter. But if he is carrying, Peter might perceive him as a direct threat, and *that* he might not be able to counter. Sifu has supplied Peter with the SMG among other weapons and presumes, rightly, that tonight those weapons are close by.

The weapon on Peter's lap is pointing towards the dividing wall. Held there casually, it doesn't seem threatening. Sifu addresses Peter directly, "Shunyuan, you will understand we all have our superiors. Mine is the consul, his the Ambassador, hers the Ministry of State Security, and on it goes. We have a slight change of plan to expedite the transfer. You will travel with me, and our 'guests' can call whoever they like to come and collect them. Shane can manage that after we have well and truly departed. Do you see any problems with the change?"

"None," replies Peter.

"Where is the Marc2, Peter?" asks Sifu.

"Right in front of me on the table." Peter's tone implies that to move it from the table would have dire consequences for anyone foolish enough to try it.

Sifu studies the bag at a distance. Two zipper handles are captured in some sort of latching system, so the contents of the backpack cannot easily or quickly be removed. The object within the bag is patently long and rectangular given the way it pushes against the fabric.

Sifu notices Peter's clipped answer but has no option but to ignore it at this stage. "I'm going back downstairs to retrieve the diplomatic plates and close the garage door."

Shane is preparing to remove the girls' hand bonds. This is his first opportunity to do so since Peter ordered him to. Unaware that Peter has already said no to any gag removal, Sifu instructs Shane to ungag them as well, but leave their legs tied for the time being.

Peter feels his hands starting to sweat on his weapon. He knows, just knows, everyone, all of them, are out to get him, to rob him of this great victory and stop his triumphant journey home. He can feel it and grows ever more certain the longer he sits there.

MARCUS IS SURREPTITIOUSLY TRYING to watch the lounge-room clock, and at the same time check for any change in Peter's behaviour or demeanour. It's only a little over two minutes since Peter sat down, a full four minutes short of the time it took the Marc2 to radically affect them in the lab trial. If Marcus guessed, he would predict Peter isn't going to last another four minutes without a major crack up. With Peter holding an automatic weapon, that's not good, not good at all.

Time 1204:05 am

Sifu goes down the stairs that access the garage via the now closed door. He practically glides down the stairs, with barely a sound as one would expect of a kung fu master. There is a light switch for the garage on either side of the door to the stairs. Sifu flicks the inside switch on, while simultaneously opening the door and stepping into the garage.

Henry is caught by surprise with the light coming on, not to mention a man appearing a mere three metres away.

Sifu hears the click as Henry cocks the hammer of his pistol back, with his thumb.

Henry has no idea who the man is, but he is one cool cucumber; he doesn't even flinch at the sight of Henry, or his gun.

Henry notices the man staring at his Walther curiously, he's never heard of anyone with a gun pointed at them doing that. This person still has hold of the door handle and quietly closes it behind him with slow, non-threatening, but somehow graceful movements.

In the absence of anything better to say, Henry murmurs just above a whisper, "Good evening."

"Good evening," comes the reply as if the man is a host greeting a guest at a dinner party. "As you don't look the type to shoot and ask questions later, may I suggest I close the garage door? We don't want some sticky-beak neighbour calling the police, do we?"

"Fair enough," responds Henry, who also judges it undesirable to have his weapon cocked when a light touch of the trigger will launch a bullet. Henry does a safety de-cock and eases the hammer forward. He can tell his surprise visitor appreciates the gesture.

The trouble is, the open garage door is behind him. Henry has to step backwards around the car to let the stranger walk by him at a safe distance. In the micro-second Henry looks down to check his footing, his gun is gone from his grasp. The speed at which this is done was breathtaking. His adversary now points the weapon at him instead. It's never a good feeling to be threatened with your own gun, not that being shot with it would hurt more, it's more the philosophical tragedy of it happening that way. Henry thinks what he imagines will be his last thought; *this man is like Bruce Lee, only for real.*

"We should still close the door, and you're closest," whispers the holder of his pistol. Henry lowers the door feeling like he is closing the lid on his own coffin.

"Tell me, what sort of gun is this?" asks Sifu.

Confused by the question, Henry answers anyway, ".25 Walther TPH."

"I thought as much, and who are you?" enquires Sifu.

"I'm the guy waiting in Peter's garage," comes the reply, "and you?"

"I'm the guy holding at gunpoint the guy who's *hiding* in Peter's garage," responds Sifu, almost light-heartedly.

"We're not getting anywhere in a hurry, are we?" points out Henry.

"So, let's speed things up then. Will you *shoot* me if I give your gun back?" asks Sifu more seriously.

"More than once, but only if you *really* make me," responds Henry truthfully.

"Fair enough, at least you're honest. Will you *trust* me if I give your gun back?" asks Sifu with no doubt as to the seriousness of his question or the answer to it.

"Maybe. But positively more than I do now," responds Henry maintaining his truthful demeanour. "But judging by how fast you disarmed me, I'm guessing you can take it back anytime you like anyway. There's a good reason for me to behave right there."

"I can work with *maybe*," replies Sifu with a grin. "By the way, if you won't tell me your name, can I call you Henry?" Sifu reverses the firearm and hands the weapon back to Henry, who is more than slightly confounded about what just happened.

"Thanks, Bruce, that's better than what I thought you were going to do to me," he says, noticing a flash of something in the other man's expression at the mention of that name. Henry doesn't want to risk aggravating him, so tries to continue their light mood. "Well, you look more like a Bruce than say a Clyde or a James, just sayin." It seems to work, and the conversation moves on.

Sifu asks Henry to *wait* in the garage, the exchange will be done shortly, then everyone can go home. Henry asks after the hostages. Have they been mistreated? Sifu responds they are fine, the worst thing that happened is Marcus had the Marc2 on him. Sifu notices the alarm on Henry's face, so follows up by telling him it didn't work.

Sifu realises the registration plates will have to stay on, and he'd better get back upstairs to try and deal with Peter's instability. He leaves with one last piece of advice for Henry, "Henry, I want you to stay with your back to the garage roller door like you were when I came down, but one step further back. Have your gun ready. Peter, your boss, has deceived you all, is mentally unstable and has an SMG. I know this is a leap of faith from someone you think is an enemy, but for all our sakes, please do this." Sifu doesn't wait for a response. In typical fluid motion, he flicks off the light and exits, leaving Henry bathed in darkness again.

It seems to Henry he has no choice but to trust this strange, seemingly highly intelligent, calm, and well-skilled man. The situation Henry finds himself in is bizarre, but he will do as he is asked. He trusts Bruce on some innate level, not just because if the stranger had wanted him dead, he didn't seem to need a gun to do it, despite borrowing his TPH! Definitely like Bruce Lee, his hands are probably registered as lethal weapons too. Yes, Bruce suits him perfectly, and he's presumably gliding back up the stairs, because there is barely a sound of him walking on them.

Time 1206:15 am

Four and a quarter minutes have passed since Peter sat down in front of his backpack. Even from the distance Marcus is sitting, he can see Peter's eyes widening, his right fingers dancing manically along the machine gun's magazine. *Fuck ... FUCK!*

Sifu re-enters the room. Marcus hopes this guy will whisk the crackpot away and they can all just go home! What Marcus doesn't realise is that Sifu and Shane are now just as afraid of Peter as he is. They know what he's capable of normally, let alone becoming unhinged.

Sifu can see his orders have not been followed as the hostages remain bound and gagged. "Shane, did you not hear me before about releasing the gags and hands of the hostages?"

Shane stares at Peter. "I did Sifu, the knife to do that is behind them on the kitchen table. I'm sorry, but you were overruled by Peter."

Peter sits still and says nothing, as if there is no need to explain his actions. To everyone in the room, Peter *is* unhinged. A pale, clammy, coiled spring about to release its pent-up kinetic energy in one, deranged, tyrannical episode.

Peter's appearance is remarkable to Sifu. The difference over the short time he's been down in the garage is chalk and cheese. Sifu decides to get the hostages out of the house as quickly as possible. He's sure the severe episode of cognitive dissonance, warned of by the two psychiatrists, is about to explode out of Peter.

"Shane, I will help you release all three of the hostages, and I want you to lead them to the front door and let them go. When you're finished, please come back upstairs to me."

Sarah has been watching Peter closely and guesses he is being disturbed by the Marc2 but has no idea as to why it should be affecting him this way. What she does know for sure is that Peter's inherent Jekyll and Hyde personality and distrust of everyone has skyrocketed in the last couple of minutes. He has become a paranoid Mr Hyde.

Peter erupts, "STOP!!! You're not in fucking charge here anymore." The thick barrel of the Type 64 is pointed directly at Sifu, whose life expectancy is imminently zero. No-one in the room doubts Peter will carry out his intention to shoot metal into flesh if one of them so much as moves an inch. Quite reasonably, no-one moves.

Time 1206.46 am

Sifu's protest falls on deaf ears, and he is too far from Peter to disarm him, as he had with Henry.

Peter seethes again, "Kill them all, Shane. You're the only one I can trust. It's just you and me now."

A chorus of 'NO, NO, NO' from Marcus and a plethora of other muffled, urgent impassioned pleas from behind gags, fill the room.

SHANE NODS COMPLIANCE to Peter and reaches around to his back pocket, withdrawing his .38. Apart from yesterday, he hasn't actually shot anyone since the Afghan war. He's never needed to, been forced to, or wanted to. But here, in the early hours of this morning, there is only one person who deserves a bullet. That man has already pointed a submachine gun at him tonight and just condemned them all. Shane is the only other person in the room with a firearm, if he can't intervene, everyone, is already dead.

Shane makes a pretence of swinging his weapon towards Sifu, but his actual intention is only to lessen the arc he has to rotate through to acquire his real target: Peter. Shane's aiming point reaches Sifu, he swivels the gun fast, accelerating his aiming point towards Peter.

PETER MAY BE CERTIFIABLY CRIMINALLY insane, but his reaction time is accelerated by a mind vigilant for such treachery.

Peter pulls the trigger as he stands slowly and swings the 7.62mm SMG from Sifu to Shane. Thirteen hundred rounds per minute of full automatic, quietened death. Both of his targets fall to the floor, motionless. The shrieks of muffled screaming terror from the two uninjured gagged women and the shouts of Marcus, echo in the room.

Peter's twisted grey matter screams at itself in return. *The others will come, defend yourself while you have the chance, there must be no mercy, finish the job and escape to those you can trust.* Without hesitation, and not quite yet fully standing, he pulls the trigger hard, swinging the weapon from left to right, until the thirty-round clip is empty. In the aftermath, he makes out rapid breathing and sobbing through the blue smoky haze produced by the magazine of large calibre bullets fired within the room. *They won't last long.*

Tunnel vision focuses him on the magazine change. He presses the release, the empty mag dropping to the floor. He reaches under his seat cushion, grasps his loaded spare, latches it home and cocks the weapon again. He may be crazy, but he acts with coordinated, steely cold speed and precision. In less than three seconds he is on the garage steps descending to his faithful car, SMG in one hand, backpack in the other.

Time 1207:38 am

It takes a couple of seconds for Henry to realise a suppressed SMG has fired two bursts upstairs. By the time he reaches the internal door to open it, he can hear someone's thumping steps on the stairs. It isn't Bruce, or whatever his name is, that's for sure. He suspects it's the gunman come to make his escape, and only one gunman has a machine gun upstairs that he knows of, and that's Peter.

Trusting his gut instinct, he takes up the position Bruce has advised and, with pistol pointed at the door, prepares himself for whomsoever is about to burst through.

Peter has both hands full and comes down the stairs on the trot, without a free hand to flick the light switch on. Henry expects the light to come on before the door opened, but it doesn't. Peter is coming from light to darkness, so his eyes take time to adjust.

Henry has the double advantage of surprise and established night vision. While there is some light coming through the open door, Henry holds a significant visual advantage, "Don't move short arse, or I'll fill your head full of holes."

The very last voice Peter expects to hear as he steps into his garage is Henry's. Although of course he is here, the world is against him and Henry is its agent!

Peter stands with his left side towards Henry, who is already pointing his weapon at him. There is no way he could swing the 4 ½ kg SMG and shoot Henry first, when all Henry has to do is pull the trigger once. "YOU DON'T UNDERSTAND WHAT YOU'RE DOING!" Peter screams, "I AM ACHIEVING GREATNESS YOU FOOL. THEY COULDN'T SEE IT. THAT'S WHY THEY ALL HAD TO DIE!!!"

Henry cannot believe he is listening to the same person he once knew. Gone is the lilt of superior intelligence, or anything resembling intellect. The beast before him is a carnivore. Despite the situation, Henry remains focused, instructing, "Lower the backpack onto the ground. Walk to the front wheel, keep your back to me and put the gun on the ground, slowly, or your next breath will be your last, I'll shoot you as quick as look at you."

Peter complies.

"Now step back two paces and open the driver's side door."

Peter opens the driver's door, which puts the driver's door between Peter and the ready-for-action SMG. Peter can't make a move towards it without first closing the car door, time he would not have before Henry double-tapped him.

Henry phones Anne in the ambulance. They are already strapped in and ready to respond. His call of multi-casualty Gunshot Wounds upstairs has precipitated their worst-case GSW scenario. He adds a command, "Enter via the front door only! Go straight up the stairs. Stay well away from the garage!"

Henry has the keys to the car in the garage in his back pocket, so it isn't going anywhere.

"Sit sideways in the driver's seat, legs on the ground, put your seatbelt on," he orders Peter. When Peter has done so, Henry throws him some cable ties he's found in the garage and makes Peter cable tie his own feet together. He then tosses the rest of the packet onto the car roof, recovers the backpack and puts it on the car roof too. He knows he has six minutes before needing to turn off the Marc2, or he will be affected himself.

Peter has started rambling insensibly, and Henry can't decipher anything he's saying. The only interpretation he can make is that it is vehement contempt spilling from his frothy mouth. But Peter's incoherent diatribe has hidden the sound of soft footsteps on the garage stairs.

Once again, the light being switched on surprises Henry. It's Bruce. Henry isn't sure if he's the walking dead or is still standing through sheer application of will. Judging by the look of Bruce's clothes, a significant volume of blood has been liberated from his body.

"Thank you for trusting me," isn't the first thing Henry expected this sticky red man to say. But he is coherent and still in the fight. The longer he stands there, the stronger he seems.

Taking advantage of Henry's distraction, Peter lowers his left hand to the driver's seat. As neither of the other men have noticed, he reaches under the seat to retrieve his 9mm pistol.

When Henry realises Peter has the pistol, he is initially startled, but keeps his Walther aimed at Peter without shooting.

Bruce believes his days are now over, after daring to believe they might not be after all.

Peter, a broken record of incoherent invective, swings the gun rapidly from man to man as if he can't work out whom to shoot first.

Against a background of Peter's frenzied gun pointing and wild insults, Bruce is as calm as always, and his wit has not abandoned him either. "Henry, you said you'd shoot me repeatedly if I gave you good enough reason to. Why haven't you shot him yet?"

Henry takes a single step forward, in doing so, blocking Peter's ability to target Sifu again. His reward is to have the 9mm pistol pointed solely and directly at his chest at insanely close range. Peter's abuse grows to a crescendo, and he pulls the trigger rapidly. Again, Again, Again, and finally, slowly, in utter disbelief, once more.

The fruits of reconnaissance should never be wasted - Henry Henderson

The loaded magazine for the dry-firing pistol is in the opposite back pocket of Henry's pants to the car keys.

Henry disarms Peter and cable-ties his hands using some of the spares from the packet on the car roof.

Time 1208:07 am

Peter is almost feral, but in the space of a few heartbeats, as Henry and Bruce watch, he transforms before their eyes from a vicious, merciless, bloodthirsty murderer to a man afraid of his own shadow.

Henry recognises the work of the Marc2 and knows Peter is now severely and adversely *Fear* affected. The Marc2 has also wreaked havoc accentuating Peter's multiple underlying mental conditions, before it even took full effect.

Henry considers opening the backpack and turning it off, but is unsure how much Bruce knows, so he leaves it as it is. In any event, Peter is safer to handle in this condition than his previous one. Henry knows he has a little over five minutes now before he will be affected himself.

Henry retrieves the SMG and drops the mag out. Knowing there is still a round in the chamber, he is about to cycle the action and eject the single bullet that's ready for firing.

Bruce interupts, "Don't bother."

Henry pauses, not knowing what he means. "Say again?"

Bruce explains, "You need to go upstairs. They need your help. In my state I'll need at least one round to guard him in case he's got any other tricks up his filthy sleeve."

Henry doesn't like it but, having assumed the worst and now being told people have survived up there, he is keen to go. He grabs the backpack and makes a beeline for the door.

"Oh, Henry," calls Bruce conversationally, "if you can trust me one more time, you've got eight minutes flat to get everyone out of the house. It should be safe on the footpath. Not quite sure ..."

Just another bizarre circumstance of this terrible night. However, Henry believes him and will drag everyone out before eight minutes are up, single-handed if necessary. Henry disappears with renewed vigour up the stairs to be confronted by the smell of gun smoke and the reek of fresh blood.

Time 1208:57 am

"Sifu, I beg you," whimpers a cowering Peter in the driver's seat.

Sifu responds gently, "After everything you have done to me, I forgive you. You don't have to beg me for anything. I remain gracious and am about to give you exactly what you have always wanted, a chance to not be afraid anymore and eternal life under the blue sky."

"Thank you, thank you," continues Peter in his emotionally deluded and grovelling state.

Sifu places the SMG barrel upwards, stock on the seat between Peter's trembling knees. "Here is your freedom, Shunyuan, here is your reward. Your ancestors call you. Can you hear them?"

Peter's face and demeanour are changing again. The fear and panic from the now missing Marc2 are no longer overriding his reactions. The untrusting Mr Hyde rears his ugly head again. "Sifu, traitor, why would I take my own life when you have betrayed *me*?"

Sifu can see this is going to be more difficult than he expected.

He repudiates the accusation, "You ... have betrayed yourself, with your, your cruelty, greed, and inhumanity. But do you know what your greatest downfall was *Peter*, do you?" Sifu emphasising Peter instead of Shunyuan.

"Suppose you tell me, traitor?"

"Gullibility," states Sifu flatly, "as definitely as the world is round."

Peter laughs like a madman, "Gullibility ... what gullibility? No-one has fooled me. You might have betrayed me, or tried to. But you're the fool, not me."

Sifu decides he is running out of time and needs to crush Peter before he finds a resolve he doesn't want him to have.

"It was me who led you to Kung Fu years ago. Who do you think put the Kwoon leaflet in your letterbox and at your local store? Who do you think the drunk fighters that dented your car, and the angry woman who called you a *short arse scaredy cat* at the post boxes worked for? It was me, it's always, been me ..."

"I bet way back then you believed you saw a random Facebook advertisement for DNA testing. I hacked your account. I sent that ad to you. You took the bait and got tested. You held yourself up to the world as a descendant of the greatest warrior king the world has known. Your DNA test and results were all fake. You're no more related to Genghis Khan than I am. Your post-birth report was one hundred per cent fake. There was no blood clot found in your hand, the whole story was fake. I paid the clerk at the hospital a paltry $150 to add the notes."

Peter isn't laughing anymore. He sits in blank silence.

"The name *Shunyuan* played on your gullibility too. That name wasn't random, or of destiny. It, like everything else, was all served to you on a platter of gullibility. It was all fabricated by me, so you would work for me, like a lapdog serves his master. You fooled yourself into living a lie, because it suited your greedy self-image, just like those it gladdened you to manipulate and rule over. You are far lesser a human than they. At least they knew who they were, and they weren't living a lie."

Peter's features soften, his intensity fading as he remains silent.

"There is no title of Sifu awaiting you in China. The night we picked up your passport, they wouldn't have let you into the consulate even if you'd asked. They only took your photo to remind them what a fool looks like. Your two and a half million in the Swiss bank account? Do you want to know if that's real?"

Peter is on the cusp of total subjugation, as he has forced others to be on so many occasions. He nods once almost unnoticeably and, without a word, his stare fixes to the garage floor.

"Oh yes, it is," continues Sifu, "but you'll never see it. You were destroyed by your own gullibility and were always destined to be, and now, you're also stone-cold broke. And, speaking of money, this is who you were really working for, all this time." Sifu, theatrically lets a bloodied note of currency fall onto the floor into Peter's gaze, followed by another, and another of the same.

Peter's downcast eyes widen as he draws a sudden rasping breath through pale lips. He is driven to that blackest of places where deep regret, disbelief, and remorse are spurred by introspection. He visits there only briefly, but that is long enough. He realises his profound self-respect and sense of superiority, the two foundations upon on which his life has been built, no longer exist, and never have. Tears of self-pity well.

He failed himself, trounced by a master deceiver, making him believe he was something … someone, else. Sifu was indeed the long game spymaster.

Peter Esser, not *Shunyuan*, utters his last words, ironically, like his persona, not his either, "Know yourself, and you will win all battles." He places the somewhat warm end of the silencer against the roof of his mouth, tastes the burnt propellant from the thirty rounds he fired upstairs, then pulls the trigger one last time.

Of all things he could have thought of, it occurs to Sifu it's lucky he's already substantially covered in blood. He removes Peter's cable ties with personal regrets anyone was killed or injured, as Peter spiralled out of control into madness tonight. *Damn the crazy bastard for going off on his demented tangents.*

Sifu leaves everything else as is.

Chapter Fifty

T
ime 1209:00am

On the other side of the door, away from Bruce's eyes, Henry turns the Marc2 off and then takes the stairs two at a time. He can already see the pale blue hue of spent bullet smoke still hugging the roof as the hot gases cool. He has no idea of the house layout. As he takes more steps, his eye level rises above the upper floor. A hallway to the right seemingly leads to bedrooms. To his left, his view is obstructed by an angled dividing wall atop the stairwell. The kitchen is in line with the top of the stairs straight ahead. He can't see anyone anywhere yet. But he can smell blood, and the smell is strong.

As he rises further, it becomes apparent the dining room and lounge room are around to the left. He completes his rapid ascent up the stairs onto the first floor, holding tight to the backpack. Pistol in right hand, he walks to the left up to the end of the dividing wall. There are at least two dozen bullet holes where the far wall meets the ceiling.

A liberal patch of blood wets the polished wood floor nearby, but he can't see anyone who might have been shot. Then two people come into view. A motionless, bloodied man, not Marcus, lies on his back near the dining table. Gun still at the ready, Henry remains on high alert. What appears to be a woman with her back to him is leaning over the immobile man. Although he can't quite see what she is doing, he guesses she is trying to stem the man's copious blood loss. *Jezzzuuusss that's Sarah!!*

Sarah spots him out of the corner of her eye and whirls to point Shane's snub-nose .38 at him. Despite what Les told him, despite what he's seeing, despite the gun pointed at him, he fights the instinct to shoot her first and save himself. Fortunately, self-preservation takes over before self-doubt kills you through inaction.

"Sarah?" was all Henry could say in disbelief.

Sarah stops turning and starts pulling the trigger, Henry fleetingly sees tears washing her eyes and is glad of them. Henry throws himself violently left and downwards towards the only piece of cover available to him, the floor at the end of the dividing wall.

The 10-gram bullet whizzes past Henry's right ear as he plunges downwards to the floorboards. At 700 feet per second, it passes close enough to feel the air moving aside to let the projectile pass. Henry lands just past the end of the wall, seeing Marcus and Maddy on the other side. Henry knows if Sarah only just missed him then, she must be a crack shot and wouldn't miss him now he was on the floor. Henry didn't throw himself down at random though, with his close quarter battle reflexes kicking in, he had landed prone, like hundreds of times before. Just like then, he automatically trained his weapon to double-tap Sarah. He knew the two bullets he aimed to shoot into her forehead wouldn't miss.

Marcus screams at the top of his lungs, "HENRY, DON'T SHOOT!!!"

SARAH IS MORE than willing to kill anyone she thinks could be Peter. She would do it before he could do to the rest of them, what he's already done to Shane.

Henry hears Marcus and sees Sarah's gun lowering, realising another round is not on its way.

"Henry? Fuck! SORRY!!" Sarah calls frantically, "Help me, Henry, help me, Shane's been shot!"

Marcus yells but not so desperately now,

"Henry, help Sarah! Maddy and I will be there in a second."

Sarah still has no idea who the woman Marcus just called 'Maddy' is.

Henry drops the backpack where he dived down at the end of the wall. He leaves it there and moves to assist Sarah.

"I nearly fuckin shot you! Since when do you carry a gun?" Henry asks.

"I don't, it was this guys. His name's Shane. He saved my life twice," responds Sarah as she continues to try to staunch the bleeding with direct pressure. "Where the fuck's Peter?"

"Peter's gone, he won't bother us again," replied Henry, as he directed Sarah where best to apply pressure.

Sarah reciprocated, "Since when do *you* carry a gun?"

This question felt tired and worn-out, just like Henry at that moment. "I'm an Aussie spy."

Sarah didn't take her eyes off Shanes bleeding as she said, "Geez Henry, one day that sense of humour of yours is going to land you in trouble big time."

Henry let it go, it was a no winner.

Noticing blue/red strobe flashes around the curtains, he says, "The ambos are here, they'll be upstairs in a sec."

Both paramedics take to the injured Shane like ducks to water. Shane has taken multiple hits from the submachine gun. For a non-medical person like Sarah, it's hard to see how many. Anne and her partner work rapidly through their protocols. In a few minutes, they have: Stopped external bleeding; Protected his airway; Set up Oxygen and IV fluids; Carried out a primary and secondary survey.

It pains Sarah somewhat more than she would have imagined seeing Shane unconscious and being worked on so feverishly by the two paramedics. But, judging by all the treatments and monitoring devices on Shane at the same time, she is reassured he is getting very advanced field care. Sarah is inspired to witness the confidence, speed and coordination as these two highly skilled artisans go about trying to save Shane's life. The medics talked about a *scoop 'n scoot*. Stabilise the patient if they can be, scoop them up and scoot to the nearest suitable hospital.

The need for speed reminds Henry of Bruce's warning. He doesn't know why, he just knows they must get out.

Time 1210:47 am

As he leaves the garage, Sifu seeks out a robe he can cover his bloodied self with. A full-length black gown is on a hanger behind the main bathroom door. He washes his face and arms off quickly. The robe will do quite nicely for someone in a hurry who wants to look like they've just got out of bed.

He knows he can't go to the hospital himself unless he is critically injured. Given he's been walking around for a while now, he reckons he'll make it through the *golden hour*. He knows the 'on the quiet' medical system his employers can call upon will be adequate. He makes a quick call. Medical attention, he's told, will be ready when he arrives at the consulate. He makes his way to the staircase.

At the foot of the stairs is an ambulance stretcher. Its silver metal guard rails are down, and the wheel brakes locked, ready to receive a patient. Sifu moves past it and ascends.

He stands on the landing, looking at the activity before him. An unconscious Shane is already on an orange backboard, ready to be carried down the stairs to the waiting stretcher. Fortunately, the staircase is wide, and the five people getting Shane ready have their backs to him. With the intense flurry of activity, he doubts anyone has noticed him.

As he takes in the scene, Sifu spies Peter's grey travel-safe backpack leaning up against the rail at the top of the stairs. It is obviously there so it will not be forgotten and can be grabbed quickly on the way out.

He sees that the zippers are still securely latched and the same rectangular object bulges out within it. Ironically, his warning to Henry has resulted in a rush to be organised to leave, indirectly making the recovery of the Marc2 child's play. Not willing to look a gift horse in the mouth, he grabs the bag and starts down the stairs to his car, as quietly as he arrived. He hears Henry reminding everyone they need to leave the house, now!

It sounds like they are all about to leave.

SIFU RECALLS UNSURPRISINGLY FINDING the self-destruct sequence for the house when he first hacked the security system. When Peter shot him, which now seems long ago, he thought he wouldn't survive, so he initiated the ten-minute countdown.

Well, it will make sure everyone is gone promptly, he thinks, and there'll be little evidence left behind. *Mind you, once I am at the consulate, no-one can touch me.*

He reaches his car and drives off, much slower than he arrived.

Time 1215:37 am

Everyone is out of the house and Shane is being loaded into the ambulance. Both paramedics are working hard in the back to have Shane a little more stable for transport. Just as Marcus starts his Honda, another car pulls up alongside Henry.

Henry hears a familiar voice. "Want a lift, honey?" It's Jane. *How the hell is Jane here? Why the hell is Jane here? Jane said she would stay at the lab!*

Henry trots to the driver's window and tries to keep his coursing mixed emotions in check.

Jane is unperturbed. She knows he'll be cranky with her on the one hand and appreciative on the other. "Wasn't sure you'd have enough transport," she says through a wide grin and the driver's window.

Marcus yells at Henry, "You go with Jane, mate. I've got the girls, meet you at the Hotel!"

Henry responds with a thumbs up.

Jane being so close to all this makes Henry unusually wound up. "I'm so mad with you at the moment ..." he says, not knowing whether he really is, just thinks he should be, or is just worried she is here. Henry restrains himself and kisses her tenderly, albeit briefly.

Jane responds with the perfect, ironic reply, "Hold that thought, honey, the make-up sex will be amazing!" He recognises she's quoting him, instantly taking the wind from his sails. He moves to the front passenger seat, closes his door, and they kiss each other passionately. Best he gets used to being outmanoeuvred.

Maddy sits in the front seat of Marcus's car, their hands holding tight, after several more longing kisses. Sarah climbs into the back. Without knowing how or why it came to be there, or caring either way, she discovers the unopened bottle of Winter Storm on the back seat and starts to noisily unwrap the fancy display carton.

"Oh yer," says Marcus, "I'd forgotten that was there. I bought it for you, well, you know, as a present, the last time I went around to your place."

"Well, thank you," replies Sarah, "I appreciate the thought, and given what we've been through, I may partake of a swig or three, if anyone would care to join me? By the way, Maddy, I don't believe we've been introduced. My name is Sarah. Marcus and I work together, it's a pleasure to meet you."

Oh fuck, thinks Marcus. *#awkward!*

Orange flames flicker in every window of the house, upstairs and downstairs. No-one has heard anything, but everyone is chilled by the synchronised arson, just glad all of them made it out alive.

The flames remind Sarah she has escaped two burning buildings in two days and the reason she has, lays on a stretcher.

"Wait", said Sarah, "I've changed my mind, I'm going in the Ambulance." With that, Sarah and the bottle of Glenfiddich disappeared into the back of the Ambulance. With only a slight delay, the Ambulance accelerates away, lights strobing, siren blaring.

Perhaps in a moment of *siren fever,* Jane pushes the accelerator to the floor, coarsely accelerating in the general direction of the hospital and Hotel. Henry finds himself once again, holding the *Jesus Handle* and bracing his legs wide. "My darling Jane, if you don't slow down right now, I might not be able to hold that thought." The effect was instantaneous. Their speeding car slows rapidly, then speeds up again as Jane realises she needs a compromise so Henry could indeed *hold that thought.* Jane doesn't want to take too long to get to the hotel, and not just for the 24 hour room service ...

Chapter Fifty-One

Live cross - morning news. "On me in, 3, 2, 1 ... We're here reporting from the scene in Lindfield. Behind me you can see the house of a Mr Shunyuan, entirely engulfed in flames despite the best efforts of firefighters wearing breathing apparatus. Mr Shunyuan's whereabouts are currently not known to authorities, and the cause of the fire is being treated as suspicious. A senior police source, who spoke on condition of anonymity, informed us that Mr Shunyuan, also known as Peter Esser, is with the Chinese Diplomatic mission. According to his diplomatic passport, and you can see a still image of that very passport here, he is a member of the consulate technical staff in Sydney. However, it appears he used the name Peter Esser while simultaneously working for the Australian Government. If we can get a zoomed-in shot of the front gate of the residence, you can see an official document attached to the entrance. It bears the seal of the People's Republic of China. It reads, *Diplomatic Notice, UN Vienna Convention on Diplomatic Relations.* Underneath is a reference to diplomatic immunity related to this private residence, and that unauthorised access is prohibited under international law.

"We contacted the Chinese Consulate here in Sydney for comment. Against a background of increasing trade sanctions against Australia, militarising the South China Sea, draconian security laws for Hong Kong, and opposition to any international inquiry into COVID-19, the consulate issued the following brief statement. Quote, 'The People's Republic of China disavows any knowledge of this matter whatsoever.' Unquote.

"We could all be forgiven for saying the evidence we've seen here tonight tells a different story. I'm sure there's going to be more developments with this storyline throughout the days and the weeks to come. Back to the studio."

Chapter Fifty-Two

With eight of them seated at the dinner table, and a roast before them, they raised their glasses and repeated the toast: "To new friends."

Rosco hadn't prepared a 'thanks for coming speech' but wanted to show his appreciation. "Anne and I would like to sincerely welcome you all. I would also be spending the night in the dog's kennel if I didn't thank my wonderful wife for putting this all together as well."

"I didn't realise you guys had a dog," said Henry.

Rosco grinned. "We don't, Hens. Anne locks me in the backyard, and I scratch on the back door until she lets me back in."

Anne chimed in, "Did you just make a joke? I'm so proud of you too, my love!"

There were rounds of appreciative: "Thank you for having us."

The ice had been broken during the pre-dinner drinks, but it never hurt to consolidate the welcoming feel for guests. Anne and Rosco would try to keep tonight upbeat and not get bogged down in what had happened if it came up. They didn't know how they would do that, but they had good intentions, and everyone seemed to be thinking that way anyway. Until …

"Rosco," asked Maddy as she took Marcus's hand in hers, "It's hard to believe it was two weeks ago, but would you mind answering something I don't understand?"

"If I can," responded Rosco.

Maddy continued, "I'm sorry, I know it's a bit of an unspoken thing we weren't going to talk about what happened, but since we were all there at one time or another … can you explain how Peter missed Sarah, me and Marcus?" It was probably fortunate Maddy had consumed a couple of glasses already, as the alcohol eased her mind in the asking.

"Well, I'll try," said Rosco, "I believe it's due to a few factors affecting a thing called muzzle rise."

"Oh."

"The muzzle of a gun rises when you shoot it. If you shoot a couple of dozen big calibre rounds in rapid succession, like Peter did, the muzzle will rise very significantly. It's something blokes like me train to be aware of and counter. But if you add in the other issues, as I understand them, it will make that rise incredibly significant. Things like, Peter was standing up when he fired. He was swinging the gun. The stock wasn't extended, making the weapon short and lacking control. Does that explain it? Oh, and the two guys who got shot were standing up, and you were all sitting, so there was another need for correction, which he thankfully, didn't make. Sorry, that seems like a very cold explanation."

"It was just the explanation I needed, thank you," said Maddy as she stared fixedly at her dinner plate. "I couldn't believe he missed. I'm sure he didn't think he had." She snapped out of it and exclaimed, "I'd like to propose a toast: To muzzle rise!"

"To muzzle rise!" came a chorus of responses.

Anne decided to ask, "Who put the two black boxes into the spare resuscitation bag?"

It was Marcus who answered, "Um, that would be me. Sorry to do that without asking."

Henry said, "Since you asked, I told Marcus to do it. So, I guess it's my fault, Anne," he added to diffuse some of the responsibility.

Anne laughed. "Just like I thought. I knew you were trouble the minute I laid eyes on you, Henry."

"Me too," said Jane as she joined in the collective uproar.

The conversation slackened off as they all devoured the delicious roast dinner their hosts had meticulously prepared for them.

Bill spoke up with his glass raised, "Helen and I were wrapped when you asked us over, and we're so glad we came. Thank you so much. A toast to new friends."

"To new friends."

Helen hadn't said much all night, but now she spoke up, "It's kind of a pity we didn't all know each other beforehand. I guess China brought us all together in some perverse way."

"Meh," escaped Jane's lips before she caught it. She also knew everyone else had caught her disagreeing syllable. Jane kept her head still and let her eyes scan the table. She felt like a television because everyone was watching her.

"O ... K ..." Henry leaned his knee against hers under the table in a gesture of solidarity. Whatever she was about to espouse was good with him.

"You don't think it was China?" Helen said, which made her exceedingly interested in what Jane might come out with next.

Jane swirled the remains of the delicious 'Pepik' Pinot Grigio in her glass, and gracefully poured it into her mouth. After savouring it a moment, she said, "You have to excuse me, Helen, I'm not in any way trying to force a disagreement, and it's not that I'm a sceptic. I just live in a world where every skerrick of information gets examined microscopically, because that's the only piece of information you might get."

Helen persisted casually with her new friend. "You think there's too much information the Chinese were pulling the strings, rather than not enough."

"Why, Helen, I do believe you're reading my mind," said Jane playfully with an infectious smile. "There's a proverb in astrophysics, well there's lots of them, but there's one, in particular, I'm thinking of. *Correlation does not imply causation*. It's a great dilemma. Can we legitimately deduce a cause-and-effect relationship between two variables solely based on observed associations between them?"

Marcus interrupted softly with a slight slurring of speech and a declaration of male bonding. "Gentlemen, we are all at the intellectual mercy of our beautiful and highly intelligent much-loved women." He squeezed Maddy's hand tenderly as he spoke in jest what he felt in truth. "May we still have some idea of what our ladies are talking about in ten minutes from now!"

"To some idea," added their male host, and they drank another impromptu toast.

The women smiled. They surmised their marvellous men, relaxed as they were, and exhibiting the initial signs of inebriation, had a fifty-fifty chance of following along in their current condition. The men smiled because they realised they had a less than even chance of *not* following along. Had they been able to compare notes, they were almost in agreement.

In the analytical computer that was Jane's brain, she was ready to make her point, but first wanted to make another sarcastically. "Yes, come on, boys, do keep up!" she giggled ... "Put another way, everyone can see all the evidence points to China, there's no piece of evidence that doesn't. But does that mean China did it?"

"Oh, like a conspiracy theory?" asked Bill, suddenly attentive.

Jane didn't answer Bill directly but acknowledged his question with a gaze in his direction. "Are any of the following points, appreciating they're right off the top of my head, any cause for reflection? A media crew got to Peter's house when it had just started burning furiously. Was the fire to destroy evidence that would implicate others? The fire didn't destroy evidence like the diplomatic plates on his car, though. Peter died in the fire and that guy Shane very nearly died afterwards. Where is the mysterious diplomatic passport now? The neighbours were on the news saying they'd never seen the sign on his front gate before that night. As for the media mysteriously being provided with a recent photo of Peter apparently leaving the Chinese Consulate, what is the context of that image, who took it and why?" The other diners were looking at Jane with great interest.

Jane had two last points to make. "In the world of calculating what goes on in the universe, we use algorithms to work out mathematical problems. These problems are linear, and you come to an answer at the end of the calculus. After a life of having to work hard for conclusions, I'm feeling spoon-fed by the solution to a non-linear equation, without even having to think about it. It's unsettling."

Bill proceeded to ask another question, "So, does anyone know of any evidence that implicates another country?" That raised a second issue in his mind, "And if there's not, that could support either side of the whodunnit fence."

Bill's questions alluded the sum total of a zero response. "Interesting ..." he concluded.

THE MEN RETIRED to the kitchen at Henry's instigation. Each held a fancy small crystal wine glass, brimming with Mr Pickwick's Particular Port. Someone, no-one was later sure who, remembered to bring the bottle with them. They took control of the dishes in a way only four socially lubricated males could. It took much longer than it should have. Their raucous, belly aching, eye-watering laughter resulted in a combined and complete inability to perform any two physical tasks simultaneously. The stories that night in the kitchen were supremely worthy of even the most competitive night at the Liebig bar.

Rosco was chief cook and bottle washer. He handed a Tupperware container he had just washed to Marcus, who was eagerly awaiting the next victim for his fresh tea towel.

Marcus looked at the familiar size and shape of the container. "What colour's the lid that goes with this Rosco?"

Rosco lifted the red lid he was washing above the soap suds in the kitchen sink, "This colour."

Henry realised where Marcus was going. "They must have sold millions of them, and I, for one, am glad they did! Gentlemen," said Henry, "for those of you who don't know, I'll tell you in a minute, but for the moment, please raise your glasses to Mr Tupper."

"To Mr Tupper!"

Bill, never one to miss the opportunity to set up a dad joke queried the others, "What are the chances of that?"

"The chances of what?" responded Henry unwittingly.

"The guy's surname who invented Tupperware was Tupper?" Bill caused another laugh-until-you-cry moment, because the joke was so incredibly stupid that it was incredibly funny.

The ladies had removed themselves to the lounge room. They were out of sight and mostly out of earshot of their clearly over-enjoying-themselves, partners. There was no shortage of jokes between the women about the weaker sex in the kitchen. Likewise, there was no lack of devotions of love and respect for their cut-above-average men. Their words of endearment descended into a series of humorous 'mere male' stories of their devoted partners, and the ladies giggled incessantly.

Anne pricked her ears up, "Did they just toast Tupperware? Maybe we should rescue the port bottle from their evil clutches?" No one moved, but everyone giggled.

The dinner party turned out to be a wonderful night of story-telling. These people from entirely different professions and back-grounds, thrust together by circumstance, had well and truly gelled.

Before they called it quits for the night, and with claps of appreciation from the other four, Rosco and Anne handed the Sara1 back to Marcus and Maddy. Marcus thanked them both for everything they had done, not to mention dinner.

With his arm firmly around Maddy, to rounds of applause and laughter, Marcus said, "Welcome to the world's most exclusive club. The Lamarr Lovers Club!"

In the end, though, this marvellous night was simply not long enough. They decreed it must happen again soon.

Epilogue

Six weeks later

The audience in Canberra had been demanded by one overly agitated Chinese Ambassador on behalf of her purportedly 'grievously transgressed' country. If the truth be known, the Ambassador had proceeded to hurl a predictable flurry of undiplomatic insults at Australia. She'd topped this off by reiterating a further reduction in trade, cooperation, and other prevailing threats such as freedom of navigation in the South China Sea.

Her departure with her extensive entourage was welcomed by all who sat through this rhetoric of familiar, bullying un-diplomacy. It would prove to be a far less pleasant and shorter meeting than the Foreign Minister's next visitor. This next visiting delegation was timed, diplomatically, to occur one hour after the Chinese were scheduled to complete their visit.

THE UNITED STATES AMBASSADOR entered the Department of Foreign Affairs and Trade, DFAT building, accompanied by an aide-de-camp and two civilians. They sat in the special secure meeting room, which was more akin to a corporate boardroom. The US Ambassador was responding to the polite diplomatic note issued by the Australian Minister for Foreign Affairs. This request for his presence was to finalise a matter already the subject of some detailed discussions between them.

"Mr Ambassador, it's a pleasure to see you again," welcomed the Minister for Foreign Affairs as she entered the special meeting room with just one other person. She extended her hand to the Ambassador, who rose with his colleagues all seated opposite at the generous conference table.

Five seconds after the entrance door closed, a pair of unmarked green lights lit up over the entrance door, indicating the room's various electronic surveillance countermeasures were active. The room was now deemed secure for secret level and above discussions.

"As it is you, Your Excellency," he replied as the two Trans-Pacific friends shook hands warmly and sat. "I have the agenda with me as discussed." He opened the folder placed in front of him by his aide-de-camp. "May I suggest we formally present those other persons we agreed to bring to the meeting, at the appropriate juncture?"

"Of course, Mr Ambassador, but it would seem by the looks on their faces the three of them have already met."

"Indeed," agreed the Ambassador unsurprised. "Shall we proceed with Agenda Item One, Ma'am?" he asked, having switched to her more informal, but still respectful, title.

The Foreign Minister removed the PRC diplomatic passport issued to Shunyuan from a folder in front of her and slid it across the table. "I believe this belongs to you. Since we are off the record,

Ambassador, this is one of the best forgeries we've seen. Your CIA station chief certainly commands fine work."

The presentation of the passport across the table, although expected by both senior representatives, brought epic realisation to one person. Consequently, the formality of the meeting was interrupted by the accent of an Australian man who now saw everything he was previously blind to. "Jezzzuuusss, of course it is ..."

"Mr Ambassador, we didn't get very far with the agenda, but since we're all friends here, this is Mr Henderson. Mr Henderson, do you wish to have the floor very briefly?"

IT WAS an unexpected offer Henry took up, since he had been warned before the meeting to say nothing until invited to. Seeing the woman and man seated directly opposite him again, and then the passport revelation, had succeeded in making it difficult for Henry to contain his astonishment since walking into the room.

Before Henry could say 'thank you,' another voice chafing at the bit to speak said, "Hello, Henry." The affection and appreciation in Sarah's voice was palpable from across the wide custom-built polished wood table.

Henry looked at her, really looked at her, to see if she was OK and she seemed to be. "We asked where you'd gone and were only told *she's alright and doing her own thing*. Are you leaving us, or were you CIA all along?"

Sarah smiled. "No, hell no! I'm just me, but I am leaving. I think we cover that on an agenda item." With emotions now verging on tearful, she thanked him. "Thank you, Henry, thank you. If it weren't for you, I doubt I'd still be here, and a couple of others besides. Shooting you would not have been a good way to say thank you."

The Foreign Minister subtly indicated it was time for Henry to move on.

Henry smiled and brushed his right ear, "Touché, you're welcome and don't worry, it's still attached. We'll miss you, come back soon."

HENRY ASKED, "How are you recovering, Bruce?" In genuine concern now that the shock of Bruce's attendance had passed.

"Well on the mend thanks, Henry," replied Bruce genially, "I really appreciate you not putting any bullets in me before Peter did," he said in good humour. "And while we're on that topic, if I may, I have something to return to you." Bruce reached down beside his chair.

Henry had no idea Bruce had anything of his at all. He couldn't think what it could possibly be.

There was a mock flourish of deliverance with his right hand, and a French-styled 'voilà' issued forth. With the fluidity of action Henry had known previously, a tall rectangular, red-lidded Tupperware container appeared on the table in front of him. The very same container he knew had replaced the Marc2 in Peter's backpack and they joked about in Rosco's kitchen. It still had its 'Pasta' label, although the pasta was tipped out two months ago. Henry had not seen Bruce smirk before, so this was a first.

"Arr ..." said Henry appreciating the gesture and reflecting briefly on the many facets of their interactions it represented. He responded appreciatively, "Thank you. I will make sure it has a good home."

"Well played, Henry, well played. If you ever need my help, just ask. Like the old Tupperware lifetime guarantee says, *I'll be there,*" said Bruce candidly.

Foreign ministers and Ambassadors are generally people

holding little emotional attachment or warmth for meetings such as these. Today was no exception.

"Shall we resume the agenda at Item Two, Mr Ambassador?" interjected the Foreign Minister, but it was a statement not a question. "Mr Henderson, would you please pass the package to Sarah, since she is the one who will be spending her time with it."

Henry rose and went to lift the specially fitted metal road case containing the Sara1 and a duplicate Marc2 from the floor and place it on the table but decided against it. "I don't want to scratch this magnificent table." Indicating one end of the table, he said, "Meet you halfway up there, Sarah?"

Sarah met Henry eagerly. There was no way he was getting away without the air being squashed from his lungs in a bear hug, "I miss you both too." Then they resumed their seats.

Bruce spoke up, quipping, "I'd check what's actually in there before he leaves if I were you, Sarah."

Even the staid diplomats chuckled at the humour, well acquainted with the irony behind it.

Sarah responded smiling, "It's OK Bruce, I trust Henry with my life."

The larrikin in Henry completely broke with any semblance of etiquette, "No way! Tell me your surname isn't Lee?"

Bruce couldn't keep the grin off his face but shook his head. It wasn't Lee.

The Ambassador was keen to regain protocol and get the next part out of the way, "Item Three, Ma'am. Contrition. As we did most harm, we will apologise first."

The Ambassador and the Foreign Minister stood facing each other. He held a prepared statement. "Your Excellency, on behalf of the President of the United States of America, I formally express my profound regret that the United States Government condoned an extended covert operation by the Central Intelligence Agency on your soil. This was for the express purpose of industrial espionage to advantage our economy at the detriment of yours. The Director CIA has personally expressed to me her deep sorrow that lives were lost, and property destroyed, during this operation. This came about as a result of a sudden increase in mental instability, suffered by an Australian recruit, Mr Peter Esser. In no way was there ever any intent to harm any person, or damage, or destroy any property.

"The President pledges this type of operation will never again be imposed upon our valued ally, Australia. It is the President's deepest wish we can put this profoundly regrettable situation behind us and move forward in a spirit of continuing friendship and cooperation."

"Thank you, Mr Ambassador. On behalf of the Australian Government, I formally accept your expression of regret without reservation. We too wish continuing friendship and cooperation."

"Thank you, Your Excellency. I will report the renewed vigour of our relationship directly to the President." The Ambassador paused, awaiting the pre-prepared comments from the Foreign Minister. They continued to stand as before.

"Mr Ambassador," began the Minister, "the Government of Australia apologises wholeheartedly for the covert activities by the Australian Secret Intelligence Service at our joint user facility located at Pine Gap. We acknowledge without our covert acquisition of your scientific invention known to us both now as the Lamarr chip, there was no rationale for CIA to conduct an extended operation within our borders. We also acknowledge we used Lamarr chips to form the electronic core of our CSIRO Lamarr project."

"I thank you again, Your Excellency, and on behalf of the Government of the United States, I accept your country's humble apology."

"Please be seated, Mr Ambassador. Item Four?" queried the

Minister. "The outlining of our respective developmental plans for the Sara1 and Marc1?"

"Yes, Minister. I have prepared a dot point list for clarity."

"Sarah and Shane will emigrate to the US and have been issued with US passports and now hold dual citizenship, as agreed.

As also agreed, Sarah will head up an innovative PTSD project, based on the Sara1. Eight million people in the US suffer this condition, one of our country's significant social blights. Shane, given his military background, will assist Sarah in this project, initially to perfect therapies, and thence to form part of the treatment liaison plan for soldiers and others."

At which, the Ambassador looked to the Foreign Minister signalling his conclusion to this point.

"Thank you, Mr Ambassador. For our part, we will maintain our Lamarr project with Marcus Hall as project manager, assisted by Mr Henry Henderson to remain for technical and security purposes. The project will move from CSIRO to DST, our more secure Defence Science and Technology facility in Sydney. Other key staff to continue the project are yet to be appointed. In our renewed spirit of co-operation, that list of prospective key staff has already been provided to you. We believe this list achieves both goals of maintaining secrecy and using specialists who already know about the capabilities of the Lamarr chip.

We will focus on developing treatments or cures for insomnia, depression, and morning sickness. We agree to full mutual disclosure of all technical data. All such data is to be, and remain, classified top secret until decided otherwise by mutual consent."

"Item Five?" queried the Minister.

The Ambassador proceeded. "Agreed. Neither the United States nor Australia will carry out any research whatsoever outside the existing, unmodified performance of the Sara1 or Marc1. Furthermore, no new research whatsoever will be conducted outside the existing, unmodified performance of the Marc2."

"Item Six? The subject of compensation."

"As discussed, the US government now agrees to provide the sum of AUD $2,485,392, being the sum held in trust in Switzerland on behalf of Mr Esser, to the Australian Government. These funds are then to be split equally between Australians not knowingly involved in the CIA operation whom Mr Esser caused to be deprived of their liberty or caused to be seriously injured. Each person is to receive $497,078.40. They being Marcus Hall, Madeleine Banner, Helen Hall, William Hall and Sarah Pease," the Ambassador concluded.

"As also discussed," added the Foreign Minister, "we have seized all assets of Mr Esser as proceeds of international crime. The sum of AUD $1M in tax-free compensation has been paid to the retirees injured in the TRG raid on their home. This sum came from monies extorted by Mr Esser from scientists, and his personal cash reserves. Coerced scientists are being offered new contracts if no other illegal activity is uncovered. No reason is being given for offering replacement contracts beyond an audit uncovering certain discrepancies. Since they had all done the wrong thing in the first place, The Crimes Act, which contains our version of the Official Secrets Act, shouldn't even be required, but they will have to sign anyway."

"Item Seven? Tidying of loose ends in Australia."

"Mr Esser's death be ruled a suicide, and he be declared an apparent spy for the People's Republic of China, but neither of our countries press the matter. This is supported by his car surveillance equipment and diplomatic plates, Chinese weaponry, diplomatic passport, building notices, photographic evidence etc."

"Agreed," responded the Foreign Minister. "Item Eight, managing media and political fallout within Australia."

"As discussed," the Minister went on, "it is proposed that with Mr Esser deceased, he be branded the head of a major spy ring which our Security Services, with assistance from the Five Eyes alliance, have now dismantled. The media were convinced of the story from the start and remain so. There is no doubt Mr Esser believed himself to be a spy for China and the additionally leaked DNA and birth documents support and further entrench this conclusion."

The Minister proceeded, "Our last item. The effect on China."

The Ambassador was happy to pick up this mantle. "The world is currently being pressured by China. Australia is feeling this even through aggressive diplomatic channels, no doubt your last meeting was one of those, loss of trade etc. The same aggressive behaviour that led them to militarise the South China Sea is being levelled at the United States, the United Kingdom, India and even France, as today's news reflects.

"China's credibility is at an all-time low, particularly in the aftermath of the coronavirus pandemic. China has for years now denied anything critical of themselves to the point where no-one outside the Chinese Communist Party, believes a word they say. In this regard, and in the situation we are discussing today, no-one will believe their denials. China only have themselves historically to blame, for making this easy for us now."

"Agreed, and meeting concluded. Thank you for coming, Mr Ambassador …"

THE POWER, and consequent danger, the Marc2 presented could not be underestimated. Both sides agreed that no new research whatsoever was permitted outside the existing, unmodified performance of the Marc2.

Politicians … well … that's what they said …

The End

From the author

First of all, thank you for purchasing Yearn to Fear. I know you could have picked any number of books to read, but you picked this book, (my first), and for that I am extremely grateful. I hope you enjoyed reading *Yearn to Fear* as much as I enjoyed writing part one of this trilogy.

I trust that it delivered a good plot and exceeded your expectations. If so, would you please share this book with your friends and family by posting your thoughts to:

Facebook: @chasmurrellauthor
Twitter: @MurrellChas
Instagram: @chasmurrellauthor

Enjoy this book? Please leave a review!

You, the reader, should know that your review is especially important to me. I would be so happy if you would leave a review on Amazon or Goodreads. Reviews help me gain visibility and they can bring my books to the attention of other readers who might enjoy them also.

I look forward to responding to all your comments and hearing from you - that will be fun! ☺

The 'next level' sequel, *Fear to Recall*, is already in process. Can you imagine a _Marc3_?

For more information; to find links to purchase this book in different formats, to leave feedback, or to reserve your first-release copy of *Fear to Recall*, please visit *chasmurrell.com.au*

Thank you very much for your support! I wish you all the best for your future success!

Please stay safe and take care of yourself.

Kind regards,

Chas

Dedication

Dedicated to my beloved and sorely missed parents.

Joseph Lynn Murrell
Born Casterton Victoria 8th Jan 1939.
Passed away 12th Dec 1999 Townsville Queensland

Margaret Ann Murrell (nee Gregson)
Born Murtoa Victoria 27th Dec 1940
Passed away 11th Sept 2020 Launceston Tasmania

About the Author

Chas Murrell has been a Police Officer, Senior Fire Commander, Customs Coastwatch surveillance mission co-ordinator, heavy machinery mechanic, emergency medical technician/instructor, film extra, and General Manager of an event company. He has published academic papers on liquid hydrogen and held a worldwide provisional patent for a nonlinear mathematical calculation. He survived Australia's largest gas BLEVE in 1987 among other "close calls" that you can read about in his blog on the website.

On a personal level he has suffered from relentless and debilitating migraines all his life, is father to four and pop to two. He and his artistically entrepreneurial wife live in Tasmania, which looks very much like Scotland and they wouldn't have it any other way. A direct descendent of Robert The Bruce (King of Scots), history runs deep in Chas's veins, along with a profound knowledge of both World Wars. You may even come across him online playing World of Tanks.

In his Australian spy thriller books you will get to know Chas's knowledge of technology, intrigue, crime, espionage, weaponry, banter, romance and even whisky... yet above all, there is a believ-ability and no loose ends.